BOOK TWO OF THE LIFE & DEATH CYCLE

A POOL
OF
PEONY

E.S. BARRISON

E.S. Barrison
www.esbarrison-author.com

Publisher's Note: This is a work of fiction. Names, characters, places, and incidents are a product of the author's imagination. Locales and public names are sometimes used for atmospheric purposes. Any resemblance to actual people, living or dead, or to businesses, companies, events, institutions, or locales is completely coincidental.

Content Warning: This book is rated 16+ due to violence, sexual content, and language.

Book Layout © 2017 BookDesignTemplates.com

A Pool of Peony/E.S. Barrison. -- 1st ed.
ISBN 978-1-7343670-5-8

Dedicated to Grandma Rhoda & Grandpa David

I'll always keep telling stories for you.

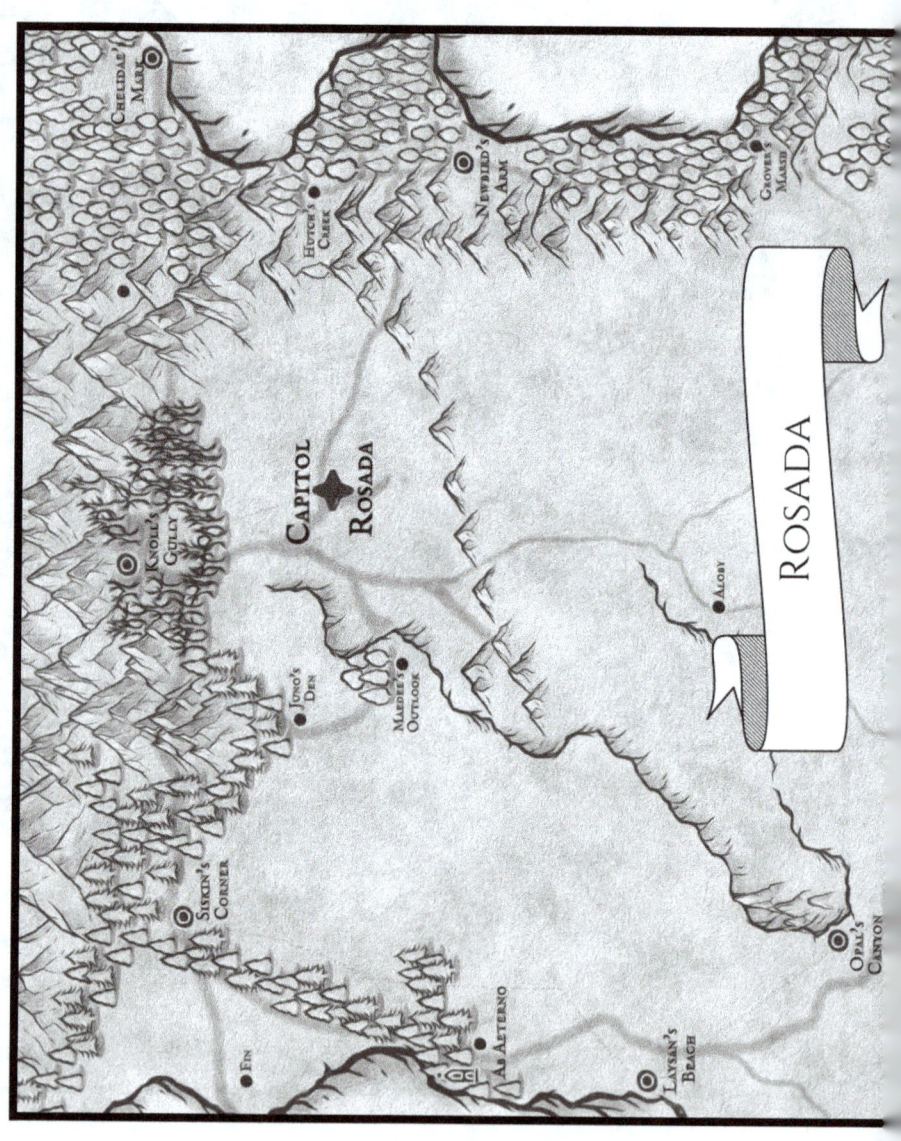

THE CITY OF MERT

LEGEND

1. Airfield
2. Station House
3. Sanitorium
4. Graveyard
5. The Apartment
6. The Shop
7. Madame Owiti

The Heights

Boardwalk District

Chessboard Plains

The Blood Sea

City Center

Industrial District

Maple
Oak
Aspen
Magnolia
Juniper
Conifer
Myrtle
Acacia
Elm
Birch
Dogwood

CHAPTER ONE

MYRTLE AND CELOSIA

Todd Dray jolted awake to the sound of glass breaking. His wife stirred beside him, mumbling something before pulling the blanket over her head. After attempting to shake her awake twice, he pulled on his pants and boots, grabbed a lantern, then rushed downstairs, cursing under his breath.

Downstairs, the front window of his little shop sat in shambles. Todd swore again.

Todd shone the light down each of the aisles, his stomach twisting in knots. "Hello? Who's there?"

Crash!

Another display toppled over, scattering an array of broken jars and vials around the room.

"Bullocks!" Todd jumped backward, stepping over the shelf and glancing down the aisle. "Who's there? Show yourself!"

Shuffling responded.

Todd passed by a few more aisles, stepping over broken displays and tattered books. The intruder's shadow lurked in the darkness, hunched over in a row of makeshift clothing and shoes. His patchwork clothes made him look like a ghost in the night, and as he lifted a giant yellow sunhat up, the color illuminated his pale face.

Todd stepped forward. "Oi! What'cha got there, mate?"

The shadow turned, revealing a young fellow with mangled hair and an uneven beard. He wore only undergarments beneath his coat, no shoes on his feet, and a tattered glove on one hand. His pockets overflowed with gems, while in his arms, he carried a box of obscure chocolates. Two distinct yellow slits sat in the place of his eyes.

Todd stepped back. "Listen, I'm not gonna harm ya mate, but you gotta put those gems back and—"

The young man approached Todd, tilting his head to the side. Mist poured from his lips with each breath. But he spoke not a word.

"Mate, c'mon. Just put 'em back—"

The shadow opened his mouth. An inhuman shriek rocked the shop, sending Todd toppling back into the wall. Once it ceased, the young man's eyes widened, and for a moment, his eyes turned gray.

"I'm...I'm sorry! Really. I'm...I'm sorry!" The boy's voice cracked as he threw his long coat behind him and dashed out of the shop.

Todd darted after him into the streets. A thick fog descended over the roadway, taking form in the miraculous shape of a ballroom dance. Images of men and women waltzing detailed the road. And, like some tale of a girl fleeing after a dance, the young man disappeared into the mist.

"What the—I hate this damn city!" Todd threw the lantern on the ground. It fizzled out, leaving a soft glow of embers on the coattails of the odd magic. A dog barked in the distance.

The Independent City of Mert was known for its tricks, enchantments, and, notably, its magic. Despite living here for nearly four years, Todd had yet to grow accustomed to its disorder. One minute, all would be calm; the next, a profuse, glowing goo covered the market square because a kid drank the wrong potion.

Todd watched as the mystical story disappeared, leaving a dense fog crowning the lampposts with halos. He grunted once more, then turned the dial on the lamp outside his shop. It shuffled through blue, white, yellow, and orange before settling on red. Once its glow captured the outline of the door, Todd reentered the shop and began cleaning the wreckage.

The floorboards creaked upstairs as he swept, and moments later, his wife emerged in the stairwell with their son on her hip. A flowing white dress trailed behind her, blending in seamlessly with her skin and hair, reminiscent of a moonbeam.

"Toddle, what in the Effluvium's name happened?" she sang. Her exhausted red eyes trailed over him.

"So, we're going with the Effluvium today? Weren't you worshipping the Giants of Yilk yesterday?" he grumbled.

"Faith changes, Toddle!"

Todd grunted again and continued to sweep.

"What happened?" she pressed.

"Go back to bed, Lex. It don't matter. I called the coppers. They'll be here soon." Todd glanced at the light outside the shop. It still hung red. "It ain't a problem. Really. Go sleep."

"Toddle, don't be coy." Lex approached him, balancing the child in her arms.

"It's a'ight, really." Todd ruffled his son's frizzy hair. The boy didn't react, staring past Todd and out the door.

Lex pouted before saying, "I saw the mist outside and...those ballroom dancers! It was the Story Collector, wasn't it? Don't they say the Story Collector brings stories in his wake? I bet it was! That's why you're being a grump!"

"That's a rumor. It ain't the Story Collector."

"How do you know?"

"I saw him! It was just some poor slob who needed money. Hell, he mighta even worked for the Pinstripes or something, tryna cause an issue or another. Not the Story Collector."

"You go that twinge in your voice, Toddle. You're not convinced." Lex poked the center of his hefty chest.

Todd groaned again.

Lex's attention turned to their son. "Right, Garrett? Daddy's in denial, right? He's so silly!"

The little boy acknowledged her with a wary glance.

"Lex—" Todd huffed.

She stopped him. "Get your head out of the sand, Toddle. This is Mert! It's filled with magic! The Story Collector was here!"

"What I saw was a kid gone mad!"

Lex turned away, her attention on Garrett instead. "C'mon Garr-bear. We'll see Madame Owiti later and tell her everything. She'll know what to do!"

Todd cursed under his breath, then said to Lex, "No, not Madame Owiti! *Please.* She's a loon. The coppers will be here any minute. We don't need to talk to her."

"And they will say what I said: it was the Story Collector." With a swift twirl, Lex waltzed into the backroom with Garrett, the beaded curtains clacking behind her.

Once she vanished, Todd muttered and returned to cleaning the shop. He took stock of inventory as he swept the floor. The kid stole at least a grand worth of jewels and broke twenty different vials filled with fake love and luck potions. The hat wasn't an immense loss, but it would take Todd at least three months to recover from all those other stolen goods!

He dwelled on Lex's strained voice as he picked up an old newspaper from the floor. For months now, the *Mertoni Times* fixated on the so-called Story Collector, recanting tales of a man with yellow slits for eyes. In his wake, stories followed. *If he came,* the paper said, *your story belonged to him.*

Nonsense, in Todd's opinion. For all the years he lived in Mert, he had never seen magic exhibit such aptitude. Glowing gems, absurd potions, and parlor tricks paraded around Mert, so the mere idea of someone casting magical stories for months on end was utterly preposterous! Whatever Todd saw couldn't be more than a trick of the light. If the kid really was the Story

Collector, then he had certainly mastered the art of a heist and illusions. Yes, illusions. That made sense.

Todd crumpled up the paper and threw it in the trash as the door chimed.

Two detectives walked into his little shop: two lovely women, carrying themselves with poise and grandeur. The Lead Detective, with her wide shoulders and pink lips, twirled a strand of auburn hair around her finger while she examined the crime scene. The other, shorter and a tad kinder with her gaze, pulled back her coarse hair as she wandered through dismantled shelving.

Neither of them said a word.

"You gonna fix this then?" Todd leaned against a shelf where a few of Garrett's drawings hung.

The Lead Detective looked at him. "Is that what you want us to do?" He didn't recognize her accent, each word pointed and direct.

"Well, yeah. I *was* robbed."

"I do indeed have eyes."

Todd didn't like the woman's tone, but instead of arguing, he crossed his arms and glowered.

She twiddled her thumbs and approached the counter. "Describe the perpetrator, please. We will try to hunt him down, although we have bigger issues on our hands than a petty robbery."

"He stole a grand of gems!"

"Please do describe him so we can carry on with our day."

Todd clenched his hands into a fist. He knew it was early, but at least she could show some sympathy! "I dunno! He was this tall, lanky kid. Early twenties. Kinda mangy looking or something. Don't think he was with one of the Pinstripes or a gang or nothing. He looked homeless."

"Anything else notable?"

"His eyes...they looked yellow for a minute." He scowled. "When he left, and I'm sure it was some stupid trick or something, there was this weird mist floating with dancers or something. Musta been an illusion..."

Her eyes ignited. "Are you implying it was the Story Collector?"

"Y'telling me you believe in that bullshite, too?"

"We do live in Mert," the shorter detective stated as she studied the bloodied footprints on the floor.

The Lead Detective nodded to herself. "We have been tracking the Story Collector for some time now. He is erratic and possibly dangerous. Once we find him, Mert can rest again."

"You're fucking me!" Todd slammed his fist on the counter. His fingers curled in pain, and he brought one of them to his lips and sucked on it, cursing once more.

The detectives ignored him and continued to comb the shop, collecting a few pieces of glass and noting the crime scene. Todd collapsed on his stool. He could see the headline now: *The Story Collector Strikes Again on the Corner of Myrtle and Celosia!* Already enough odd business came to his shop. The last thing he needed was to become the latest talk of the town – or a tourist trap for that matter.

He doodled on a piece of blank paper as the detectives finished their rounds. The bare space between his knuckles taunted him, and Todd needed a fresh idea for a tattoo to complement the dragon traveling down his arm. But the caricature he drew up of the tall detective, with a large chin and enormous hands, would not be the tattoo for that spot.

As the Detective came back over, he tore the paper into pieces and threw the scraps into the bin. She didn't notice. "Thank you, Mister...?"

"Dray."

"Thank you, Mr. Dray, for reporting this incident." The Detective leaned back on her heels. "Do you have anything else you need to note for our investigation?"

"Just do your damn job and get my gems back."

"Very well. If you think of anything, though, please do come by the Station House and ask for my partner or me."

"Yeah, that's gonna be hard without a name."

The Detective smirked, puckering her lips in a way that caused Todd's stomach to turn. "My name is Detective Walsh, and this is my partner Detective Locasta." The shorter detective waved from the doorway. "We are overseeing the investigation surrounding the Story Collector. So, if you learn anything at all, please do not hesitate to let us know. Is that understood?"

"A'ight. Fine. Whatever."

Detective Walsh and her partner left the shop as the sun's rays blessed the streets of Mert. As they left, Detective Locasta twisted the knobs of the red glowing lantern outside, returning it to its usual yellow before disappearing into the street's early morning commotion.

With the detectives gone, Lex reemerged from the backroom. "Well? What'd they say?"

Todd grunted.

"Hm?"

"They said it's the Story Collector."

"Told you!"

"That don't mean nothing. They're a bunch of loon detectives if you ask me."

"Why are you such a curmudgeon?" Lex tapped her fingers along the dragon tattoo on his arm, pausing at the Black Stamp hidden amongst the design's teeth.

Todd spent years creating the tattoo to hide that hideous Black Stamp, two black triangles that forever marked him as a vagrant in the country of Rosada in the west. In Mert, the Black Stamp didn't matter. But if he ever ventured back to any nation where the Order of the Effluvium maintained its stronghold, it was key to hide it.

"You know why!" Todd heaved out. He changed the subject. "Where'd Garrett run off to?"

"He's coloring with Preston."

"You shouldn't encourage—"

Lex held up her hand. "Madame Owiti says it's good for him. Besides, didn't you ever have an imaginary friend, Toddle?"

"Madame Owiti shouldn't be making calls on our child!"

"She is my friend, Toddle! And I trust her."

"She's a nutter!"

Lex placed her hands on her hips. "Well, I disagree! And she said if we keep being so negative, we're not gonna make rent. So, excuse me while I go spruce up. Day is here, and I must change. Clientele expect a certain persona!"

"You haven't had a client in weeks!"

"If I negate your negativity with positivity, Madame Owiti says I will. And, she says, we will embark on a grand journey soon."

"Load of bullshite."

"Well, I'll be positive for both of us then!" Lex patted his cheek before wandering again into the backroom. Her steps came with tremors, and as Todd watched her take a step behind the curtain, his heart fell. He knew he should go easier on her, but she always befriended the oddest folk. Madame Owiti was no exception to this rule. She'd be by later today, that much he was certain, but every time the old woman showed her face, he worried that Lex fell deeper into her blanket of lies.

He grumbled and finished straightening up the shop, turning the sign out front to say *OPEN*. After grabbing the latest newspaper off the doorstep, he collapsed again behind his counter.

Details of the recent senate elections in Rosada filled the front page. Most notably, a newcomer had taken the seat for the Knoll Region, a radical member of the Order by the name of Donovan Cordova. He built his following out of nowhere, arriving one day by train and decreeing his wish to protect the nation from the uprising of magic across the region. Todd usually ignored the politics of his home country, but Mr. Cordova's election fueled disquiet in Mert. It threatened the city's notorious sanctuary of magic, sending rumors flurrying about Rosada's desire to annex them in the shadows. Mr. Cordova, political columnists thought, would lead the charge.

Todd hated to admit that he agreed.

He flipped the page to an article about airship construction. Before he could delve into it, though, the shop's bell rang again. A small, young woman with eyes like oak trees walked in with her head bowed. For a second, she stared at the broken window. She wore a jacket at least thrice her size, torn at the bottom, with baggy pants and a men's shirt. Her hair hung in an uneven braid at her shoulder. He'd seen her come in a few other times; she always hid her dark face, and with each visit, she looked thinner. Yet, despite her roughness, she was far too well put together to be living on the streets.

The girl perused the aisles, stopping before the toppled shelves, then turning to the hats.

"You need any help?" Todd called.

"No, not today..." The girl shook her head and glanced around the shop, then said, "You were robbed."

"Great, it's already getting around." Todd groaned and slammed the newspaper on the counter. Just what he needed!

"No, it's just...they broke your gem case and stole your yellow hat." The girl scowled. "Why would he take that?"

"At least someone wanted it."

She touched one of the other displays and frowned, "Did he say anything?"

"I'm sorry?"

"Oh, uh, nothing. Sorry."

"A'ight, whatever."

"I...I should go..." Before Todd said anything else, she dashed from the shop, vanishing into the now crowded streets without looking back.

Todd grumbled and returned to his paper. It wasn't the weirdest thing he'd seen that day. He wasn't sure if he would ever get used to the peculiar disorder of Mert, but for some reason, he called it home.

CHAPTER TWO

CHASING STORIES

B ria rushed out of the little shop on the Corner of
Myrtle and Celosia. She raised her hand in the
air as she ran past a nearby cedar tree, letting the
branches lift her onto the rooftops. She had seen these
signs before: the shop's broken window, bloodied footprints, and a flustered shopkeeper only meant one
thing.

It meant he'd appeared again.

She had chased him across the world. From Rosada
to Yilk to Perenes and to Spinoza, Bria refused to give
up on him.

It'd been almost six months since Brent lost his mind
to the Diabolo during the Storm of Nightmares. Six
long, terrible months. After chasing him in circles, Bria

trapped him in the City of Mert. She contained him to the streets of the city, blocking the magical tunnels beneath the earth with lattices of vines and roots, cornering him in alleyways and streets. He often fled like a shadow before she got close enough. He didn't know his name. He didn't know her name.

He almost wasn't human.

Yet deep down, Bria knew Brent continued to fight. On those rare occasions when she managed to corner him, she saw that glimmer of fear in his eyes or hints of his authentic voice peppered in with the Diabolo's snarls and shrieks. He always darted away before she reached for him, though.

These little moments gave her hope.

For his safety and for hers, she had to make sure no one followed.

Notably, the Council of Mist Keepers.

Her encounters with the Council continued to haunt her. She hadn't seen them since Brent's eyes turned yellow. Sure, they seemed friendly at first, giving Brent a much-needed escape from his destined life in Newbird's Pit. They rid his fate of vagrancy and offered him an alternative path: become a Mist Keeper, a gatekeeper of the afterlife and protector of the mist that circumnavigated the globe.

But like the Order of the Effluvium in Rosada, the moment Brent decided to be different, their amiableness vanished. They saw his friendship and romance with Bria as a threat, his mistakes as the enemy, and his exposure to the hellish beast known as the Diabolo as a villainous transformation.

No. Bria couldn't trust them now. If they captured Brent, there was no telling what they would do.

Well, she had an inclination. Her thoughts went to her little branch behind her ear. She once used the branch as a mask, allowing it to expand across her face to hide her identity. Not anymore. It still didn't flourish the same way after the crooked architect of the Council, Alojzy, imprisoned her so their all-knowing God-of-Death, Ningursu, could use her as a puppet. Brent, now wrapped in the yellow embrace of the Diabolo's stories, would be Ningursu's new toy. They would take a piece of him and turn him into a weapon.

She shook off the fear as she darted along the rooftops to search for Brent. How many times had this hopeful adrenaline led her to thoughts of flight? How many false leads made her nearly concede? But even if she lost hope, it wasn't like she could return to Rosada. After she instigated riots across the province from a mere broken wall in Newbird's Arm, the song of *Rhodana the Forest Queen* became the call of rebellion throughout Rosada. And Bria was their saint.

She should have expected as such. She used the identity of Rho to hide her face and her magic. Of course, they latched onto the same tale.

Now, everyone knew her, and flyers plastered with her face covered the walls throughout Rosada. The only place she was safe, where she could practice her magic in plain sight, was far away from her home. Where else could she go but the Independent City of Mert?

So here she stayed. And here, she shuffled through survival.

Alone.

As she reached the edge of the rooftop, she felt the hopeful bout of adrenaline bequeathing her body. The Story Collector vanished in a blink of an eye, whisked away by mist-filled stories into the night after his jaunts.

"Brent!?!" Bria called into the street.

Only the hustle and bustle of the city replied.

Bria sank against the roof tile, digging her fingers into the dirt-filled crevasses. Moss and mildew flourished by her fingertips. Why did she bother trying to run after him when each search ended with such dismay?

She lay there for a few minutes, watching the Mertonians stroll along the boardwalk. A group of children pointed at the golden whales emerging in the cool red waters of the Blood Sea. Meanwhile, a few large individuals in pinstriped suits walked by, speaking in vociferous Mertoni. Coppers pushed past them, pasting flyers up on the wall, smiling to the patrons in a way that foiled the Guard of Newbird's Arm from Bria's childhood.

Once the coppers vanished down Conifer Street and the patrons along the boardwalk dispersed, Bria hopped from her rooftop and grabbed a couple flyers from the wall. The first two were for members of the Pinstripe Gang. The third flyer was the only one that mattered to Bria.

WANTED
For robbery, indecency, and disturbing the peace:
The Story Collector
Reward: 500 Notes

Beneath it sat a caricature of Brent's face with snakelike slits for eyes. Bria blinked a few times, almost laughing. *Five hundred notes? That's a big reward for Brent. He'd like that!*

The detriment of the situation kept her from laughing. Once again, Brent Harley faced certain scrutiny. In Rosada, the Order branded him with the Black Stamp because of his silver eyes and his talent for storytelling. Here in Mert, no one considered him anything but a nuisance.

But a nuisance was better than a demon.

After pocketing the flyer, Bria trailed along the boardwalk away from Conifer and up toward Juniper. Once again, she'd gotten her hopes up over another false lead. Brent was gone by the time she arrived at the little shop.

She'd try again tomorrow.

And the next day.

And the next.

Bria scuffed her feet along the path as she walked, running her fingers along the bark of the cedar trees. They whispered affirmations that her barricade beneath the earth in her tunnels stood. For now, they were safe.

The sun had yet to reach its pinnacle in the sky, the morning young and filled with opportunities. Bria followed the pathway of colorful homes along the water. Ivy, flowers, and evergreens decorated their yards in contrast to the brown and yellow musk highlighting the edges of the city.

Just like the rest of the world, most of Mert basked in the death of wildflowers and crumpled leaves. Only those with money and patience kept gardens. And as always, gardens needed a gardener. Even without her powers, Bria's experience helping Mr. West in the Senator's Gardens while growing up came with an insurmountable amount of knowledge. She won over the wealthy owners of these homes with her knowledge, but under Bria's magic the past few months, the gardens not only bloomed...they bolstered.

Yet today, Bria found no desire to nurture the gardens.

As she passed by the white fence of a pink house, an elderly woman waved to her from the porch. "Rho! How are you today?"

"I'm okay, thanks." Bria smiled candidly. "Do you want me to come by tomorrow? I'm all booked up right now." The lie tasted fresh on her tongue, like an unripe tangerine.

"Perhaps next week, love. All is right with weeds and prosper. May your day be grand!"

Bria waved goodbye to the old woman and continued along the path towards her apartment. As she walked, surrounded again by the tranquility of the residential road, a cramp poked at her insides, and she crumpled by the wall. She cursed under her breath, then forced herself along the road, panting every few steps. At first, she thought it came from stress or the negligible amount she'd eaten in the past few days, but as she reached her building, the cramps reaffirmed her fears.

Her monthly bleed arrived again with a vengeance.

She managed up the stairs and into the apartment before collapsing on the disheveled bed. She lay there, counting the lights on the ceiling, unable to move. At least the lights were always the same. It became a habit after her interrogation with Captain Carver many moons ago: always count the lights. If she identified the true number each time, then no one would convince her of their propaganda. They grounded her in the present, where she intended to remain.

The rest of the apartment sat unkempt: plates cluttered the counters, dead plants hung from the walls, and dirty clothes lived on the floors. On the kitchen table, three books collected dust from prior months when Brent sat there fidgeting with the pages. Bria tried reading them, but their riddles left her with a headache. Whenever she came upon a page he'd bookmarked or written a note, her own heart sank. While Bria couldn't see stories like Brent, she still felt his presence: their laughter in the kitchen, dances down the stairwell, and embraces deep beneath the covers haunted the apartment. But Bria couldn't bring herself to leave.

She gathered herself and limped into the lavatory, filling the tub, so steam basked about the room. The windows dripped in the humidity, wrapping around her.

Cradling...

Drifting...

Dreaming...

Every time she closed her eyes, she traveled back to that fateful day in Newbird's Arm. Around her, the world spun, her magic reaching every crevasse of the forest. A guard chased her; he tried to cut her open; her magic defended her. And the forest collapsed.

A cramp yanked her from the nightmare. Bria gagged and leaned her head over the toilet bowl.

She stayed in the tub until the water turned lukewarm, bringing her fingers along the jagged scar on her chin. Her mind went back to those events. Every day, she recalled how Cadet Chet Lawry's body lay in the middle of the forest, his mouth ajar, eyes vacant. Could she have fought him off any other way?

I'm not a killer.

Not only did Cadet Lawry's death weigh heavily on her soul, but so did all the events that followed that day. She helped destroy the town and caused riots. Instead of fixing it, she fled.

Now all she could do was lie in this tub while cramps riddled her sides and abdomen.

Slowly, she climbed out of the tub, listening as the drain spun. As she dressed, she lit the two gas lanterns on the counter, then circled the apartment to check for food. The icebox sat empty. Even the oranges on her counter went bad, fizzling out at her touch.

Bria collapsed in the chair and held her head. *You need to take better care of yourself. What would your Grandmama say?*

Stop with the self-pity. Make it pretty.

A clumsy knock on her door pulled Bria from her defeat. It tapped on the door two times. No call followed.

"Who's there?" Bria called, catching the knot in her throat.

No reply.

She grabbed a dead orange from the table and squeezed it in her hand, tiptoeing to the doorway.

"Hello?"

Still nothing.

She gulped and unlatched the lock, peaking through the crack.

Her heart nearly jumped from her chest.

"Brent?!?"

He stood in the doorway, his eyes glossed over and unfocused, a box of chocolates in his hands. He didn't look like himself: mangled hair, chartreuse eyes, and pale chapped lips captured his face, hidden beneath an uneven scratchy beard. His coat pockets overflowed with random objects while his fingers twitched with each breath.

Bria gawked at him, holding up her guard as she pushed the door open a tad more. He stumbled backward in shock.

"Help... help... help me... help... help..." he repeated, gripping the box of chocolate tight.

"Brent...are you in there? You always come back." Bria held out her hand, trembling. "Come inside. Please."

Brent took a step forward. A childlike curiosity captured his face, and he held out the chocolates. For a moment, Bria saw the fearful young man she'd fallen in love with, kissing beneath the forest's canopy on a brisk spring day. He had to still be in there somewhere. Why else would he show up like this?

Why did he ever show up at all?

She reached for him. "It's okay. You're safe."

As soon as his fingers grazed her hand, he hissed, dropped the box of chocolates, and darted down the stairs.

"Brent! Wait!" Bria raced after him into the streets as another cramp stitched its way along her left side. She winced.

Brent already vanished into the evening crowds. Mist-like stories danced in the streets. Men in tall hats and women in swaying dresses, children play with snowballs, and a cat jumping from the top window; all stories disappearing and intertwining as told by the Story Collector.

When the Council selected Brent as the next Mist Keeper, his powers manifested in a way where he could see, create, remember, and visualize stories in the world's mist. Bria only sometimes could see the mist, but from what he told her long ago, it never left.

No wonder the monster's story drove him mad when he ultimately defeated it.

How many more stories had he collected since he lost his mind?

Bria jumped back as a story of three individuals in suits ran past her, sending a few real people stumbling.

This is worse than usual! Bria darted down Juniper and up Elm, past the corners of Magnolia and Aspen, toward the heart of Mert.

But save for the few coppers lounging by City Hall, the City Square sat silent. Airships whirred in the shipyard behind it while different colored lanterns flickered in the window of the Station House. A few flyers rustled through the air, advertising the magical talents of seers, potion masters, and parlor magicians. A few whisked by with Brent's caricature.

Where are you? She slowed at the end of the plaza and dug her fingers into a tree. For once, Bria wished she had Brent's magic, then she could see where he had been. After all, the trees didn't tell stories like the mist.

The wind caught her hair as if answering her prayers and turned her attention down an alleyway where the mist thickened. It whispered to her, pushing her along the path with one last bit of hope. Bria followed it past the sterile white bricks of the Sanatorium, nearly running into a doctor removing a beak-like plague mask from their face for a smoke. Bria apologized in haste, then continued down the road.

The mist led her to the rural edge of the city where the white and black tulips of the Chessboard Battlefield dominated the fields. At their border, a yard of crystalized stones embossed with the names of those long dead glistened in the moonlight. The mist congregated around the gravesite.

And there stood Brent, walking from headstone to headstone, the mist trickling beneath his bare feet. He still strode with that glass look in his eye, his face twitching in ways not matching his movements. As he touched each headstone, the mist wove with the stories of the long-dead. After each one, he loosened his shoulders and sent a new spirit of mist twisting into the air where it vanished.

Bria crouched behind a tree. *He's still releasing the dead. He's still in there.*

After another release, Brent slumped against one crystal. He brought his hands to his face and clawed at his cheeks, producing an inhuman sob.

Bria hopped between the bushes. This was the first time she had ever caught up with him. Most times, after his brief visits, he disappeared into the onslaught of stories. Finally, luck was on her side!

As she neared him, Bria got a better look than during the brief encounter at the apartment. One of his eyes fluttered open, revealing the nightmarish yellow that haunted her even now. She saw it in her sleep: holding him in the tunnels, watching him come to life not as Brent Harley but as the Diabolo of Newbird's Arm. Still, there sat a glimmer reminiscent of Brent Harley in the twinkling edges of his irises.

As she neared, the true harrowing effect of the Diabolo's story became obvious. Away from his face and down his skin, scratches covered his face and arms while blisters ate away at his bare feet.

"Brent," she whispered.

He curled in on himself as she approached.

"I'm not going to hurt you..." Bria knelt before him. "I want to help."

He shook his head.

"Do you know who I am?"

Still no response.

"Do you know who you are?"

A blink.

Bria reached for his cheek. She half expected him to back away, but like a lost puppy, he leaned into her touch. As he inhaled, the mist pummeled over him.

"Lonely," he mumbled.

"I'm sure you have been..." She gulped down her tears.

"No. You. Lonely."

Bria stared at him.

"There once was a girl with a flower on her head," Brent mumbled, failing to make eye contact as he spoke. "She'd help. She'll help you."

"Brent..."

He closed his eyes. "She always helps."

"She tries..." Bria took his hands. "If you come with me...she can help you too."

"No...she can't...she can't...she—" Brent scrunched his face. It was almost as if a hundred personalities washed over him at once. "Cut her—no, no, I can't—she an evil lass—rip her—rape her." He fell backward, mist forming around him as he tore at his hair. "No...I can't. I won't. It's—I—stop—I can't!" He pushed Bria to the ground and stumbled back from her. "Go away!"

"Brent!"

He screamed into her face, "Go away!"

Bria commanded the few white and black tulips in the gravesite to expand, their petals and leaves exploding towards Brent's ankles and wrists. At their touch, he shrieked again, falling backward on his bottom. A couple gems fell out of his coat pocket, rolling against one of the crystallized stones. When he tried to retrieve them, Bria sent another tulip after his wrist. He screeched.

"Brent!" She climbed to her feet again. "Please! Come back!"

"Get away!" He slashed at her face with his overgrown nails.

Bria recoiled, holding her hands up in the air. "Brent! This isn't you!"

"No! No! No!" He banged his fists to his forehead. "Get away! Get away, ya bitch—damn—shite!"

"Brent!"

"I can't control it." The voice belonged to Brent this time. For a fleeting moment, his eyes lost the yellow and returned to that kind silver. "I can't—I dunno when it will be ba—ACK!" He stumbled backward, and with a snarl, his eyes transformed into those nefarious yellow slits.

"No! Brent! Come back!"

He screeched again in an inhuman tone, then bolted out of the gravesite, disappearing into a whirlwind of mist.

CHAPTER THREE

NAMELESS

Was it night?
Or day?
It was yellow.

Empty.

Alone.

He saw nothing else but yellow.

His knees buckled. He pulled his hair; he sobbed aloud, and he begged for it to end. His fingers smelled of blood, fresh, cut from skin.

She was there. Right there! Why did I scare her?

Or did she scare him?

Kill her...

Kill her...

No.

He listened to the decrees. He heard the demands.

He focused on his footsteps hitting the cobblestone instead.

I am...

A man cutting his children into pieces?

A woman who set her town ablaze?

A young soldier who raped and killed two girls in the snow?

I am all of them.

Or none.

He fought it day in and day out; the monster tried to cling to his mind, but he knew it was but a story.

"Shite!" He screamed, and the yellow passed. Mist exploded around him, masking his surroundings, dragging him into the darkness of an alley. Were those voices just beyond the veil?

Where was he?

Who was he?

I hurt her.

Who? He remembered her voice, a safe voice, a kind voice, sitting in his chest.

She left.

Because she hates you...

No. No! No!

He tried focusing again. In the distance, a dog barked.

Get back. You need to get back. They're expecting you.
You got information for them.
Get back.

Where?

When?

Who was he?

Fog covered everything.

Why did the dog keep barking?

Why did everything seem so far away?

I'm not supposed to be here.

I need to get back.

Where is here?

Then the mist parted, and for a moment, he could see. His breathing rocked his chest, his throat tightened, and his eyes watered. Before him stood an alley of white stones lining the walls.

So bright.

Too bright.

Nauseating even.

He remembered, just for a moment.

The mist belonged to someone else.

A Council.

Like Death.

They were called the Mist Keepers.

What are their names?

Like whispers, their names whisked through his head.

Caroline, his teacher, the Masquerading Illusionist.

Alojzy, the Architect of the Library.

Malaika, the Cartographer of the Mist.

Jiang, who denied magic on all counts.

Julietta, the Painter who Forgot.

Tomás, the Mind-reader and Peacemaker, with a lie in his tone.

Aelia, the Healer with no bedside manner.

And of course, Ningursu, the Skeletal Head that led the Council to greatness.

But what is the girl's name? What is my name? Who am I?

His stomach churned with excitement. It was there. He could feel it reaching to him.

It came to him in the parting mist.

My name is Brent Harley. I'm twenty-one years old. My name is Brent...my name is...my name—

Then it vanished, once again leaving him alone.

No! Come back. Come back! That's my name!

It's not your name. You're nothing. You're a vessel.

My name is...my name is...

He howled and banged his hand against the nearby wall. Agony rippled through it, and he brought it to his lips.

"My name is...my name is—" He sobbed. Would he ever remember?

He rose to his feet and stepped forward. It hurt to peer past the white bricks. A hundred stories of men and women filled the path; they would stop, talk, enjoy, and laugh. Their voices buzzed in his head.

"No, no, no, no!" He closed his eyes and knocked his forehead with his fist. "No...she can help. The girl—the girl with the flower on her head." As he stepped forward, mist followed his footsteps, showing a young woman darting past him as if she'd walked this same road earlier. "Her name...it was...her name is Bria Smidt. And Brent Harley loved her. He brought her chocolates once." He glanced down the road. "She's good...she'll help..."

His feet felt like anchors as he walked. The stories mingled with the tale of Bria Smidt, running down the alley back toward whence he came. Were those actual stories? Were they real? Who was alive? Who was dead?

She won't help you.

You slashed her face.

"Shut it." He gritted his teeth.

She won't find you.

She won't save you.

Monster.

Demon.

Diabolo.

He clutched the wall. *My name is...my name is...*

Who am I?

A robber. You robbed today.

No.

I am—

Who am—

I am—

He wandered back into the yellow fog. A thousand stories called to him.

Was he their vessel?

He didn't know.

"Help." He stumbled again, reaching forward for something, someone, anything that could keep him standing.

To his surprise, someone reached back.

The individual came to him through the yellow smoke. Their face reminded him of a bird.

Who has a beak that long? They must be a bird.

"Help me." He pleaded again.

Their voice laced through the air like a spider on its web. "Oh, you terrified thing. It's okay; you're safe now."

"Who—"

"It's all fine now. We'll take care of you here." The figure draped an arm over his shoulder and walked him towards a fuzzy light, hidden by the musk of the fog. "You're safe with us."

As he followed the figure, a sterile white light blinded him.

Perhaps I'm finally dying.

CHAPTER FOUR

DEATH'S MOURN

D eath's Mourn arrived with a pyre. It illuminated the Newbird's Arm's market square, towering over the shambles of the Pit. Above, the newly repaired Year Glass shimmered with the embrace of each flame, its ruby glow creating a permanent sunset over the town.

Beneath it, the townsfolk quivered, avoiding its gaze. Except for Jemma Reds.

Jemma stood beneath the Year Glass on the steps to the Temple, her head held high and shoulders stiff. She didn't fear the gaze of the Order, not now that she'd she became a Sister herself. Since she was a child, the Order helped her feel safe, always there as a guide in times of trouble. She assumed she did them well by accepting a betrothal to a boy who needed help; it turned out; he did not need her help, and through him, Jemma came to understand the Order in full.

Determined to change it, she joined as Sister Jey Ma.

Then came the Storm of Nightmares.

It ravaged Newbird's Arm, stuffing everyone's minds with their worst fears, leaving a blanket of fear over the town. Her old betrothed stopped the storm with the help of a young woman who commanded plants. It was too late, though. The Storm of Nightmares destroyed the Temple and left shambles in its wake.

Since then, no one had seen the *saviors* of Newbird's Arm, Brent Harley and Bria Smidt.

Though some saviors they were! Jemma couldn't help but scoff; they'd abandoned the town after the disarray, never to return. She thought Brent had changed; she thought Bria was noble! But they left without a word. Now their faces occupied bulletins across town.

And in their wake, the nightmares remained, leaving an odd taste over the town in the months that followed. People walked with their heads down, never making eye contact and avoiding small talk. At night, Jemma remembered the tendrils of incubi climbing over her skin, leaving a constant feeling of failure in her throat. Perhaps failure was her destiny.

Newbird's Arm had not reached its former glory again. With the Pit's walls in shambles, vagrants occupied the market square, begging for coin and other gratuitous delights. Most people avoided eye contact with them, while few others acknowledged the vagrants as equals.

At night, the vagrants returned to the Pit, chanting songs of rebellion on their lips.

Ey oh
We have come back
We have come back
Ey oh
She came, she wreaked
She saw, she pleased
Ey oh
We will see
We will see
Ey oh
Rhodana will be
She will be free.

They didn't stop singing for their savior, Rhodana the Forest Queen, the lass who broke their walls. Some days, they started riots, leaving the market square empty for the following weeks.

The town rebuilt from the ashes. While dilapidated buildings and charred walkways adorned Newbird's Arm, greenery thrived. The Senator's Gardens and neighboring forests maintained their glamor. Filled with luster, basking in the Senator's immortal camellias, they told Jemma one thing: The Effluvium watched them all, and in its hands, Newbird's Arm would survive.

Death's Mourn waltzed through town, riding the gray cape of the Effluvium. The mountains sank into a dusty white while the trees descended into a restful hibernation. Jemma maintained her stance on the step with Brother Roy Al, watching as the townsfolk offered heirlooms to dump in the fire. While the richest members of town deposited old jewelry, gems, books, and antiques, the vagrants dumped old clothes and wood, coming together for one reason and one reason alone.

Mourning.

Grief always brought everyone together, young and old, poor and rich, for sadness, in some ways, was a universal emotion. Jemma had learned that much in a short time as a Sister of the Order; sadness always found a way into the happiest hearts.

Jemma directed her gaze towards Brother Roy Al. He always kept his head up high, a smile on his lips whenever a patron passed. But she recognized the depleting flame in his eyes, filled with sadness and unease.

"Are you mourning for your brother and nephew today, Brother?" Jemma asked.

"I do not believe they died in the Storm," Brother Roy Al stated. "We already know Elder Don Van survived; that much is certain. It is likely they did as well."

"But what if they did not? Do you not wish them to be welcome into the Effluvium?" Jemma read the reports in the paper about Elder Don Van's survival. How he'd escaped the collapsing Temple, Jemma still didn't know. The commotion from the Storm of Nightmares masked most of the events in a deep yellow haze.

"That, Sister Jey Ma, is for Death's guiding hand to decide."

She bowed her head as another vagrant walked by, dumping an old teddy bear into the fire. Its plush face burned in the flame, two coal-like eyes watching her. *Be mindful, be pure, be callous. You are here for the Order and the Effluvium; stay strong.*

As the townsfolk came and went, she kept her stance firm. She paid due smiles to those in their mourning grays and assisted those who stepped away from the fire with tears in their eyes. A kerchief became her saving grace, each person sniffling a thank you as they left the pyre.

"Come on, Alexandria!"

Mrs. Janette Harley approached the pyre, carrying a pile of tattered books and two mud-caked boots. Her young daughter, Alexandria, plodded at her side, two long braids swinging against her shoulders, her new-minted round glasses reflecting the fire's fury.

"Ma! What're you doing with Brent's books?" Alexandria yanked at her mother's hand. "He'll be mad!"

"Brent's not coming back, I told you!" Mrs. Harley spat at her daughter.

The girl recoiled.

Mrs. Harley turned away from her daughter and held the books over the fire, tears shimmering on her cheeks.

"Wait!" From up the path, Old Madame Gonzo limped after them. The woman let out a heave, leaning her hand on one tree, before speaking again. "What are you doing? You must have hope!"

Janette glared back at her. "He'd be home by now if he were alive! He was a wonderful boy! That damn...that girl! She took him away! We worked everything out. He was going to marry Jemma! He was going to be right!"

Jemma continued to stand tall, but part of her wanted to shrink into her robe and brush her red hair behind her face. She remembered back when she and Brent first agreed to the arrangement under Brother Roy Al's guise. Mrs. Harley's face lit up with hope. Only Brent still carried the black stamp, still had silver eyes that attracted demons, and still, no matter what anyone pleaded, kept telling stories.

Per the Order, per the Guard, stories attracted demons. They belonged under lock.

Though even Jemma had to admit, Brent Harley told a marvelous tale.

She pushed away the confession at once.

For the good of the Effluvium, she couldn't get distracted by petty tales. As much as she wanted to open her heart to the stories, her desire to change the Order from within meant maintaining poise and composure. Brother Roy Al taught her that.

Stories and magic would be a distraction. She had to keep looking forward.

Madame Gonzo placed a hand on Janette's shoulder. "He and Briannabella were always fond of each other. They were bound to run away—"

"Why should I trust you? You said your granddaughter was dead! You damn liar! I thought we were friends, Beatriz!"

"It was for—"

"For what? Her safety?" Janette threw one of the three books into the fire as she screamed. "Well, it done screwed over my son then, right?"

"Jan—"

Jemma cracked her neck and stepped forward. "Mrs. Harley—"

"Oh! Sister Jey Ma!" Mrs. Harley stopped, holding a picture book over the flames, "I apologize for the disturbance, dear."

"Your son and I called off the betrothal weeks before he vanished. I gave him and Miss Smidt my blessing. They were always going to run off together. It was just a matter of when."

"I don't believe that."

"Please, Janette, you are being irrational. Come. I'll make tea." Madame Gonzo offered a hand to her.

"I'd rather spend time with my vagrant husband than you!" Janette barked. She dropped the remaining books on the ground, steps away from the fire, before storming off.

Alexandria stared at the ground, her cheeks pale, gray eyes reminiscent of her brother's kind stare. She scratched at the black stamp on her wrist, the one given to her the day before the Storm of Nightmares. With Brother Roy Al's help, she did not face the same discrimination her brother endured, left instead with a bitter reminder that the Order watched.

Though sometimes, that was for the best.

Jemma picked the books off the ground, dusted them off, and handed them to Alexandria.

The girl smiled.

"Alexandria!"

"I'm coming!" She darted off behind her mother.

Silence drizzled after Alexandria fled, only broken by Madame Gonzo's single sigh. Brother Roy Al finally left his spot on the stairs, approaching the old woman with his usual grace and candor. He took both of her hands. "I am sure your granddaughter is safe."

Everyone knew the truth now. Briannabella Smidt was Madame Gonzo's long-believed dead granddaughter, the girl she'd named Rhodana, born with a flower on her head.

Madame Gonzo's head fell as she said, "I may never see her again. She's wanted throughout Rosada for terrorism...not that she has done anything wrong! She protected this town—"

"Only after causing destruction," Brother Roy Al reminded her. "I have spoken with Senator Heartz. She wishes to pardon your granddaughter, but the Senate sees this as a national threat, so the case must be heard at that level. There are too many of the Order's puppets in the High Chambers to pardon a girl of magic."

"I am aware, Brother!" Madame Gonzo snapped. "But her father is struggling more than you can imagine! And I am withering. But..." She glanced towards the garden where the Senator's immortal camellia bushes highlighted the path. "As long as the camellias keep blooming, I know she'll be okay."

After the pyre weakened to a soft evening glow, plumes of smoke bubbling over the ashes, Jemma retired with Brother Roy Al to the Year Glass Atrium above the pews. The Temple had yet to reach its former glory, merely a shadow of its former self, scarred with charred furniture and a few saddened patrons.

Brother Roy Al knelt before the Year Glass, watching as the strange red-metallic liquid swirled in its confinement, not speaking a word. Sometimes, when Jemma watched it with the other Brothers and Sisters of the Order, she swore someone stared back at her.

Perhaps the eyes of the Effluvium itself.

Brother Roy Al rubbed his glasses and sighed. Though only a decade older than Jemma, wrinkles embedded themselves around his eyes. He'd been more flustered lately, pacing well into the evening after conducting prayer, and though always a man of few words, he'd grown quieter. The stress of mending faith in the Domicile weighed on his shoulders. Jemma stood by his side through it all, even as other Brothers and Sisters traveled to the Capitol Rosada and the Holy City of Ab Aeterno in protest.

Together, she believed, they could bring Newbird's Arm back to its Golden Age.

Brother Roy Al repositioned his glasses, peering down at the pews. "The town continues to distrust the Order. People do not come to services. They see the scar that Elder Don Van left. It has tainted us."

Jemma knelt beside the Brother and took his hands. "Pardon, Brother Roy Al, but we have made great strides in the past few months. The riots are slowing. The vagrants are calm. If we host a glorious Year Birth Festival after Winter's Wane, I think the town will rejoice!"

Brother Roy Al shook his head. "It will not matter—"

"We must try!"

"Sister Jey Ma, let me finish my sentence!" Brother Roy Al snapped.

Jemma bit her tongue.

He shook his head and closed his eyes. "I apologize, Sister, but you are too naïve to understand this. Too hopeful. But you must listen now, for our time together is limited."

"What do you mean, Brother?"

"I received word from the Order after the elections a few nights ago. They are sending Elder Lau Rel here from Knoll's Gully. Upon her arrival, they asked that I return to Ab Aeterno for reeducation. They claim I cannot run the town unless I know the doctrine in purity and entirety."

Jemma gawked at him, flabbergasted by the sudden announcement. Everything had been going so well! "But if you're not here, who will I train with? Brother Mar Van and Sister Reb Ka are not as knowledgeable. I chose to be your apprentice for a reason, Brother."

"Elder Lau Rel will tend to your training, Sister Jey Ma, do not fret. She is knowledgeable, and if you follow her guise, you will succeed. Do not be afraid. You will be a sister of the Order yet."

Jemma's heart fell to the pit of her stomach. After all their work, the Order reclaimed Newbird's Arm. And this time, they wouldn't let magic and disorder slip through their fingers.

"Can I come with you?" she asked.

"Nay, dear Sister, this is my quest. It is for the best that you stay here." He squeezed her hands. "For if you leave, who will carry the torch of change?"

CHAPTER FIVE

THE ORB

B ria stayed in her small apartment until her monthly bleed ended, only leaving twice to get food and cottons to prevent her sheets from staining. The cramps proved nightmarish, and any time she dared to leave for more than an hour, nausea ripped through her body. Instead, she let sleep take her away, dreaming of living on a cloud, wrapped in the wind, away from trouble.

Until her nightmares pried open the wounds from the past, sending her running through a collapsing forest and away from all she held dear.

The morning it passed, and after watching streaks of light catch the curtains, she forced herself out of bed, sulking over to the cupboard in search of something to eat. All she found was a stale loaf of bread and a moldy lemon. *Grandmama would yell at you. What would she think of you now?*

She'd think you're behaving foolishly.

But what am I supposed to do? It's not like I can go home.

Her hunger pangs forced her to dress. Bria left the apartment with her cowl acting as a hood and headed outside and down Celosia towards the shops. Sleet drizzled through the air, producing a white film on the cobblestone. Few patrons, to Bria's relief, braved the depressing weather. Many shops had closed early, with restaurants operating on a ghost staff, and even beggars took shelter in their makeshift tents in the alleys.

The Little Shop on the Corner of Myrtle and Celosia remained open. Boards covered the broken window, with its single lantern flickering in front of the entrance. As usual, the shop was quiet. It was much like all the other shops, especially by the city square: petty potions, over-priced gems, and traditional goods and wares. Whenever Bria went inside, the unremarkable nature of the shop masked her. And like always, the shopkeeper with dragon tattoos on his arms didn't look up as the bell rang, engrossed in the newspaper spread out before him.

Bria nodded in his direction then meandered down the rows, running her fingers along the shelves of jams and honeys before reaching the strange gimmicky potions. With titles like "love potion," "honor elixir," and "forget-me-not," she couldn't take any of them seriously. But what wonders it would do to forget her troubles and be carefree.

Don't be foolish. It doesn't work like that. Bria shook her head and gathered up her groceries.

An empty counter greeted Bria when she returned to the front of the shop, a lone bell sitting on the counter. She looked around twice, waiting for the shopkeeper to reemerge, and then tapped it.

A voice sang from behind the curtain. "Toddle! There's a customer!"

"Can you get it?!?" the shopkeeper's voice boomed from upstairs.

"I'm with Madame Owiti!"

"And I am in the loo!"

Bria almost laughed.

"Fine! If you insist!" Out waltzed a woman as striking as moonlight. Decorated in a purple dress speckled like a starry night, her pale skin and white hair reflected the candlelight, while her red-stained eyes lit up like fire. A smile punctuated her round face. "Ah! Hello! You're back."

"Just these, please." Bria shifted, looking down at her feet.

"You always get the same things, don't you? Wheat bread? Lackluster honey? Frowning oranges? This is food for sad people! Are you sad?" the shopkeeper's wife prodded as she recorded the items in her notepad. "You need not be sad."

Bria still didn't meet the woman's gaze as she responded, "I'm fine."

The woman stopped bagging the items and placed her hand on Bria's wrist. "That's the answer of a sad person too."

Bria stepped back and met the woman's gaze. She was striking, really, with a smile punctuated by two dimples, eyes like crimson, and hair as white as snow.

"Oh, and your poor eyes! There's such little hope in them! You're looking for something, right?"

Bria blinked.

"I can help! Have you ever had a reading done?"

"A reading?" Bria recited the words to herself.

"Come, the first one is free! I think it will help!"

Bria hesitated. Her own paranoia told her to leave with her things and not return, but curiosity got the better of her. What did she have to lose? Nothing at this point. Perhaps a reading would give her clarity on Brent.

Or peace of her own mind.

She followed the shopkeeper's wife through the curtain. Bria half expected to enter a magical chamber, but the room behind it was nothing but a bland storage closet, with a single lantern hanging on the wall. A silver orb waited on a pedestal in the center of the room as the only remarkable object. Behind it sat an old ochre-toned woman with candid crimson eyes and a wide smile holding a young boy with similar red eyes on her knee. When Bria blinked, she swore a second child rested on the woman's other knee.

"By the way, my name is Lex." The shopkeeper's wife curtsied, then motioned to the old woman. "This is my friend Madame Owiti and my sons Garrett," she pointed to the boy bouncing on the woman's lap, "and Preston." She indicated to the woman's empty knee where an ephemeral mist gathered.

Bria tried to focus, but without Brent there, her sight had gotten weaker. Bria knew throughout Mert, the mere existence of second-world sight was stronger and more popular because of the hefty presence of Magii and Seers. Yet, beyond the known visitation of Mist Keepers and a thick flickering mist, it was hard to get a stable glimpse without a guide.

Bria recollected her thoughts. "You can call me...Rho."

"Very well, Rho. Please have a seat."

Rho. The name made her stomach turn. An uneasiness followed her with any insinuation that she was still

Rho. After all, Rho knocked down the wall in Newbird's Arm, Rho killed Cadet Lawry, and Rho fought off monsters and Mist Keepers. Would Rho waste away in Mert?

No. She'd search for answers.

Bria lowered herself onto the pillow before the orb. Lex sat opposite her, moving her fingers over the sphere before guiding Bria's own hand over the surface and resting it on top.

Madame Owiti called from her seat in the corner. "Remember what I told you, Lex. Focus and the visions will come."

"Yes, yes, very well. Rho, focus with me." Lex pressured.

Bria gawked at Lex, still uncertain about what was happening. "I'm sorry...on what? What are we reading?"

"Oh, you aren't a Mert native, are you? Did you not read pamphlets in the square about our Signature Seer Readings?"

"I haven't been paying attention much..." Bria looked away again.

"How can you not know? Mert's known for her sight!" Lex laughed, smooth like melted chocolate. "You haven't heard the stories? Or seen the flyers?"

"I might have, but...I don't know. It's not something I paid attention to, I guess." Bria slumped. She'd seen the flyers. Once, she even mentioned to Brent about talking with a seer and seeing if they could find answers about his supposed death curse. Later, she abandoned that notion as preposterous and hopeless. Brent's fate seemed sealed...even if it went down the unlikely path.

Why hadn't she thought of returning?

Madame Owiti interjected with a kind chuckle, reaching over and patting Bria's hand. "Now now, it's alrighty. Madame Owiti understands. Life gets in the way, and we funnel our way into our heads, yes, yes?"

Bria recoiled and pulled her hand back, not meeting Madame Owiti's gaze.

"In Mert, we're always here to help. Mert has been a haven for seers for almost two thousand years. Our namesake, the lovely Merta, was a seer, and while she is long gone, she is not forgotten. We seers congregate here to conduct readings and help young lasses like yourself, you understand, yes? We sense your emotions, your aura. We can speak to the dead and examine the past. So, we can help you, yes? Do you agree, yes?" Madame Owiti grinned, a twinkle in her eyes that reminded Bria of her grandmama.

"Madame Owiti tells me I have the gift!" Lex added. "I've got the red eyes and an aura of gold. So, I've been training and would love to help you find answers. Maybe you'll be the one I can finally see!"

Bria pondered for a second, then agreed. "Okay."

"So will you let me do the reading?"

Bria nodded.

Lex clapped her hands, beaming at Madame Owiti like a child, then turned back to the orb. She reached for Bria's hands and guided them over the orb's surface again. "Focus. What do you want to know?"

Bria tensed at Lex's touch but focused her attention on her reflection twisting in the orb. She looked tired, even in the distorted image. Hopeless. "I want to know how to have a normal life."

"That is not an answerable question, dear. Since what is normal, yes yes?" Madame Owiti asked.

"Oh. Um. Then I want to know how to save him." Bria gulped. She held onto the silly notion that saving Brent would give her normalcy.

"Save who?" Lex pressured.

"Brent."

"And what is wrong with this Brent?" As Lex spoke, she glanced once at Madame Owiti for reassurance. The old woman nodded.

Choosing her words proved difficult, but Bria managed the next sentence in a hoarse whisper. "He lost his mind."

"Oh! I think that's enough for me to work with. Let us focus together on finding your answer."

Bria wasn't sure what to make of the performance, but she did as she was told, gazing deep into the silver orb. Lex hummed a prayer to the Constable Gelida of Heims and the Sun God of Yilk. As she sang, the surface moved beneath her fingertips, liquid-like, reminiscent of the strange liquid that counted the passing days in the Order's year glasses.

While Lex closed her eyes, tracing the orb's surface and humming out loud, Bria found herself entirely entranced by the orb. As Lex's fingers danced across it, the liquid followed. Magnetic. Enchanted.

Then it fell still.

And like a window, two dark eyes stared back at Bria. They blinked once and vanished.

Bria jumped, her fingers locked in place, glued to the orb. The silver liquid within it continued gathering around her fingertips. Why was it pulling at her? Did Lex feel it?

It had to be in her head, right? It was just a fixture. A prop for Lex's performance. Nothing more. It couldn't be anything more.

But she couldn't pull her fingers away.

Lex was unphased, finally breaking out of her song. "Love...love is the answer."

"Huh?" Bria gawked.

"To save Brent. You must love him, and he will be well. That is what the orb tells me."

"No...I didn't see that. I saw...didn't you see the eyes?"

"What are you talking about?" Lex's lips parted into an asymmetric smile.

Behind her, Madame Owiti's attention piqued.

"Someone was looking at me!" Bria tugged again, but her hand remained latched to the glass. "And I can't move my hand!"

"What? What do you mean?"

Madame Owiti's placed Garrett and his mist-brother on the ground then hurried over to Bria. She placed her callused hand on Bria's arm and gave a tug. "Do you have magic?"

"Yes," Bria replied. It was weird being candid about it, but in Mert, it didn't matter.

"And you have some form of sight, correct?"

"I guess?"

"I see." The old woman glanced at Lex. "Go upstairs with Garrett and Preston. I'll handle this."

"But this is my reading!" Lex argued.

"This is more than a simple reading, my dear. Remember, I told you to be wary of who you expose to the orb? Yes, yes, you must remember?"

"But—"

"Please go upstairs. I'll explain later."

"I want to help!" Lex objected.

Bria closed her eyes tighter, ignoring the argument. The magnetic pull from the orb drew her fingers closer. Her arm hurt. Her head spun. She wanted it to stop.

Go away. Go away. Please go away!

Was someone trying to get in her head? No. It couldn't be. She was only tired. She wouldn't go through that again!

But her head continued to buzz. It shrieked even.

It was almost as if flowers cried out to her.

Were they drowning?

Was *she* drowning?

Everything screamed.

And Bria did too.

"Stop! Let go of me!"

She pulled back. The orb ruptured. But glass didn't go flying.

Instead, the silver liquid exploded around the room, painting the walls chrome. It splattered on Madame Owiti and Lex as they argued. The children laughed with excitement.

Bria gasped, stumbling backward.

There, where the orb once sat, twelve red peonies bloomed in a silver pool.

PHANTOM ROT

An odd silver goo covered Todd.

It dripped from his fingers and arms like tendrils while his ears popped from the mild explosion that ruptured behind the curtain.

Todd huffed. This was the last straw! He was putting an end to this madness; Madame Owiti had done enough! Every day the woman showed up, Lex ended up either flustered, over-confident, or exhausted. While she curled up in the bed without dinner, Todd alone cleaned the shop and tending to Garrett. Lex floundered in a pool filled with lies. The old woman was mad! She consistently put in Lex's head that Garrett's brother, Preston, was a ghost hanging around in the shop. If that were the case, then why didn't he show himself? A load of malarkey, in Todd's opinion!

He stomped into the back room and glared. The liquid covered the walls and the floor. Garrett sat on the floor, tracing his fingers through the liquid like paint. Meanwhile, Madame Owiti stood in the center of the room, dripping in the liquid, while beside her sat that petite girl who frequented the shop. A bundle of red flowers congregated at her knees.

"What the hell is going on in—" He stopped himself, his attention falling onto Lex. She stumbled forward from against the wall, paler than a sheet of paper, her eyes wide and dilated. She opened and closed her mouth. Then, with a dramatic gasp, she fell forward with a thud.

"LEX!"

He rushed forward, pushing Madame Owiti aside. Lex's lips bubbled, the silver goo around her mouth popping and comingling with blood. Todd raised her head as she choked. "Lex? Lex! Are you a'ight? What...what happened? Lex!" He turned to Madame Owiti and the girl, "WHAT DID YOU DO!?!"

"I don't know," the girl squeaked. "It just exploded...I couldn't control it!

Todd glared at her. "You tried to KILL HER!"

"No...I didn't mean to, I swear!"

Todd grabbed the girl's wrist, hoisting her up like a rag doll. She squirmed, face paling, and pulled out of his grip. He noticed a Rosadian betrothal mark stamped into the back of her hand. "I'll have you arrested and sent back to Rosada—"

"Toddle! You're scaring your sons!" Madame Owiti diffused him with a single glare, holding Garrett close to her. The boy hid his face in her legs.

He dropped the girl to the ground. She withered, hugging herself and looking away. The silver liquid bubbled at her feet.

"I—" He stared at Garrett, then back at Lex.

Madame Owiti continued, "Instead of screaming at this poor girl, why don't you get your wife some help, yes, yes?"

"But what HAPPENED?"

"Rho's magic reacted poorly to the reading." Madame Owiti motioned to the girl.

"So she attacked my wife!?!"

"Stop asking questions and go get help, you numb-skull!"

Todd blinked, then rushed out of the backroom and out the front door. In haste, he flicked through the different color flames in the lantern: yellow, white, green, red, and then blue. Once the flame reached a constant glow, he rushed back inside the shop.

Madame Owiti had propped Lex up on a pillow. Todd shot a glare at her before lifting Lex, her breaths shallow and skin clammy, into his arms. "Sirens will be here soon. I expect you gone when I return."

"Toddle—" Madame Owiti objected.

"BOTH of you! You've messed with Lex and Garrett more than I like. It's not good for her!"

"Toddle, listen—"

"And clean up this mess before you leave, and lock up on your way out!" He snarled, then glanced at his little son. "Garrett! Come!"

Garrett waddled behind him, pouting. Todd felt bad for snapping, but he'd find time to apologize later; for now, his thoughts remained only on Lex. They came to Mert for protection, but this wasn't what he had in mind.

It didn't take long for the siren to arrive. A hunky piece of machinery with a loud bell and flashing blue lights, it pulled up in front of his shop with a *screech*. The medicks rushed out and hauled Lex onto a stretcher and into the back of the siren, where Todd joined them, holding Garrett on his lap.

Riding in the siren, with its odd chugging gears, smelled of rubber and smoke. The medicks acted fast, almost mechanically, hooking Lex up to an oxygen tank while counting out her pulse and speaking in fast Mertoni. Todd understood not a word, never bothering to learn the language himself when the Common Tongue was so prevalent.

The Sanatorium waited in the northeastern corner of Mert, past the City Square, before the paved roads turned out towards the Chessboard Plains. It glistened with pearl white stone, four stories tall, sprawling over the cross streets, a beacon of both hope and death. Todd never liked it; each time he came here, he left with only heartache.

Upon arrival, the medicks wheeled Lex into the primary facility without saying a word to Todd. He chased after them, Garrett on his hip. The receptionist stopped them by closing the ward door with a snap of their fingers.

"Oi!" Todd spat.

The receptionist didn't look up from the newspaper. "We'll call you when she is stable."

"But—"

"Please take a seat, sir."

Todd cursed under his breath and collapsed in the chair, bouncing his son on one knee. He tried to focus, placing his attention on the bare space between his knuckles. His elaborate dragon tattoo, interwoven with the old black stamp on his wrist, stopped just above his knuckles. Why hadn't he filled it in yet? He could have dedicated the tattoo to Lex! Now she might die, and he had never even thought to garnish his skin for her.

Garrett pulled Todd from his thoughts, tugging on his shirt.

"What? What is it? Todd grunted at the wall.

Garret pointed at the floor.

"You want down?"

Garrett shook his head. "Pres!"

"Preston? No." Todd growled, "He stayed home."

"No! No!" Garrett protested.

"Then go on the floor and play with him!" Todd snapped. His voice bounced around the empty lobby. Oh, how he despised the way Madame Owiti encouraged Garrett to play with his imaginary friend! The last thing the little boy needed was to think his younger brother was alive, of all things!

Garrett stared at his father, tears budding in the corners of his eyes. Slowly, he climbed from Todd's lap and onto the floor, crossing his arm and pouting.

Todd looked away, tapping his foot and fingers. A few times, he went to say something to his son, but the little boy had either forgotten the outburst or was content on the floor playing with *Preston*. Todd just had to remind himself that it was okay; boys his age had imaginary friends.

But he won't grow up if he can't move past this.

Todd glared at the clock on the wall. Time passed with no updates.

He inquired with the receptionist every few minutes. Had they stabilized her yet? They'd already changed shifts! Surely, she should be okay by now...right? The receptionist barked back, more annoyed with each question, before pointedly saying that if he didn't sit down, they would escort him out of the Sanitorium.

Todd collapsed again on the bench and resumed tapping his foot.

He lost track of how long it took for the doctor to emerge from the double doors. But when the doors finally parted, a bulky doctor with short curly hair and olive-toned skin greeted him. They wore a pointed, bird-like mask on their face. Upon noticing Todd, they removed the mask. Their eyes looked like pits on their face, made even darker by the white light bouncing from their jacket. Round lips pursed, they marched across the room and held a hand to Todd.

"Mr. Dray? I'm Dr. Kafele."

"Yes, thanks." Todd shook their hand. "How is she? Is she a'ight?"

"She is stable. We have put her in the Intensive Care Unit for observation, but I believe she will recover."

Todd exhaled in relief.

"But I do need to mention—"

Todd interjected, "Can I see her?"

"She needs her rest, Mr. Dray."

"Can I see her!?!" Todd pried again.

"Yes, but—"

Todd didn't hear what Dr. Kafele said next. He picked Garrett up in his arms, then rushed past them and through the double doors. Garrett whined and fidgeted as the undeniable smell of blood and death lingered in the halls. He quickened his pace as he rushed past the magical and non-magical wards, beyond the psych ward, towards the Intensive Care Unit. This wasn't the first time he'd been there. Between Preston's illness and Lex's occasional outbursts, he was all too familiar with this path.

Intensive Care lingered down a hallway wreaking of urine and a twinge of magic. Here, magical and non-magical ailments collided. In one bed lay a man with his fingers turned to icicles, while in another lay a man with half his face burned sideways.

Lex lay in the bed beside the two men. Dry blood coated her lips, her hair sticking up at all angles, fingers trembling as she inhaled and exhaled.

Her veins wove through her skin like black tree branches, crossing her arms and up to ward her chest.

"Lex!" Todd raced forward. A towering nurse stepped in front of him before he could pass through the doors.

He hadn't even seen the man, but he emerged from the pristine walls, hand outstretched to keep Todd from running forward. Todd glared. "Oi! Let me see her!"

The nurse's voice hung heavy. "This unit is highly vulnerable. Please stay behind the glass."

"That's my wife, though!"

"She's recovering."

"But the doctor said she was stable!"

"With a caveat!" Dr. Kafele's voice purred from behind Todd.

Todd glared.

The doctor disregarded it and looked up at the nurse. "Mr. Varden, please tend to the patient in Ward Nine. Miss Edith is finishing her therapies with him presently."

"Yes, Dr. Kafele." The tall nurse bowed. Even with his head lowered, he still towered over Todd.

A bitter silence loitered in the hallway as the nurse left. The ticking clock echoed while a muffled moan from the icicle-finger man in the intensive care ward sang with it. Todd pressed one hand to the glass, watching Lex's chest rise and fall in sync with the clock's ticks and tocks.

Todd clenched his fist. "You said she is stable! This don't look stable!"

"She is stable. She is recovering." Dr. Kafele placed a gentle hand on his arm. "We need to run further tests to see the extent of the damage."

"From what?" Todd barred his teeth. He would find that girl who caused this and hand her over to the authorities. First the so-called Story Collector, now this! What a week!

Dr. Kafele continued, "Your wife has what we call Retrogressive Phantom Rot."

"What now?"

"It's a magical degenerative disorder. It is due to multiple reasons, but more often than not, it means... To put it simply, your wife is allergic to magic."

"Wha-what? We've lived in Mert for years! She's been fine until today!" Todd's stomach turned as he spoke. "It was just some freakish Magii! She caused some orb-thing to explode!"

"Was the orb magical?"

"How the fuck should I know? What does it matter!?!"

"We saw signs of it in her bloodwork and on her clothes. With that heavy a dose, it was enough to trigger the allergy. So, her entire body attacked the magic. And then it attacked her too."

Dr. Kafele's blunt tone did not soften the blow. Todd felt his lunch rising into his throat again, but he swallowed it down, instead resorting to a series of profanity-laden sentences. He always hated magic! Of course, this would happen to *his* family! This was that girl's fault...and Madame Owiti! It was both of their fault! If he ever saw them again, he would call the coppers in a heartbeat. How dare they hurt her!

Todd squeezed Garrett closer, holding back another stream of curses, dropping his voice instead to ask, "She'll be fine, right?"

Dr. Kafele stared at Lex through the glass. "Unfortunately, Phantom Rot is a chronic disease that does not go away. Once exposed to a heavy dosage of magic, it activates inside an individual's body. In other nations, it doesn't matter as much. But when it activates in Mert...it is deadly. We can stabilize her and provide her medications once we discover how far she has progressed. She can live a long and happy life under the right circumstances. So, Mr. Dray, I would highly advise you to get your wife on the first airship you can afford. Head to Kainan or Rosada, a nation where magic is almost extinct. The only way to prolong your wife's life is to get her as far away from magic as possible. Is that understood?"

Todd's knees gave out, and he slid to the floor, cradling Garrett close. The little boy fidgeted out of his father's arms, walking over to the glass and staring at his mother through it. He pointed at her once, a smile across his face.

"Not now, Garrett. Mama's sleeping," Todd croaked.

Dr. Kafele guided the boy back to Todd as they spoke. "If it is not too far along, she will recover and could live a long life. Do not fret, Mr. Dray."

"You don't understand!" Todd glared at Dr. Kafele, tears filling his eyes. His voice cracked. "I brought her here for safety! If we stayed in Rosada, she never would've gotten sick! She'd be *fine!*"

"Well, now you will find her new safety." Dr. Kafele said without flinching. "You are welcome to stay on this side of the glass, but visiting hours end soon. It might be best for you to go home and rest yourself until the morning."

"But—"

"Plus, this is no place for your son."

Todd knew the doctor was right. He pulled Garrett back over and squeezed him, continuing to stare at his wife through the glass.

I'm so sorry, Lex.

He stayed by the glass long after the doctor left, closing his eyes and tempering his emotions. Long ago, when he'd been a guard in Rosada, he trained himself not to cry. This pulled hard on his heartstrings, though, and he had to blink twice to keep the tears at bay.

Did he even have enough money to afford an airship ticket? They'd have to sell the shop first. Business hadn't been doing well. Myrtle and Celosia were no longer the tourist hotspots. Most attention was on the performers by the Blood Sea and the merchants in the City Centre. But he could probably find someone to take over the business.

Especially once he got those damn gems back.

Todd pressed his hand against the glass one last time before turning away, shuffling a restless Garrett in his arms. The boy didn't ask questions. He never did.

"Garrett, Ma will be a'ight, a'ight?" Todd finally said.

The little boy frowned.

"I promise."

His son still said nothing.

It'll be okay, Todd reminded himself. It'd been a long, terrifying afternoon. By the morning, Garrett would spend time entertaining his imaginary friend again. Lex would be okay. They wouldn't be apart long. He'd be back in the morning.

A crash derailed his thoughts.

The door down the hall to the psych-ward burst open.

A young man with gray-toned skin and haunted yellow eyes ran forward and grabbed Todd's arms. The man shook him once, his chapped lips opening and closing, mist oozing from his skin. A small incision bled from the top of his head, with pieces of glass woven into his mangy hair.

Todd recognized him in an instant.

"You! You stole my gems!"

The boy flinched, eyes narrowing as he stared at Todd. "It's not your fault...not your fault...stop being sad...stop being sad." He strained his neck, and next, his voice changed, pernicious and sharp. "But it's your fault! You murderer! You killed them in cold blood, and you do just the same to her! Your fault!"

Todd's stomach dropped. "What?"

"You killed three people, Mr. Dray. Three people! You naughty bastard—" As the boy spoke, mist wrapped around him, and a shadow of a man holding a pistol formed against the wall. With a single bang, the mist exploded, and the story reeled out in five different directions.

Todd stumbled back. "What're you—what!?!"

"I... I see it... I'm the... stories... I... please stop... please... stop... shite... stop... I wanna go home." The boy sobbed. The mist swayed. "I wanna be... I wanna... I don't... I don't know who I am. I don't know. I don't."

The door flew open. Dr. Kafele rushed out with two other nurses, the tall one from before and a small woman with puffy red hair. They rushed past the doctor and pulled the young man away. He went with them without a fight, tears dripping down his cheeks, the mist flailing about like ghostly vines. The stories followed them back through the ward: tales of a guard shooting down three defenseless individuals, a child crying for their mother, and two lovers dancing through the clouds.

"Thank you for catching him, Mr. Dray." Dr. Kafele remarked.

"He's the Story Collector," Todd stated. He felt stupid making a comment on it, though. Surely the doctor knew that by now.

As staid as ever, Dr. Kafele stated, "I have no clue what you're talking about." Then, without another word, they vanished back into the psych ward.

Todd watched them disappear and blinked. How did the doctor not know? With flyers plastered through the city, everyone kept watch for the Story Collector! There was a hefty bounty—

That's it!

The bounty! He could use the bounty to buy passage out of Mert. When morning came, he would rush to the Station House and tell Detective Walsh and Detective Locasta everything he uncovered!

Finally, they could leave this damn city!

CHAPTER SEVEN

MADAME OWITI

B ria stared, still like a statue, her heart thudding in her ears. She looked around the room. The silver liquid continued to drip from the walls. On the wall, the single lantern flickered, illuminating the red peonies on the table. The flowers pulsated, the liquid echoed, and the room creaked. She still couldn't wrap her head around what happened.

Nor did she know how they would clean up this mess.

Madame Owiti seemed unphased. After the shopkeeper left, she sat down on the cushion and stared at the liquid. At first, all remained still. Then the liquid started to move. As if pulled by a magnetic attraction, it gathered around the peonies, reforming in the shape of the orb. Except for a few speckled drops on the pillows and floor, it was as if silver hadn't coated the room moments ago.

Bria gawked, transfixed.

"Magic." Madame Owiti winked. "Just like you."

Bria fidgeted, unsure what to say to the old woman.

"You're extraordinarily strong. I've seen the orb react to other Magii, of course, but never like this. It was like you felt its heart."

"The peonies?"

"Yes, yes, the peonies."

"It was like they were pulling me..."

Madame Owiti tilted her head to the side, "What is your magic, if I may ask?"

Bria stared at the woman. Usually, she didn't enjoy answering questions about her magic. Even in Mert, a powerful Magii caught eyes. Brent had been the prime example. The last thing she needed was more people knowing.

But Madame Owiti had a strange comfort about her that reminded Bria of her grandmama.

She chose her next words carefully. "I am in tune with nature."

Madame Owiti nodded to herself. "Ah, yes, that explains why you can feel the heart. You are in tune with flowers, yes yes?"

"More than that, I think." Bria reached behind her ear and stroked her little branch. It sighed against her skin, barely moving at her own touch. "I used to think it was just plants, but a few months ago, I discovered I could sometimes cause rain and sinkholes and...and other disasters. And I'm too afraid to find out what else I can do."

"Why?"

"Because there's no one to help me understand," Bria admitted. She never said it aloud, but it was true. At least Brent had the other Mist Keepers. At least seers had other seers. But a powerful Magii? And one with plants? She met no one else with the same magic.

Even after everything, Bria was still alone.

"Deary, you're in the City of Mert! There are plenty of people to help you!"

"No, not this time. Not in this situation."

"Why do you say that?"

"Because what if I lose control? What if I...what if I hurt someone?" Bria shook her head. "I'm already not allowed to go home. My *normal* was torn from me! My best friend is the Story Collector! And I'm...I'm so...I'm lonely. I'm alone. There's no one who can help. I'm...I'm alone."

She dropped her head. It was the first time she'd admitted it. She didn't have anyone to tell: not her grandmama, her father, or Mr. West. Daily, she yearned to be with them, surrounded by the stench of warm lemon cakes and of tea brewing in the kettle. She longed for the market and the Senator's Gardens. She pined for the nights she spent sitting by the cow pasture, naming the newborn calves with Brent. She desired the greenery, the mountains, and the immortal camellias along the paths to her house.

"I want to go home," Bria croaked.

Madame Owiti pulled her into a tight embrace. At first, Bria stiffened. No one had hugged her so closely in months. Yet, its warmth rocked her, and she accepted the hug with open arms. With it, the floodgates opened, and Bria cried. A deepening humidity decorated the room, and as if the room were sweating, moisture gathered on each piece of furniture and glass.

"There there, girly, there there. Why don't we go outside before we cover Toddle's place in mold, yes yes?"

Bria wiped her eyes. "Oh...okay."

Madame Owiti gathered the now-reformed silver orb in her arms, leading Bria out of the shop and down Myrtle, locking the door on her way out.

Once the shop disappeared from their sight, Madame Owiti spoke, "Why don't you come to my place for tea, yes yes? You look like you need some company."

Bria's instincts usually would have said no, but she liked the old woman. Tea, a warm home, and a chance to act normal appealed to her. "I'd like that. Thank you."

Madame Owiti lived in a small apartment on the corner of Myrtle and Maple. It smelled like Bria's grandmama's home, with a few dying plants on the table, a porcelain lamp on the table, and old crocheted blankets covering the couches and chairs. Bria draped her fingers over the plants, letting their leaves bolster again, as Madame Owiti bumbled into the kitchen. Life came easily to the plants, and they curled toward the dimming sunlight in the window at her fingertips.

Madame Owiti returned with a tea kettle and a jar of honey. It wasn't the typical lemon tea Bria had grown up around but a more herbal-based one, sweetened with honey and hibiscus flowers.

"I think tea is the universal language of comfort." Madame Owiti smiled as she poured Bria a cup.

"My grandmama would say the same thing." Bria stared into the cracked cup. The old porcelain even looked like her grandmama's dishware.

"Your grandmama sounds like a wise woman."

Bria managed to smile.

Madame Owiti poured herself a cup and glanced around the room. "You brought my spider plants back to life!"

"Oh...yeah. They just needed a bit of love." Bria ran her fingers across the plant on the table. The leaves curled and crooned at her touch.

"Yes yes, love. Like what Lex recommended for your missing man?"

Bria looked away. "That's different."

"How?"

"Because...he lost his mind."

As if the story were being coaxed out of her, Bria launched into a half-truth about Brent's current state, the same ways she would tell her grandmama. She skipped the entire part about the Mist Keepers but kept the truth about the monster and Brent's ability to collect stories.

When Bria came to the end of her explanation, filled with lack-luster descriptions that would have been better told by Brent, she redirected her attention to her lukewarm tea. "Sorry. I haven't been able to talk to anyone about this. It just came out."

Madame Owiti patted her hand. "Seers have a way of helping people open up. True seers. Like myself. You've never met a true seer? Here in Mert, I mean? We're everywhere, yes yes."

"I've been keeping to myself."

"That's no way to live."

"I've always lived that way. I'm from Rosada. People don't like magic there..."

"Ah, Rosada. Yes, yes, they are quite prejudiced if I say so myself. Yes, yes." Madame Owiti refocused on Bria. "But you must let those thoughts run off you like water. You're in Mert, yes yes? It is time to discover who you are, dear. I see your aura. Your potential is brimming. Why are you so determined to save this boy when you have so much more to live for?"

Bria turned to the window. Orange streaks decorated the rooftops, with evening beginning its lustful descent into the night. "All I ever wanted was a quiet life with the cottage in the woods, a family, just...normalcy. Yes, I wanted to travel, but I wanted it to be by choice and with people I cared about before settling down in a comfortable home. I almost had that too...and I guess I'm just clinging to it."

"But maybe you are destined for more."

"I don't want more! I never wanted more! I...I'm a gardener!" Bria clutched the cup. "Sure, I tried being a hero...but it landed me here, alone, because I'm wanted across Rosada. Did you see in the paper about how Newbird's Pit was destroyed? That was me! It made things worse. I killed someone...I started riots. But I didn't *win*. I tried to be more than a gardener...but what good did that do? I've been a ghost for months! So, I thought maybe if I saved Brent, I could, I don't know, be normal!" Bria closed her eyes to stop another round of tears from forming. "And I love him. He's my best friend, and I love him. I can't let him...vanish."

Madame Owiti joined Bria by the window and placed a hand on her arm, "What has happened in the past doesn't define you now, deary dear. You made your choices, but now it is time to move forward."

They stood there in silence for a few minutes longer. Bria nursed her lukewarm tea, fingers shaking. She didn't revel in being so open. It made her feel vulnerable...but it also gave her heart reprieve. The weight removed itself from her chest, and for a moment, she breathed.

She wasn't alone.

Madame Owiti ultimately broke the silence. "I may have a way to help you, dear."

"You don't have to—"

"It is my job and duty as a seer to help. We see problems, and we try to fix them. So don't stop me. I'll be back in a jiffy!" The woman rushed out of the lounge with her teacup in hand. Clattering in the kitchen followed before the slamming of a door down the tight hallway brought silence.

Bria curled up in the chair, hugging her knees to her chest as she scoured her surroundings. The apartment was comfortable, and she wondered if she fell asleep, if she'd wake up in her grandmama's home instead. Had Bria made herself a prison in her little apartment? Why didn't she ever try to make it a home? But despite the comfort in Madame Owiti's sitting room, Bria's paranoia remained, nagging at the back of her mind. *I should leave. This is too risky. What am I doing here?*

The woman must be tricking her! Why should she trust a seer she just met? She might be working for the Council! Or be an Order spy sent from Rosada!

Or she may be someone legitimately trying to help, Bria reminded herself. But her legs still carried her off the chair and over to the front door. She expected it not to budge, but to her surprise, the door opened when she turned the knob. *She's not keeping you as a prisoner.*

Madame Owiti's call pulled her back. "Rho! Come here!"

Bria hesitantly followed the woman's voice into the lavatory. Madame Owiti knelt before the toilet, staring into the bowl. Bria approached it. The water bubbled with silver, red petals decorating the edges of the porcelain throne.

After a few seconds, the silver substance twirled before stabilizing like it had in the orb a couple hours earlier. There, an image formed of an umber-skinned woman with eyes as red as Madame Owiti's and long coarse hair pulled back in a thick ponytail. The two could have been mother and daughter.

"Tilda!" Madame Owiti clapped her hands. "I was hoping I would get you! I hate dealing with the others. Especially Varden. He is always so formal and enigmatic, yes?"

Tilda chuckled, her voice bubbling from beneath the water's surface. "Yeah, that ain't happening today. Bunch of stuff going on, for sard's sake. Haven't heard the details, though. Been busy derailing some investigations."

Bria noticed the detective badge on Tilda's shirt. *What investigations?*

"Well, I want to introduce you to someone if you have a moment, yes yes." Madame Owiti motioned Bria forward. "This is Rho."

Tilda clapped. "Oh, her aura is beautiful! All that green! Is she a Magii?"

"Yes."

Bria shifted uncomfortably.

Madame Owiti gasped. "Oh! So, so sorry, dear! I forgot to introduce you. This is Tilda Locasta. She is my great-great-great-great-grandmother. She works for the—"

"Wait...what?" Bria gaped at Tilda, then at Madame Owiti. Tilda looked at least fifty years younger than Madame Owiti.

Tilda chuckled. "There're ways to extend life-spans, far beyond your wildest dreams, hun."

"But...immortality...that's a myth!" Bria's mind spun. She believed in Mist Keepers, Diabolo, and ghosts...but the prospect of Tilda being Madame Owiti's senior relative seemed impossible!

Madame Owiti squeezed Bria's wrist. "There are more mysteries in this world than you can imagine, my deary dear. So much of it lies here in Mert too."

"And I have taken the job to protect it as a detective in the Mertoni Police Department," Tilda added.

Bria gawked in disbelief.

Tilda continued, "There are many of us in the city who are doing our best to keep the interests of Magii and Seers alive...here and across the world!"

"Are they all...*immortal?*" The word tasted strange on Bria's tongue. Why couldn't someone be immortal? Mist Keepers existed. Wasn't that already a form of immortality?

"There are four immortals in Mert, but we work with others such as Madame Owiti to create the safety net." Tilda said all of this without hesitation, as if the secret meant nothing, as if it were common knowledge.

"But how? I mean...is it a spell? Or...how?"

"Alchemy." Tilda didn't show signs of explaining much more than that.

Madame Owiti brought the conversation back on track. "Tilda, you've been working on the Story Collector case, haven't you, yes yes?"

Bria perked up at the statement.

"Our leads are few and far between, but yes."

"Rho knows the Story Collector." Madame Owiti glanced at Bria. Once again, the way her burgundy eyes traced Bria's skin felt like a violation of privacy.

"Oh! Kek will be delighted to hear that. They haven't told me much, but they keep saying to make sure my partner and the other coppers ain't on his trail."

"Why?" Bria asked, pushing down the droves of other questions bubbling at the tip of her tongue.

"Not sure, honestly. Ain't any of my business. Kek's got a way of working. Guess they don't think the kid is that bad or anything. Though don't know why they're all so fixated on that pathetic sap. Your aura is way more interesting. The Story Collector's aura is this disgusting yellow."

Madame Owiti agreed, "I think Kek would be very interested in getting to know her, don't you, yes yes?"

"Oh indeed. For more reasons than one."

Bria looked away from the toilet bowl for a moment. Her head raced. Her heart fluttered. Six months ago, she'd been looking for answers like this. All the possibilities bounced through her head. Could the immortals hold the truth behind her magic? Could they save Brent from himself? Or would they hate him like everyone else? Did they know about the Mist Keepers?

Madame Owiti took her hand. "I know this is a lot, Rho; I apologize for springing this on you so quickly."

"But I think we gotta act fast. I'mma gonna talk with the others and get you clearance and all." Tilda beamed, showing off one silver tooth.

"Trust us," Madame Owiti finished.

"I'll try. It's a lot to take in..." Bria blinked. "But I'll try."

"Excellent. I'll reach out to—" A muffled shout came from inside the toilet bowl, and Tilda turned. "I'm coming, love! Be right there!" Tilda turned back and laughed. "Sorry, promised my lady we'd eat some fresh fish she caught. Sorry 'bout that. No matter. I'll reach out once I get contact, yes?"

"You got a new woman?" Madame Owiti pried.

"Sort of..." Tilda blushed.

"Oh, are you flirting with coworkers again?"

"Be quiet, Awiti, or I'll tell your mama on you!"

"My mama is dead."

"We're seers. I can tell her whenever I want."

Bria couldn't help but smile.

"Aw! What a pretty smile you have, Rho." Another muffled shout cut off Tilda. She turned to the door, bellowed in a foreign language, then returned to Bria and Madame Owiti. "I best get going. It was wonderful meeting you, Rho." Tilda waved, and the pool went dark.

Madame Owiti motioned with her hand, and the silver liquid raised out of the water, captured the peony petals, and reformed into a sphere.

Bria eyed the orb. She continued to process what had happened, running the conversation through her head a few times.

"Go home, dear. I'll stop by once Tilda has an update." Madame Owiti beamed. "You live on Celosia and Conifer, yes? About two blocks from the shop?"

"How did you—"

"I'm a seer. I know things."

Bria didn't like that answer, but her walls of defense had fallen. Instead, she merely bowed her head, thanked Madame Owiti, and left the apartment into Mert's brisk night air.

CHAPTER EIGHT

ELDER LAU REL

J emma woke before the roosters crowed. She made her bed, with her teddy bear Miss Porridge positioned in the center of the two pillows, before joining her parents and younger brother, James, in the kitchen for breakfast. Neither of them looked up, engaged in a conversation about the cow pastures while clinking away with their silverware and glasses. They barely said a word to her since her betrothal became void. It disappointed her parents; as a Sister of the Order, she would never bear children. Sure, she could marry and have relations if she desired, but her existence would be nothing more than a ghost in the Effluvium to them, no matter the pull she obtained in Rosada.

Jemma had never been all that close with her parents. Growing up, her mother spent most days tending to the field while her father completed odd jobs around town. They left Jemma to her own devices, trusting her to complete her studies and occupy her time. At a young age, she found solace in the Temple after playing an elaborate game of *Come Find Me*. When Brother Roy Al found her, rather than scolding her, he introduced her to the scripture and the Effluvium. She spent her days admiring the architecture, sketching out patterns in her notebook. For a time, she wanted to be an architect, but her mother scoffed at that idea. They wanted her to take over the farm, raise a family...be them.

But Jemma continued to go back to the Temple and embrace the scripture. Her parents thought it a pipe dream, but as she grew older, she espoused the Temple's teachings. The betrothal was her parents' way of stopping that.

They never expected everything to fall apart.

Now, as Sister Jey Ma, her parents disregarded her, treating her like a guest in their household rather than their daughter. At first, Jemma's heart sank when her mother didn't meet her gaze or her father refused to speak her name. But was it that much different compared to her childhood? They had always been so busy; when James was born, all their attention fell onto him.

Now, they could mold him into exactly what they wanted: the heir to the Reds Family Farm.

So be it.

"Towers are coming today." Her father broke the silence as he read over the Gazette, pushing back his thick-rimmed glasses and grunting.

Her mother didn't glance up from her meal. "We aren't allowing them on the fields. I already sent a telegram to the Senator reinforcing that. They get the shite water near the Pit and the old train tracks. That's it."

"All because that damn Roy Carver can't keep his mouth shut."

Jemma dropped her fork and glared. "Brother Roy Al is doing what's best for Newbird's Arm!"

"If he was, then he'd keep his damn mouth shut. He's a petty fucking low-tier Brother. He shouldn't be questioning jackshite."

"Father, he—"

"Jemma Abby Reds, do not argue with me!" Her father slammed his fist on the table. That stopped the discussion in an instant. With the silence staying, he didn't humor the topic any further, flipping to the next page and commenting on the weather down in Grover's Marsh.

Jemma scowled, pushing away her untouched meal and excusing herself from the table. Her parents acknowledged her with a small grumble, and James didn't even meet her gaze. Not that it mattered. She was twenty-one now. They had no say over her.

She pulled on her coat and left the house without another word. Just one more year, she kept reminding herself. Once her training to become a sister of the Order ended, she'd be able to move into the Temple's cloister and be free of her parents' judgment.

Even her parents' plantation, decorated with a glamorous mansion and sprawling fields, left a bitter taste in her mouth. She grew up surrounded by the fortune and privilege of a well-off family. It shocked everyone that she considered a life enthralled with the Order. Why give up such glamor?

To help. That was always Jemma's reasoning. She wanted to help cleanse the vagrants of their demons, she wanted to help Brent have a future, and now, she wanted to help Brother Roy Al bring change. So, if that meant abandoning her parents, so be it. There were bigger things out there than a rich plantation overlooking the vagrants as they worked day in and out.

The roads bustled with curious townsfolk awaiting the Tower. It'd been nearly twenty-two years since a tower arrived in Newbird's Arm. An ominous chill ran through the market square, and even the vagrants did not dare cross over their broken fence. People whispered, waiting, wondering, but cautious all the same.

Jemma joined Brother Roy Al on the bottom steps of the Temple and pressed her fingers to her lips, holding them up to the ruby embezzled Year Glass. Just past it, from the mountains, steam rose into the air, riding on the back of a train emerging from the foothills. A shadow of a tower moved behind it along the train tracks, like a beast born from the mountain range. Its dark exterior, composed of stone and pipes, whistled behind the train.

Where the Newbird River crossed the tracks, the Tower slowed and unhinged itself from the train. Two stilt-like fixtures pushed it over the tracks, then lowered it into the water. The rivers flooded its banks, pooling into the creases between the bricks in the market square, dampening the flyers strewn across the walkway.

Patrons in the market square backed away in awe, both enchanted and distraught by the arrival. Madame Gonzo motioned from her porch in anger, pointing to the flooded market, while mothers guided their children away from the scene. Vagrants rushed into the Pit.

Brother Roy Al, as determined as ever, motioned for Jemma to follow him through the market. She lifted her skirt up to her ankles, sloshing through each of the puddles. *So much for these shoes,* she scowled as she stepped through another puddle. *I should have known better and put on my boots!*

Captain Randal and his men waited at the base of the Tower to greet their counterparts. Guards draped in the traditional gray uniforms of Knoll with the hourglass insignia on their pockets marched out from the giant steel doors with anger and determination in their gazes. Knoll's Captain towered over Captain Randal, a big man with sleek silver hair that towered over the other Guards.

Jemma didn't hear much of what the Guards said before they trooped into town. The two captains detouring towards the Senator's Gardens. Brother Roy Al motioned for Jemma to follow him towards the train station. She kept her head high, ignoring the nerves clawing at her back. Just like when they arrived nearly a year earlier, the Guards of Knoll brought with them a darkness that made even the happiest people glum. Children stopped dancing in the streets. Every smile felt forced.

They rode on the coattails of the Storm of Nightmares. It was as if the yellow clouds never left.

By the time Jemma and Brother Roy Al reached the platform, Elder Lau Rel had already exited the train and stood there waiting in her ruby decorated robe. She didn't look how Jemma imagined her, her wide lips drawn in a frown across her lips, reminiscent of an alligator. When Jemma researched the woman in the Temple's archives, she'd pictured someone with much more grandeur and wisdom, like an owl. Elder Lau Rel had been a sister in almost every major city across Rosada, led the conversion mission out in Heims Norte, and became the first female Elder in Knoll. Jemma admired her perseverance.

The poignant conversation that followed cut her excitement short.

"Elder," Brother Roy Al bowed to the woman, "it has been a long time."

"Enough with the formalities, Roy. You know why I am here." Elder Lau Rel's voice sliced the air. "The train leaves in an hour. I expect you to be on it."

Brother Roy Al shrank. "Oh. I need to get my things then. Sister Jey Ma, can you show Elder Lau Rel to the Temple?"

Jemma glanced at Brother Roy Al, then straightened her back and bowed to the Elder. "Of course."

Elder Lau Rel waved her hand. "Good. I hope your reeducation goes smoothly.

"Thank you, Elder. I hope so."

The Elder strode down the platform. Jemma glanced back one last time at Brother Roy Al. He smiled at her, enough to quell the nerves in her stomach, before ushering her along after the Elder. Jemma only had one moment to mouth the words, "Good luck," before joining the Elder at the bottom of the platform.

Elder Lau Rel ignored Jemma as she marched through the streets. The newly arrived Guards from Knoll bowed in her direction, and the residents of Newbird's Arm gazed at her in awe. She carried candor and dignity about her that demanded attention.

"Sister Jey Ma, we need to make adjustments as soon as possible. Brother Roy Al has tainted the Effluvium, and if we want to maintain order, then we must eradicate his influence," the Elder said.

Jemma blinked. Elder Lau Rel took no time getting to the point. Already, Brother Roy Al had mentioned the Order's displeasure with his stance.

Jemma chose her response carefully. "I'm sorry, Elder, but I must inquire...what has Brother Roy Al done wrong? The people of Newbird's Arm love him."

"He has not facilitated the reconstruction of order in this town. It is in the hands of vagrants and demons." Elder Lau Rel gazed at Jemma with her stone eyes unmoved. "I imagine you see it; otherwise, I may need to send you for reeducation as well."

"No, of course not. I serve the Effluvium." Jemma selected each word. The only way to ease change would be through the Effluvium. She had to keep her lips closed and tight.

"Good, good. Then we must act with haste to save Newbird's Arm from the demons and smog." Elder Lau Rel paused at the steps of the Temple, glaring at the charred structure. "I doubt the Temple's infrastructure will be up to par for mass cleansings."

Jemma could feel the blood leave her cheeks. It was hard to put together her next question. "Mass cleansings?"

"Senator Cordova has already begun this in Knoll, and we have seen miraculous results. Once he makes his proposition to the Senate and it passes, we will implement it throughout the province."

"I'm sorry, Elder, but after what happened a few months ago, the people of Newbird's Arm might be wary."

"The men of Knoll won't give them a choice. If they value their families and livelihood, they will oblige." Elder Lau Rel stroked the stair's handrails with a tubby finger. "But first, we must clean up this mess. How do you worship in such squalor?"

"We turn our hearts to the Effluvium, Elder," Jemma squeaked.

"Pah! What good have your prayers done during these hard times?" She brushed her fingers on Jemma's robe, scowling at the soot. "Get this place looking spotless, yes? We will become the crowned jewel on this side of the country yet again."

With a spin, Elder Lau Rel trudged into the Temple, leaving Jemma alone on the steps.

Jemma stared after her, then up at the Year Glass, before turning to face the Tower, casting a shadow over the market square. It sat perfectly, blocking out the sun from the town, an ominous reminder that the Order always watched.

CHAPTER NINE

REAPER

Bright lights.

So bright.

It hurt to open his eyes. Shadows danced over him.

His head roared.

Searing.

He missed yellow.

He looked away. Mist pulsed from his blood-crusted fingers, casting stories on the walls. One figure grabbed his hand to stop the tales.

Then his head exploded. A thousand years of stories fled through his mind.

War. So much war. And blood. Death. Suffering. Broken hearts.

So much death.

He screamed out.

The light faded.

And he sat in a room masked in fog. His wrist itched, and his head pounded. Two shadows stood above him again.

When he turned, he noticed an intravenous line digging into his arm with leather straps wrapped around both his wrists.

"Relax," a voice cooed.

He shook his head. "Let me go...let me go..."

That voice, the one that exited his mouth, this time it sounded human. Not like the monster that latched onto his throat, not like the thousands of stories that flooded the corners of his mind. No, like an individual. A single person pleading.

His voice.

"Relax. You'll be able to think clearly in a moment." The voice came from a figure in a long white coat and a pointed bird-like mask.

It's a talking bird.

He blinked, the fog continuing to nestle in his head, shoving the stories back to the shadows. The figure's image stabilized: a bulky doctor with short curly hair wearing a plague mask on their face. Beside them stood a small but broad-shouldered nurse with long red hair sneering down at him.

"Good." The doctor's voice rose with a smile. "Very good."

"Where...where am...where am I?" His words tasted stale.

"You are in the Sanatorium of Mert, magical psychiatric ward. I am Dr. Kafele, and this is Nurse Edith. We've been taking care of you for the past week."

"I don't...I don't...I don't remember." He racked his brain. All he saw was yellow. Nothing else.

Just yellow.

Dr. Kafele shook their head. "Of course not; you were very disoriented. It took multiple tonics, elixirs, and sedatives to get this right. But you seem clearer now, yes?"

"I think...I mean...I guess."

"You'll get there." Dr. Kafele joined his side. Though he couldn't see their eyes, he felt them scanning his body, leaving him exposed beneath their gaze. Nurse Edith wandered to the other side of the bed, taking a seat beside a metallic table covered with syringes and scalpels. She picked one up and turned it over in her hand.

His eyes widened. "What is all...what is all that?"

"It only helps to give you clarity. It is not to harm you." Dr. Kafele took his hand in their gloved one, their voice as smooth as silk. "This tonic should have helped. Just take a deep breath. Do you remember anything?"

"I...um...I..." He gulped and shook his head.

"Think. What is your name?"

"My name...My name is—" When did he last say his name? How long had he been drowning beneath the disarray of the yellow fog and nightmares? "My name...um...it is...I...I don't know. I don't know who I am."

"Let us help." Dr. Kafele motioned to Nurse Edith. The nurse removed one of the syringes from the table, flicked its tip, and guided it to his vein.

"N-N-No!" He recoiled. "No more!"

"It is only to help." The doctor's voice remained calm.

Nurse Edith put the syringe in his arm before he protested again. The tonic washed through him, pushing back a few more clouds so he could delve deeper into his memories. He finally saw a town, a monster, and a beautiful young woman running towards him. Then darkness, running and screaming. What happened? Where was he? Who was he?

Dr. Kafele asked him again. "Do you remember your name?"

"It's...um... it's..." He licked his lips and tried again. "I think...I mean, I think it's... it's Brent."

"Brent?" Nurse Edith cackled. "What kind of name is Brent? Especially for a—"

"Not now, Edith!" Dr. Kafele waved their hand.

Brent—yes, that was his name—glanced between the two.

Dr. Kafele caused his confusion to fall to the back of his mind as they asked the next question. "What happened to you, Brent?"

"I...I, uh...there was...I...I don't...I..." He gritted his teeth and counted backward from ten. "I was fighting a monster, and I absorbed its stories." *And then I was running...and I was on the streets...and her... what's her name? Where is she?*

"What does that mean?"

Brent struggled to form a coherent story, the memory more like a distant nightmare. "I don't... I don't know. It's all so...so fuzzy. And I...I...I dunno."

"Edith." Dr. Kafele nodded to the nurse. Another syringe appeared from the table.

Brent squirmed. "Please, I don't wanna...I wanna remember normally. That stuff...I don't...what...please, I don't wanna."

"One more dosage, Brent. It'll be okay."

The needle hurt more this time, sending his veins aflame. Brent withered, cursing once. But for one beautiful moment, everything was clear. He remembered fleeing through the tunnels, lost in the haze of the monster's story. Under its guise, he saw the world. He released more souls, but Brent Harley remained trapped beneath the monster's clutches. Some days, a beautiful queen with eyes as dark as her skin came to him and nurtured him before he escaped from her.

A beautiful queen who ruled the forests.

His queen.

"Bria," he moaned. His heart broke thinking about her. Did he hurt her? Had she conceded? Where was she? "I need to find Bria."

"Who is Bria?" Dr. Kafele asked.

The words fell from Brent's mouth, uncontrolled as if a lasso wrapped around each truthful word and pulled them out of him. "She's my...I...I love her...and I dunno if she loves me anymore because I dunno what I've done and...and...and..." He closed his eyes and held back tears. "I don't know what I did. I don't know who I am anymore."

Dr. Kafele said nothing for a moment. Already, he sensed his mind would not stay stable for long. The fog trickled into his head again.

"What happened, Brent?" Dr. Kafele asked.

"I...there was a...a monster..." He blinked a couple times, visualizing as it descended over Newbird's Arm. "It's called...they call it a diabolo. I...I accidentally released it and then tried to destroy it, but it destroyed me instead. I don't know how...who...I don't know what is happening anymore."

"Diabolo?"

"It's a monster thing that the Council of Mist Keepers created or something, and I... I'm talking nonsense. Because what's a Mist Keeper, right?" Brent laughed. The words fell out unhindered. With each sentence, they came out faster, more truthful, and more lucid than the next. "Apparently, I'm a Mist Keeper, and I do things with mist and save dead people. But I also see stories everywhere, and the Diabolo tried to infiltrate my mind. And it did. I don't know for how long...I don't know...I don't! Fuck!"

Silence followed. Brent gritted his teeth, straining his neck to look around the sterile room. There stood no windows. Only a door and a buzzing light above them. His clothes lay on a single chair in the corner of the room.

Edith broke the silence, snarling. "I told you he was a reaper."

Brent stared at her, his stomach dropping.

"Now, Edith, we haven't heard his full story yet." Dr. Kafele brushed back Brent's hair. This time, their fingers didn't feel as welcoming, more like a spider nestling into his head. "Tell us more, Brent. Why are you not with the Council right now?"

"How do you...I mean...how do you... they're secret..." He flinched. While the fog had finally dissipated, a blazing rod prodded at his thoughts, pushing them to the forefront of his mind. Tears trickled down his cheeks. "I can't...who are...what are...who...I don't...I don't know."

"Tell us what happened from start to finish. We won't hurt you." The smoothness in Dr. Kafele's tone rocked Brent's stomach. Could he trust them?

Could he trust himself?

"I can't..."

"Yes, you can." They nodded towards Edith.

The nurse took the last syringe and sank it into Brent's arm. He squirmed, trying to avoid it, but it was for naught. This time, the inoculation burned like ice, spreading out through his arteries and latching onto every single chain of thought and pulling it forward. Every word, every tale sat but inches from his lips. Was it his story? Or the story of a young man who once had hope?

He didn't recall.

The young man named Brent died in Newbird's Arm when he struck down the Diabolo.

Now he had no recollection of his story.

He closed his eyes. "I don't know...I don't...I don't know where to begin."

"Tell us...when did you first become a Mist Keeper?"

"I don't know. I mean...it...I... it's jumbled...I mean... it's been...I don't know."

The nurse spat, "He's clueless, ain't he?"

"Edith. Be patient." Dr. Kafele glared, then turned back to Brent.

"I...uh...I remember seeing...fallen leaves or something. Is it almost winter?" Brent asked.

Dr. Kafele nodded.

Brent closed his eyes and whispered to himself, "So, it has almost been a year since I met her."

Brent launched into the story. Whatever they had injected him with wove through each of his thoughts, dragging out the truths and slaughtering all lies. The tale came out of him like the story of a gorilla once named Mr. G working in the treasury. He described the misty exterior of Newbird's Arm, the day that Caroline arrived as a stain on the landscape, and his discovery of the tunnels.

Slowly, he recalled each of the Mist Keepers: he met Alojzy, Tomás, and Aelia, the Architect, Mind-Reader, and Healer, respectively. Over time, the rest of the Council appeared to him: Jiang the Giant, Julietta the Forgetful, Malaika the Cartographer, and finally, the mysterious head of the Council himself, Ningursu. But only after he dared release the monster from its prison, the nefarious created known as the Diabolo, did he discover the Council's true guise.

With details down to the monster's teeth, he described how the Diabolo rose from its jar deep in the Library. He recalled the trepidation held by the Council over the monster's release. In a lull, his story changed, detailing his own adventures with his newfound mistmagic with Bria before returning home to battle the Diabolo one last time.

Only to lose himself for good.

Sweat coated his body as the tale concluded with him touching on his whirlwind of memories over the last few months. He remembered running, he recollected Bria, he recalled living on the streets with others, and he reminisced about a dog licking his feet. Other than that, the past few months wore a shroud of mystery.

His bottom lip quivered. Already, his story began to slip, the monstrous storm clouds returning from the back of his mind.

"Thank you, Brent." Dr. Kafele dabbed his brow. "I realize that was difficult."

"Please, let me stay...please. I don't want to go away again...please...please." He sobbed, flexing his fingers as if trying to reach for something, anything even, to latch him into place.

"Yes, it seems it is wearing off. I will make you a stronger dosage...but that takes time, unfortunately." Dr. Kafele rose, staring down at him. He yearned to meet their eyes behind the darkness of the mask. Did fear gloss them? Or fury?

Brent sputtered. "But...but what was the serum? What'd you do...I couldn't...I wasn't...what was it?"

"Clarity." Dr. Kafele turned away. "It cleared everything. No lies. No falsities. Only clarity."

"Clarity..." Brent repeated the word to himself. Any other time, he'd be able to make sense of this. But the fog continued to settle around him. Why did this doctor care so much? Was this magic? Was he even in a hospital?

Where was he?

What happened?

Who was he?

"Nurse Edith, please make a note that our patient here is Priority One. I need to discuss these events with Nurse Varden."

"You want me to label him?" Edith cackled.

"I do not want you to *harm* him."

"I understand." Edith's voice reminded Brent of a snake wrapped around a tree branch, blending in seamlessly with the canopy of the forest.

"Rest, Brent. We will get your head in order." With that, Dr. Kafele pushed open the doors on the far side of the room. A golden light trickled into the sterile room from the hallway where Dr. Kafele vanished, leaving Brent alone with Edith.

It was the first time he got a good look at the nurse. Her red hair puffed out over her head, a smile on her face showcasing her sharp teeth. She ran her fingers over the metal tray. The different knives and scalpels danced around them before appearing to meld together into a thin and precise-looking carving knife.

Magic.

"What are you...what is that...what is...please don't." He squirmed. The leather bands around his wrists dug deeper.

"All Dr. Kafele asked was that I do not harm you. This will only hurt for a moment, and it's just so we don't forget who you are." Edith held the precision instrument up to the light. "I think this will go well with your other two brands."

He recalled the two black triangles that formed an hourglass on his wrist and the stenciled single triangle on his hand.

"What's another mark to all your others, right?" Edith dragged the blade down his left arm, testing its sharpness and precision in random spaces between his veins. Once the knife produced a satisfying cut, she celebrated with a high-pitched giggle and circled to Brent's right side.

He bit his lip, holding back another scream as the pain ripped up his arm. He felt the blood trickle down his arm to his fingers.

"If you thought that was painful love, you don't know the half of it."

"Please...please don't..." Brent choked.

"Oh, *poor baby*." Edith stroked his cheek, her sharp nails stinging his skin. "It's a shame you're a reaper. You're not half bad looking. Guess you're not the hardiest, though. That's okay. Soon we'll all know who you are."

Brent asked one last question. "Who is *we*?"

"Oh, that doesn't matter anymore. Hold still now. Let's have a bit of fun."

The blade carved into his skin. As blood seeped out, pain soared through his head, creating a wave of dizziness and sweat. His lips quivered; his throat tightened. Even if he wanted to scream, he couldn't.

Once again, he was being branded.

But this time, he didn't know why.

And soon, he wouldn't even remember his name.

CHAPTER TEN

TRANSFER

Madame Owiti did not reach out to Bria for a couple days. She didn't mind, instead tending to the gardens on the boardwalk for extra money during the day while scouring the streets at night for Brent with no success. The Story Collector had vanished.

And that silence frightened her.

Each night, she returned to her small apartment after another fruitless search. No new windows broken. No red lights lit outside shops. No stories. When she heard the sirens screaming, she followed them, only to end up at a crime scene left behind by the Pinstripes and other scoundrels.

Exhausted and defeated, she unlaced one of her shoes by the kitchen table and turned on a single lamp. On the table sat the dust-covered books Brent left there many months ago. He folded multiple pages over, with notes along their borders. Yet, he still hadn't touched one book, inscribed with the golden numeral *I* on the cover.

Curious, Bria grabbed the book and an apple and collapsed on her bed. She pined through the pages, but as she expected, the pages belonged to riddles, metaphors, and languages gone awry.

In the plains of death and prosper, where thy light be yonder and frayed, Life and Death done meet...young both, new, and incomplete.

She flipped to another page, hoping for a clearer phrase, but each one was more confusing than the next.

A babe. A babe! Born at last.
Slayed, a slayed, death born of that.

Bria groaned and bit into her apple. Brent would have the patience for this, but she didn't. She scoured through a few more pages, stopping at a random line in the book.

They drank the blood to see the world.
Forever. Forever.
Immortally bold.

"Immortals..." Bria trailed off, glancing towards the window again where the sky basked in orange. This book, however daunting, must have answers in it. Why else would Brent have grabbed it? Sure, he might have snatched it on a whim, but she liked to believe he was more calculated than that.

Who am I kidding? Brent Harley's a spastic goof.

A knock broke her thoughts.

"Rho, deary dear! It's Madame Owiti! Open up!"

Bria reassembled herself, placing the book on the bed, then unlocked the door. The old woman beamed at her, and without waiting for the invitation, pushed past Bria and into the small apartment.

"Oh dear, oh dear, this place is a pigsty! You don't care for it at all, do you? Are these rotten oranges? Rho! You have plant magic!" Madame Owiti scoured through the kitchen as she spoke, shaking her head in disgust. She picked through the cabinets for a cup before venturing into the bathroom with no real invite.

Bria gawked after the woman, following her into the lavatory. "What's going on?"

Madame Owiti filled Bria's tub with water, pulled the odd silver orb out of her bag, and spooned a cup out of the orb with the glassware. "They're ready for you."

"The immortals?"

"Of course, deary dear! Isn't that what you want? To meet them and finally master your magic? Yes, yes?"

Bria paused. Yes, that was what she wanted.

That was always what she wanted.

But her heart sank, worrying about Brent. What if she left, and he came knocking on the door moments later?

"I know, I know, you don't want to give up on this little lover boy of yours. But deary dear, you can't keep living like this." Madame Owiti motioned out towards the kitchen again. "You can come back whenever your heart desires. But it is time to tackle bigger things."

Bria stared at the clutter on the table. She hugged herself, bringing her oversized coat tight around her frame. It smelled stale. Empty. Like the apartment.

She knew Madame Owiti was right. The longer she lived in squalor, the further she would fall. But she couldn't give up on that small bit of hope that one day, someday, normalcy might return.

Bria pushed away the anxiety and knelt beside the tub. Madame Owiti dumped the cup of silver liquid into the basin. It swirled in with the pouring water, like a whirlpool in the sea, before resting on the surface.

Madame Owiti removed a peony flower from her bag and placed it in the center of the tub. "Rho, dear, could you turn this one peony into twenty? We need a bigger heart."

"Oh, um, yes." Bria cradled the peony in her hand, letting the silver liquid drip from her fingers, feeling the flower pulsate. The seed pods beneath the petals brimmed at her touch and exploded, sending the red flowers across the surface of the water. Around each of the new flowers, the silver liquid circled. The flowers sank to the bottom of the tub like an anchor in the sea.

Madame Owiti smiled at Bria. "We need to give the tub half an hour to regulate. Then we'll establish the connection, and you'll be able to meet them, yes, yes?"

"I'm going to meet *immortals*." Bria shook her head in disbelief. "I wouldn't have thought."

"It is best you think of them as only Magii, dear. Yes, they have lived long...but they do not differ from the rest of us." Madame Owiti cackled. "In fact, in my opinion, they have their head in their arses, yes, yes?"

Bria glanced back at the tub, then followed Madame Owiti into the main room. The old woman went over to the bed and sat down, then scowled in discomfort and paced to the opposite end of the room.

"You could have told me you were coming." Bria shifted and stared at her feet.

Madame Owiti chuckled. "I should come here to say I was coming, go back and get my things, then return? No, I don't think so. I'm too old for all that back and forth."

"A telegram?"

"I don't trust those children. No, this was easiest. Besides, we needed a bigger tub than mine, and yours does nicely. Knew you would have one. I used to live in a building like this one, yes yes, I did."

"But why me? I'm just a gardener. This seems...unproductive."

"I see your aura. So did Tilda. You are so much more than that."

Bria looked away. She still didn't like being called different. What made her different from any other Magii? She had the luck of the draw: a grandmother who encouraged her to practice magic, a father who turned a blind eye, and the world at her fingertips.

It didn't mean she was special.

"Trust me, Rho, deary dear. They know exactly who they are looking for." Madame Owiti patted Bria's hand. "You will meet them soon."

"Are you calling them to come here?"

"Not at all!"

"Then why do you need my tub? The toilet worked fine with Tilda..."

"Cause you're not gonna fit in a toilet, dear." Madame Owiti laughed, a deep-hearted one that warmed Bria when she heard it. Like her grandmama or like Ric's laugh, it was pure, never forced.

Bria almost smiled back. "What do you mean?"

"This might alarm you, but there are magical ways of hopping between locations. We're establishing a two-way door, so to speak, between Tilda's connections and us. Even with them right here in the city, they like to keep their location under locks."

Bria was familiar with these magical ways of traveling. She'd grown up playing in magic tunnels her entire life, exploring all corners of the earth. They belonged to her...at least until she met the Council.

This sounded more direct, though. A door opened to lead to one place. And one place alone.

"So that liquid can be used to communicate and also travel?" Bria asked.

"We use it for many things. We seers often use it only to see, but it is also used for communication, traveling, and other elixirs. Seers have passed this orb down for generations. It's our lifeblood."

"And today, we will use it as a door?"

"Yes, yes."

Bria's hands grew clammy. What if this was an obscure way of murdering her? Would the old woman push her beneath the surface, and she wouldn't be able to come up for air?

No, no, that's ridiculous! Madame Owiti had only been kind. She couldn't let her paranoia get in the way.

She wouldn't.

"Have you done this before?" Bria asked.

"I did once, many years ago, with this crazy young man named Fritjof. Or was it Joffrey? Or Fritz? I don't remember anymore. He was a weird one. But yes, I did, don't fret, dear." Madame Owiti grinned at Bria. "And remember, it's just a door. All you need to do is turn around and come back through to be home. It is not a death sentence."

"Okay." Bria stared at her bare feet, kicking up dust on the floor. It wasn't like this apartment was much of a home, anyway. Why should it matter if she left?

Because Brent might come back.

Wishful thinking, at this rate. But she couldn't let him go.

He'd want me to go, though. He'd want me to find out more about myself.

"It is probably about ready now. Why don't you get anything you want to bring and come join me in the lavatory? Yes, yes?"

Bria obliged, gathering her boots and cowl. Her heart thudded in her ears as she entered the bathroom. Madame Owiti leaned over the tub, stirring it with her crooked finger. When she removed her finger, the liquid dripped off her skin. Well, it wasn't truly liquid, but a mimicry of sorts. It didn't stain. It was its own creation.

"Ready, dear?" Madame Owiti beamed.

Bria nodded. "I guess so."

She joined Madame Owiti by the tub, watching as the liquid swirled. It wasn't as clear this time, thick like mercury with the peonies floating on its surface.

"Remove any loose articles of clothing. We'll send those in first as a trial, make sure it doesn't burn you alive."

"What?!" Bria jumped back.

"I'm joking, deary dear." Madame Owiti chortled. "But it's always good to test the door first, yes yes?"

Exhaling in relief, Bria agreed, then removed her coat and cowl. One at a time, she dropped the articles into the tub, and they sank beneath the surface.

And vanished.

In its place, a white ribbon floated to the top.

Bria gasped. Magic never ceased to amaze her. "Did it work?"

"Yes, that's the sign Tilda told me to look for. They're ready.".

Bria continued staring at the tub. She couldn't believe what was happening. For years she'd been looking for answers. This might finally give them to her.

Perhaps.

She glanced back into the main room one last time. Empty. No ghosts haunted the walls. No mist.

No Brent.

"Alright, let's do this."

Madame Owiti offered Bria a hand, helping her into the tub.

The liquid gathered around her. Bria expected it to burn like ice, but it cocooned her like a blanket, rocking her into a half-sleep. Despite her nerves and fears, she even closed her eyes, holding her breath as the liquid covered her face.

She drifted.

Sank.

Floated.

Dreamed.

A foggy light surrounded her.

And she came up for air.

Bria emerged from the liquid, panting.

She sat in a tub in the center of a sterile white room. A tall man with dull red hair stood over her. A smile crossed his face, and when he spoke, a warm voice coated the room.

"Hello, Rho! My name is Varden. It's a pleasure to meet you at long last."

CHAPTER ELEVEN

THE SANITORIUM

B ria blinked away the liquid and stared at Varden. He was taller than anyone she ever met, even the Mist Keepers' Giant, Jiang, with his head nearly hitting the ceiling.

Varden offered her a huge hand out of the tub. Bria gazed at it for a moment, then placed her hand in it, letting him lift her from the basin with little effort at all.

Shivering, Bria glanced around the room as she collected her coat and cowl from the floor. She'd resurfaced from the tub in an operating theatre, with tiered seats gazing down toward her in the middle of the room. Six musty lights hung from above, and shadows danced on the walls.

"It's okay, miss. I know passing through the pool can cause disorientation the first time. Well, the first few times. You're safe." Varden's lips parted into a smile again.

"Where am I?" she asked.

"The Mertoni Sanatorium."

"Oh...um...why?"

"The Palaver has made its home here for many seasons to help those suffering from untamed magic."

"The Palaver?"

"Did Tilda not use our formal name?"

Bria shook her head.

"She's a chowderhead." Varden chuckled and shook his straw-like red hair from his eyes. "I, as well as the others, am a member of the Immortal Palaver of Kek. We've taken quite an interest in you, Rho."

"But...I only met Tilda and Madame Owiti a couple days ago."

"We can see many things. Once we learned about you, Tilda and I did some additional research. You've left signatures of your aura around the city. You were the one making all those gardens pretty, yes?"

Bria hugged herself. "Yes."

"It's impressive, Rho, really." There was that smile again, highlighting his immortal youthfulness. "But enough idle tittle-tattle. Even though you were right here in the city, traveling through the Pool here gives us a safeguard from unwanted intruders. So, I imagine you'll probably want to wash up and get your bearings. Once you're all cleaned, I'll introduce you to Dr. Kafele. They'll be exuberant to meet you."

"Oh. Okay."

Bria took two steps for every one of Varden's strides as she followed him out of the operating theatre. A dusty hallway with more blinking lights waited beyond it. Old cots and trays lined the walls. Bria always imagined the Sanatorium being, well, sanitary, but this place reminded her more of a ghost town.

Until Varden pushed open the next set of double doors at the end of the hall.

The next corridor held to the Sanatorium's name. White walls with numbered rooms and glass windows lined the path, and the tile was so clean, Bria worried her boots would scuff it. A multitude of fluorescent lights captured the area in an eerie glow. As they walked, the lights flickered, and their steps echoed, dancing with the pacing of doctors and nurses. Varden exchanged humorous jabs with a few of them, his hefty laugh echoing through the hallway.

"This way, Rho." He motioned her through a door and up a dark stairwell pivoting out of the hallway. "Watch your step here. It's loose." Varden pointed to a step. He continued blathering. "We keep our pool in the old ward. No one goes in there anymore, so it makes a perfect location. Plus, if there are any problems, we can get you all checked out since it connects to the minor magical injury department. Up ahead are the more...intense cases of magic dysphoria. We like keeping our personal suites right above them because they require the most upfront care."

At the top, beneath a single swinging lamp, Varden unlocked five different hinges, then turned back to Bria. "As a warning, these cases can be alarming."

"I'm okay," Bria lied. *Intense cases? Like what?*

Her mind fled to Brent. Perhaps they took him in after a moment of dysphoria. It was a dream, but it was better than the alternatives.

At least then, he'd be safe.

Varden unlocked the door.

It wasn't dark like a prison or a crypt. On the front end, the ward looked the same as any other floor in the hospital: sterile, with bright lights hanging overhead. Yet, it seemed different. No chatter. No life. Lonely. Empty.

Bria wondered what stories lived in these walls.

Interest got the best of her, and she approached the window to the first room. An old woman sat in the center of it, playing the violin. Sheet music covered her walls, a serenity on her face, unaware that she was being watched through the glass.

Varden joined Bria's side. "That's Miss One. She was our first patient. She was involved in some orchestra accident where she got stuck in a loop playing her violin. No matter what we do, she can't stop."

"How long has she been here?" Bria whispered, worried to break the song.

"Sixty years in Dr. Kafele's care."

"Sixty? No one claimed her?"

"Many of our patients are forgotten. Dr. Kafele tries...but there is only so much we can do. We treat them well here, though. If we let them go, they'd end up in jail...or worse." Varden lowered his voice as they passed another room. The man inside slept, his beard reaching the floor, his mouth hanging ajar. Just another forgotten soul lost in the hospital.

Alone.

Each room they passed looked more depressing than the last, and the further they ventured, the darker they became. Shrieks plastered the hallway with steam boiling out of the cracks in one door, while in another, a woman paced while sparks flung from her fingers. The rooms with the most detrimental screams often had their curtains closed, hiding whatever monster lay behind the walls.

No. Bria wouldn't call them monsters.

They were no different from her. No different than Brent.

Struggling. Yearning. Begging.

Bria stopped in her tracks as one door opened. A nurse with frizzy red hair wheeled a cart out of a room. Blood stained her apron. She didn't seem to notice Varden or Bria, too focused on the scalpel in her hand. It oozed with blood, and with a smirk on her face, she squeezed her hand around it. When she opened her hand again, the scalpel had vanished.

"Edith!" Varden called out.

The nurse turned and curtsied. "Varden."

"Is room twenty-seven acting up again?"

"Unfortunately. I've sedated them for now. No need to worry."

Bria glanced to the room where Edith exited. Like its neighbors, the curtain hung shut.

"Rho," Varden nudged her, "this is Edith, one of our members and a nurse here on the ward."

Bria turned back to the woman. She was about the same height as Bria, with more hair than she seemed to know what to do with and green eyes that pierced the air.

"Why's she here?" Edith snapped.

"Dr. Kafele has taken an interest in her. She has a powerful aura."

"You damn seers and your auras. Ridiculous. What has she done to warrant interest is the better question?"

Bria squirmed.

"She has a strong connection with nature. She's the one responsible for all the flourishing gardens on the boardwalk."

"Nature? I see." Edith glared down the hallway. "Interesting."

Bria followed Edith's angry gaze.

The woman shrugged, then readjusted the tray of tools, hissing as she walked past them. "Well, it is nice to meet you, *Bria*. I'm sure Dr. Kafele will be entranced by you."

Before Bria could respond, Edith left. Even if she hadn't, Bria wasn't sure what she would say. How did Edith know her name? Unless...unless...

Brent.

Varden hadn't heard Edith, though. Or if he did, he ignored it. "Sorry about her. She isn't the most welcoming."

Bria didn't reply.

She followed Varden in silence towards the end of the ward, where he unlocked another door. This staircase greeted her with a warm embrace, like home.

But before she dared step inside, she glanced down the corridor one last time. "Varden?"

"Hm?"

"Is the Story Collector here?"

"The who?"

"Nothing. Forget it." Maybe a crazed storyteller wouldn't fall on their radar.

Varden left Bria alone in a small bedroom suite with a washroom and a single bed, promising that the doctor would be up in a few minutes. As soon as he left, Bria took stock of the five lanterns on the wall. Once sure their shadows didn't change, she went into the washroom to clean, spending a long moment staring at herself in the mirror. Her hair rested in a matted braid on her shoulders, while dirt mingled with her freckles, acne, and scars. One strand at a time, she unwound her braid, letting the coarse locks fall against her back.

She'd tried to avoid looking at herself. But she'd lost weight, her ribs popping from her sides, and she almost didn't recognize herself. She used to think of herself as pretty, but without the happiness of others to feed off, she recognized nothing but her imperfections. Her overbite misshaped her mouth, her blemishes stained her face, and her hair frizzled at the top of her head.

Loneliness had worked its way through her veins and transformed her into a shadow on the wall.

The shower filled the room with steam, and she stepped inside, washing away the grime and few silver bits of liquid that remained in her hair. As she sat on the edge of the latrine, brushing her hair and watching the water spiral down the drain, she observed those little bits of silver. They didn't follow the water, instead mingling together into a small orb in the center of the tub.

Bria put the brush down and lifted the orb, no bigger than her thumb, into her palm. She twirled it in her hand. It didn't disperse, resting in her palm like a marble. When she peered long enough at it, she thought she saw shadows moving around inside the silver surface.

She placed it in her coat pocket, then put on the white dress Varden left her. Vulnerability latched onto her again as though everyone could see her. Not just her aura, but her soul too. Bria pulled her jacket and cowl on over it, shaking back her hair into a single ponytail before leaving the small suite.

A large common room connected the bedroom with a kitchen and a few other suites. All remained quiet, giving Bria the chance to explore. She examined the candle-lit bookshelves towering to the ceiling, reminiscent of the Library of Mist Keepers. An array of old devices telling time cluttered the shelves, from a ticking clock to a year glass from the Order. Beside them waited a few orbs, all composed of the same silvery liquid as Madame Owiti's orb. Their peony-shaped hearts vibrated in their core, calling for Bria with their soft voices and humming a distant tune.

She approached one of them and placed her hand against it. In her pocket, the miniature orb tremored. As she peered into the larger orb on the shelf, she swore she saw a beach, wrapped in the wind, dancing with palm fronds and sand. Peaceful. Serene. Like a dream.

Each orb showed a different scene. Forests, cities, and fields. Bria reached for them. She longed for a new adventure, for the ability to travel again and see the world.

Like she had since her childhood.

"Rho?"

Bria turned. A doctor entered the room, a pristine white coat over their bulky body. They wore a silver, beaked plague mask.

"My name is Dr. Tehuti Thema Tarek Kamilah Kafele Kek. You can call me Kek. Or Dr. Kafele. Or whichever of those names. I hold each in high regard." They removed their mask and offered Bria a hand.

Bria met Kek's dark beady gaze, then hesitantly took their hand. "Nice to meet you."

Kek squeezed Bria's hand tight. "Ah, yes, I sense your magic. It is brimming, isn't it?"

"Are you a seer too?" Bria retreated, once again feeling exposed beneath the doctor's gaze.

A chuckle. Deep. Warm. Like chocolate. "No, no. I am a doctor and an alchemist. But when you've been around as long as I have, you get a sense of who has potent magic."

"Of course," Bria realized. "You're the Kek that Varden mention. So that means...you're immortal, right?"

"I turn...two-thousand-seven-hundred-and-eighteen around the Spring Equinox if memory serves correct."

Bria lowered herself onto the sofa, gawking at Kek. Yes, she had met the Council. They were just as old, but they were god-like, almost inhuman. In contrast, Kek was a person on equal playing field with Bria despite their age. A Magii.

Kek, still smiling, sat down across from Bria. "We've been watching you, Rho."

Bria squirmed again, "As I've been told."

"It's been for quite a while. Your magic is stunning. I've heard about what you did in that little Rosadian town. And the way you have tended to these gardens here in Mert...well, it's fantastic. You have this touch I have not seen in over a thousand years. It's stunning, quite stunning, really."

"You know about me?" Bria squeaked.

"Only a bit. Enough to know I would like to take you under my wing, see what we can unlock inside of you." Kek raised their hands. "Only if you want to. I am sure this is overwhelming for you."

Bria's mind raced, and then the next words slipped from her mouth before she could control them. "So you can help me figure out why my powers are like this? And why, for the longest time, I was the only one in the tunnels? I've just...never understood any of it. And I was trying to find answers and...things happened. I—" She stopped herself, bringing her fingers to her lips. She hoped Kek didn't hear everything. *Why did I bring up the tunnels?*

Kek narrowed their eyes. With the smile gone, their pupils looked more like beetles than starless nights. Hollow. Ageless. Empty.

But the smile returned as soon as it left.

"Yes. We can help you understand all of that." Kek's voice remained warm and welcoming.

"Really?" Bria stared for a moment. There had to be a catch to the proposition; surely, a powerful Magii like Kek wouldn't just offer a hand. "What do I need to do, though?"

"Nothing. I want to see you flourish."

"Oh." Bria's nerves slid to a halt in her throat. Nausea sank into her stomach. *You need to stop thinking people are out to get you. Grandmama used to say that most everyone is good. You should believe it too.*

"We'll begin exploring *you* in the morning, yes? It sounds like you haven't had the proper guidance, and there is much we need to learn about."

Bria shuffled her feet. "Okay."

Kek pressed Bria's hand once more. "Varden will bring you food soon. I promise you're found now. You do not have to hunt for answers alone."

Bria said nothing else, removing her hands from Kek's grip and clasping them to her chest. Kek smiled once more, then left the room, their long coat scraping the floor.

Bria couldn't bring herself to leave the common room. Her mind continued to race. She wasn't a prisoner, but she felt trapped.

Vulnerable.

Powerless.

And as usual...alone.

CHAPTER TWELVE

A CALL TO ORDER

Sunlight danced through the pews, casting an orange glow around the shadow of the Year Glass. Jemma waited towards the back of the auditorium, her head bowed, listening as Elder Lau Rel finished her third prayer of the day. More townsfolk filled the benches than she had seen in months, while the Guards of Knoll lined the walls in their steel gray uniforms and gruff faces. Whenever vagrants entered the Temple, they dragged them out with the ferocity of bears.

"And thus," Elder Lau Rel continued, "the day has ended once more. We raise our arms to the Effluvium, and with a smile wide, we plea to be free of a demon's embrace. For we are what?"

The congregation chanted, "The Effluvium's Soul!"

A hum echoed about the room, and Elder Lau Rel smiled widely, so her face expanded like a crocodile. It reminded Jemma of a story Brent once told about a pernicious witch in the woods, brewing potions with toadstools and animal bones, luring children into the forest—

Jemma shook her head. She wouldn't get herself wrapped up in the old stories. Even if stories didn't belong to demons, didn't cater to liars, and didn't misguide children, they were a distraction. Now was not the time for such minutia.

Elder Lau Rel flexed her hands, eyes tracing over the audience. "I am so happy to see the people of Newbird's Arm returning, at last, to our Temple. With the demons eradicated from the town, we can return to the Effluvium's welcoming arms if she will have us. Thus," her eyes went over to the guards lined along the walls, "we must prove our worth and rid the rest of Newbird's Arm from demons and horror. That is why I am here to pick up where Elder Don Van left off."

The congregation murmured. A few glanced toward the guards. Jemma's chest tightened. Elder Don Van's cleansing ritual, which forced all those with the Black Stamp and silver eyes to undergo the procedure, remained fresh on the minds of the town. They dragged children with silver eyes from their homes, stamping them for the first time in twenty years. The guards hauled the vagrants, both the vilest and the kindest, from their homes in the Pit and forced them to endure the cleansing ritual. And in it, the town and vagrants grew bitter and afraid.

Riots broke out.

So did the Forest Queen.

But would they fight the same way with the Guard of Knoll occupying every street? Last time, Knoll sent only a handful of young cadets. Now, big burly men with wide shoulders and chiseled jawlines marked the streets. Disobeying them meant certain punishment.

Elder Lau Rel continued, "I hope each of you will come willingly. We want everyone in the Newbird Region to undergo the cleansing. We do not have the manpower to do everyone on this side of the mountains yet. But here, in Newbird's Arm, we can facilitate the change."

At the front of the congregation, not to Jemma's surprise, Madame Gonzo rose. She carried this presence that shook the room, confidence in her smooth voice. "Did Senator Heartz sanction this, Elder?"

"It will not matter if the Senator approves or not." Elder Lau Rel nodded to the guards. They straightened their positions along the wall, pistols in hand, arms crossed. "Senator Cordova is working on passing his first series of laws in the Senate as we speak. We will welcome the Effluvium back. And if you resist..." Elder Lau Rel tilted her head, the corners of her mouth rising. "We have our ways of forcing you."

Jemma tensed, squirming as Sister Lau Rel's smile spread across her face. The congregation shifted uneasily, hushed conversations bouncing about the room.

Madame Gonzo didn't budge.

Elder Lau Rel persisted. "I highly encourage everyone to cooperate. The Guards have produced a list of names for the first round of cleansing. We do not recommend resisting."

Beside Madame Gonzo, the Senator's gardener, Mr. West, rose. His voice scratched the air, all eyes on him. "We do not need to be cleansed. Newbird's Arm has been moving to restore peace. We are almost there. Senator Heartz and the Domicile Council have been working hard to—"

Smack!

Jemma blinked. The noise ricocheted about the Temple.

Mr. West crumbled to the ground, holding his bloodied face. A guard stood over him, a club in hand, a snarl on his lips.

"Anyone else?" He snarled, tugging Mr. West up by the collar of his shirt.

"No!" Noah Smidt rose. Madame Gonzo placed a hand over his chest to stop him.

The Guard dragged Mr. West away from his family, along the floor, and down towards the crypt. Jemma kept looking forward, refusing to make eye contact with the man.

The cleansings need to happen. Remember that. Do not break your stride.

Yet, silence did not follow this time. More and more people in the congregation shouted and screamed, belting for justice. Others stared in horror, mouths ajar, as the Guards tightened around the congregate.

"We didn't ask for you here!"

"Bring back Roy!"

"This is Rhodana's territory now!"

"We will stand by the Forest Queen!"

"LEAVE!"

Their bellows silenced Elder Lau Rel's voice. Jemma stood frozen, watching the scene unfold, her lips quivering, her head racing. She froze.

On one hand, she knew forced cleansings led to torture and disarray. She saw it with Brent and other vagrants those months ago.

But on the other, she alone could not stop these riots.

She was a mere Sister of the Order still training to learn the way of the scripture and open her heart to the Effluvium. Every day, she listened to the mist on the mountain tops, but they never spoke to her. How could she help lead a change alone?

Bang!

Gunfire assaulted the air. Shrieks followed. Smoke rose.

Jemma ducked to the floor. Her ears buzzed. She couldn't see. She couldn't think. Feet ran past her.

It was like the Storm of Nightmares all over again. Townsfolk pushed each other out of the way, knocking into Jemma and running into the market square. Guards raced after them, further gunshots ringing about the square. Fixtures fell.

Once she climbed to her feet, Jemma rushed out with the Temple. She didn't know what compelled her to follow, but she did, her heart racing in her breast. She skidded to a halt on the top step, ducking behind the railing to avoid one guard dragging two women up by the scruffs of their hair. One bore the black stamp as clear as day on her wrist.

Meanwhile, the vagrants climbed from their broken wall, chanting.

Ey oh

She has come back
We'll paint it black
And keep odds stacked
Ey oh
We have come back
We have come back
Ey oh
Ey oh

"Sister! What're you doing!?!" one brother called from the doorway.

Jemma wasn't sure how to answer the question. She gawked at him. "I..."

"We have space in the cloister! C'mon! You'll be safe down there!"

She hesitated.

"Sister!"

"Right, of course." Jemma straightened her back and stared hard at the Brother. "Thank you."

She glanced back one last time as the scene unfolding in the market square beneath the shadow of the Guard's Tower.

There was no running from its gaze.

It watched everything.

CHAPTER THIRTEEN

THE STATION HOUSE

As much as Todd wanted to rush to the Station House the day after he saw the Story Collector, life had other ideas. For the following days, Garrett woke him in fits of distress, begging for his mama and drawing furious pictures on the walls and furniture. Todd only quelled the toddler by carrying him to the Sanitorium to visit his mother...and by giving him ice cream. But those days proved too long and harrowing, and with daily rainstorms bombarding the streets, it was harder to get to both the Station House and ice cream after visiting hours.

Under the guise of Dr. Kafele, Lex recovered. The medication brought life back into her cheeks, and once again, she spoke with lust and calm in her voice. Normal, almost. Yet, Dr. Kafele urged her to stay for a few days under observation, and Todd reluctantly agreed.

Todd hoped this outbreak would deter Lex from further interest in magic, yet it seemed to spark the exact opposite reaction. She listened in awe as her ward mates talked about dazzling light shows, blazing auras, and weaving vines throughout the city. Her excitement wrapped Garrett in smiles again, so at least that was something. But as Todd listened to her talk, his own heart sank. These stories rocked her into newfound fantasies, ones that had every ability to destroy her. Why did she cling to them? Why did she let them fill her dreams?

He didn't pry. She still recovered, and she needed her strength for healing...not arguing. Instead, he listened with intent until her own rambles sent her into slumber.

Once Lex fell asleep after praying to the Dueling Princess of Spinoza, Todd kissed her forehead and pried Garrett from her. The boy squirmed, sniffling and whining for his mother, before crossing his arms and pouting in Todd's general direction. Todd soothed him, reminding him that Lex would be home soon. But as usual, his son went off on a tirade about his imaginary friend and ask when "Witi" would return.

Todd hadn't let Madame Owiti back in his home since the incident. He spent each evening lying in bed, debating whether to tell the coppers about the events that led to his wife's hospitalization.

But he'd already waited too long to report his discovery of the Story Collector. By now, the kid could be free again. Or worse, someone else might have turned him in and collected the bounty, although that seemed unlikely. Wouldn't it be on the cover of the paper?

Now that the sky was finally clear, no storm clouds looming over the city, Todd had a chance to hit the Station House before the ice cream parlor. If he didn't, Detectives Walsh and Locasta might brush off his statement as mere hearsay.

Todd rounded the bend towards Dogwood, pausing as a siren and three buggies stormed across the road. Once they passed, he traversed the street towards the City Centre. A few flyers lay on the ground, muddled by puddles and footprints. But he could still see the awful caricature of that so-called Story Collector. Beneath it, the reward number gazed up at him.

"Five hundred," Todd mumbled to himself.

That was enough to book an airship out of Mert, with some to spare! Why had he waited so long to turn in this criminal? He could save his family!

"I gotta run an errand, a'ight Garr-bear?" Todd shuffled the child in his arms.

"Ice cream!" Garrett demanded.

"If you behave, yes."

Garrett smiled half-heartedly towards the ground. "Pres wants strawberry."

"We'll get strawberry then." Todd ignored the statement about Preston. Now wasn't the time to argue about imaginary friends.

The City Centre bustled with restaurants, vendors, performers, and magic. He ignored their acts, focusing ahead where the Capitol Building sat defending the airship field in the west. Beneath its giant dome, smaller buildings and departments speckled the path: the treasury and stock exchange, the business bureau, the Department of Magical Affairs, and the Station House.

Todd took a deep breath and approached the Station House. The front of the small building glowed with miniature gas lamps outside the window, dancing with beats of red, green, blue, and yellow. Each represented a different home or business calling for help somewhere in the city, just as he had in the past weeks.

Inside, five others sat on the bench. He strode past them to the giant with a long black braid at the front desk.

Todd leaned forward. "Ahem. 'Scuse me."

The man looked up at Todd. "What d'ya want?"

"Hi, um," he glanced at the man's nametag. "John. I, um, have information about the Story Collector."

"You and the rest. Sign in and sit down. We'll be with you shortly."

"Detective Walsh said I should come—"

"I said sit down. We'll call you when we're ready."

Todd grumbled, signed in, and then sat down on the bench next to a bird-like woman with mousey hair. She smiled at him briefly, then returned to her knitting.

Waiting had this strange way of creating its own magic. Time dragged. Todd swore the stubble on his chin and neck grew. Ridiculous, but except for Garrett's garbled conversation with his imaginary friend on the floor, Todd had no way to pass the time.

The bench emptied. Todd occupied himself by scanning over the different wanted posters on the wall. While the Story Collector's face garnished most of them, the Pinstripe Gang popped up on quite a few, wanted for stolen identity, theft, and disrupting the peace. *They gotta be more of a menace than this damn kid. Too bad they ain't got a good bounty.*

In fact, most of the Pinstripes' bounties weren't even worth a week of rent. Todd wouldn't care one way or another if he saw one of those men on the street.

The primary focus of the police precinct was obvious: The Story Collector. Todd didn't question why. He was here for one reason.

After what felt like hours, though Todd realized based on the way the moon hung that it hadn't been that long, the receptionist called his name, then led him and Garrett into the back. A few officers watched as he followed the somewhat inebriated receptionist through the hall. He recognized Detective Locasta among them. She stared at him as he walked down the hall in a way that made him feel vulnerable.

The receptionist sat Todd down in a small room with a wooden table and two chairs, then left without a word. Garrett once again squirmed out of Todd's arms to play beneath the table. Left to wait, with no windows to tell time, the slamming of doors and echoes in the hallway became his only companion.

This waiting game didn't last as long. Sooner than he expected, the door swung open again, and in marched Detective Walsh.

She looked different than Todd remembered. While she still had the same alarming gaze, she'd dyed her hair blonde, and her eyes now shone with a pristine green. At first glance, Todd might not have recognized her if not for her badge and uniform.

"Mr. Dray, it is a pleasure to see you again." Detective Walsh didn't sit, instead pacing the room, so her heels clicked. "I hope you have brought reputable information. Some stories I have heard today might as well have come from the Story Collector himself! Absolute hogwash if you ask me!"

"Yes...the Story Collector..." Todd tapped his fingers on the table, looking again at the space between his knuckles. "I, um, think I know where he is."

He launched into an explanation, describing the day of Lex's Phantom Rot diagnosis. Detective Walsh said not a word as Todd spoke about the girl who caused that weird orb to explode. But his story didn't take root until he told Detective Walsh about seeing that boy—the so-called Story Collector—running distraught through the hospital ward.

"I know that it was a few days ago or whatever, but I've been too distraught to deal with it. My wife's sick and all, and I've got a kid, y'know?"

Detective Walsh nodded to herself, finally collapsing in a chair and closing her eyes. She twiddled her thumbs as she opened her mouth to speak, closing it again when no noise came out.

"I could be wrong...I dunno. I thought you outta know, though." Todd glanced down at his feet. Garrett sat between his shoes, pointing at a speck of dirt on the ground and mumbling incoherently.

Detective Walsh opened her eyes. Briefly, they turned bright blue, then turned back to green. "This is the best lead we have had in a long time. I will need to consult with my superiors on how to handle this. But yes, the hospital makes perfect sense. Why had we not thought of that?"

Todd didn't have an answer.

Detective Walsh rose, pursing her deep red lips. "Thank you, Mr. Dray."

As Detective Walsh turned, Todd stopped her. "Wait. What about the reward money?"

The detective chuckled. "That is all any of you ever care about."

Blood rushed to Todd's cheeks. Yes, he only cared about the money; he wouldn't deny that. But why else would anyone come forward? Out of the goodness of their heart? For the most part, did the Story Collector really do anything?

He robbed you. He's a menace. You needed to report him.

Detective Walsh smiled, a sharp smile with an uneven bite. "Once we confirm that your information is accurate, we will be in touch regarding the reward money. Is that fair?"

Todd grunted, "Yeah, fine."

The detective said nothing more, beaming once again before leaving the room. As she left, a cold air bit Todd's skin. His stomach dropped, and sweat pulled at his palms. He was so certain this was the right thing.

But now, as the detective shut the door, he wondered if he'd made a mistake.

The Story Collector was just a kid. Couldn't be much older than twenty-one or so. What would Lex say?

She'd say that it's just a bit of magic. Just let them be. His eyes fell to Garrett. *But I need to protect you and Garrett. This is the right thing to do.*

Garrett glanced up at Todd and giggled. "Hi, Daddy."

It was the first time Garrett addressed him like that since Lex's outbreak.

I had to do this. For my family.

Todd grinned. "Hey, bud. Let's go get you some of that strawberry ice cream, a'ight?"

CHAPTER FOURTEEN

WARD NINE

B ria lay in the dark, rotating the marble-like orb in her hands, listening as silence crept over the suite. She didn't hear anyone rummaging about, and since Kek left, only Varden appeared once with a plate of food. Despite her stomach's growling, Bria picked at the platter before climbing into bed to count the lights on the ceiling.

She counted them over fifty-six times before giving up and rolling onto her side to watch the light fizzle out in the common area. Each time she closed her eyes, she drowned in silver. Was she deep beneath the surface? Was she falling? Or were the trees? Who was that climbing into her head?

Why did her ears buzz?

She lurched forward, gasping.

You're safe. Relax. They won't hurt you. Have trust.

Trust them.

Her mind continued racing, and she squeezed the miniature orb tighter. *I need to trust them.*

But how could she when Edith blatantly stated her name?

Maybe they've been watching you for a long time. If Kek is as old as they say, they might know about the Council and the Mist Keepers. Don't get any ridiculous ideas in your head!

She swung her legs over the side of the bed. It was pointless to try sleeping. Her head swirled in five different directions.

Bria didn't expect the door to open, but it did without hesitation. *I'm not a prisoner. I'm free to come and go as I please. Stop being afraid.* Yet she continued to squeeze the orb as she headed down the stairwell. It creaked and moaned with each step, and the walls seemed like they could collapse.

But then the door at the bottom opened, and there she stood in the long, sterile ward. It extended into flickering darkness haunted by gas lanterns. The dripping, moaning, and clanking battled with the emptiness.

What are you doing here? Bria let her feet carry her forward while her heart and mind reached back towards the stairs. Curiosity led her forward, past the first few empty rooms. She paused at one of them, staring at the vacant cot. Who had been on that bed? Did they get better? Was their story still loitering in the walls of the hospital?

Bria shook away the questions and continued walking.

She came across the first occupied room a few doors away from the stairwell. A magician sat in the center of the room, playing with a pile of coins. With each of the magician's laughs, the coins multiplied, filling the corners of the floors.

Bria watched the magician fall back into the coins and throw them in the air. She smiled at the childish nature and continued along the hallway. At each room, she stopped and peeked through the curtains. In most rooms, the individuals slept. Some breathed their magic, sending sparks or tricks flying, while others didn't move.

Bria passed by a few more rooms before pausing at room twenty-seven, where she met Edith earlier that day. Her heart rose in her ears, remembering the blood on Edith's hands as she put away a scalpel. Slowly, she opened the curtain.

Inside lay a woman whose fingernails extended beyond the length of her arm. Cuts dug into her skin, commingling with the bandages around her wrists.

Relief washed over Bria. She closed the curtain and caught herself from sobbing. *Don't be stupid! Edith isn't torturing Brent!* No, this was just a poor woman with a plague of uncontrollable nail growth. Edith might've known Bria's name, but what did that have to do with Brent?

Bria wiped her eyes and took another step forward. Exhaustion had already paid its dues, but she wanted to keep going. Just for peace of mind, really. What did she have to lose? It helped her have more faith in this Palaver. They wanted to help. That's all.

She checked another couple of rooms, pulling aside each curtain with care. Once again, most slept. People resting, healing from whatever deep ailment washed over them.

How many loitered in these rooms? How long had they been here?

Bria exhaled and leaned against the wall. Her exhaustion caught up with her. Perhaps now was the time to end her excursion and return to bed.

Even if he is here, he's safe. Take care of yourself. Think about what your grandmama would say—

A door opened down the hallway. Bria flattened herself behind a cart, watching as light poured out and painted the hall in white. She recognized Edith, her hair glowing like fire upon her head, staring back into the room.

"Sleep tight, love. We'll try again tomorrow," she called, her voice as pointed as a blade as she closed the door. "Heavens know you'll need it."

With a swift movement, she turned and strode down the hall with a long thin saber at her hip.

Once Edith disappeared, Bria bolted to the room from where she came from. The curtains hung closed. She reached for them, hands clammy and heart racing.

Thudding and bumping.

There he lay, like all the other patients, his chest rising and falling in uneven beats beneath the cover. His face was pale, glowing under the dimmed lantern, contorting in odd shapes as he breathed. Mist wove around his fingers in obtuse tales.

His curls sat matted on his head while stubble decorated his chin and upper lips. An intravenous line of silver liquid ran down his visible arm.

"Brent..." She pressed her fingers to the glass.

Bria yanked at the door. It didn't budge, locked tight. Her mind raced. Edith probably had the key, so that wouldn't help.

She paced before the door, checking on Brent every few seconds. He didn't wake, his breathing still heavy. *I will get to you; don't worry. I'm coming.* She glanced down the hall. An empty stretcher lay a few doors away, sheets and towels stacked on top of it. Bria ran over and pushed it towards the door with all her might.

It still didn't budge.

"Fuck!" she cursed, running back to the window. Brent stirred slightly.

Bria shook her head. The little branch behind her ear, for the first time in months, rustled.

Slowly, Bria touched the branch, letting a small flower gather at her fingertips. With a mild pang, she plucked it. The petals wilted away, leaving the seed pods alive and pulsating in her hand.

She smiled.

Bria allowed each of the seeds to grow, twisting around each other into a thick braided branch. Once they wove together, Bria hoisted the new club up and slammed it into the glass window.

Clang!

The window cracked.

Brent shifted again on the other side. A thick mist poured out of his mouth for a moment before dissipating around the room.

A few more times, and it'll break. Bria hoisted the club up again.

A door down the hall opened. Out walked Edith, swinging her saber side-to-side. Bria paused, staring at her.

Edith glared back. "What are YOU doing here?"

Bria pushed away her fear and met the woman's gaze, keeping her grip tight around her club. "I was going for a walk and—"

Edith rushed forward, eye level with Bria, her saber extending. "Don't lie to me, *Bria*. He's told me everything about you."

Bria didn't budge. Edith wouldn't think of hurting her, would she?

"You are Bria Smidt, the reaper fucker, right?" Edith placed the tip of her blade on Bria's chest. "How does it feel knowing you have Death wrapped around your finger? Or well, you did until he went crazy, didn't you? You tried to mold him into a model citizen, but look at him now! An utter demonic disaster!"

"He only started acting like this because he saved the day," Bria retorted.

"Or perhaps the monster brought out his true nature. A crazy, malicious, wild fucker, ain't he?" Edith tilted her head to the side, laughing as she twisted at her blade.

Bria stepped back, gripping her foliage bat.

"Reapers," Edith continued, "should be eradicated. He's nothing but a monster."

"He's your patient!" Bria swung the bat.

Edith hit back with her saber, as smooth and trained as any warrior. The bat fell to the floor with a clatter and withered.

"That won't do you any good, Bria." Edith dropped her saber, and it melted into the ground. "You can't save your monster."

"He's not a monster!"

"Are you sure? Are you so sure?" Edith leaned in and snagged Bria's wrist. Her nails tightened around Bria's wrist, almost like miniature knives digging into her skin. "Prove it."

"Wha-What?"

Edith kicked open the door and threw Bria into the wall with a clatter. Before Bria could find her footing, Edith rushed over to where Brent slept and unhooked his intravenous line and the leather cusps around his wrists. With a single grunt, she shoved him onto the floor.

Brent gasped, curling up into the fetal position as he brought his hands to his head. Bandages garnished his right arm.

"Time to play, Reaper," Edith hissed.

Bria glowered at Edith.

With another loud cackle, Edith retreated from the room and gathered herself at the window, smirking as the door locked behind her.

The room dimmed.

A thick smog filled the room, and Brent's body contorted. His eyes blinked rapidly. At first glance, they were a glossy silver, but after a few more blinks, yellow slits replaced them.

"Brent...Brent, it's me. Please," Bria begged. "It's me. It's Bria."

He rose to his feet, hunched over, the fog drifting around his ankles. As he moved, the mist told stories of monsters, of horrors, of murderers, and of demons. They climbed on the walls, inches along the floor, slithering toward her with the veracity of the Diabolo.

Bria backed into the corner.

"Brent, please, I know you're in there!" Her voice bounced against the walls.

Brent—no, not Brent, but his body—continued towards her. More stories poured from the walls. Tales of past patients continued to fill the room. All of them surrounded her until Brent himself stood mere inches from Bria. He picked her up by her throat.

"Brent!"

He tilted his head and spat into her face.

Bria squirmed.

As Brent's fingers dug into her neck, more stories filled the surrounding areas. She could see herself in the tales, running between cities, crying in alleyways, and lying alone in the apartment. The sadness reverberated throughout the room. It grew thick, like the humidity of a summer storm.

Brent's fingers tightened around her throat. The stories closed in around them.

"Please..." Bria grabbed his wrist.

To her surprise, she yanked his hand loose.

His face softened, the stories completely washing over him.

Bria used that moment to her advantage. She shoved him backward, and he toppled to the floor.

In haste, Bria searched her pockets for something—anything—to use against Brent. *He's not frightening! He's just bigger than me!* The stories guided him, but at the heart of it, he was still physically Brent Harley. And if there was one thing Bria knew for certain: Brent Harley was a klutz.

Only the single silver orb occupied her pocket. She removed it, and without thinking, she smashed it into the center of Brent's forehead.

The silver liquid exploded over his face. He shrieked and grabbed at his head, withering against the floor. Around them, the mist dispersed.

"Help me," Brent begged. His voice belonged to him for once.

"I'm trying. I'm trying." Bria cupped his face.

He met her gaze for a moment. Then, his eyes rolled backward, and he collapsed on the ground with a thud.

CHAPTER FIFTEEN

THROUGH THE
MORGUE

Bria dragged Brent back onto the cot, cuffing his hands to the bed with the leather straps before collapsing on the floor with an angry sob. She dug her face into her hands, heaving and sputtering, trying to get her emotions under control. With each exhausted cry, the humidity in the room thickened, and the little branch behind her ear grew.

She glanced at Brent. The silver liquid remained splattered on his face, yet to reform into a sphere. Brent had stopped twisting and churning, though, drifting into a rhythmic sleep.

"What did they do to you, Brent?" She sniffled. Finally, she got a good look at him in the dim light. Scratches covered his arms and legs from weeks on the street, some deep and gnarled, while others looked like pinpricks on his skin. With acne scars and chapped lips decorating his thinned-out face, he almost looked like a skeleton but for his uneven curls. She hoisted herself up and placed a hand to his cheek. Stubble tickled her fingertips. *You never could grow a beard.*

But then her attention fell to the bloody bandages on his right arm. Bria couldn't help herself. With care, she unwounded each bandage.

More tears fell as she traced the wound on his skin.

REAPER.

The word scarred his arm, deep cuts painting his skin red, mingling with his Black Stamp.

Trembling, Bria rose. *How dare they!*

Anger replaced her fear. Her little branch crawled from her ear, climbing through the room and the door. Nature reclaimed everything, and the branch wrapped around the doorknob and into its keyhole. Her emotions took hold, and with a single flick of her neck, her little branch broke open the lock.

As the door swung open, the branch rescinded, leaving debris of foliage in its wake. Bria hurried back over to Brent's bed, unlocking the wheels on the cot, then pushed it into the hallway.

To her relief, no one occupied the corridor. Only the flickering lights above provided company.

I will get you out of here, okay? She stared down at him. He rested peacefully, undisturbed by the recent change in events.

She pushed his bed along the hallway, stopping every few steps to listen for Edith. Either the woman had ventured off into another poor patient's room, or she had gone to bed, but Bria didn't want to take any chances. The sooner they left this place, the better.

At the end of the corridor, Bria slowed, checking the leather straps around Brent's wrists. The doorway to the stairwell taunted her, laughing even. How would she get Brent downstairs?

There must be another way. How else would they get patients upstairs?

She scanned the wall. A few feet away from the stairwell sat another door. Instead of a traditional wood fixture, metallic lattices served as the barrier. When Bria pushed it aside, it opened into a small room just big enough for a stretcher and one other person. A single lightbulb hung overhead, illuminating the dial against the wall.

It's a hoist! Bria saw them a few times during her travels. A pulley system lowered and raised these small rooms inside buildings, so individuals didn't need to use the stairs. Bria never rode in one herself, but looking at the dial and the ropes, she had an idea how it might work.

She pushed Brent into the shaft and closed the lattice door. With all her strength, she rotated the dial counter-clockwise.

Then, with a loud creak, the hoist descended.

Sweat built on Bria's brow, her arms aching with each churn of the lever. After what felt like a never-ending cycle of turning, the hoist hit the bottom floor with an uneven thud. Bria checked Brent again, then pushed him out of the shaft.

They arrived in a frigid room lined with stone. Bria pulled her cowl closer to her chin and squinted in the hazy light. A few carts lay empty while multiple metallic boxes lined the walls.

Brent squirmed on the cot. His eyes remained shut.

Mist gathered around his fingertips.

"Brent?" Bria nudged him. "Are you okay?"

He fidgeted more, arching his back as he tried freeing himself from the restraints on his wrists. His legs shook, more mist swallowing him like a storm.

"Let me...let me," he whispered.

"What?" Bria stared at him.

"They're...they're...they call me and...they...they need to be...they..." His eyes shot open. Glassed over, they darted back and forth, a slight tinge of yellow in his irises. "Let me help them."

"Who?" Bria's heart pattered with hope. He almost sounded like himself. There was still that scratchy noise in his throat, dancing with voices of a thousand others as he spoke, but his stutter and self-righteousness were there. Brent was alive, deep down, past the Diabolo's mask.

"THEM!" Brent screamed. "I need to help them! They're screaming...they're...they're crying! They need...they're stuck in Hell, and they need...they need me...they need me because...they're trapped, and they need me!"

Bria glanced around the room. She only saw the metal boxes. No one else but mist filling the floor.

Unless...

Bria gasped, "We're in a morgue."

"Let me help. Let me help!" Brent's screams turned into sobs, his face contorting like a child.

"I—"

"They keep screaming! Please...PLEASE! They need help...they need...please..."

Bria's heart sank, and she gave into Brent, removing the cuff from his right hand. Before she made it to the other side, he raised his hand outwards.

Mist spiraled around the room, brandishing the walls, picking at the doors, and wrapping around cots and trays. As it danced, mystical figures joined in from the walls. The air breathed in relief. Happiness swung, the celebration of prisoners at last free darting about the room. Colors overflowed the mist. For a moment, Bria saw the figures clear as day. Not just shadows loitering in the mist, but people at peace with their death.

Bria often forgot the true nature of Brent's magic. It did not come out of innate talent but under the promise that he guarded the gate between Life and Death. Without him or the other Mist Keepers, the dead floundered forever in a Hell constructed of their worst nightmares.

She'd seen Brent release a few dead souls before, each time leaving him in a terrifying state of dysphoria. But she never saw him release multiple souls as he did now. All at once, the souls waltzed together, then dispersed as if part of the same tale.

Brent lowered his hand to his side. He cursed under his breath. His entire body trembled.

"Shite," he croaked.

Bria took his hand. "Brent?"

He glanced at her. His eyes remained glossy as he spoke, "Hi."

"Do you know who I am?" She choked on her words. Was it too much to hope he'd recognize her?

"Yeah...you're—" He stopped, gritting his teeth. After a moment, his lips turned upwards into a cynical smile. "Missy! You damn slut! How could you cheat on me! You deserve what you got—gah!" His hand shot outwards, pushing Bria away from the cart. He threw his voice higher at the next word. "No, Reginald, I didn't mean it! I promise I didn't mean it! I thought—YOU THOUGHT NOTHING!"

Bria stared. She collected her thoughts slowly, trying to stay calm as Brent continued his back-and-forth conversation between 'Reginald' and 'Missy.' His eyes flickered with each person, but she still saw the confused young man hiding behind the altercation, like a lost child.

She inched back to him. "Brent..."

"Go away, you...you slut!" he cried.

"Brent," she said with more force this time. "Look at me."

"I said go away!"

Bria grabbed his hand. "I said look at me."

He closed his eyes and shook his head.

She guided his face back to her. Gentle, one finger at a time, she placed a hand against his cheek. "Look at me."

After prodding him for a few more minutes, slow with beats between each request, Brent finally opened one eye. Tears washed down his cheeks, his lips quivering, his breaths rampant.

"What is your name?" Bria asked.

"Reg...Aur...Quin...Bo...Pa...Ma...I...I don't...I dunno..." He burst into tears. "I don't know...I don't know! There are so many...they're all...they're yellow and...FUCK! Shite! FUCK! HELP ME!"

Bria let him cry, lulling him until he finally fell asleep like a child. She held back her desire to cry with him and flood the morgue with a series of raw emotional storms. *Stay strong.*

Once he fell back to sleep, Bria cuffed his right hand again for safety and pushed his stretcher towards the far end of the morgue where the doors waited. With the dead released, the weight of the morgue vanished.

Part of Bria expected to find the morgue locked, but the doors swung open without hesitating into a utility hallway on the ground floor. She checked each door one at a time. A closet contained an array of supplies and uniforms. Bria took advantage of a spare nurse's uniform, shoving her jacket and cowl under Brent's blanket after changing before continuing along the hallway, looking for an exit.

She didn't have a plan once she got Brent out of the hospital. It was possible that it would end up the same as before, chasing him across the world with no end in sight. *Love can't stop a monster like this.* But to leave Brent here, in the hospital where someone like Edith would torment him, seemed worse.

Finally, Bria found a door leading into another hallway. Brighter, a skeleton crew of nurses and doctors walked in and out of rooms. None paid heed to Bria as she pushed Brent along on the stretcher, much to her relief.

Not that it lasted long.

Her stomach dropped as she rounded the bend. At the end of the hallway stood a giant figure with its back towards Bria.

Shit. Varden.

She slowed, pushed Brent's stretcher against the wall, covered his face with the blanket, and ducked behind the cart. From her position, she barely made out Varden's voice.

"Do you have a warrant?" he asked, crossing his arms.

Bria couldn't hear or see who he spoke to, but his reactions spoke volumes.

"I don't care if the so-called *Story Collector* is wanted. Without the proper warrant, you cannot search our hospital."

A pause. Bria held her breath.

"I'd be happy to get our Chief Doctor, but they will say the same thing."

One more beat.

"Very well. Please wait in the lobby, Detective. Dr. Kafele will be with you shortly."

The doors slammed, and Varden turned, pouting. He stood there for a moment, scanning the hallway. A few of the other doctors and nurses gawked at him, then as the giant took a step forward, they returned to their work in haste. He didn't move, though, continuing to glance over the hallway before his eyes rested on Brent's stretcher.

"Rho?" he called.

Bria's stomach dropped.

"You can come out. I see your aura."

Her nerves tight, Bria rose from behind the stretcher. What was he going to do to her now?

Varden approached her and knelt to her level. "What are you doing, Rho? You can talk to me."

Bria stared at him. "You were torturing Brent!"

"Pardon?"

Bria pulled back Brent's blanket, so his REAPER scar sat visibly on his arm. "You've been torturing him!"

Varden's eyes widened. "Damn her..."

Bria blinked.

"She wasn't supposed to harm him. He's our patient. Which must mean that you're..." Varden gasped. "You're the Bria he spoke about! I imagined you being taller!"

"Is that supposed to make me feel better?"

"Bria," Varden pressed, "we've been working on a cure for him. He's been getting better."

"I don't trust you. He tried...he tried to attack me. He doesn't remember his name..."

"It's a long process. When he's hooked up to the intravenous line, he is much more lucid. Please," Varden held out his hand, "trust me. I can prove it to you."

Bria stared at his hand, then glared up at him. "If you're wrong, will you let us leave?"

"Yes, I promise."

Varden carried Brent with ease back up to the suite at the top of the hospital. He lay Brent's body onto Bria's bed then vanished for a few minutes before returning with an intravenous line of silver fluid. Without a word, he tightened a band around Brent's arm, inserted the needle into his veins, then adjusted the dial on the line, so the liquid flowed with ease. Once Brent relaxed, Varden waved his hand over the splattered orb on Brent's head. It reformed into a sphere which Varden plucked off Brent's head and put into his pocket.

"Don't remove the line. I have a few issues to attend to, but I promise you will see an improvement in him within the next couple of hours." Varden smiled. "I promise."

Bria said nothing as Varden left. She curled up in an armchair next to the bed, watching as Brent inhaled and exhaled. His rhythmic breathing was almost soothing, like a gentle hum rocking the air...

Calm.

Tranquil.

A knock jolted her from sleep. She gasped, flinching as she glanced around the room, recollecting herself. Brent continued to sleep on the bed. Color had returned to his cheeks, and while each breath arrived with tremors, he looked human.

The knock followed again.

"Come in!" she called, straightening herself in the armchair.

Kek strolled in with a plate of boiled eggs, cheese, and fruits in their hands. They motioned with their chin at Brent. "He's looking better."

"No thanks to you." Bria crossed her arms.

Kek approached Brent, handed Bria the plate, and examined his arm with care. Their frown stayed. "I have not been paying enough attention to him. I was a fool to leave him in Edith's care. She has such distaste for Mist Keepers that she could not ignore that to treat him right."

"So, you know about the Mist Keepers?"

"I've known them for many thousands of years." Kek nodded. "Brent told me what happened to him with the Diabolo."

"Then...you must know who I am," Bria whispered. "Why didn't you tell me he was here?"

"I didn't want to get your hopes up. He has...not been responding well to treatments. Stable, yes, but no improvement." Kek adjusted Brent's intravenous line, their expression still downcast. "I can get him talking, but I need to sacrifice more of the elixir than I'd like. The current dosage is enough to keep him stable, but he is stuck in a void between the monster and himself."

"But maybe he'll get better around someone he knows. Someone like...me?"

"It is possible. This is all uncharted territory for me. I have never treated a Mist Keeper; the Council has always cast a tight net around their own, even when I could help. I am surprised they haven't caught up with him yet, to be frank."

"That's because of me. I blocked the tunnels."

"You blocked the tunnels?"

"Yes."

"So you can enter the tunnels?"

Bria hesitated. "Um...yes."

"Interesting." Kek said nothing else on the topic, glancing back at Brent. "I've known the Mist Keepers for a long time. We have a tenuous relationship. I want to help Brent, but more importantly...I want to protect you, Bria. Or do you prefer Rho?"

"Bria's fine," she replied. "But...but why? What does it matter who I am?"

"I've seen what you can do. This has nothing to do with your *aura*, as the Seers call it. I've been watching you."

"You've been watching me?" Bria held back a scream. Kek knew about her? Why didn't they come and help? Why didn't they answer her pleas in the tunnels when she was alone?

Kek almost seemed to read her mind. "I watch many Magii. I have my ways of getting details, so I get a sense of their abilities from afar. Usually, I don't pursue them unless one of my Seers brings them to me, for they make the best judgment calls. If I were left to my own devices, I would end up with an army of trickery rather than talent."

Kek paused, giving Bria a chance to process what they said before continuing. "I didn't pay much mind to you until I learned about how you rejuvenated your hometown. And more importantly, you angered the Order of the Effluvium...and per Brent, the Council! Ha! If I had known you were tormenting them in the tunnels, I would have latched onto you years ago!"

"I'm not proud of that." Bria looked away, focusing on Brent's steady breathing.

"You should be. It takes a lot to anger them. And if you can do that much without proper training, how much stronger could you be with it? I want to see you thrive, Bria. Let me help you."

Bria pondered what Kek said. Fear tugged at her wish to reach beyond her comfort levels, but wasn't this what she'd always wanted?

Kek patted Bria's hand. "I don't expect an answer today. Think on it. You're processing trauma—"

"I'm not traumatized!"

"You've been through a lot. Take a few days to reconnect with yourself. Only then will your powers thrive." Kek rose. "If you need anything, Varden will be around shortly. I need to do my rounds and then research potential elixirs for Brent. Hopefully, we can get him more himself in a matter of weeks."

Bria watched Kek leave, then curled up again in the armchair. She picked away at the eggs and cheese, not quite feeling hungry but knowing she needed to eat.

She didn't move for quite some time, only budging when Varden came in and dropped off Brent's things. Bria recognized the long overcoat Brent had been wearing around the city, the pockets weighed down by random items he collected.

She shuffled through them, discovering a handful of glistening gems throbbing with emotions on their surfaces. A lemon quartz radiated with happiness, a sapphire gem with melancholy, a ruby with lust and love, and an emerald with rebirth. Bria lay them along the end table, stroking each one with her fingers. It was strange, feeling the different emotions breaking through the wall she'd kept around her. *No wonder Brent stole them.*

Bria wrapped Brent's coat, clean now after months of wear, around her. She stared at the wall. Waiting.

For what? She wasn't certain.

Until she heard Brent mumble.

"Brent?" she whispered.

His eyes flickered open, squinting against the light.

Silver.

Bria inhaled.

"Birds," he said without hesitating.

"Birds?"

"Smells like birds."

"What?"

He raised a trembling finger and pointed at Bria's half-eaten breakfast. "Birds."

"You mean eggs?"

"Yeah." His hand fell again.

Bria stared at him for a moment, then at the eggs, and then back at him. "Are you...hungry?"

He nodded.

With care, Bria helped Brent sit up on the bed. He moved like an uncoordinated hatchling, lulling to the side at first. Bria stuffed a few pillows behind him before sitting across the bed from him with the plate of food.

Brent's fingers trembled as he picked up an egg. He sniffed it once, then picked away at it with his uneven nails. He left the yolk on the plate.

It was strange watching him eat. He behaved like a curious child, experiencing new foods for the first time. What had he eaten on the streets?

He picked up a piece of pineapple, tasted it, then threw it across the room. "Demon fruit! Vile! Begone!"

"You still don't like pineapple." Bria almost laughed.

"Evil fruit. Demon. Evil."

"That's something you always used to say. I'm glad there's...some of you left." She dabbed his face with a napkin. She tried to keep her voice steady as she spoke, focusing on normal topics. She hoped the more she introduced normalcy, the more he would remember something. "You really need to shave. A beard doesn't work on you."

"Makes me look like a regal fool...or a...cat...or...walrus. Yeah. A walrus." He chuckled and placed his fingers in front of his mouth like fangs. "Bark bark!"

"Do walruses bark?"

"I've been studying walruses for years, Gail! You know that! Of course, they—no..." His smile fell. "That's not me."

Bria waited to see if he would say anything else. He dropped his head, staring at his hands, drawing his fingers over his wrist and up to his REAPER scar. He recited the word to himself, then glanced up at Bria.

For the first time in months, he met her gaze. Not some half-conscious version of himself, but Brent himself.

"I know you," he said.

Bria's throat knotted. "Yes."

"And you know me?"

"Yes."

His eyes fell to his wrist again. "My name...my name is....it's...shite...it's...I'm..." He cursed. "Shite! It's on the tip of my tongue. Gotta...I need...I mean...I wanna rip my tongue out and lecture it 'cause this is...it's not...why don't I remember my name?"

Bria stopped him from reaching into his mouth and pulling at his tongue. "Brent. Your name is Brent."

"Brent." He repeated. "Yeah, that's right. I'm Brent...and you're...you're...fuck. I...you're..."

"I'm Br—"

"NO! I wanna get it myself!" Brent cursed again, closing his eyes while he focused.

Bria watched in silence. He was trying his best to climb out of the hole in his mind. She wanted to reach in, yank him up, and hold him tight. But this was his battle now.

"My name is...Brent...Brenton...Brenton Rob Harley," Brent muttered to himself. "I'm...I'm from...I'm from Newbird's Arm. My parents are...they're...they're names are...Janette and Robert Harley. I have a sister. Alex...Alexandria. And my one...my one constant...the one thing in my life that's always there has been...it's always been..." His eyes locked with hers. "Bria. You're...you're Bria."

Bria reached forward, squeezing Brent's fingers tight, as tears dampened the corners of her eyes. "Yes. I'm Bria. That's me."

CHAPTER SIXTEEN

A YARD OF TENSION

The nights grew longer in Newbird's Arm and not because of the solstice. Riots overtook the streets while the Guards of Knoll dragged vagrants and townsfolk into the Temple for the cleansing. Jemma helped quell the townsfolk as they sought refuge from the violence. Meanwhile, Elder Lau Rel and other brothers and sisters from Knoll suffocated the screams from the forced cleansings in the crevasses beneath the pews. It was a double-edged sword; while the cleansing would rid those tortured by sin, the ritual was synonymous with torture for those unprepared. But weren't these same individuals causing chaos in the town, singing the song of Rhodana the Forest Queen as a battle chant? Didn't they understand she wasn't coming back?

Jemma wanted to support their cause. But, upon leaving the Temple one early morning after hiding out again in the cloister with the rest of the brothers and sisters, she struggled to find her sympathy. The night itself had been long and treacherous, and while many brothers and sisters found comfort in each other, Jemma was left as an outlier, counting the moments until morning's arrival.

As the sun rose in the sky, she stepped out into the market square, where trucks and autos lay flipped on the ground, the evergreen trees sat charred, and merchant carts hung dismantled throughout the market. Flyers bearing caricatures of Bria's face fluttered through the air. The Guard did not react with kindness. Instead, they escalated further, thriving on the disarray in their tiny town.

She argued with her parents about riots multiple times. Whenever she arrived home from nights of prayer and protection, her mother waited for her in the foyer, launching into a whole tirade about the disgracefulness of the Order. If they genuinely treasured peace, they'd be on the side of the protestors, her mother insisted, not the oppressive hand of this Elder from Knoll. Jemma didn't totally disagree, but it was not her place to stand up against Elder Lau Rel.

Not yet, at least.

She needed a plan to bring Brother Roy Al's words back to Newbird's Arm. He had guided the town with poise and dignity. Could she emulate it? Not until she memorized the scripture and grasped what Elder Lau Rel stood for in the Order. Only then could she lead the Order to newfound greatness.

Well, at least in Newbird's Arm.

Jemma decided, with the town quiet after another night of unrest, to take a long way home. She wanted to avoid the altercation with her mother for as long as possible. Their bickering led nowhere; Jemma wouldn't budge from her goal, and neither would her mother. They were two sides of the same coin.

She glowered up at the Tower as she left the market that morning. It buzzed with electricity, the Guards who marched in and out with smirks on their faces reminiscent of Captain Carver's cadets. Relief washed over Jemma when those goons disappeared, but now new ones marched along the river, smirks on their face and thoughts of demons in their heads.

She circled around the Tower to where the guard parked their automobiles, trailing back towards the field. Jemma saw nothing like these vehicles until the men from Knoll arrived. Gears, wheels, and motors created the machine's body. Like a monster, when it moved, it exhaled puffs of smog, mingling with the Effluvium and sending waves of smoke through town.

An odd clanking, matched with equally vile cursing, exited from the shadows between the automobiles. As Jemma rounded the last bend around the yard, she saw someone crouched over the front of a vehicle. Their puffy hair blew in the wind, their round belly pressed to the machine, their fingers dancing over the engine.

She slowed and peered past the fence. When the individual looked up from the hood, she relaxed.

"Micca Fein? Is that you?" she called.

The man jumped and turned to her. "Ah! Jem! Ain't seen ya in years!"

Jemma approached the fence. She hadn't seen Micca since the Guard threw him into the Pit nearly four years earlier. While his stomach protruded much further out now, his hair remained in its wiry and knotted descent to his shoulders. Rough stubble masked his face, and when he smiled, his yellowing teeth almost glowed in the lantern light.

"What are you doing out of the Pit, Mr. Fein?" Jemma pressed.

"Oh, Jem, drop the formalities. We done known each other since we were babes. Come now. Lighten up." Micca leaned against the car.

"I don't want you to get in trouble, that's all." That was true. Under Elder Lau Rel's domain, it was far safer for vagrants to stay in the Pit.

"I bought my way outta the Pit there a month ago. Right after the first leaves changed, saved me up a ton of money and pow! Out I went! So I got all the right to be here." He scowled. "But now with these damn Knoll guards, it won't last long with my stamp and all."

"You will be fine if you don't have magic...and as long as you behave," Jemma stated. "If you're out of the Pit legally, they can't force you back."

"What if I do, though? Brent didn't know he had magic 'til recently and now he done destroyed the town. What if the Order pulls my teeth out and I discover I got a magic tongue shaped like a snake or something like that? Huh?" Micca leaned forward. The smell of smoke poured from his mouth.

Jemma crossed her arms and scowled. "The Order doesn't pull out teeth."

"You know what I mean."

"You do not have magic, Micca."

"How do you know? Did you know that 'bout Brent? Or Beebelle? Did ya'll share some secrets I ain't known about? Didn't think you were close."

"We weren't! He didn't tell me anything. But if you say you don't have magic, I believe you!" Jemma glanced up to the Tower, not wanting to face Micca. He raised a good point, though. How many, like Brent Harley, had magic lurking in their bones, hidden and tame?

Micca scoffed. "It don't matter if you do or not. Cause they ain't gonna see me and think 'that boy done paid his debts. I should, y'know, ignore that there stamp and all.' No. They gonna see me as a fucking dirty-ass vag. So you hear what I'm gonna do?"

Jemma glanced between Micca and the car. "Don't tell me you're going to—"

"Yeah! I'm gonna steal it! What'cha gonna do? Put the guard on me or something? C'mon Jem. I bet ya better than that, yeah?"

Jemma glanced back at the automobiles, then towards the empty train tracks.

"Trust me, I got this bullshite all worked out too! Was gonna hop on that circus train that was coming! But as soon as the damn Guards of Knoll came marching, the circus canceled and chugged straight on past Newbird's Arm and all. And it ain't gonna come for a long while. And even if it does, who's gonna let a vag like me even with my freedom bought on it? Nope. Gotta steal this thing. What'cha gonna do about it?"

"I can't let you."

"C'mon, Jem! Don't be like that!"

"It's my duty as a Sister of the Order—"

"Blah blah blah! C'mon! We've known each other forever!"

"I'm sorry, Micca." Jemma bowed her head. She was sorry, but if anyone discovered she let him get away with the truck, it could end her studies. Then where would she stand?

Worthless, talentless, alone.

"I can't let me turn you in, Jem!" Micca grabbed her wrist. "Please. I don't wanna do this...but if ya gonna turn me in, I'll gotta."

"What will you do?"

"I'll drag you along with me. Run you over. I dunno! I'm a fucking filthy vagrant. I'll do whatever I can, y'know?" Micca seemed uncertain as he spoke. Jemma almost felt bad for him. He reminded her of an animal in a cage, looking for a way out.

Weren't all the vagrants like that? Begging for freedom?

The Order put them on display behind these fences so everyone could gawk and stare. They dehumanized them, turned them into nothing but a show.

Jemma watched it too.

She tugged her hand out of Micca's grip. "You have done nothing wrong yet. There is still time for you to be save—"

"I don't need your damn salvation! I just want freedom!" Micca raised his hands in the air. "Don't you get it? I just wanna get outta here!"

Jemma searched for a response. Sometimes, she didn't understand the vagrants; why was it so hard to go get cleansed and find peace? It was invigorating. She shook off the wish to convince him otherwise, refocusing her thoughts and asking, "Do you even know how to drive an automobile?"

Micca's face changed, replaced with a wide smile. "I bet it ain't that hard. Like, I dunno, riding a bike or something."

"You mean like the one you built when you were twelve and crashed into the river?"

"I'm more coordinated now. And this got more than two wheels!"

Jemma straightened her back. This was all ridiculous, but...she realized that Micca might have the right idea. There were few ways out of Newbird's Arm now. While walking was possible, navigating the mountains in the early winter could take weeks! But stealing from the Guard? It almost seemed preposterous!

Yet...it might be preposterous enough to work.

Jemma chose her next question carefully. "Are you leaving tonight?"

"Nah. Probably a couple days. Been familiarizing my-self in parts and all cause the Guards got this routine. Disguised myself as one of their maintenance boys." Micca pointed to his chest. The Black Stamp rested on the corner of his overalls. "I almost got myself an understanding. Need to figure out how to jump-start this fucker, but I studied what the parts are and such. Like this here is the brake, and here is the shifter, and—" Micca droned on, pointing to the different parts of the automobile.

Jemma held up her hand. "I understand."

"You ain't gonna tell on me, right, Jem? You gonna let me be and all, right? I need another couple nights, then I'll disappear, and no one will realize. Just a missing car from these damn Guards. C'mon Jem...they ain't what you worship, right? Didn't you wanna join the Order to be good? That's what you said when we was kids."

Jemma stared at Micca. Yes, she remembered their childhood acquaintanceship. Micca had always been friends with everyone, remembering little things about them and how to push their buttons.

No, she wouldn't tell the Guard. This was a man who had bought his way out of the Pit. Why should they throw him back for his hard work? Jemma always assumed that the Pit belonged only to the true vagrants.

Those who showed the desire to change...well, they deserved freedom.

Perhaps Micca had really changed.

Though, why he ended up in the Pit in the first place still eluded Jemma. No matter the reason, it didn't matter. Micca was smart; he would find out how to drive this beast of a machine. The world would be at his fingertips. He could go anywhere.

Even across the country to Ab Aeterno and to Brother Roy Al.

She could almost see it, the car pulling up along the rumored marble-paved road of the Holy City, basking in the arms of the Effluvium. The Tower of Ab Aeterno would greet him with open arms.

No...it would greet the both of them.

"No, I won't tell," Jemma replied.

Micca sighed in relief. "Good, 'cause I really didn't want to hurt ya or nothing."

"But..." Jemma stared hard at him, "I want to come with you."

Micca jumped back. "What? Why?"

"I need to get to Ab Aeterno to speak with Brother Roy Al. I have no way of contacting him, but that is where he is. If I do not turn you in, you will take me there. Is that agreed?"

"I ain't thought of you as someone who'd wanna get away like that and all. Thought you were all about *saving* this town or some bullshite like that?"

"Going to Ab Aeterno will help me accomplish that. But you don't have to take me if you don't want to." Jemma sighed dramatically. "I'll inform the Guard that someone is sneaking around in their automobiles. Who do you think they'll listen to – an ex-vagrant or a Sister of the Order?"

Micca opened his mouth to protest, then relaxed. "A'ight. Deal."

"Good. I expect you'll be ready in three days?"

"Um, yeah. A'ight. I can try."

"Good. Thank you, Micca." Jemma turned with a swift wave. Her heart thudded in her ears as she left. She kept her composure as Micca's gaze clung to her back. Although her nerves continued to course through her body, battling away at the confident façade, she wore as a mask.

She prayed this was the right choice.

CHAPTER SEVENTEEN

COPPER PERIWINKLES

Bria preoccupied herself with Brent's care over the next few days. Some days, he welled better than others, but mostly he went through the motions of existing, with brief flickers of himself bubbling to consciousness. She often got him talking, though, even when nonsensical. When he spoke, at least he stayed; silence was the clown that dragged him down into his nightmares screaming.

Bria's own exhaustion weighed heavily on her mind. She hadn't slept well, anxiety keeping her awake with every pattering movement. Would Brent slip again? Would the detective return with a warrant? Did Kek tell her the truth?

Everything will be okay. She counted the lights in the room as she tried to quell her anxiety.

Closing her eyes sent her back into her nightmares, though.

One morning, Bria woke up to Brent scratching at his face, his eyes wide like two silver moons. "A cat is clinging to my face. I hate cats. They're monsters."

"You mean your beard?" Bria yawned. Her head hurt from another night of buzzing nightmares. She dreamt she ran through a forest again, unable to see beyond her tears. The trees grew denser with every passing moment.

It was a relief when Brent woke her.

"Yeah, my cat."

Bria climbed out of the armchair, proceeded into the bathroom, and rummaged through the lower cabinet where Varden had stocked up the toiletries. She removed a sterile razor and returned to Brent, placing her fingers on his cheek. "Here. Let's shave your beard."

He sat on the edge of the bed, and Bria gently shaved his face. His gaze never left her, fingers trembling as one hand touched her arm. His lips opened and closed.

"Shite!" He jumped back. The razor cut into his cheek. "Stop...stop stop stop...get out of my...stop!"

Bria dropped the razor. "Brent! Calm down!"

He hissed like a cat.

What could she do to make this better? Some people claimed that love cured...but not this. Never this.

Patience. Kindness. Love. It all helped. But a cure? No.

Brent gulped, shaking his head back and forth. "I wanna...I know...I'm Brent...but...but...the voices. They want me to do terrible things. Ugly wretched things. I can't...I won't."

"I know you can fight it." Bria clutched his hands.

Brent reached for Bria, stopping himself short, but Bria pulled him into a hug. He dropped his half-shaven face onto her shoulder while shaking like a leaf. His breaths arrived in heavy bouts.

You're not a monster. Bria clutched him tight. "Focus. Fight it. You're a storyteller. All the voices...they're just other ideas in your head. You're still you."

Brent gritted his teeth. "I can't. They're too real."

She didn't pressure him. How could she imagine what tormented his head?

Instead, she finished shaving away the last bit of Brent's stubble and then helped him lie back in bed. Sleep soon washed over Brent's eyes. He fought it off with multiple blinks before succumbing to the wave of exhaustion.

Once Bria was sure he'd fallen asleep, she gently kissed his forehead and whispered, "I'll be back. I'm going to get some fresh air."

He didn't stir.

Bria scribbled the same message on a piece of paper. Then she pulled on her boots, coat, and cowl over the white dress they had given her before exiting into the living suite.

Varden left a platter of cheese and crackers out on the table for her, but that was the only evidence someone had been there. Bria hadn't seen Edith since her run-in downstairs, not that she was complaining, and she knew Kek was busy.

The silence wasn't a bad thing.

Bria opened the blinds and peered down into the alleyway below the Sanitorium. Save for a few pedestrians, the alley stayed silent, the winter clouds hanging with a gloomy aura over the rooftops. She knew she wasn't a prisoner, that she could leave any time, but she certainly felt trapped. Why was hard to place.

Perhaps it was her inability to help, stuck once again in the same cycle.

The door opened behind her. "Ah, Bria! Just who I wanted to see."

Bria turned to face Kek and Varden in the doorway. "Oh, hi."

Kek removed their mask. "I am glad to see you up and about! I am sure you are getting stir crazy."

"How did you know?"

"You have nature-oriented magic. I cannot imagine staying indoors does you well." Kek beamed at her, a wide grin on their face. "I was actually coming to ask if you would you like to get out for a bit? I need your help."

Bria glanced at the bedroom door.

Varden must have known exactly what she thought. "Do not fret; I'll monitor him."

She pondered for a moment, then agreed. "Okay. Thank you, Varden."

The giant smiled.

Kek placed a hand on Bria's shoulder, and after one last glance towards the bedroom door, they headed down the stairwell together.

They entered the magic-ward, where doctors and nurses bustled among the afflicted patients. During the day, the ward frolicked with energy, bustling with activities from the patients, nurses, and doctors. Edith heralded the bunch. She stopped shouting as Bria walked by, glaring at her with eyes like daggers. Bria tugged on her cowl to hide her face. She'd dealt with profuse individuals for years, but Edith was different. Was it the magic? Her hatred for Brent? No... Bria couldn't put her finger on it, but something made her stomach queasy. It was as if the woman's moral compass spun in circles. A nurse, yes, but with lust for blood.

Bria shrunk as Edith glowered at her. Edith's existence taunted her; she wasn't tall, but she carried the same presence as Varden. If Bria saw auras, she imagined that Edith's was dark red, like blood seeping along the walls, never stopping.

Bria and Kek didn't stay long in the ward, queuing down the second set of stairs towards the operating theater from where Bria had arrived. It was brighter than Bria remembered, the lightbulbs on the walls causing the white ground to glow. In the center of the room sat the odd white tub.

Untouched.

Still.

Vacant.

Kek walked to a cabinet on the far side of the room and unlocked it, humming an unrhythmic tune. Inside, at least fifty different orbs, silver at their base but swirling with unique images, waited. Kek rolled their finger over one row and smiled to themselves as they removed a sphere.

"Where are we going?" Bria finally asked.

"I've been in contact with one of my people. I think I found a way to help poor Brent."

"What?" Bria's heart leapt.

"There are rumors that there is a flower called the Copper Periwinkle on an island off the coast of the region of Delilah. If my research is correct, it has properties that should help with Brent's symptoms...especially when mixed by a talented alchemist like yours truly." Kek winked. "I've already had my comrade out there gather a bunch. He's been running a few trials for me. If all goes well, we may have a stronger medication for Brent."

"So...a cure?" Bria asked. She didn't want to get hopeful. Not again.

"It will be some a serum or tablet he will need to ingest regularly while conducting the proper therapy. But yes, it should stabilize him at least." Kek turned the orb over in their hands, then placed it in the tub. "It is quite a shame the Council consists of such pricks. Someone like that mind reader or memory eater or whoever else is there now would do him wonders."

"They are a bunch of pricks..." Bria touched the little branch behind her ear and cringed. "They tried to unleash my powers months ago." The words hung for a second. She hadn't mentioned this to anyone. But she remembered it so plainly every day. The truth remained clear. "I...I lost control. I tried to fight, but instead...my powers got out of hand. They attracted the Diabolo. It means...Brent's like this because of me. If I had just gone elsewhere, the Order wouldn't have taken him, and he wouldn't have been so weak when taking on the Diabolo."

"To me, it sounds like the Council is to blame, not you," Kek asserted.

"The Council isn't to blame for everything! Sure, they set my powers into a frenzy, but I...I went home! I attracted the Diabolo. And then I killed someone!" She tried to avoid thinking about the lifeless body of the cadet in the forest. Sure, Cadet Lawry represented the worst of the Guard, but did he deserve a tree falling on him and crushing his body? Even Bria didn't know. "I couldn't control it, and I killed him."

Kek turned on the faucet. "That is why you are coming with me. We will learn to control it. But we will only go as far as you desire."

Bria reached forward, holding her hand out in front of her, watching the tendons in her hands flex as she moved her fingers. She'd been told to keep her powers under lock for years, to never reach out beyond the confines of her tunnels. Kek was offering her a chance to explore at last.

"Think about it; that's all, Bria." Kek switched off the water and spun their finger around in the tub. "Though I have one question for you?"

"Yes?"

"Why did you call yourself Rho?"

Bria looked past Kek at the wall. Her throat tightened as she spoke. "I was born with a flower growing from my head. My mother was angry; she had turned against magic and all of it. She tried to kill me by burying me in the ground, but...I flourished." Bria closed her eyes for a moment. Whenever she spoke of her mother, she saw a malevolent witch digging a hole in the ground, cackling as she shoved the body of a newborn between the roots. Angelana Gonzo, as far as it concerned Bria, was not her mother. "My grandmama found me beneath a camellia bush. But by then, the Guard had declared me dead, and they'd arrested my mother for murder. They used the name Rhodana on my birth and death records. That's why I call myself Rho, I guess. Because it's also my name."

Kek replied with one word only: "Interesting."

"Why?"

"Nothing, nothing." Kek shook back their head. "Come. We are already running late."

Bria didn't ask anything else, and Kek ushered her into the bathtub in haste.

The silver liquid washed over her.

Traveling through the pool left Bria exhausted. This time, she felt the peony seeds blossoming around her and kept her eyes open as her gaze turned from clear, to silver, to red, and back to silver. Two small hands reached into the abyss and pulled her to dry land.

After she blinked a few times, her vision returned.

Forest.

She was in a forest!

Trees towered above her. Humidity rocked the air, spiraling between the shrieking calls of birds and shaking branches of trees. Chattering lemurs barked from the trees. For a moment, Bria could breathe for the first time in months. Free from smog and smoke. Free from human-made structures.

And everything green.

But not pure green. It was the type of green that lingered between summer and autumn, just before the leaves changed. This green existed in the mountains, in the snow; it didn't belong in the tropics.

"Here." Someone spoke, handing her a washcloth.

Bria took it and wiped her face, then followed the small hand holding it. A man who must have stood no taller than her shoulders grinned at her. His oak skin and hazel eyes bolstered in the sunlight while black stubble traced the wrinkles and crooks of his face. Uneven, coarse hair fell to his ears.

"Thank you," Bria replied. She turned as the liquid behind her started bubbling.

Kek emerged moments later like a monster in one of Brent's stories coming from the silver lake. The water dripped from their limbs, and a smile once more paraded on their lips. "Ah, good! We're all here now. Bria, I'd like you to meet Yusef."

The squat man bowed. "Pleasure. Kek has told me of you."

Kek kept beaming. "Yes indeed! You see, Yusef is also in tune with nature."

Bria stared at Yusef. Her heart once again climbed into her ears. Her shoulders released in excitement. "Really?"

"Nowhere near as powerful as I heard you are. A rainstorm? Vines everywhere? And giving life to the dead? Nah. I'm a tracker."

"A tracker?"

"Basically, I can find different...uh, what's the word?" He started mumbling to himself in a foreign language before jumping up in satisfaction. "Ah yes! I can find distinct elements, plants, minerals...you know, things that belong in nature."

"So, for instance, I gave Yusef a Copper Periwinkle and asked him to find them for me. He led us here," Kek explained.

"Oh. I see." Bria's excitement tamed. *So much for someone with the same abilities.*

"I can also expedite the growth of some plants, but not to your extent. Everyone I have ever known to have these types of nature-oriented powers manifests in different ways."

"You've known others?"

"When you're around twelve hundred years old, you don't see something only once."

"Are there any now?"

"Maybe." Yusef shrugged. "I'm sure they're out there. Magic emerges in different ways. Nature and elemental magic, mind and body magic, illusion and disillusion magic, and so on and so forth."

But there are no others in the tunnels. Bria paused. She remembered Kek's brief respite when discussing the tunnels earlier. What made her special?

"Enough chit-chat!" Kek clapped their hands. "I imagine you've located the flower, yes?"

"Yes, fine, yes." Yusef reached into the pouch on his side and removed a gorgeous bronze-colored flower with five petals. He squeezed it in his hand, and around his feet, the ground sprouted with a few blades of grass, pointing in front of them like an arrow. "Follow me."

Bria stayed a few paces behind Kek and Yusef. Despite his height, Yusef moved with alacrity; even Kek struggled to keep pace. Bria didn't mind hanging back, though, watching each blade of grass break through the forest floor while the canopy above bathed the ground with a tint of green. It was as if the forest sparkled, birds fluttering by, flowers grappling towards the sky, and the hissing fusa cats crouching in the brambles.

Despite the liveliness of the forest, each time it breathed came in a detrimental huff. Bria sensed each time it exhaled, begging for clean air, demanding a bit of hope and magic for its own survival.

They continued along, stepping through mud and over fallen trees. A golden-faced puma peaked from the shadows, a mist squirrel bounded in the trees, and a few miniature water-breathing dragons fluttered in the air. Bria caught one on her hand and let it sit for a minute before sending it back to the air.

Magic and life hid in this forest.

What had once been in the forests of Rosada and Mert? Did they ever harbor the same delight? Had they always been so dead?

Here, Bria detected the truth. At its core, the Earth was dying. Bria brought life again to the Senator's gardens growing up and to the boardwalks in Mert, but she couldn't stop the world from heaving. It was outside her ability, and it left a pit of sadness and despair in her stomach.

Why did it die? Why did it cry?

Why did she abandon it all to hide in a city of smog?

You forgot who you were. She brushed her fingers along a tree, letting the moss gather beneath her fingers. *You became a shadow while fighting for a dream. A normal life was never for you.* Even as the thoughts whistled through her head, she didn't shake the desire; she wanted a quiet life with her grandmama, her father, Mr. West...and Brent. All of them together, safe, and okay.

Just okay.

"Bria, are you with us?" Kek called back.

"Yeah, I'm coming!" She fought back the tendrils of the forest's humidity and caught up with Yusef and Kek.

As she approached, Yusef slowed his walk, watching the blades of sprouting grass and moss extend towards a small clearing. When they arrived, all that remained were long grasses and mud. Light created a curtain of shimmering streaks from the treetops. Amid it all sat a singular bush blossoming with a dozen Copper Periwinkles like the one in Yusef's hand.

"Is that it?" Kek asked. "I thought there'd be more. That won't last a year."

"The forest is struggling. There might be more on another island, but here...that's it."

Bria walked towards the bush, staring down at the copper flowers. She traced her fingers across the petals, letting them croon, bask, and flourish. Then, she moved to the leaves and listened to their voices. They sang in harmony, reaching to the roots buried beneath the earth. Some had long since died, others gone dormant, and others had merely forgotten how to bloom.

But Bria didn't forget.

She reached for the roots, for the leaves, and for the flowers that lay dormant. Her fingers trembled as she tickled them awake. They belonged to her heartbeat, and her breaths belonged to their voice. She pushed away the fear in the bushes, replacing them with love and care. With a gentle sigh, her magic flooded the surroundings. The periwinkle bush grew, spreading out within the clearing, and giving birth to hundreds of copper flowers.

They glistened like bronze in the streaks of early evening sun.

"Will that be enough?" Bria asked, digging her fingers into the dirt.

Kek clenched their hands together. "That's perfect!"

Bria smiled widely. *I've still got it.*

CHAPTER EIGHTEEN

REIGNITED

After collecting the copper periwinkles, Kek and Yusef led Bria away from the clearing and into a small tree house above the forest floor. Bria leaned out the window, letting the humidity brush against her cheeks. Kek and Yusef worked at a table, speaking in a foreign tongue while diluting the flowers and herbs in a vial. She loved the heat on her face, the way the wind bickered with the leaves, and the way the sun sank below the canopy. It brought her peace.

Tranquility.

Serenity.

Kek called her over. "Bria, can you help us pull apart these petals for the serum? I'm going to prepare lunch."

"You mean supper," Yusef corrected Kek.

"Semantics. It's lunch for Bria and me."

Bria joined them by the workbench, picking apart each petal from the flower's center. Kek grinned, then leapt out of the treehouse.

At first, she and Yusef worked in silence. The small man worked just like he walked: with haste and focus, pulling each petal and diluting it in the silver water. He heated it over a burner, humming to himself, never once breaking his stride. Bria followed along only for Yusef to stop her and take the petals, shaking his head.

"Your powers are causing the flowers to stay alive. We need them dead. And you're fumbling. Let me do it." Yusef pulled off the remaining petals and dropped them into the liquid, letting them disintegrate in the silver liquid.

Bria listened as the flowers sang their withering melody. Did Yusef hear the song? Did others dance beneath nature's voice the way she did as a child?

Before she asked, Yusef redirected the conversation. "You know, you're lucky Tehuti has taken an interest in you."

"Tehuti?

"You call them Kek."

Right, that's one of their names. "Why do they have so many names?" Bria's curiosity spiked.

"One for each of their kills." Yusef held a vial up to the light, unflinching.

"Kek murdered people?" Bria glanced at her feet, running the word 'murder' over her tongue. It shouldn't have surprised her. Besides, even good people killed.

She knew that better than anyone.

"You'd have to ask the nature of such deaths. They have killed no one for over a thousand years, though. And if you ask me, six kills in two-thousand years isn't that bad."

"I guess..."

Yusef tapered the flame beneath one vial. "I fundamentally believe that Tehuti is good. They help others. They're helping your fellow now, too. Murders and harm in a war do not speak of true character unless done for pleasure."

Like Edith did... Bria clenched her fists.

Yusef didn't say much else, focused again on his work, occasionally mumbling as he continued mixing and diluting the plant in the silver base. Bria crouched down against the wall, watching, waiting, and wondering. She thrived by the power of nature, but could a simple copper flower coated in a magic silver liquid make Brent's head clear?

But more so, she wondered about Kek: what stories did they hide, who had they met, and what truths could they answer? Sure, she'd met a few members of the Council, many as old as Kek if not older, but they did little to harbor her trust. But Kek...they were here for the Magii.

And her.

She rose to greet Kek as they entered the treehouse, carrying a basket of roasted papayas, mangos, and pine-apple. Bria's stomach growled at the sight.

They sat across from Bria on the floor and placed the basket between them. Bria picked at the array of fruits before settling on a slice of pineapple. She smiled before eating it. *Brent hates pineapples. He'll hate me for this.*

"You look much more rested," Kek stated, cutting in-to a piece of papaya.

"I didn't realize I missed this. The forest and nature." Bria blinked, picking away at a piece of pineapple and placing it in her mouth.

"What Magii cannot realize, especially in this day and age, is how deeply ingrained their magic is in their soul and aura; for you, being one with nature is key to your survival."

"It's why I stay here on these types of islands!" Yusef barked from his table.

"I was always closer to the forest back in Newbird's Arm. There's not a lot in the city or anything." Bria pulled a strand of pineapple from her teeth before continuing, "I used to think Mert would be escape but... it's not. I'm...trapped."

"As I would imagine. Your magic does not equip you for the city life, even in one filled with charm."

"Lucky for you, though, being in Mert will help your mate, yeah?" Yusef held the vial out to Kek. "You're up, Tehuti!"

Kek rose from their spot and joined Yusef by the table. Bria watched as they stood over the vials and dipped their fingers into the silver liquid. Slowly, one at a time, Kek's fingers glowed, brightening the room with light. The liquid then trickled from their fingers and onto the plate below, forming puddles upon the glass.

For a few minutes, Kek continued to do this until a half-sphere sat upon the plate, bobbing like a boat upon the water.

Kek grinned. "There. Now we must wait a couple of hours."

Bria gawked at Kek, butterflies fluttering in her stomach. "Is that it then? The cure?"

"It should dull his outbreaks and keep his head clear. Time will tell its full effects."

Bria continued to watch the liquid fizzle. "But you created it. Shouldn't you know?"

"I'm an alchemist in my core, but ultimately, what comes of my creations is up to the different elements. In this, I focused on elements of soothing. The Copper Periwinkle contains antipsychotic properties, and diluted properly in the Pools of Peony, it should help render some sort of normalcy in Brent's mind. But it is hard to be certain."

"Stop bragging, Tehuti. We are all aware of your talent." Yusef chuckled as he put away the remaining vials.

Bria continued to smile, staring at her reflection in the half sphere. Her images curved upwards, making her chin appear twice its size. She'd seen so much in the past few days. Magic had no limits. *What am I capable of doing?*

Kek read Bria like a book. "Fascinating, isn't it? My offer still stands. We can test it."

"I'm not sure..."

"Tehuti knows what they're doing. They helped me discover my full potential. Trust me," Yusef barked from the table and winked, "they won't let you do anything destructive. Not at first, anyway."

Bria pondered it for a second. What did she have to lose?

"Okay. We can try."

Kek led Bria through the forest, leaving Yusef behind to pick apart more flowers. As they walked in the early evening glow, the ferns along the pathway opened their leaves, glowing like moonbeams against the ground. Bria tracked her fingers along their blades, letting each leaf bend beneath her touch. The forest watched her, breathed with her, and she bled back into it.

Kek took her on a path of lost livelihood, just as the sun set and the purple tints of dusk faded into black. Stars stared down at them, telling stories in their patterns of hikers upon the mountains and dragons fighting bears. A few miniature dragons flew by, catching in Bria's hair before flying off towards the top of the mountain.

Bria and Kek didn't speak much during the ascent. With each step, though, the prowess and laughter of the forest disappeared, leaving Bria with emptiness in her stomach. The ground lost its greenery, replaced by soot, rock, and charred lumber. Steam pummeled from the mountaintop.

"Where are we going?" Bria finally asked.

"To where life is dormant."

Kek did not give any further details, hopping over a rock and climbing further up the mountain. Bria drifted in the dormancy lingering around her, like a deep sleep. The fatigue battered her bones, and by the time they reached the top, her breaths grew flimsy, her body aching with each step.

Yet the mountain didn't end at the top. Instead, a hole sat in the center, gazing into the center of the earth. Bria sensed the tunnels echoing deep beneath it, calling for her. *Come home...come home...*

"This is a dormant volcano," Kek stated, gazing down into the hole. "The world around it is dead. You feel it, don't you?"

"Yes." Bria winced, inhaling sharply, and hugged herself. "I do. It...hurts."

"Is it calling you? The Earth? It wants you to bring it back. Focus. Just focus." Kek spoke with such furor, their entire demeanor changed. They fixated entirely on Bria, unmoved, unblinking, like the empty pit of the volcano.

"On what? What do I do?"

"Do what your name suggests. The name you chose...*Rhodana*."

"But that's just a story."

"A story? Or a prophecy? It is told across cultures. How does it go? Oh yes, like so...

Rhodana
The Forest Queen
She loves to laugh
She hates to scream
She promised the world a reverie
Rhodana

"But the ending always changes based on cultures and beliefs. It's hard to know the true end of the story since it changes like you. What ending do you prefer, Bria? Don't you want the one where you, well, win?"

"I want..." Bria choked. "I want the one my grand-mama used to sing."

"What is the verse?"

Bria recalled the verse deep in the back of her mind, speaking each line slowly.

She gave birth to spring,
summer and fall.
She lives life fully enthralled.
Surrounded by flowers,
a smile of bliss.
It's in the forest she lives
for years like this.
Rhodana.

"So peace, prosperity...love and beauty, yes?" Kek asked.

Bria nodded.

"Reach for that in this dormant land. It's there; can you sense it?"

Yes. It vibrated beneath her fingertips. Each dying root breathed out, climbing towards her, while the seeds that lay dormant beneath the dirt quivered. Yet, around the seeds, it was more than just dirt; Bria sensed the way the earthworms squiggled, the mongoose dug, and the ants stacked leaves in their underground tunnels. Beneath their tunnels, she heard *her* tunnels calling her name again. But this time, the crackling of flames and bubbling of liquid muffled their music. Magma, molten lava, screaming beneath the surface. It reached for her through a wave of sweat on her brow.

"What do you feel?" Kek asked, though their voice sounded far in the distance, like the wind riding the waves of the sea.

"Everything," Bria huffed.

"Focus on all those elements. Let them slip through you. Become one with your magic. For you are a Magii...and no one can change that."

Bria knelt to the ground. Closing her eyes, she moved her attention away from the core of the earth and out to the seas. She rode the wind breezes, reached the sky, touched the clouds. She was everywhere on the small island. Like a dragon soaring, like a mongoose burrowing, and like a snake slithering, she moved around it. Life decorated the canopies, vanishing in the sands, weaving through the mountains.

Green.

Green bloomed.

All the way to the sea, she knew it. It pulsed through her, beating with her heart.

Thump.

Thump.

Thump.

She was everywhere. Nowhere. Everything. Nothing.

Like she'd been that fateful day in Newbird's Arm.

Bria let out a scream. The ground shook. A thundercloud clapped.

I can't control it.

She cried out again, but the wind picked up her voice. What would happen if she couldn't let go? The earth pulled her. It clung to her. It ravaged her.

I can't breathe. Someone help. Someone—

She gasped, finally coming up for air and pushing away from the ground. The earth let go of her. Her muscles relaxed, and she fell forward into the dirt.

"I'm sorry...I couldn't do... I'm sorry..." Bria sobbed into the ground. As she cried, blades of grass wiped away her tears while a gentle rain fell.

"Bria!" Kek's laughter made her uneasy. "That was amazing!"

"What do you mean?" Bria opened her eyes. Greenery covered charred ground. The smoke thickened where the mountain peaked. Clouds trembled above the forest.

She turned to face down the mountain.

Everything had changed. The canopy glowed beneath the moonlight while the lunar ferns glistened like lanterns. Birds took flight against their new backdrop, and even with the trembling clouds and light rain, the moon looked just a tad bit brighter. Trailing up the mountain towards her, a rainbow of flowers decorated the path, dazzling as if made of gemstones.

The ground tremored again.

"What happened?" Bria glanced back at Kek. "What'd I do?"

Kek's grin never left their face. "You reactivated everything dead and dying...and more. I knew you had great potential...but nothing like this!"

"More?"

"You caused those clouds to gather, you rocked the earth back to life, and now this volcano is once more active! What else can you do, Bria? If we just tapped a bit further, what else could you bring back to life?"

Bria looked away. "I don't know. I can't do anymore today."

"Of course. Let's get back to Yusef. The medicine should be ready soon." Kek offered Bria a hand, helping her off the ground and back down the mountain. She might have marveled at her own creation, but tremors rocked her body, leaving her nauseous and unsure. Despite the silence coming through the forest, but for the chirping of insects and the cawing of birds, she still heard the world beneath her. It called to her and pulled to her. Every step might have been a heartbeat.

Bria reached behind her ear for her little branch. For the first time in a long time, it wove out from the back of her head and down towards her shoulder without her commanding it.

A single camellia flower bloomed from the end of her branch.

CHAPTER NINETEEN

TOO MANY STORIES

hy does my head hurt? He squinted at the bright light above his head. Everything spun as he tried to sit up before slumping back against his pillow on the...floor? He blinked a few times, trying to remember...well...anything, really. He closed his eyes, trying to remember something, anything, only to receive visions of red hair whisking about his face, nails clawing into his skin, and a kind set of oak-colored eyes. As he reached for those kind eyes, his head blazed.

Slice the bitch at your next chance.

Kill her. Fuck her. Rape her.

Throttle her.

Slice!

"Stop! I don't wanna! I wanna...I wanna...stop!" He sobbed. "Stop...I wanna...stop."

Like a bolt of electricity, a sudden wave of clarity struck the voices down, giving Brent a moment to breathe. Someone moved beside him, tightening the intravenous line in his arm, whistling to themselves as they refilled the bag.

Brent lay on his back in the middle of the living suite, half-dressed, his head pounding. His mouth tasted like blood. In his hand, he held a green gem, pulsating with a distant, soothing song.

The Giant knelt beside him.

It took a few moments for Brent to remember how to speak. "What...what happened?"

"You came storming out here under the guise of an angry chef. It would have been amusing if you hadn't run into the kitchen and hit your face with a pan." Varden, Brent recalled his name now, adjusted the intravenous line as he spoke.

"Oh." Brent sank into the ground and closed his eyes, avoiding the stark white light overhead. His mind fled to the girl with kind eyes, the girl he loved. *Her name...what is her name?* "Where's... where's...um...her? The girl...her name is...I—"

"Bria?"

That's right. "Yeah."

"She went with Kek. Don't worry. She'll be back soon."

"Bria," Brent recited to himself.

"You're struggling to remember still, aren't you?"

"Everything is...foggy."

"I've been telling Kek that you need a stronger dosage. They claim to be searching for a new cure, but until then, you deserve more humanity. So I've upped it, but that will be our little secret, yes?" Varden tapped the intravenous line and winked.

Brent sat up and stared at the needle in his arm. The fluid climbed up his veins, chilling his core. As it entered his heart, it dispersed throughout his body, and a sensation of relief washed over him. It was slow, but there, unwinding the knot in his head.

Slit his throat! He's killing us!

Do it before it's too late!

Brent pushed the voices back. "Thank...Thank you."

"Do you want anything to eat? Or drink? I'm sure you're famished." Varden's head hit the top of the ceiling as he stood.

"Oh. Um. Yes, please. Thanks."

Stories followed Varden out of the room. Hundreds of stories. Thousands, maybe. They danced around the man's feet. Repeatedly, he visualized Kek, Varden, and Edith. His heart stopped at the sight of the woman with her frizzed red hair, her violent smile, and sharp irredeemable nails. She stared at him, eyes like stone.

Just a story. It's just a story.

But when he shut his eyes, she appeared again in a haze. She stood over him with a knife and dug into his arm. The next time, she took her nails and cut into his chest. And then the next—

Each time, more vulnerable.

Each time, less himself.

Ravenous.

Monstrous.

Brent dropped the green gem in his hand and bolted into the bathroom, the intravenous line dragging behind him as he pushed open the door and vomited into the toilet. He stayed there for a moment before hauling himself up to the mirror and staring at his reflection.

His glassy eyes stared back. A slight tint of yellow haunted the rims of his pupils, but mostly, his eyes were his own. His face appeared hollow, almost skeletal, his lips thin and chapped, while the cut from this morning's shave dug into his cheek. He started unbuttoning his shirt. To his dismay, he didn't remember how buttons worked and resorted instead to plucking them from the shirt. The material split open.

"Get it off...get it off of me...stop!" He threw his arms back and removed his shirt. It felt like spiders crawled over his skin. Try as he might, the stories escalated around him.

They pushed him deep into his nightmares.

They forced their way into his head.

His heart.

His mind.

Edith's cackle haunted the air.

Was that her behind him in the mirror? Did she see him crying here now?

"GO AWAY!" Brent slammed his fist into the mirror. Glass shattered.

"Brent!" Varden rushed into the bathroom and pulled him back.

"They don't stop...the stories don't stop...they don't—" Brent sobbed into Varden's arms. Why couldn't his mind be quiet for five minutes?

My name is...

My name is...

My name is Brent Harley.

Right?

He winced.

Stupid boy doesn't remember.

But I DO!

Varden guided Brent to the couch and handed him a cup of water. "I apologize. I should not have left you alone for so long."

Brent stared into his cup.

"I believe the higher dosage upped your story sensibility. It must be why Kek didn't increase it. But you also are more alert than I have seen you since you've been here. I think it's a valuable trade-off." Varden picked the gem Brent dropped off the floor and held it to the light. A green shadow danced around the room.

Brent found a question at the edge of his disorientation. "How long have I been here?"

"About two weeks. You were not in good shape when we found you, I promise. Thin, discombobulated, rabid; Kek got you under control. But the stories? That's something new. Or new to us. Perhaps the Mist Keepers understand why you see them."

"Mist Keepers...right...them." Brent winced. Other than their names, he struggled to remember much about them, but he recalled one thing: they were responsible for his current state.

"I don't expect you to remember right now, although I am not giving you the heaviest dosage like Kek did last week."

"I told them things, didn't I? Kek. With the powerful thing?" Brent asked.

"Yes." Varden scowled. "It was a truth serum. I didn't approve of its use, but Kek believed it would help you."

"But they tortured me. Edith—"

"Acted of her own accord. Kek did not want any violence against you." Varden sighed and rolled the gem between his fingers, then placed it on top of Brent's knee. "It's a shame, really, that Kek and the Council don't get along. I am sure that they could help."

Brent poked at the gem. "They don't like me. They think...they think I'll...fail."

Pieces of his memory returned as he poked the gem. He remembered the library, he remembered releasing a monster from its shelves, and he remembered the Council's anger. No matter how hard he tried, their faces blurred into the mist. They were but shadows watching on the walls.

Except for the woman in black. She stood plain as day at the forefront of his mind, her stark blue eyes glistening and red painted lips hiding a smile.

"There are members of the Council who aren't that cunning. I know a couple of them quite well." Varden's cheeks flushed.

"Like Caroline," Brent recalled.

"No...not her. I am not acquainted with her." Varden shrugged. "I was thinking of another. It really is a shame because he could help you get that head of yours in order. I can always attempt to contact him."

Brent shook his head, but Varden didn't seem to notice, continuing to babble. His words mixed with the stories in the air, and Brent lost his ability to listen. Instead, he watched as the stories poured around Varden. He caught glimpses of the giant in a checkered battlefield, walking hand-in-hand with another man.

For a brief second, everything was calm and sedated.

Then came war, and fleeing, and sobbing.

Blades clanked.

Shouts.

Blood poured out.

An eye removed.

A head chopped.

The story spun and spun. Brent fought past his confusion to put the pieces together, but as much as he tried, he only received an incomplete tale of an apparent war. Individual players were missing, acting only as shadows. Why couldn't he see them? Why did everything blur together?

"Dammit, I'm a storyteller!" Brent tightened his hand around the gem.

Varden blinked. "What?"

Brent relaxed. "The stories...I can't make sense of them... they're everywhere. And dammit, they should make sense! I mean... I'm...the real me...the me me... I'm a storyteller, and I should be able to figure this out, and I can't. I'm...not me."

If Varden had an answer prepared, he never had time to say it. The door to the living suite flew open. A woman in a copper's uniform, her coarse hair woven back in braids, stomped into the room. Her deep red eyes scanned the room.

Varden rose. "Oh, hello, Tilda. I wasn't expecting you to visit today."

The woman didn't exchange any pleasantries, cutting straight to the point. "Varden, is the Story Collector in the Sanitorium?"

"You mean him?" Varden pointed at Brent.

Tilda cursed.

Brent blinked. *Story Collector?*

"What? What's wrong?" Varden's face paled like marble.

"My partner got the consarn warrant approved. They're coming here. Today."

"Who... who's coming? What's going on?" Brent asked. "Did I do something wrong?"

Tilda and Varden ignored Brent, speaking quick amongst themselves.

"We'll get him out of here." Varden turned to Brent. "It's all right, young man. You're safe."

"From what?!?"

Tilda didn't allow Varden to answer. "They're already on their way here! I ran here as fast as I—"

"Don't you have a pool? Wouldn't that have been faster?"

"I was already out and about! I didn't have time to find a pool!" Tilda rolled her eyes, fixating at the bookshelf on the far end of the wall comprising an array of orbs. "But a pool... that's a good idea! I can contact Madame Owiti."

"And I shall reach out to my contact to negate this chaos," Varden added.

Brent interjected, "What is going on!?! Who's coming!?!"

"It'll be fine, Brent. We'll get you out of here."

"TELL ME!" Brent gritted his teeth. His head spun again.

Feed on the anger.

Live it.

Eat it.

You're nothing but a monster in a shell.

Be angry.

Varden placed a hand on Brent's arm. It was a single, kind gesture, but the storm already began in Brent's head. Like a tsunami, a thousand stories wrapped around him. He choked, trying to swim out of the undertow, but they continued to shove him beneath the waves.

Around him, the past reverberated through stories of lovers.

Of fighters.

Of wars.

They mingled around him. He kept trying to swim, searching...

Searching...

Who was lying? He had to search deep into the undertow, past the weeds. But there were too many voices. Too many years. He saw only the past, stuck...locked...thrown into battles. Of blood. Of mercy. And of hatred and love.

And then silence...

Silence...

Silence.

He gasped out, begging for air. His identity slipped with the countless stories.

He couldn't breathe.

He couldn't think.

I don't know who I am...

I don't know...

I don't...

CHAPTER TWENTY

THE STORY COLLECTOR'S RETURN

After a week at the Sanitorium, Lex returned home with a newfound bounce in her step and a glow in her cheeks. Much to Todd's dismay, she continued to marvel at magic, not deterred by her bout of Phantom Rot. As Todd walked her home with Garrett, he tried on multiple occasions to bring up the prospect of leaving Mert, only to have Lex shoot it down at every step.

By the next day, she danced amid their shop's shelves with Garrett on her hip. She moved like streaks of sunlight in the sky, caught in the lantern's embrace, a smile on her lips. Todd loved seeing her happy, but he wished she understood how detrimental her illness was to her wellbeing. Mert was a drug, and she inhaled it. He thought overdosing would be enough to sway her, but like any addiction, it wasn't so easy to break.

She remained entirely unphased, continuing to dance with Garrett through the aisles before approaching Todd at the front of the shop. She sang rather than spoke, her eyes catching the light like rubies. "You should reopen the shop tomorrow, Toddle!"

"Lex, we don't got any product. It's not the best idea." Todd leaned against the counter, fixated on the tattoo needle in his hand. He had poked away at the skin on his left hand, letting the ink seep into the cuts. After days of fretting, he'd settled on a simple heart for the space between his two knuckles. For Lex. He followed her into this hellish city; he'd never leave her.

But damn, he wished that she would use her head.

"We have plenty to sell! I think I can improve my readings now and—"

"Lex!" Todd dropped the needle. "Enough!"

"Why? Toddle! We need money!"

"We're leaving Mert!" He couldn't bear listening to her anymore. Why didn't she think? "Magic hurts you! We can't stay here!"

"Some people are allergic to milk, and they do not go avoiding cows."

"That's not the point!"

Lex smiled, candid and calm. "I don't know why you hate magic so much. Magic saved me from this Phantom Rot, and by the grace of the Guardians of Perennes and Proveniro, I continue to thrive."

"Science saved you from it! It wasn't magic or...or one of your damn gods or whatever!" Todd slammed his hand on the table.

Garrett whimpered.

Lex lulled him, then turned back to Todd. "Will you control your temper? You're upsetting Garrett!"

"Sorry..." He recoiled and pressed his fingers to his brow.

"Don't just say sorry. Do. Be the role model you want for Garrett."

"Yeah, yeah, I know."

Lex waltzed over to a cabinet. "We can fill this here up with potions! I am sure Madame Owiti has some—"

"Lex! Please hear me out before you start talking about that crazy old woman again! We need to leave Mert. You're sick! You can't stay here."

Lex lost her usual serenity, flames in her eyes illuminating the paleness in her face. Todd rarely saw her lit up like this, but when she did, she transformed from the moon to the sun. "We came here to escape the hand of the Order...but you're starting to sound like them if you ask me!"

Todd looked back at his hand. "It's hard to shake what they've put in my head for so long, y'know?"

"We left that life years ago. I thought you liked Mert."

"I did...I do!"

"Then what happened?"

"It's magic...it killed Preston...and it will kill you!"

"Dr. Kafele gave me medication. I'll be fine!" Lex straightened her back, standing at near eye level with Todd as he slumped against the counter. Her anger stabbed him in the chest. Lex continued, "You never trust my judgment, Toddle. Trust me now. This world is too beautiful to run back home and give up."

Todd didn't reply.

"I shall set up for tomorrow since we need the money. Madame Owiti is coming by--"

"I don't want her here!"

"Too bad! She's my friend!"

"Lex..."

"I'm done talking about this. I'm staying, and I will continue spending time with my *friend*. You can go back to Rosada and their hateful Order. I don't care."

She stormed into the backroom with Garrett. With her gone, the little shop seemed darker than usual.

He and Lex had created an unspoken rule to never bring up Todd's time in the Guard. It brought shame into his core, a strange heat that made him nauseous and vulnerable. He regretted everything from those years. But he'd been a boy, coerced into prejudice and hatred. What did he know?

They didn't totally take away his morals. He still pushed back, he still received a black stamp, and he still had to flee.

But magic still scared him. He tried to ignore it. Now it was killing Lex.

Even if she didn't agree.

Todd fixated again on finishing his heart tattoo, a detailed image of the organ with a few leaves detailed around it. The ink bled into his skin, serving as a permanent reminder of this argument. His actions came from his heart; he would do anything to protect Lex and Garrett. Couldn't they see that? Could anyone?

Todd looked up only once when the bell rang. Madame Owiti wobbled into the shop with that strange silver orb at her side. She met Todd's glower with a smile and continued past him in silence.

He almost stopped her but decided against it; the last thing he wanted was to further anger Lex.

She'll get sick again; then she'll learn. Todd continued to mutter to himself for a time, adding the last details onto the heart before finally slamming the needle down on the counter. Something about the heart seemed off, and he couldn't put his finger on it. Was it lopsided? Misshapen? Why did he even bother working on these damn tattoos anymore? No one ever wanted a normal tattoo. Not in Mert. Not when tattoo artists created moving images on their skin.

Todd's thoughts broke with a thud. He jumped, rushing past the curtain to the back room. Garrett sat on the floor, drawing with his imaginary friend. He beamed at Todd and held up the picture of two squiggles.

Todd waved the drawing away. He focused solely on the light glowing beneath the lavatory door. Another thud echoed from behind it. Todd's fears grew in his throat, and he raced into the bathroom.

"LEX—the fuck?"

To his relief, Lex was fine, standing beside Madame Owiti in the bathroom

To his dismay, the tub was overflowing with an odd silver liquid.

And to his utter horror, there stood the Story Collector.

Yes, it was definitely him. He'd recognize that kid anywhere. He stood hunched over, his curly hair matted to his forehead, eyes wide and distraught. While they didn't have the same yellow tinge as last time, the kid continued to stare with that piercing gaze.

"WHAT THE HELL IS HE DOING HERE?" Todd bellowed.

"Toddle—" Lex raised her hands.

The Story Collector recoiled at Todd's shouts, falling back into the tub as he mumbled, "Please stop being a mirror. No more mirrors. No more..."

Todd pushed past Lex and Madame Owiti, yanking the Story Collector out of the tub and hoisting him up into the air. The kid didn't fight back, holding an intravenous fluid bag to his chest, shrinking beneath Todd's grip. "What the FUCK are you doing here? Didn't you mess with my family enough already?"

The Story Collector stared at Todd and chuckled. "Your nose is lopsided. Twisty nose. Like a...like a tree stump."

Todd blinked.

"You look kinda like a tree." The Story Collector laughed harder. "Tree man. Kinda like...like Bri. She's a tree woman. Tree lady. Pretty tree girl."

"What the hell is wrong with you!?!" Todd shoved the Story Collector to the ground.

The kid continued laughing, bringing his knees up to his chest and throwing back his head in amusement.

Todd gripped his fists tight. The kid stole his gems, destroyed his shop, and now he acted like a twat? This was more than I could handle.

"Toddle, please, calm down!" Madame Owiti pleaded. "This young man is ill—"

"Shut the HELL up! I didn't ask you to come or for you to cause this...this bullshite!" Todd slammed his fist against the wall. The Story Collector tried to hide behind the toilet bowl like a cat as the sound chanted around the small lavatory.

"Nothing bad has happened yet, Toddle. Yes, yes. Everything is fine here." Madame Owiti knelt beside the kid on the floor and pulled him away from the toilet.

"No, it's not! You keep bringing this magic into the house. Don't you get it!?! Lex has Phantom Rot, and she will die with shite like this around!"

Lex interjected, "Toddle! It's under control! I don't need to avoid all magic!"

"Dr. Kafele said you shouldn't be around it!"

"But I want to be!"

"But I don't!" Todd slammed his hands against the wall again. The Story Collector once again ducked behind the toilet. If Todd hadn't been so angry, he would have found the sight amusing. "I hate this fucking magic, and Madame Owiti and this kid—" he pointed at the Story Collector "—have continued to fuck our lives in a matter of weeks! And you let Madame Owiti back into our home, and she causes...causes this! Dammit, Lex! We have a son! We're married! Stop doing shite like this!"

"Yes, we're married, and that's why we need to talk about these things! But you don't listen!"

"You don't either!"

Lex's eyes narrowed. She no longer looked like a candle but like a bonfire, ready to explode. Twice in one day! How stupid could Todd be! He didn't need to lose Lex over something as petty as this.

"Excuse me?" the Story Collector choked out.

Todd glared back at him.

"There's a story...about a man. He was a guard out in Knoll, but he fell in love with a white dove. They spoke for hours...and hours...and fell deeply in love. So, he cast aside his shadow to run away with her. Where did that man go...the one with the dreams? I see his shadow in this room, but...but... he's not here and I...I mean...I...shite!" The Story Collector hunched his shoulders and shook his head back and forth. "I can't finish it."

Fury burst inside Todd's stomach. "Don't you dare collect my story!"

"I'm—I'm not. It's... it's strong in here and I...I—"

Todd leaned forward, inches from the kid's face, and hissed. "It'd be best if you let it go."

"Toddle!" Lex shouted. "You're being rude to our guest!"

"Our guest!?! More like your guest!"

"Enough, enough!" Madame Owiti stepped into the conversation. "I will take the Story Collector and go. We do not want to cause any more problems."

Madame Owiti turned to the tub and waved her fingers over the silver liquid, once again forming that firm orb she'd carried into the home. Tension skidded through the room as she helped the Story Collector climb off the floor.

Lex didn't look at Todd as she walked Madame Owiti and the Story Collector from the back room. Todd followed a few paces behind, glancing once at Garrett playing on the floor. The boy was unphased by the turn of events. Todd supposed that was for the best.

He watched from the counter as Madame Owiti left with the Story Collector down Myrtle. Lex bid them farewell, striding away from the entrance, saying nothing.

"Lex..." He reached for her.

"I don't want to talk to you right now." She threw open the curtain and went into the back room, not daring to meet Todd's eyes.

He cursed under his breath, then left his spot at the counter and walked towards the entrance. An eerie mist trailed over the dusky road. Images of children playing filled the mist, wandering behind the path of the Story Collector. Todd watched it for a moment before turning to the gas lantern.

He flipped the switch, so it glowed red.

CHAPTER TWENTY-ONE

A TASTE OF VICTORY AND RACOONS

W here's Brent?" Bria asked as she arrived in the suite with Kek. Disarray marked their arrival back to the Sanitorium. While no one noticed as they left the vacant operating suite, a few coppers in the main ward caused Kek to take the hoist rather than the stairwell upstairs. They dragged Bria along without a word, the tension so thin it might break.

Upon arriving in the suite, they found Tilda standing in the room. She looked exactly like the image in the orb, although stouter than Bria imagined, and when she turned to greet them, her eyes showed with haste and uncertainty.

"What is going on, Tildy?" Kek inquired.

Tilda answered Bria's question first. "Brent's safe. We sent him to Madame Owiti."

Before Bria asked why, Tilda answered that question too.

"I tried to hold them off for as long as possible, but the coppers have a warrant to search the hospital. Varden is detouring them for now, but it may be wise for you to deal with them." Tilda stared hard at Kek. They exchanged a look that Bria didn't understand.

"Your partner is leading this, yes?" Kek asked.

"Yes."

"And you couldn't stop her?"

"No. I swear, I tried so hard!" Tilda shook her head. "She's a stubborn consarn woman, and no matter what I did, she kept her head high! Her aura has turned to muck. It used to be so blue too! Really, I don't know what is happening with her. For a while, she was fine, monitoring more than anything. But there's been a change...I can't quite explain it. It is as if—"

Kek cut Tilda off. "Very well. I'll deal with it."

"What about Brent?" Bria glanced between Kek and Tilda.

Kek stared at her for a second and removed an elongated vial from their bag as well as a handful of sterile syringes. They held it up to the light. "Go. Give him two injections a day to start. We may reduce it over time, but I think the hefty dose is necessary to clear his head." They handed Bria the vial and syringes. "Make sure he doesn't smoke or drink while taking this. I don't know the reaction it will have yet."

Bria pocketed the supplies and met Kek's gaze. "Thank you. For everything."

"I'm not done with you yet. Don't worry; once we get this sorted out with the coppers, I'll be knocking on your door." Kek winked.

Bria managed a half-smile. She hadn't felt this hopeful in months.

After Bria collected her and Brent's remaining items in the bedroom, Kek showed her the way to the fire escape. With the coppers already in the building, they agreed it would be safer for Bria to take to the rooftops than try to send her through a pool. Based on what Tilda told them, they had missed Brent by about twenty minutes. Varden took him down to the tub, connected him with Madame Owiti, then switched the orbs back for Bria and Kek's return. When Bria asked about Brent's state, the only word Tilda supplied was "disoriented," and she left it at that.

Bria waited until Kek and Tilda's shadow vanished from the window, then ascended the fire escape to the top of the Sanitorium. The city was dead and dry beneath her, streetlamps flickering on and off in the road. She reached out to the few trees, letting their branches carry her over the rooftops and down Elm. It wasn't the same as the forest. Each movement creaked. The branches groaned, and between every few roofs, she had to stop to give the trees a chance to breathe.

She peered over the edge of one shop on the corner of Elm and Aspen. A few coppers stood in the streets around the Sanitorium. None of them noticed her, most lounging about the steps, disinterested in the events that no doubt occurred beyond the hospital's doors.

Bria didn't stop for long. Once the trees breathed with ease again, she continued her voyage along the rooftops, down Elm towards Myrtle. She stopped every few moments, hiding behind chimneys and awnings, before continuing onward. Her fingers reached into her coat pockets, tracing the vials Kek gave her. They soothed her, promising that everything would be okay.

Things were about to get better.

She followed along Myrtle, watching the people meandering in the streets below with dogs running about and children playing. She slowed on the corner of Celosia and Myrtle, just above the little shop. Everything started there; even if the shopkeeper disliked her, even after Lex ended up in the hospital, if she hadn't gone inside that day, she might not have found Brent.

Her heart sank. How selfish had she been? She hadn't even wondered about Lex. Her mind was so wrapped up in finding Brent and uncovering her own magic that she forgot that she'd sent the woman to the hospital.

How did I forget? She stared at the shop from the rooftop across the street. *Has killing Cadet Lawry made me numb to other harm? Why didn't I stop by to find out? She could be dead.*

Bria hopped off the roof and approached the shop. A sign hung in the window.

Closed.

Bria peered inside the store. The shopkeeper leaned against the counter, poking at his finger with a tattoo needle. She pondered going inside to ask if his wife was okay. To her relief, the curtain swung open behind the shopkeeper, and Lex strode out, not looking at her husband. The light cast a white glow around her body.

At least she's okay. Bria hugged herself and walked away from the shop. *I'll stop by to apologize later.*

Bria strode down Myrtle, each step heavy. She wasn't sure what Brent would be like when she arrived at Madame Owiti's apartment, but she braved the walk, her head up, nodding slightly to those passing by her. In contrast to Newbird's Arm, no one really made eye contact with her, keeping their heads down, uninterested in who or what she was. If home had been like this, magic might have gone unnoticed. She might have been normal.

Bria shook off the thoughts as she approached the building on the corner of Myrtle and Maple. All was quiet except for her footsteps.

It remained until she reached Madame Owiti's door. She knocked on it once, letting it echo around the hallway.

"HARK! AN INTRUDER!"

The voice behind the door belonged to Brent.

Oh, dear. Bria held her breath as the front door open.

Madame Owiti's beam filled her face. "Ah! Rho!"

Brent peaked out from behind the cushions. His face softened, whatever story assaulting him at that moment vanishing. "You…"

Bria approached him, "Do you recognize me?"

"Yeah. You're… you're—the slut that…NO, STOP!" Brent collapsed on the couch and held his head.

Madame Owiti joined Bria's side. "He has been jumping between stories a lot since he arrived, yes. He hasn't been easy to pin down. His aura is mucky too. Yuck! It's like vomit with a hundred different stories."

"I expected that." Bria reached for Brent's arm.

He flinched. "No…"

"Brent, I have something that will help. You need to sit still, okay?"

Brent shook his head, but he let her sit beside him. Slowly, she removed the vial and needle Kek gave her.

"No...no...I don't...no!" Brent backed up, falling off the edge of the couch and hiding behind a plant.

"Brent, please, it will help you." Bria kept her voice low as she spoke. "It's not a narcotic. Please. Let me help you."

"No..."

"Brent. Please."

He shook his head again.

"I'll get you ice cream."

Brent dug his fingers into the floor. "Ice...cream?"

"Yes. I promise." Bria crawled onto the floor with him. Carefully, she took his arm. She left the intravenous line in as a safe fail and traced along his worn skin to a visible vein in the crux of his elbow. Then, she filled the needle, tapped it twice, and inserted it into his skin.

Brent screeched. Inhuman almost. He tried to move away, but only his head moved, thrown back against the wall. His legs remained locked while his body quivered.

"STOP!" he screamed.

His eyes flew open. For a moment, they turned bright yellow, then circled through orange, red, brown, black, and then...silver, where they remained.

He was still there.

As the elixir exited the needle, Brent's thrashing slowed.

"Done," Bria whispered as she handed the needle to Madame Owiti and dabbed the injection site with a rag. She didn't expect a sudden change in Brent. That would come with time. She fully expected Brent to sink into the wall and pass out.

But Brent Harley was always full of surprises.

He blinked a few times, then met Bria's gaze. "Did you know raccoons taste like chicken?"

"Wha—what?"

"Yeah, tastes like chicken. Better than pineapple, at least. I mean, really, I'm glad I haven't had pineapple in months. What sort of person thought pineapple was a good idea?" He grumbled. "But what about that ice cream you promised me?"

It was the first time Brent sounded like himself in months.

CHAPTER TWENTY-TWO

A BOY AND HIS TRUCK

Jemma closed her suitcase, packing away the last of her essential belongings: a few long gowns, her year glass, bare-bones necessities, and one of her father's pistols for safety. It wasn't much, and she had no clue how to use the pistol, but she didn't have a reason to carry anything else. Once she arrived at the Grand Tower of Ab Aeterno and found Brother Roy Al, she wouldn't need such petty, sentimental objects.

She stroked her plush bear's fur once, smiling half-heartedly. "I'm sorry I have to leave you behind, Miss Porridge. The road is no place for a sweet old bear like you." Jemma gulped down the knot in her throat as she placed the letter she'd written for her parents on Miss Porridge's lap.

After three days of planning, she and Micca were ready to leave. It had been a couple days, filled with anxiety and nerves as the Guards continued dragging vagrants and townsfolk to the Temple for cleansing. The riots continued beyond the new makeshift wall of the Pit. Newbird's Arm was falling. Jemma knew that it was her duty to fix it.

She had to leave.

Jemma moved like a mouse, tiptoeing across the tile to avoid waking her parents. The old wooden door creaked as she opened it, but no one woke, letting her slip into the night.

Once more, she glanced back at the small farmhouse. *It's for the best.*

She detoured the long way through the fields. The chilled air battered her face, and she brought her thick scarf up to cover her lips and nose. To be frank, she didn't know what to expect when she reached the yard behind the Tower. Who knew if Micca could even *start* this automobile? *Have faith, Jemma. The Effluvium will guide you.*

Newbird's Arm slept beneath the mountains. Jemma crept between the trees. She'd stolen her mother's brown overalls and a dark turtleneck, blending seamlessly in with the surroundings.

The Tower stood dark over the scenery. She tiptoed between the bushes where few guards sat drinking and laughing, smokes lit between their fingers. Their words proved disgraceful to the Effluvium. How did they think they were better than the vagrants who came to pray each day? Jemma wanted to forget such slanders even existed, but profanity slaughtered the air and cut open the guards' mouths. *Despicable!*

She waited for one guard to finish his patrol of the yard. Once he joined his friends by the steps, Jemma slipped out of the trees and approached the fence. To her dismay, unlike during the day, a padlock guarded the gate.

Oh, crud. She shook the gate lightly, but it didn't budge.

"Psst! Jem!"

She turned. Micca appeared from between the trees.

"What'cha doing? You're gonna get caught. C'mon! There's another way."

Jemma said nothing as she followed Micca back into the brush. He hopped between his feet, carrying nothing but a small canvas bag on his side. His frizzy brown hair blew in the breeze.

I can't believe I'm doing this. With Micca Fein of all people! Perhaps I should go home.

She shook her head. No, she had to get to Ab Aeterno. There were no trains. No transport. No way to get back to Brother Roy Al. This was her only choice.

Though her gut told her to stay. Fight the Elders. Win.

You could just write a letter, Jemma. Tell him to come back. We need his leadership now more than ever.

As they approached the fence on the far end of the yard, she didn't have time to change her decision. Either haste and irrationality or determination and pride marked her choice. If she had chosen wrong, it was too late.

Micca motioned her over to a hole beneath the fence. He slid across the ground like a rotund snake, kicking his legs and shoving himself through to the other side. Jemma scowled, glancing at her overalls and back at the hole.

"What? You afraid of a little dirt?" Micca smirked.

Jemma snapped. "No! That looks tight is all."

"If I can get on through there, you can fit too. Don't be so pathetic."

"Fine, I'm coming!" She tossed Micca her bag, then crawled to the ground on her hands and knees. Her throat tightened, and her heartbeat pattered as she slithered against the ground. What if she got stuck? Or the fence collapsed?

But within seconds, she was through, sitting beside Micca in the yard.

"Was that so bad?" Micca goaded.

"Can we please get the automobile and proceed on our way?" Jemma brushed off her overalls and rose, taking her bag from Micca before stepping towards one truck. "This one looks fine—"

"I got one picked out, a'ight? Been learning all 'bout it. Keep your head on." Micca poked her forehead. "Don't be so antsy. We got this shite."

"Can you please stop cussing?"

"For someone once betrothed to Brent *'my favorite word is shite'* Harley, you sure don't like these cuss words, do you?"

"Brent and I had nothing in common. You know that, Micca."

"Yeah, whatever," Micca grunted and scanned the yard. "Let's go steal a truck."

Before Jemma could stop him, he bolted down an aisle. "Micca!"

He jumped between each of the trucks, examining each of them in haste, before darting down the next lane. Jemma's nerves danced on her skin as she followed him. What if the Guard saw them? Why did Micca take such a long time choosing a truck? With every flickering light, every gust of wind, Jemma's throat continued to tighten. Why did they have to park the trucks so close together? Someone would find them!

"Where the shite is it?" Micca hissed as he passed another truck. "It ain't here!"

"What does it matter?" Jemma crossed her arms, "We will get caught if you don't choose one already!"

"This one was older. More simplistic...easier to steal. All these others are new models and shite. It's the one I learned about! Where the shite did they park it?"

"Micca!"

Footsteps pattered a few rows from them. The light shifted again.

"Give me three minutes, a'ight? Three minutes!"

"They're going to find us!"

"It's fine!"

"Micca!"

A voice boomed from over the trucks, "WHO GOES THERE?"

"Shite!"

"Phooey!" Jemma darted behind one of the trucks with Micca. Her heart performed swing dances in the center of her chest, roaring against her sternum and buzzing in her ears. Micca's own breaths caught the air. Visible drops of sweat gathered on his brow despite the cool winter winds.

"Look what you did!" Micca hissed.

"What I did? You're the one who cannot settle on a truck!"

"If you were quiet, they ain't woulda heard us."

"If you found a truck, we'd be out of here by now!" Jemma pinched the bridge of her nose. "This was a mistake. I should have stayed home. What am I thinking?"

"I dunno, but it's too late to turn back now, girly."

"What do you propose we do?"

Micca tapped his fingers against the truck next to them. "I'll try to start this one, I guess."

"You guess!?!"

"Yep!" Micca hopped into the truck and began fumbling with the dashboard. Jemma muttered and climbed into the backseat, hanging over Micca's shoulder as he tried to start up the engine. He cursed a few more times as he finagled with the levers and gears, removed a few tools from his bag, and poked at the screws and wires.

Jemma dug her fingers into the seat, glancing out the window as light seeped from a lantern a few trucks away. "Hurry up, Micca! The guard is approaching!"

"I'm trying. This piece of shite needs a damn key, and I don't have that. The other one didn't need one. Just some levers and—gotcha!"

Jemma had no clue what Micca did, but he rose from beneath the dashboard with a grin extended across his face. He tied two wires together and jammed his screwdriver into the ignition. With a puff of smoke, the truck's engine chugged to life.

Brrrroooom.

The truck growled with excitement. Micca shifted one of the gear sticks, and the truck's wheels turned, then shifted backward with a jolt.

"Micca!" Jemma gripped the seat.

"Hold on, I got it—I got it!"

"I thought you knew how to drive—"

Thud.

Then a scream.

The vehicle stopped, screeched, then skidded forward as Micca adjusted the gears.

The truck's trajectory changed, starting forward as it clunked one more time. Jemma refused to take her eyes off the ground behind them.

A guard lay on the ground, breathing hard, body twisted in an unnatural shape. Blood stained the back window of the truck.

"Micca! You killed him!" Jemma held back a shriek.

"So what? He's a fucking Guard!"

"Micca! This isn't right...I..." *I should go help him! This is wrong! What am I doing?*

Before she could react, Micca pressed down on the foot lever. The truck sputtered and roared.

And crashed through the fence.

"Yeehaw!" Micca bolstered, his hideous smile reaching from cheek to cheek.

The truck shook off the fencing and continued chugging along the road.

Jemma glanced behind them. Shouts rang in the distance. A few lights flickered on in the yard. But no one followed.

Not yet, at least.

"Mi-Micca...we...what..." Jemma sank into the seat and hugged her suitcase close to her chest. *I wish I'd brought Miss Porridge with me.*

Micca seemed unphased. "We're heading west, yeah?"

"I...um..."

"Jemma, if you wanna go to Ab Aeterno, tell me where the shite we're going! Otherwise, the guard might catch us or some shite like that!"

"Sorry, um..." Jemma shook her head and removed a map from her bag. "Yes, west. To Ab Aeterno."

"Got it." Micca swerved onto the road bordering the train tracks and increased speed. He guffawed at the top of his lungs, gaining speed as the Tower and the Temple became mere specks in the distance. "They thought they got everything, but they ain't ready for Micca Abe Fein!"

Jemma finally exhaled, her pulse shaking her entire body, her chest tight. They were on their way. No one could stop them now.

Except perhaps the Tower, glowing red in the distance, like a monster from a story.

Or a nightmare.

CHAPTER TWENTY-THREE

TRUE HISTORY

S leep did not play well with Brent over the next few days. He often woke up in the middle of the night, covered in sweat or confusing shadows with stories. Bria grounded him in the present by placing that strange green gem into the palm of his hand and talking to him even as exhaustion pulled on her eyelids.

Since the first dosage of the strange elixir, which Bria dubbed 'the periwinkle medicine,' his thoughts had gotten clearer. He rambled, going off on non sequiturs mostly to himself while playing with the gems he allegedly stole. As he rambled, each random topic helped him rediscover himself: a hatred for pineapples, a confusing opinion about cats, and his undeniable love for Bria.

That he remembered her name meant everything to him. When she slept, he paced, running her name over his lips, and smiling. *Briannabella*. It was such a pretty name. How could he forget it? He could say it for ages.

And to make it better, she stayed with him through all the terrible stories. He watched them now in the studio apartment as he paced: the stories of a lonely girl, magic dying, and tears filled the small apartment. But behind those tales hid remnants of smiles, kisses, and dances. He tried to pull those stories to the forefront, but the mist kept them back. Why did the strongest stories belong to putrid and evil people? Why couldn't people holding hands and kissing be the dominant story?

Brent slid into a chair and covered his face with his hands. Whenever he focused on a story, even just a small one hidden in the corner of an apartment, every single tale bombarded him, threatening to tear him away from reality. Despite the treatment with the periwinkle medication and Kek's three visits to adjust the dosage, he still wasn't completely himself. There was that quiet nagging of the Diabolo in the back of his head, trying to scream its way back to the front of his mind. It taunted him for being weak before laughing that the periwinkle medication would be a dependency that would never make Brent whole.

So, Brent would turn his attention to the streets, but that didn't stop his mind from racing. Stories beckoned him, luring him with a tightrope: tales of men in pinstripes shooting up the stores, of dogs running, and of monsters screaming. If he didn't see the stories, the dead begged for mercy in his ears. It seemed impossible to help. Instead, his mind trapped him between the monster and himself. And some days, the Diabolo almost won, dragging him through self-deprecating thoughts.

You abandoned your home, your ma, and your sister. You're worthless.

Not on purpose.

You ran away with some girl.

They're better off without me.

It'd be better if you were dead.

Brent tried his best to ignore the Diabolo's snide remarks, instead focusing on things safe from the monster's touch.

Like Bria.

"Brent?"

The hair on his arm rose at Bria's voice, but he didn't turn to her. "Go back to sleep."

The floorboards creaked as Bria approached him and took both his hands. There was still a slight wall up between them. They hadn't shared a bed or touched beyond the handholding. Whenever Brent tried to embrace her or kiss her, it sent him spiraling with guilt and fear.

But the way she took his hands and squeezed into his knuckles still soothed him.

And her voice cooed like a gentle breeze. "You're okay. It's okay."

He closed his eyes. His voice betrayed him, breaking with each word. "I still hear everything...and the stories...they're...they're pulling me in five directions. Like...I mean...they're everywhere. I hear them in the streets, beneath the floorboards, on the ceiling, in this room. The dead...they're calling me. But so are the living and the past. It...It doesn't stop. Please...please, make it stop...please."

"We're trying. Just keep taking the medication—"

"And become an addict like my father!?" Brent gritted his teeth and pulled away. "Bri...I'm...I'm a stranger in my body. I don't have control of my limbs or my thoughts, or my words. They...the stories, the Diabolo, or whatever...they push me down, hide me in the darkest corners of my mind. It's like...I mean...it's like when you're dreaming. You know what's going on, but at the same time, you slip away. And sometimes, on a rare occasion, you know you're dreaming, so you try to wake up...and when you do, you're groggy and want to hide in your bed. The dreams fade..." He gulped. "I still dunno who I am. Well, I do...but...I mean...I know my name and what happened, but...I'm not...I don't feel like me. Some days I am me, but other days I'm some criminal named Reginald, or a woman named Missy, or a...a father...a child...I don't...it's too much."

Bria squeezed his hands tighter. Her care and compassion danced with a story of a girl in the gardens, but Brent pushed it back, keeping focus on Bria as she spoke. "I know you're afraid the medication will mess with you, but it's making you better." She caressed his cheek. "My father takes something like this to control his tremors and anxiety. No one will think less of you if you need something to help you."

"I guess so." Brent let his head fall as he ran his fingers over Bria's hand. Her skin still felt so soft...but not fragile. She was a cloud on the horizon, brewing a storm in its belly. One wrong move and she had the ability to destroy a city like a tornado or flood a plain like a monsoon.

But why was Brent so scared to touch her then?

Why did he worry for her safety over his?

She'd be a nice prize. A feisty prize, the voice of Reginald the Murderer crooned.

A woman he named Missy added, *She's a blossoming woman. Lay her down and strip her and show her how to be a woman. Just like—*

Shut up! Shut up! Shut up! Brent banged his head with his fists. "Please stop!"

Bria, unafraid as always, took Brent's hands away from his head. "Hitting yourself won't solve the problem."

"They don't stop. They don't...they...want me to...I mean...they claim that I...and that...shite!" Brent gave up talking.

"I think it's time for another dose. It's been a bit." Bria retrieved the vials and needles from the bathroom. Brent hated this process.

Or the Diabolo did.

Brent fidgeted in the chair. Bria carefully traced along his arm for a vein, then without a moment's notice, injected the elixir into his skin. A cold sensation worked its way through his arteries and veins, then back into his heart.

Brent lowered his head to the table. "Shite..."

Once Bria removed the needle, she knelt beside him and stroked back his hair. He closed his eyes tighter, reveling in her touch but too worried to look at her.

Bria kneaded her fingers into his back. "I'm going to wash up. You rest."

Brent didn't move as Bria went back into the lavatory. His head spun, and his eyelids seared. If only that odd serum would just stop leaving him so cold.

Empty.

Numb.

But it acted fast, and after the cold anesthetized his emotions, a fire ignited around the commotion in his head. All those wild thoughts, the ones of rapists and murderers, of heathens and tyrants, backed into a corner, quivering from the flames. And as the stories became but a small flickering candle in the darkest crevasses, Brent found his breath.

He traced the veins on his arm, resting them where the needle left a small prick in his inner elbow. It reminded him of the time he spent in the Pit, months ago, where people gathered on the streets injecting themselves with liquids both soothing and filled with anger. His father partook in such endeavors, leaving the festivities wearing the mask of a different man, one Brent had never seen.

A man of sleaze, of disgust, of vulgarity...the man Brent didn't want to become.

Bria told him he wouldn't, that this serum would help. But every time the needle entered Brent's skin, he worried.

Would it ever stop?

Would he ever get rid of the monster in his head?

The sound of the water running from the bathroom soothed him. It was almost normal, listening to Bria as she hummed to herself in the shower. He rose as he listened to her, imagining the off-tuned song as the ballad in a dance hall. His partner became a broom, and as the shower played a tune of pitters and patters, he strutted across the kitchen and asked the broom for a dance.

The jig comprised a waltz across the kitchen, picking up plates and rinsing them. The faucet sounded like a tambourine, and as the water hit the plate, a cymbal played.

And as he danced through the housework, a story wrapped around him. He was back in the dance hall once again, dressed in an old suit too short for him, and Bria in a beautiful green dress that swished whenever she walked. He saw them dancing and listened to their laughter.

Was it a memory or a story? Had it really happened to him?

"Brent?"

He turned, still holding his broom. Bria watched him from the bathroom door, dressed in her usual sweater and baggy pants.

Brent beamed. "You look beautiful!"

"What's going on with you? You seem...happy."

"I am happy! I just...I mean...it's like my head is clear again. For a bit. Maybe. I dunno." He dropped the broom. "I might've cheated on you with a broom, though."

"I knew you would find someone better one day." Bria returned his grin.

He loved the way she smiled. The genuine smile. The one with dimples and a slight overbite. It lit up her face. And it ignited his heart. "I can kick the old broom to the street. You're way prettier."

Bria took his hands. They finished the dance together in the kitchen, putting the last plate in the cupboard like the last beat of a drum. With the vibrations ringing in Brent's heart, he collapsed on the bed next to Bria and stroked back her hair.

Everything about her made him want to hug her, touch her, and kiss her. Months ago, it was easy. Now, even the mere thought brought the monsters out of hiding.

She's vulnerable. Take her.

Push her!

Slice her!

"No...no, no, no...shite!" He jumped up and hugged himself. "Please just shut up!"

"Brent? Brent! What is it? What's wrong?" Bria rose with him.

"I wanna... I want to...to hold you and everything. But the voices...they keep...I hear them, and they tell me to do things. Like Cadet Lawry keeps whispering in my ear about how...I mean...he hates you."

"Cadet Lawry is in your head?" Bria's face paled.

Brent nodded. She never brought up how much the Cadet's death hurt her. But Brent understood. He saw it in the Cadet's story deep in his head and in her eyes. "I dunno if it was...I mean, it's not exactly him. The Diabolo must've done something with his soul. Eaten it or something."

Bria shook her head. "But...you're not Cadet Lawry."

"Yeah...but if I kiss you, what if I eat your lips?"

She sputtered. "I'm sorry?"

"I mean...what if I...what if I eat them?" Blood rushed to his ears. "Like chew them off or...or I mean, I wouldn't want to stop kissing you and kill your lips or something or...yeah."

"Brent Harley, you are a goof!"

He smiled back.

"We'll take it slow." Bria relaxed and squeezed his hands. "We're together. That's all that matters. We'll figure out who we are again. Okay?"

"A'ight. Yeah, a'ight."

Bria pulled him into a hug.

And Brent never wanted to let her go.

Brent and Bria whispered into the morning, hands entwined, foreheads pressed together. While Brent never pried, Bria made succinct statements about her time searching for him across the world. He followed whiffs of her story through the air, the sadness and loneliness like stains against the panels in the room. Why did she chase him? Why didn't she just let him go?

Because she loves you, you fool, a voice whispered. To whom did it belong? That didn't matter. It reassured him that some things were always, without a doubt, constant.

Bria climbed out of bed once the sun painted the room yellow. She smiled at him, tired and empty.

"Listen," Bria whispered, "I'm going to go out for a few minutes to run some errands. We need some money to get by, and I have a few gardens to fix anyway. Kek also told me to stop by the hospital for an additional dosage for you too."

Brent pouted.

"You'll be okay for a couple hours, right?" Bria pressed.

"Yeah, I'll be a'ight."

Bria didn't look convinced.

"I promise, a'ight? Really."

She leaned forward and kissed his cheek. Brent flinched, eyes wide, before turning to face Bria. This time, she smiled so her dimples showed, and she bopped his nose with her finger.

"I'll be back soon. I promise."

"And I'll be right here." Brent grinned.

Bria pulled on her boots with a smile, then vanished down the stairwell.

The moment she disappeared left Brent with an odd hollowness. The room bounced with stories, with sadness and happiness, and sitting too long in silence left his head buzzing. Voices returned in strips, whispering nonsense and obscenities, assuring him that none of this mattered.

But he recited his name.

He recited Bria's name.

And he recited truths.

"I will be okay," he said aloud, moving across the room to the table. Brent ran his fingers over the books on the table. He now realized how to build a monster, as told by the storybook the Mist Keeper Julietta shared with him back in the Library. Like the story, he was transformed into the vessel, swallowed by the stories and the monster's embrace. But he had escaped it; now, he just had to figure out how to destroy it.

Unless it couldn't be.

He stroked the spine. Didn't stories, no matter how terrible, live on forever? The moment they entered the air, they thrived. It was why the Order banished them; stories had the power to change the world. They lifted people out of the haze of the Effluvium and into the arms of ideas, truth, and rebellion. By controlling stories, they controlled imagination; it meant stopping people from dreaming; it meant preventing people from growing.

Brent reached for the other book, with the golden numeral *I* embellished on the cover. Back when he first looked it over, it gave him a headache. Now, his head scorched touching it, the history of the book weaving around the room in a mist-filled tale of a figure hunched over, scribing the words. He recognized the figure with slicked-back hair and scarred face. The man scribbled out the history of a war, not moving for days, wearing the weight of truth on his shoulders.

As the story subsided, the man closed the book. He dropped his quill to the floor and looked away from his desk.

"Tomás..." Brent stumbled backward and shook his head. *He's not here. The Council can't see you. You're safe. You're safe. Dammit, you're safe!*

Why don't you go into the Tunnels and destroy 'em all then? a voice barked.

You can show them what you can do, another added.

"I don't want anything to do with them!" He threw the book at the wall. As soon as it landed, he rushed over, apologizing profusely to the book as he picked it off the ground. It opened on a page with a watercolor painting of the Chessboard Field north of Mert. In the center stood a man cloaked in black while another individual in a white gown stood holding a sword.

They gathered in that last hour, face-to-face and tall. An army of monsters stood behind Death while Life rode with a brigade of humanity. The innocent watched in horror as Death and Life clashed.

Half the tulips wilted while the others bloomed beneath the prowess of Life and Death. Magic seared through the sky, painting the world red with blood and ash.

There are few who can say what happened that day. But records dictate the truth: a battle, two gods clashing, begging to oversee the fate of humanity.

Of those immortals and mortals, they thus tried to reign.

Only to lose themselves in the whirlwind of demise.

Neither deserved to thrive. One chose the path of deception, the other of manipulation. Both sides of the same coin.

History won't be kind.

Brent stared at the page. The words drew him in, tightening around him as he read each sentence. But the longer he held the book, the more detrimental the story became, and before he flipped the page, he dropped the book.

For a moment, the story-version of Tomás stared at him through the mist. Then the image vanished.

Unless it wasn't a story? Was Tomás entering his head, manipulating him?

Brent stumbled backward, trying to shake off the stories protruding from the books. This was ridiculous! Why couldn't he just focus on one story at a time? Why did they scratch at his head? Sure, the medication helped. But his head continued to thunder.

He stumbled over to the end table, picking up his green gem and holding it. Briefly, the room stopped spinning, calmness reigned.

I need fresh air. I'll just step out. It'll be a'ight. I'll be a'ight.

He stumbled down the stairway, realizing halfway through his descent that he forgot to put on his shoes. After debating for a moment, he shrugged off his bare feet, then stepped into the midday bustle of the street.

Everything whirled around him the moment he stepped onto the road. People strode past, unphased as stories mingled in the air, while the dead drifted in and out of the mist.

He often failed to tell apart reality from fiction. Or history. Or stories.

Or something.

He gripped the wall as he walked along, taking each breath slowly. *I know who I am!* With each step, he recited his mantra. His name. His history. His story.

And he watched on the way the fog danced along his face, the way the half-living bushes gathered about his feet, and the way the stone skid beneath his toes. He was alive. He was aware.

Things would be okay.

Brent wandered around the block and into a square where a few vendors gathered. A woman played the cello, and a few people danced between the benches.

But beside them swayed similar stories of orchestras and the dead, all mingling among the benches and circling a statuesque fountain in the center of it all.

Someone carved a few sentences into the stone, written in an old Mertoni dialect. Brent squinted. The residuals from a few releases gave him the ability to understand other languages. But it'd been so long, hadn't it? Sure, he'd conducted releases in his Diabolo-state, but did the residuals stick?

To his surprise, they did. After a moment of focusing, he understood the words.

To her, our flower, our lovely one.
To her known as Merta, our pride,
Our lady.
Our seer.
May the city glisten for eternity.

"Merta," Brent recited and glanced at the statue. It resembled a middle-aged woman with long hair, wide eyes, and a steady frown. He half expected the stories to tell him more about the woman, but he only saw the tale of the sculptor creating the statue.

Brent tried to focus more on the story. He wanted to learn; he wanted to listen; it was something to embrace rather than fight. But as he focused, the mist retreated. The story vanished.

"Huh?" Brent blinked. He wasn't used to seeing the stories retreat so readily.

But as soon as they disappeared, in their place stood a flickering ghost. A man with a long wiry black beard with dark eyes and knotted hair stood there, his mouth pursed into a distinct frown.

Brent squinted. "Who are you?

The ghost stared up at the statute.

Brent stared at him harder. Sadness embellished the ghost, decorated with a soft story of wandering, slavery, and duty. Had Brent met him before all of this? He looked so familiar.

The man did not speak, instead motioning with his hands. It took Brent a few seconds, but a story battered his mind about a little girl speaking in the same manner. Her language bubbled into him like any other, and he understood the ghost standing before him.

"We need to speak," the man said.

"About what?"

"You're in danger."

"What?"

"They're coming. You're not safe here."

"I'm...I'm sorry? Do you mean the Council? Or...the Order? Or..." Brent's mind raced with the possibilities. "What do you mean?"

"I need to go," the man stated. "He'll be waking up soon."

Before Brent could stop him, the ghost vanished into the mist.

CHAPTER TWENTY-FOUR

PINSTRIPES

Brent sat on the edge of the statue for a couple hours, watching people dance, shop, and dine without a care in the world. He turned the green gem over in his hand, going through his story every few minutes to stay grounded. His thoughts kept returning to that mysterious ghost. Why did he seem so familiar?

He paced around the statue, trying to recall his memories. Instead, old stories of construction and lovers kissing beneath the statue's gaze followed him. Once again, he collapsed on a bench beside a crumpled day-old newspaper. The newspaper felt different from the book at the apartment. The stories attached to it were mundane: a printing press, a delivery girl, and a woman flipping through the pages before throwing it halfway in the trash bin.

Everything carried a story. He couldn't shake them anymore.

No wonder he hadn't been able to rationalize before the periwinkle medication.

He skimmed over the first pages, detailing how the Mertoni State Police gathered forces on the plains because of annexation threats from the east. Usually, that type of story drew him in, but at the bottom of the second page, something else caught his eye. A wanted ad with his face, drawn as a hideous caricature, with the words 'THE STORY COLLECTOR' beneath it cut off half the page.

Story Collector? Right, that's what they're calling me. He chuckled to himself. *I like that. Good thing the drawing looks nothing like me.*

He chuckled to himself before flipping it to the next page. A blurry photograph of tall birds with wide eyes, balding heads, and misty wings stared at him. Brent gazed back, unable to shake their gaze. The caption beneath them read 'Hypnotic Ostriches,' and their gaze was something for that matter. In another picture, they stood at least twice the height of their handler, their long necks curved downwards. Their eyes never left Brent, even as he attempted to turn the page.

They may even be worse than cats. Brent paused before turning the page. He poked the image three times. "You don't scare me."

His voice quavered as he spoke.

He continued flipping through the paper, focusing on each word. It reminded him of the days before the Mist Keepers when he used to salvage every word of the paper for his own stories. Now, though, he was free. He told stories without fear. There were bigger things to fear.

A dog barking caught his attention.

"Nix, what ya doin'!?!"

Brent glanced over in the direction of the voices. A gray box-headed dog, shifting in and out of the mist in a state of semi-permanence, came bounding towards him.

"Nix!" An individual in a pinstriped suit came bounding out of the crowd. The dog leapt right at Brent, pushing him back into the fountain.

Brent landed with a splash. The dog gnarled its teeth.

Then slurped Brent's face.

"Oi! Nix! Stop! Bad dog! Bad!" The pinstriped man pulled the dog off Brent.

"Shite..." Brent grunted. A hand helped him out of the water.

"Sorry about that—REGGIE!" The man pulled Brent into a hug. "REGGIE, WHERE YA BEEN!?!"

"Oi Billie." A small woman in a pinstripe suit joined the larger individual's side, "What'cha—REGGIE!"

Brent gawked. "I—"

As the one called Billie continued to hug him, stories flashed over Brent.

He sat on a stool in the bar with a dog at his heels, clinking glasses and laughing with others. They all wore pinstripes, except him. He was the outsider, the one in a brown jacket, laughing over their crime and choices.

"Atta boy, Reggie!" one of them called, "You got us another story. We gonna get a foothold in the government yet."

He raised his glass and shifted. The dog lay on his feet, snoring away, a half comfort.

"Oh, Reggie!" A woman danced over to him and threw her legs over his lap. She stroked his face with her fingers. "You don't look like yourself anymore, but you still got talent, I'd say. Why not a kiss for old times' sake, hm?"

He shook his head, "Not now, doll."

"But Reggie!"

"I said not now/" He slammed his fist against the table. "I got things to do."

"Mitzi!" a pinstripe cried, "Leave the poor kid alone. He ain't your Reggie."

"He knows everything that Reggie knows!" the woman cried.

As the bickering commenced, he lifted a glass to his lips. The bitter taste of whiskey burned his throat.

It brought him to a simpler time, sitting by a fence and naming the cows.

"Bri..." he mumbled.

Mitzi glared. "Oh, there you go again, going on and on about some dame! Just admit you done cheated on me, Reggie!"

"I..." He opened his mouth to protest, but a banging roared against the basement door.

"Shit! Coppers!" a pinstripe screamed.

He took to the floor as the door flung open. The pinstripes dispersed, crawling this way and that.

Yet, he no longer saw them. Fear washed over him.

Then all he saw was mist, flinging stories through the air.

He couldn't see anything.

But in his confusion, he slipped through the tales and into the street.

He wandered. He mumbled.

He gawked.

He stared.

He lost his head.

Until he found solace in a quiet alley on Celosia, beneath the glowing window of a familiar apartment building.

He made a nest out of a pile of newspapers and his jacket.

And there, he drifted to sleep.
Alone.

Brent gasped and pulled out of the hug, blinking away the vivid tale. He glanced around, once again back in the square. A dog lay at his feet while two semi-familiar pinstripes stared at him.

That was my story... Brent blinked a few times and shook his head. I *spent time with the Pinstripes?*

"We've been lookin' everywhere for ya, Reggie," the smaller one continued, unphased by Brent's change. "Ya promised to get us some good stories, ya 'member? 'Bout some ministers? Ya went all crazy, robbin' that little shop like a madman. That ain't gonna help us, ya see. Ya gotta do what we ask."

"Coun—Council members?"

"Ya! The City Council! There'd been some new ministers added. Like Ms. Helios and Mr. Nursing! Ya said you was gonna poke around with their stories."

"I...um...I dunno what you're talking about."

"Oi, Freddie." The big fellow poked at Brent's chest. "Reggie don't look like himself, don'tcha think?"

"Ya right, Billie. He ain't got that crazy eye look he usually does. What's up with that? You still there, Reggie? Y'know that Mitzi won't be happy if ya ditch on her. Ya been missing for a month now!"

Brent blinked. "Mit—Mitzi?"

"Ya don't remember? Guess you really did lose your mind!"

"Maybe he done got too many stories in his head now or something, Freddie." The big one continued poking Brent's chest. "Huh, Reggie? You eat too many stories?"

"I—I don't know what you're saying. I'm sorry..." Brent gulped, his mind racing as he tried to recall the past couple months. "I'm...I wasn't myself the past few months and...and I kind of...I mean...I found myself and...and..."

"See! What'd I tell ya! Reggie ain't back!" Freddie continued, "He just a crazed loon! We ain't able to trust a loon!"

"He ain't a loon, Freddie. He's a bit confused is all. He has all those stories. Remember, he used to go by Geraldine for a bit too but had that switcheroo over to Reggie! Didn't think it was actually Reggie's ghost!"

"That's true, Billie! I done forgot about that. So, what d'ya go by now, Reggie? Ya not remember your Reggie days?"

Brent blinked, "Oh, um, sorry, but...um...my name is Brent. That's...that's my actual name. I...I got help. And I'm sorry, but I really remember nothing that happened. I...who's Mitzi? Who are you?"

The short-one bellowed, "Ya such a buffoon! Reggie—I mean, Brent, if that's your name now! Ya don't remember nothing? We was hanging around ya for about a month. Kept ya alive and everything!"

"We had a nice little deal. You found us stories and goods; we gave ya food and a place in the basement," the bigger one added.

"I found you...stories?" Brent blinked.

Freddie stopped laughing. "Ya really don't know?"

Brent shook his head.

"We found ya here in this plaza, kinda looking pathetic and everything, about three months ago before you up and gone missing again," Billie said. "You was rabid. Like crazy rabid. We got ya healed up and some food in ya over yonder past the canal, and ya bolted again. Ya came back every now and again, saying different names and such. Reggie was ya last one, and all...thought ya was channeling ghosts 'cause Reggie was our brother and all. But then you started collecting these stories and shite of other living people, like Mitzi! It freaked her out so much, I tell ya!"

"We thought we could use ya, though, cause ain't no one gonna take advantage of us. So we asked ya to go find us stories," Freddi added. "Ya know, ones we could use to...get our way and all, ya see bub?"

"You mean blackmail?" Brent whispered. *So, I spent days with the Pinstripe Gang, doing their bidding, committing crimes. I don't remember any of it...*He wracked his brain, but his memories of those days were so foggy. A vague recollection resurfaced of him standing in a tent city with a few individuals in striped suits. But beyond the mere image at the forefront of his mind of a group of pinstripes gathering in the basement of some saloon, he couldn't reach into the story beyond it.

"If ya wanna use the word blackmail, sure." Freddi rolled his eyes. "I miss Reggie. He ain't got a moral compass. Just grunted and said 'kay' all the time. Was a funny guy."

"Oh, um...sorry." Brent looked down at his feet. The dog rolled on her side so he could rub her belly.

"It's all good, fella. We ain't gonna go knock ya down cause ya found your head or something."

"Besides, you got us a ton of nice stories," Billie said. "We'll be able to make 'em work for years, isn't that right, Freddie?"

"That's right, Billie!"

"Real...really?" Brent stared at them. "You're not going to...force me to get more or something?"

"Nah, we ain't like that. Mitzi ain't gonna be happy that you're not comin' round again, but that's her problem if ya ask me!"

Brent grew quiet. His fingers tightened around the newspaper, finding home again on the page with the wide-eyed ostrich. One question remained on his tongue, though. "Who...who's Mitzi?"

Freddie chortled, "My sissy. She always fawned after Reggie, then she started after ya, no matter ya name or nothing. Thought ya was a good-looking fellow or something like that. Don't really get it, but whatever. Ya not my type." Freddie winked and laughed again. "Ya going pale there, fellow! Don't worry, don't worry! You did nothing with Mitzi. Was always talking about someone. Mumbling and all. Who was it? Ya remember, Billie?"

"A Bee or something." Billie shrugged.

"Bri...Bria?"

"That's it. Yeah. You was sappy about her. Hope you found her cause it was kinda pathetic. *I wanna find my Beeeee!*"

Brent hid his face behind the newspaper. "Yeah, I did. I have, I mean. Yeah."

"Atta boy." Freddie smiled. "Hope ya been kissing her silly cause you was crazy bout it."

"Yeah, I...I will. I will." Brent picked at the edges of the newspaper.

"Good." Freddie raised their eyebrows at Billie and nodded. "I'm sure we'll see ya around, Brent. Know we're on ya side though if ya need it, okay?"

"Oh, um...thanks."

"See ya!" Billie waved.

Billie and Freddie began to leave. The dog didn't budge.

"Wait! Your dog!" Brent called.

"She ain't our dog!" Billie shouted back. "You brought her with ya! She's been barking like crazy looking for ya!"

"My...my dog?" Brent glanced at Nix again.

"Yeah, keep her. She's been driving Mitzi crazy!"

Before Brent could object, the two pinstripes left the square, marching off with pride and guile. They didn't look back at him. It left Brent with an odd warmth in his stomach. He was so used to people dragging him into bad situations, kicking him to the curb, and forcing him to be something greater. But these two mobsters, for lack of a better word, treated him as a human. As family.

He brought his hand to the REAPER scar on his arm, then to his black stamp. *I'm not defined by marks on my skin.*

And I have a dog.

He scratched Nix's head. The dog hung her head back, tongue hanging lopsided out of her mouth. For a moment, Brent saw the story. A dog ran up to a per-plexed man in the street. As the man screamed, the dog licked his hand, and all fear vanished. The man was free to breathe for a short time.

That man was his shadow. When Brent pulled at his memories, he remembered the bark and the sniffing, he remembered sleeping with his head on the dog's fur, and he remembered the dog's cocked head. It was distant, like a dream, but Nix was there.

A shadow, but there.

"C'mon, Nix." Brent smiled at the dog. "Let's go home."

CHAPTER TWENTY-FIVE

SOME PIZZA OVER BROKEN TREATIES

B rent?" Bria called as she opened the apartment door. It sat empty, waiting for her with a book on the floor, the lights turned off, and Brent's shoes sitting by the bed. She dropped the bags to the floor. A few vials of the silver liquid and a lemon rolled out. "Brent? Stop playing games and come out."

She didn't expect a reply, but the silence left her with a knot in her stomach. Without waiting, she bolted out the door, leaving it hanging ajar, and raced into the street.

"BRENT?!"

She glanced left, scanning the crowd, before turning right.

Her heart nearly broke from relief.

Brent strode towards her with a dog on his heels. A smile filled his face.

"Oh, thank goodness..." Bria raced over to him and threw her arms around his neck. "Don't do that! I was...I was scared." She buried her face into his chest and gulped back a few tears. "I was so worried that you ran off again or that the stories overpowered you or something. Please don't scare me like that."

"I'm sorry." He squeezed her. "Just...I needed fresh air. I should have left a note."

"It's okay...it's fine. You're allowed to go out." She glanced at the dog, "Who's your friend?"

"Um, Nix. I guess I...I adopted her when I was in my Diabolo state or something."

"Oh!" Bria remarked and reached for the dog, "Nice to meet you, Nix."

Nix promptly gave Bria her paw.

"Good girl!"

Laughing, they headed back into the apartment. Brent detailed his day with the admiration of a storyteller. He described how he saw Tomás's story, his run in the odd ghost in the square, and his encounter with the

Pinstripes Billie and Freddie, who reunited him with Nix.

He continued babbling while in the shower. At the top of his lungs, he pondered the warning from the ghost while Bria sat on the bed with Nix. The dog reminded her of Gato, her father's dog, except for the strange misty coat covering her fur. *We couldn't have a normal dog.* She grinned and scratched behind Nix's ears.

Brent circled back to his rambling about the mysterious ghost as he waltzed out of the shower, steam painting the room, a towel wrapped around his waist. He sat down at the table and finished saying, "Dunno what he meant. I...I recognized him, but I can't put a name on him. Must've seen him in the Library or something...but my head is shite right now."

"Do you think we'll need to leave?" Bria approached Brent and brushed back his knotted hair with her fingers.

"I dunno...it's...OW! You're pulling too hard!" He flinched. "I didn't really get a read on his story or anything. What if...I mean...is it a trick?"

Bria grimaced. "We can always mention it to Kek..."

"Can we trust Kek, though? I mean..." Brent's fingers went to his arm, tracing along the jagged REAPER scar.

"I think so. At least, I hope so. They've been helping us so far. Who's saying they'll stop?"

Brent continued to touch the scar on his arm.

"Edith isn't like Kek. She acted on her own accord. Whatever happened...Kek won't let it happen again." Bria caught his hand and squeezed it. "I'm sure of it."

Brent huffed an agreement, turning back to the bag on the table and parsing through it for a lemon. With a jagged nail, he cut into the peel.

Lemons! He really is himself. Bria relaxed her shoulders. The nagging sensation that something bad might have happened while he was out remained, the endless pang that if she looked away for too long, her good fortune would end. "You could've left a note..."

"I was going stir crazy," Brent said without looking up at her. "Sorry. I mean...I know I should've, but...it just...it happened."

"But...what if the Diabolo won? I wouldn't have been able to find you."

"Well, that fuckwad didn't get me this time, did he?"

"Fuckwad?"

"Yeah." Brent didn't even flinch at the ridiculousness of the statement. "It's a wad of fuck that messes with my head and...shite." He finished cutting into the lemon and placed a piece in his mouth.

Bria snorted as she put away the groceries in the now clean kitchen. It was nice being able to look at the little home without being repulsed.

She glanced at Brent and smiled. He sat there like he had months earlier, flipping through an old newspaper. He stopped in the classified section, running his finger over an advertisement for a restaurant on the other side of the city. He fixated on the image of a doughy creation coated in red sauce and cheese.

"You ever explore the city while you were trying to...I mean...while I was going crazy?" Brent turned back to Bria. "Like, did you ever try this thing? The bread monstrosity with sauce and all?"

Bria looked at the image and shook her head. "I didn't really do much of anything."

"Bri! Why didn't you? I mean...you could have done so much!"

"I couldn't."

"Then we're going!" Brent lunged to his feet. "You need to have fun!"

"Brent..." Bria stared at him.

"No! Don't *Brent* me! We're going!" He spoke with animation in a way that Bria hadn't seen in months.

"I'm not objecting. It's just that—"

"Not hearing it, nope!" Brent opened the door to the apartment.

An old woman coming down the stairs screamed. Nix raised her head, woofed once, then fell back to sleep.

Bria covered her face and flushed. "You're not wearing any clothes."

Brent slammed the door, his face as ripe as a tomato.

Restraining the urge to laugh, Bria helped Brent get dressed and clean-shaven. She even changed out of her baggy clothes into the luminescent dress Brent bought for her all those months ago. For a moment, she stared at herself in the mirror; it was like looking at a stranger.

I'm happy, almost, for the first time in months. She spun in a circle, watching as the skirt flared around her, before joining Brent in the entranceway.

She glanced him up and down for a moment. Even cleaned up, he stood out like a blossoming tree in the middle of winter. His face, plastered throughout Mert, would gather the attention of many people throughout the city. *He was lucky to not be caught while I was out.*

"Hold on." Bria went back to the pile of clothes on the floor and pulled out a worn-down scarf and yellow bowler hat. She placed the hat on his head and wrapped the scarf around his neck.

"What's this for?"

"It's kind of hard to miss your dumb face. Remember? The Mertoni coppers want you?"

"Oh. Right. Yeah." Brent adjusted the scarf around his chin. "There. How do I look?"

"Ridiculous." Bria laced her fingers around his hand.

"Oi! You wear scarves all the time!"

"But I make them look good."

Laughing, with their arms laced together, they walked out together into the city. Nix didn't budge, fast asleep.

Bria still worried for Brent with each step, watching as he would get distracted by what she was certain were stories frolicking through the alleys. Sure, he'd been out and about, but how much of that had been in a craze?

Sometimes as they walked, Brent stopped in the middle of the road with a laugh, and other times he'd curl in on himself and mumble a few incomprehensible phrases. Kek's potion was working, but would he ever be free of the Diabolo's effects? Or would he ever be able to ignore the stories?

But, undeniably, he was Brent Harley.

He insisted they take the long way through Mert, stopping to peruse different vendors in the City Centre while marveling at different statues written in old Mertoni. On more than one occasion, Bria worried she'd lost him only for Brent to reappear a few vendors down, his smiling reassuring her that he hadn't gone awry. He never got to explore the market like this back home, and after being trapped in his head for all those months, it was okay to let him live.

He is okay. Bria kept reminding herself of that one truth. *He's himself.*

After losing him a fourth time, Bria swore he needed a leash, but her anger vanished quick. There Brent stood in front of a vendor, weaving a story using the mist. It was a story he'd already told once before, the tale of Mr. G in the Treasury, but at least he was sharing something. A few children gathered around him, eyes wide with wonder and laughing as the mist flourished around Brent.

Bria almost bolted over. *Why is he using the mist? That's going to draw attention!*

Neither the vendors nor the children flinched, though, watching with awe. Brent's behavior was methodical, ending the story on the same note as before: the ultimate twist, Mr. G was a gorilla! This caused a ruckus of laughter out of the children. The vendor clapped his hands together, then handed Brent a shawl reminiscent of the sea.

He returned to Bria, a half-smile on his face, and draped the shawl around her shoulders. "You need more color. And I thought you'd...I mean...it looks good on you and all."

Bria stared at him in disbelief, "That wasn't smart."

"Wha...what?"

"Brent, come on. The coppers have been looking for you. Don't you think telling a story with your magic might attract attention?"

Brent's face fell, "I...um...sorry. It just...it came out and...it felt natural and...yeah."

Guilt seeped into Bria's heart.

"I...I haven't told a story like that in months, and I...I wanted to...and...yeah. I...it was dumb. Just..." He turned away, "I couldn't help thinking about Alexandria and how she loved the stories, and I wanted to...I dunno, make another kid smile cause of the stories or something. I...I miss her."

"I know," Bria whispered, "I know. But if you get caught, you won't ever see her again."

Brent agreed with a single nod.

Bria touched the shawl, examining the stitching. The design reminded her of the shawl her grandmama knitted many years ago. One that she'd left behind in Newbird's Arm. Brent probably saw this one and thought to buy it for her because of that exact reason.

He always paid attention to the weirdest details.

It must have frustrated him beyond measures to no longer have that same perception.

"The shawl is beautiful, though. Thank you. Really," Bria said.

Brent sucked in his lips. "Worth the attention, though?"

"You always told stories...no matter how irresponsible. It's not like anyone could stop you. It's who you are."

Brent's shoulders loosened. "So you're not mad?"

"Why would I be mad? You told a story. You were *you*."

As they left the City Centre and headed towards the restaurant district, Bria nestled beneath Brent's arm. At first, they said nothing else, listening as the birds flew by, the sky whistling with the wind, and magic dance through the road. Bria heard the way the trees spoke. She was sure Brent saw the stories dance. Two sides of the same coin; they both saw the worlds through a different lens, but together, it was the same.

Brent broke the song, his voice soft. "I...back there...I couldn't tell a story."

"What are you talking about? You just told a story about Mr. G!"

"'Cause I remembered it." His voice cracked. "But I couldn't...when I tried to think of a new story, my head screamed and all, and I...I mean...I couldn't."

Bria had never seen Brent so defeated. He turned into an alleyway and crouched down, holding his head and mumbling.

"There's too much. There's too much. I can't...there's...I mean...there's too much..."

Bria knelt beside him. "Look at me."

He shook his head.

"Brenton Harley, look at me."

He raised his head. "What am I if I can't tell a story?"

"It will return. I promise."

"But what if it doesn't?"

"It will."

They sat there until Brent was ready to leave. He didn't speak much, staring past Bria into the market outside the alley. Bria wondered how many stories spun around him and if the medication continued to dull the constant screaming the stories carried. If his eyes remained silver, he was there.

And if he was there, he would keep fighting.

Once Brent recollected himself, they walked hand in hand along the canal towards the restaurant from the article. They took a seat along the canal, watching the sunset weave down against the blood sea. A waiter came by to take their orders: two Mertoni delicacies of dough layered with tomato sauce, cheese, and other toppings known as pizza. They ordered one Mertoni special and one plain. While waiting, Brent played with the word on his tongue, extending out the sound of each letter.

"Pizza. Pee-zah. Pi-zuh." Brent laughed to himself and grinned that goofy smile in Bria's direction.

The smile disappeared when the pizza arrived.

While Bria's looked exactly like the one in the picture, Brent's Mertoni Special included an array of toppings.

Including pineapple.

He hissed at it.

"Just try it!" Bria urged as she cut a slice of her own pizza.

"It's *pineapple*."

"Brent!"

"I'm gonna throw it to the gulls." He lifted the pizza in the air.

"No! No! We're not wasting food. Switch with me." Bria snagged the pizza from him and pushed the plain pie over his way.

After avoiding a crisis of pineapple and food waste, the meal was an absolute delight. Brent dug into the pizza and devoured it like someone who hadn't eaten in months. Bria supposed he really hadn't eaten well for that long, and a meal as filling and wonderful as these delicacies made him happy.

And although Brent despised pineapple, Bria found it added a pleasant taste to the meal.

Brent gagged as she put a piece in her mouth.

They finished the meal by sharing an ice cream sundae, sitting on the edge of the boardwalk, watching the water thrash against the shoreline. When Bria leaned in to kiss his cheek, Brent shied away, holding a hand to her face.

"Gross! You smell like pineapple. Go away!"

"Too bad. I got you ice cream!"

"Only 'cause you promised!"

"Nope. You're still getting a kiss!" Bria kissed his cheek three times. He was back! He was really back! Her heart fluttered like a schoolgirl as she nestled her nose into his neck. For a moment, she was back in the Newbird Forest, sitting next to him on a picnic blanket, teaching him how to kiss. She remembered it as clear as day. It was a few days after their first kiss, and hesitant, hand in hand, they strolled into the forest. Brent didn't understand back then why she would ever like him, but she affirmed her feelings. And they practiced kissing until the sun fell.

She wanted to kiss him now more than anything. She yearned for the closeness, the caressing, and the intimacy.

But there was a wall between them. A fear, as Brent put it, that he would do something wrong.

Bria didn't believe it possible.

But he was right; he had only started his ascent out of the Diabolo's grasp. One wrong step and he would fall back again.

Instead, Bria rested her head on Brent's shoulder, watching the sunset paint the waves of the sea. "It's beautiful here..."

"But?"

"But what?"

"You don't seem entirely satisfied." Brent peered at the water.

"Well..." Bria sighed. "I don't know. Something is missing."

"Like what?"

"The forest, perhaps?" She thought about her time on the island with Kek. "I miss the way the green strokes my skin. Or the trees sing songs to me. Yes, I love the magic in this city, but it's a manmade jungle. It's not home for me." Bria eyed the water. "Part of me wants to go back to Newbird's Arm, but I spent my entire life wanting to run away."

"This time, you ran without a choice. It's not the same."

"I guess so. But, if we had to leave Mert – as in if there is some danger like the ghost said...I don't even know where we would go."

Brent furrowed his brow. "Yeah, I dunno. Someplace where people will leave us alone would be nice."

"That might be hard."

"Yeah..."

"But...if we do leave..." Bria traced his fingers. "I would like to go someplace with a forest. I need it back."

"There'd be less commotion."

"Less stories."

"Mmm," Brent's face hardened as he nodded in agreement. "But there's still one terrible fact..."

Bria's heart sank. "Please don't start going on about the curse again. If you can survive the Diabolo, you can survive some curse that a bunch of grumpy Death gods claimed to put on you!"

"No, not the curse. Fuck the curse. I've beaten things worse." He smiled that goofy half-smile that Bria loved. A twinkle lit up the corners of his eyes. "What I mean is...even without the curse, I'm still kinda a Mist Keeper, I guess? I mean...I still hear the dead screaming..." He let out a single nervous chuckle. "And mingling with the stories. I don't think that will go away, I mean."

"And knowing you, you're not going to walk away from people needing help, are you?"

"Probably not."

"And that's what I love about you. You're so damn kind. You still are. I wasn't sure if you would still be...*you*...even after you recovered. You went to Hell and back."

Brent didn't take his eyes off the sea. "In those brief moments of...self-awareness, I clung to what I remembered. I might not have known my name, but I knew who I was sorta. Because I'm not a murderer. I'm...I'm me."

"And no one can take that away from you."

"I guess not." His shoulders relaxed, and he draped his arm around Bria's waist.

Bria watched with Brent as the sun fell, leaving a purple tinge against the horizon. Once night settled, they strode together along the water, letting the sand tickled their toes.

Brent fidgeted a lot. This normally would have been a time where he would tell a story, but he struggled to come up with a new tale. Bria didn't need Brent to tell her, she saw it in his face, and it hurt more than anything. *Someday, you'll tell a story again, Brent. I don't doubt that. But it'll take time.*

They left the beach and headed back through the city, ignoring the passage of time told only by the streets growing vacant. Brent often paused in random spots to collect a story. He sometimes mentioned what he saw: a girl playing with dolls in front of the shop, a couple dancing in the moonlight, and a boy chasing cats in alleyways.

Brent shuddered when he spoke about the cats.

"Why do you hate cats so much? You never really cared, it seemed." Bria asked, leaning into Brent's side as they rounded the bend back onto Juniper.

"The first time I helped with a release, with Caroline, it was some woman who really hated cats, and I guess it just sorta...stuck." Brent scowled. "But c'mon, dogs are better."

Bria smiled, thinking of Nix sleeping on the bed at home.

"Once we find a better place, we'll be able to settle down, and I dunno...adopt five dogs or something. I mean, Nix needs friends, right?" Brent shrugged. "A nice quiet house in the forest with dogs. Someday we can get..." His face suddenly turned red. "I mean, we'll be together and all."

"Yeah, I know. Maybe we'll even get married."

The color in Brent's cheeks deepened to scarlet.

Bria squeezed Brent's fingers. "Really, though, it's so great hearing you talk about the *future*."

"Yeah, cause I might be a self-deprecating bastard, but, I mean, if I can fight back a Diabolo...then I guess I can have a future." Brent relaxed as they reached the corner of Juniper and Celosia.

"You always had a future."

"Yeah, but now I get a say in it."

Bria wanted to throw her arms around Brent, kiss him like her life depended on it, and hold him close.

But before she opened herself up, she noticed a tall figure at the front of the building.

"Ah! There you two are!"

Bria stepped back. "Varden? What're you doing here?"

Varden stepped out under the streetlamp. "I need to talk to both of you...in private."

"At this hour?"

"It can't wait."

Bria glanced at Brent. They exchanged a mutual glance of confusion, then let Varden into the building and up to their small studio apartment.

Nix jumped off the bed the moment the door opened. She barked once at Varden, then cowered beneath the bed, ears pulled back.

Varden's presence made the apartment feel even smaller. He bent his head down as he walked in, nearly stomping on a chair as he entered the room. Bria collapsed on the bed while Brent climbed onto the floor with the Nix. They watched as the giant mulled about the room as if searching for his best way to broach the subject.

Finally, he spoke, his eyes hard on Brent. "We have reason to believe that you're in danger."

"Yeah, I know that already." Brent shrugged. "Already spoke with the ghost you sent this way."

"Ghost?" Varden shook his head. "I didn't send a ghost."

"Well, someone did. Or something. He was some bearded fellow. Mute. Spoke with his hands."

Varden nodded. "My contact must have sent him..."

"Your contact?" Bria inquired.

"There's...a lot going on." Varden picked at a patch on his coat. He looked strange out of his nurse's uniform, almost as if he shoved himself into a pair of ill-fitting pants. His hair, usually slicked back, stuck out at all angles, and his freckles almost looked like smudges of dirt. "And it is not fair to either of you that I am being elusive, but I do not have the time to go into detail. I can say this: I have a contact in the Council, and we've been tracking a few of the other Mist Keepers for some time. We believe they discovered where Brent is and that they intend to claim him."

Brent leaned forward, scratching at his wrist as he spoke. "Is that what was going on the other day? I mean, when Tilda came and said—"

"Yes."

"We wanted to leave the city anyway." Bria looked at Brent as she spoke. "I guess this gives us a reason?"

"Kek has already made arrangements for the two of you on an island off the coast of Perennes. It should divert the Council for a bit."

Bria watched Brent as Varden spoke. He didn't flinch, only focused on the area past the giant's shoulder. It sounded too perfect: a quiet place away from the commotion, an island by the sea. It probably had a forest, few stories, and at last...peace. But could she trust Varden? There remained that bit of uncertainty. She could tell by the way Brent watched Varden that he felt it too.

When neither of them replied, Varden continued, "My contact and I will attempt to refurbish the treaty, prevent this altercation from further escalation."

Brent met Varden's gaze. "Treaty? You mean...you and Kek and the Magii had an altercation with the Council?"

Varden nodded. "Yes. The One War was an endless battle for hundreds of years between the Mist Keepers and Kek's Palaver of Magii. Part of the treaty that ended it was the agreement that Ningursu must abolish the Diabolo. Ningursu did not respect that half of the treaty. But this isn't a reason to rekindle the flame of war."

"I remember some of that. I think Caroline mentioned it to me early on..." Brent nodded to himself. "But why does the Council care about me then?"

"You're the one who found the Diabolo, didn't you? Ningursu never liked rogue players."

Bria waited for Brent to reply. He said nothing, though, eyes falling to the floor. She wondered what danced through his head; she hoped it wasn't guilt. There was no reason to bask in that guilt anymore! He restrained the Diabolo! It was no longer loose! For the most part now, Brent was himself! Everything else was the Council's fault.

Varden didn't wait long, already rising from his seat so his head brushed the top of the ceiling. "Madame Owiti will meet you tomorrow morning at, and I quote, 'Toddle's shop.' Kek has provided her with the proper communication line to get you to the island. Don't worry. You'll both be safe."

"Thank you, Varden," Bria whispered.

The giant bowed his head once, then exited the small studio apartment, leaving Bria and Brent alone to prepare.

CHAPTER TWENTY-SIX

MASKS

Brent didn't sleep that night. He lay awake, staring at the ceiling, one arm draped around Bria and the other hand pressed against Nix's fur. It had been hard to focus with Varden in the room, and after he left, the stories continued to spin. They pounded against Brent's consciousness and yanked at the tendril-like fingers of the Diabolo. There were too many stories: tales of loves, tales of warriors, tales of doctors, tales of patients, and tales of belonging. They swirled around Varden as he walked about the room, but Brent knew before Varden told them what was wrong.

Because, of course, the Council would be watching.

As morning settled, Brent climbed out of bed. His head pounded. His eyes hung. The stories twirled around him, screaming and begging for his attention.

Give in to the stories.

Brent shook his head. He fumbled over to Bria's bag and removed one syringe and a vial of the Periwinkle Medication. His fingers trembled as he guided it to his skin.

What're you doing?!

Stop!

Go away!

"Shite!" Brent gritted his teeth, forcing the voices back into their hideaway in the basement of his mind.

"Brent?" Bria called from the bed. "What's wrong?"

He shut his eyes tight as the last voices finally subsided before looking up to meet Bria's gaze. "Just...I was...I'm a'ight. Needed the meds."

"Are you sure?"

"Yeah. I'm a'ight. Really."

She approached him, taking her fingers and dragging them over his arm. A smile punctuated by a single dimple highlighted her face. Brent pulled her close, pressing his lips to her forehead and listening as her breaths rose and fell in her chest.

"Once you're ready, we should head over to the shop," Bria whispered.

"Are we actually gonna go? Can we trust Varden?"

"I think so. He seems genuine at least." Her face hardened. "If anything, I do trust Madame Owiti. Without her, I don't know if I would have found you. It's worth something to meet up with her."

Brent agreed. He vaguely remembered Madame Owiti. His head spun during the time he spent in her apartment, and each movement sent him on edge, but the old woman had been kind. She treated him like a human.

He and Bria spent the morning packing. They straightened up the blankets and silverware, only packing some clothes, the books on the table, and other essential items. Bria layered the Periwinkle Medication on top of that, each vile wrapped carefully in a tunic to protect it from breaking. Nix paced around the room, begging for food as they ate and stealing a pillow and hiding under the table. She tore it to bits, sending fluff everywhere, deterring their chores for a few minutes with laughter.

Once they finally got the apartment in order, Brent pulled on his long coat. Gems continued to weigh down the pockets, and as his nerves heightened, his fingers at once went to the green gem in his front pocket. He traced it once. Even now, it still calmed his nerves; it reminded him to breathe and focus. Whether or not it was magic, he couldn't figure it out. But it helped.

Together, they walked down the road with Nix looping in and out of their heels. Brent found that focusing on random objects helped him stay sane: the lamppost down the road, a bird flying in the sky, and the way Bria spoke, to name a few.

They rounded the bend where the little shop on the corner of Myrtle and Celosia waited. Boards covered the windows. Brent's mind raced; for a moment, he remembered that window shattering, running inside and turning over cases, before settling on the gems now in his pockets.

He also recalled arriving in the shop through that weird silver pool. The shopkeeper boomed in a fit of anger at Brent's arrival, forcing him to leave as he cursed and raved.

To his relief, when they entered the shop, the shopkeeper's wife tended the counter instead.

"Oh!" Her pale face lightened. Despite the clear smile, her eyes hung heavy while involuntary tremors shook her body. "Hello! I didn't think I'd ever see you again, Rho! It's a lovely day brought to us by the Gods of Sol, is it not?"

"Hi, Lex. I'm glad you're better." Bria forced a smile. "I meant to stop in, but...a lot has been going on. I'm sorry about what happened."

Brent glanced at Bria and raised an eyebrow. She hadn't mentioned this to him.

"Oh, it wasn't your fault! I had no way of knowing I had Phantom Rot. In fact, maybe causing the orb to explode was a blessing in disguise! Now I can take care of myself the right way, even if Toddle is a curmudgeon and says otherwise."

Brent glimpsed at the story now. The siren pulled up in front of the shop and wheeled Lex out on a stretcher, covered in silver liquid. She lay there like a paper doll. Her husband chased after her with a child on his hip. Moments later, Bria and Madame Owiti emerged from the backroom.

"What's Phantom Rot?" Bria asked, pulling Brent out of the story.

"Dr. Kafele said it's some degenerative magic disorder. As long as I take my medication, I'll be fine, though. There's no reason to avoid this beautiful, magical world, right?" Lex blathered. "Personally, I am envious of you...and your friend! He's the Story Collector, right?"

"Yes, Brent's the Story Collector." Bria patted his arm.

Brent flushed and tried to hide his face. It was odd talking about magic in the open, even after all the time he'd lost in Mert.

"I really thought I had the gift of sight...but I guess not." Lex sighed. "Perhaps my son does. He plays with his brother all the time, but I can't see him. At least that's what Madame Owiti says." Lex jumped from her trance. "Oh right! You're here to see Madame Owiti! She came by last night and said she'd need to use my tub again. Of course, I allowed her. Toddle threw another fit. The foolish, selfish...oh, never mind him. Please, browse the shop or have a seat or something. You're not imposing! I love company!"

Lex continued rambling, catching them in her net of words. While Bria remained captive in the web, Brent wiggled his way free, redirecting his attention to the stories in the shop. The tale of a man breaking open the window caught his attention, and his own story bled into his soul. Now he saw his destruction in a broken glass case. His fingers reached for the gems in his pockets, a knot of regret pulsating in his stomach. *I can return them now.*

He approached the case as two children raced past him with Nix on their heels. One of the boys had a mist-like quality about him, patting the dog with excitement and smiling at his twin brother.

When they noticed Brent looking at them, the living boy hurried behind one shelf while the mist-like one stayed beside Nix, pointing to a bug on the floor.

"Garrett! Preston! Watch where you're going!" Lex called from the counter.

The living boy peeked out from behind the cases.

"Be careful!"

"It's a'ight," Brent said as he knelt beside the boy. "You playing with my dog?"

Garrett nodded, then pointed to the bug.

"Chasing bugs too?"

"Me and Pres, yeah," the little boy mumbled.

The ghost boy, Preston, bowed his head. He didn't dare look in Brent's direction.

He must be used to no one seeing him. Brent followed the little ant crawling on the floor. "Hey Preston, Garrett, wanna hear a story?"

Both boys turned. Preston's eyes widened while Garrett took his brother's hand and continued beaming.

Brent smiled back. "Let me tell you a story about that little ant there, a'ight? Did you know that there used to be ants the size of dragons! Once upon a time, though, there was an evil scientist in the land where ants were huge. He hated feeling small compared to the ants, so one day, he built a machine to shrink anything bigger than him! With wires and light, the machine came together, and he lured an ant into his laboratory and shrank it down to this tiny-tiny size." Brent pointed at the ant and grinned. "But! The princess disliked the evil man's ways. How dare he defy nature? The scientist laughed, 'Ha ha ha! You can't stop me, Princess!'" Brent threw his voice and cackled. "He captured the princess and hooked her up to the shrinking machine. But what the scientist didn't expect was that the princess understood wires and lights. So at a flick of the switch...the machine buzzed and flinched...until then...then the...I mean the...it....um..."

He closed his eyes. The story rushed out of him so fast, so naturally, but then it came to a grinding halt. The Diabolo mocked him.

What a stupid story, boy.

It's not true.

Liar liar! Into the Pit, you go!

Ants, huge? Give me a break.

"I mean...I...I...the..." He gritted his teeth.

"What happened? What happened?!" the boys asked in unison.

Bria came to Brent's rescue, joining him in the aisle, her hand on his back as she crouched down to the boys. "What do you think happened?"

Garrett hid his face in his hands.

Preston stepped forward and replied, "Maybe the princess made the machine make everything huge and big! So, everyone got big, and the ants and bugs stayed the same size! And then the...so then the ants aren't big, but they're small, and they didn't get hurt at all."

Garrett added, his voice meek, "But the evil scientist stayed small and got even smaller, and the ants ate him!"

"Ants don't eat people!"

"These do!"

The boys bickered. Brent half smiled, but his head and heart hurt. *How could I not finish a story?*

"It's alright," Bria reiterated as she kneaded her hand between his shoulder blades. "You're alright."

"I couldn't finish the story..."

"You're still returning to yourself. It will come back."

Nix licked his hand to reassure him.

Brent climbed to his feet and gulped down the nausea. His eyes were heavy, his heart weighed more, and any time his eyes closed, he saw mere whisps of the past year of his life.

Lex joined them. "That was an adorable story! Why didn't you finish it, though?"

"Oh...um...Preston ended it."

"You saw Preston?!"

"I, um, have...sight." Brent grimaced and fidgeted with his fingers. "Yeah. I can see Preston."

A sadness climbed over Lex's face. She gazed down at Garrett, then at Preston. Her expression remained vacant. "Do both of you have sight?"

"Brent's is stronger than mine," Bria said, "but yes...we do."

Lex's sunny demeanor changed, reminding Brent of a sudden snowstorm. Heartbreak loitered in her face.

"I'm guessing your Phantom Rot doesn't allow you to have sight?" Bria asked.

"Unfortunately..." Her gaze trailed to the windows. "Oh! Toddle is home!"

Brent turned. The sour-faced shopkeeper stood outside the shop with a few bags in his arms. He adjusted something on the lamppost right outside the door, then walked inside, glaring at Brent and Bria with cold stone eyes.

"What're you two doing here?" the man called Toddle barked.

"Toddle! I told you! Madame Owiti is having guests here today!"

"I didn't know it was *them! She* hurt you, Lex!" Todd pointed at Bria, "and *he*," Todd turned to Brent, "stole from us!"

"Blah blah blah. They seem fine now, Toddle!"

"They're criminals!"

Brent spoke up. "Excuse me—"

"What?!" Todd barked.

"Do you...I mean...are these what I stole?" Brent reached into his pockets and removed a handful of gems. He held them out, letting their array of colors glisten. Each one passed on a different array of emotions: his mind drifted between anger, lust, serenity, and passion. He only kept the green gem secure in his pocket. "I'm sorry. I didn't mean...I mean...I didn't mean to take them."

Todd's eyes narrowed. He grabbed Brent by the collar of his shirt and glared at him. The gems toppled to the ground. "What makes *you* think that returning these gems, after a month of HELL, that I will accept some bullshite apology like that!?!"

"Toddle!"

Todd shoved Brent to the ground. At his touch, Todd's story wallowed around him.

Brent's head spun. He saw it all for that brief second of touch: a boy growing up on a farm, a boy's mother dead, a boy joining the guard. The boy became a man.

Then the boy learned to shoot. To kill. To strike.

The boy defied orders.

Branded...

Branded...

Branded...

Brent gasped for air as he toppled backward into a shelf.

"What the shite is your problem, kid?" Todd barked.

"Huh? What did...I mean..." Brent gawked, "Please don't...the story is...it's heavy!"

"I told ya to keep your head outta my story, you fuck-er!"

"I can't. It was so strong and...I mean..."

Todd kicked him again. "You've caused enough SHITE for my family! You destroyed my shop! And then you—" Todd turned to Bria. "You gave my wife Phantom Rot!"

"TODDLE, ENOUGH!" Lex cried out.

Brent hung his head in shame. The two twin boys scurried behind a couple shelves. Nix growled at Todd.

"Stop it!" Bria spat. "You remind me of the Guard back home! You think one person causes all your prob-lems. We're not causing them, though! We're..." She glanced at Brent. "We're leaving. We'll wait outside for Madame Owiti. She can use our apartment instead." She helped Brent climb to his feet, her glare continuing to trace Todd.

"You ain't going nowhere," Todd spat.

As if on cue, the door chimed open behind them.

Brent turned and followed his gaze.

His stomach dropped.

In walked a detective with long blonde hair and piercing eyes.

Todd darted over to the visitor. An uncertainty painted his voice. "Oh, um, hello...Detective Walsh?"

"Mr. Dray, fantastic work," the detective remarked. As she strode in, mist followed her, gathering up around her hair and passing over her face.

Bria gasped beside Brent. "You turned us in!?!"

"TODDLE!" Lex shouted.

Brent didn't hear if Todd responded. He instead approached the detective and squinted. At first, the mist danced around her like a story. But it was fuller, more distinct.

And it kept dancing around her face.

Brent chuckled.

"What is so humorous, young man?" The detective glared.

"Drop the act. This isn't working."

"Pardon?"

Brent waved his hand through the mist, inches from the woman's face. Her skin loosened as the mist dispersed, reshaping into a pointed face with a set of ruby red lips. Her blonde hair turned black, and her eyes dazzled like the sky over the sea.

Brent leaned forward. "Hello, Caroline. How have you been?"

CHAPTER TWENTY-SEVEN

THE ILLUSIONIST'S RETURN

B ria froze. There she stood, their notorious woman in black, the God of Death herself: Caroline, the Eighth Member of the Council of Mist Keepers, the Illusionist. Brent stood over the woman, looking a tad more confident than he had in a long time, glowering close to his old master's face. Nix snarled at her feet.

"Well, hello, Brent." Caroline tossed back her hair. "I am glad you are...you."

"Are you? Are you really?" Brent raised his voice. Bria had never seen him angry like this, his face scrunching up as if he were about to explode. His voice scratched the air. "You left me to die! You didn't care! You could have helped me!"

"That is why I am here. To help."

"*This* is helping?"

"You're here to arrest him!" Bria joined Brent. Heavy mist filled the room, wearing down the shelves and hiding Todd and Lex in the background. She pushed her anger over the shopkeeper to the back of her mind. That was an issue for later.

"Yes, I am here to retrieve him. The Council can help—"

"I've gotten plenty of help! You abandoned me!" Brent's hands shook, continuing to grit his teeth. Bria worried he would erupt like a volcano. She'd never seen him this upset.

"It was hard to track you. You were...erratic." Caroline seemed to choose each word carefully.

"But don't you have work to do? Aren't you Madame Death or whatever? What is...you should have let me be!"

"I cannot let you be."

"Yes, you can!"

"No...I cannot," Caroline reiterated. "You behaving as a lunatic has endangered *me*."

"What are you talking about?"

Caroline shook back her hair. The mist shifted around her, and rather than the proper and prim face of the Goddess of Death, a bloated, drenched, rotting face reminiscent of a sea monster stared back. Only Caroline's striking blue eyes remained while her usually lush hair hung in dead strands at her side. "This is who I really am. When I died, I drowned, and my body withered away. The mist reclaimed me as a monster, and my illusions helped transform me back into my youthful self. But now, my magic is festering. I am fading because the mist has a new fixation. I cannot do my routes. You should have died six months ago. But you are here, and I am fading like one of your stories."

Anger bubbled inside of Bria, listening to Caroline. "This is all about you, isn't it? So, you can look...pretty?! I should have known you never cared about Brent! You didn't help back in Newbird's Arm, because you're a selfish, lying—" She shook her head, unable to finish the sentence. Brent placed a hand on her shoulder, and Bria recollected herself. "So it's you, a three hundred something-year-old woman, or Brent, someone who has his life ahead of him? That doesn't seem right!"

"No! It is Brent or the hundreds and thousands of souls I cannot release!"

"Bullshite. You can still conduct releases." Brent said.

"It is getting harder to do on my own."

Bria continued to dance on burning coals, her anger turning into tremors. "Then why can't others help? There's a whole Council! It doesn't make sense that one person would be in charge of the world!"

"It is more complicated than that, Bria."

"Is it? Or is it a spoon-fed lie like the rest of this?"

Caroline stared at the floor.

Brent interjected, "I'm able to release souls. I've been doing it...I can do it. Aren't I still a Mist Keeper, even if I'm not dead? I mean...why can't I still be a Mist Keeper?"

"You should be dead," Caroline stated.

"But I'm not. The curse hasn't killed me."

"Hence, the mist is struggling."

Bria struggled to believe Caroline. All of this seemed like a lure to her, a way to play on Brent's emotions. He always thought of others before himself; this was bait.

But Brent's confidence remained. "Do you really believe that?"

"It is what Ningursu says is true."

"Yeah, but do you believe it?"

Caroline said nothing.

Bria glanced at Brent. He kept his composure, though the exhaustion in his face showed he was losing focus. *Come on, Brent, hold your ground. I have faith in you. You can do this.*

"Brent, please," Caroline begged, her voice bubbling as if she was still underwater, rotting away like her face. "Come with me. We can talk about this. The Council wants to help you—"

"No! Stop lying!" Brent shook his head, taking a few steps back. "Your story... you're lying! You wanna...you wanna get rid of me! You wanna...the Diabolo...you fear the Diabolo. But it's too late. You can't hide it from your enemies...you can't hide it because they know, and I don't care! I'm not... you're not allowed to... you're lying!"

He collapsed on the ground, holding his head. Nix ran over and licked his hand. Bria knelt beside him and kneaded his knuckles, pressing her forehead against his brow. "Deep breaths. It's okay."

"They just wanna...they just wanna take me...eradicate and...and... they're scared of the Diabolo and the magic and...they want it gone." He sniffed. "Caroline doesn't understand it, but the mist... it's strong. It's like there's another person dancing around her and...and...I think Ningursu is watching."

Bria glared at Caroline. "Leave."

"I cannot."

"Yes, you can! If you care about Brent like you claim, you'll leave him be."

"Even if I wanted to, I cannot."

"Then we will." Bria helped Brent off the floor and marched towards the shop exit with Nix on her heels. The mist had finally settled, leaving a strange residue on the ground. Past it all, she glanced back at Todd, who gawked in their direction. His wife and kids waited in the half-opened curtain as if frozen by a spell.

"I cannot let you do that either. Please. Let us talk," Caroline pleaded, her voice cracking. Her face continued to droop as she spoke, her blue eyes shimmering with nerves and anger. "Please. Just talk with me. Let me explain."

Bria turned, but Brent stayed, gazing at Caroline. He reached into his pocket and pulled out his green gem, running it through his fingers.

"Brent? What's wrong?" Bria tugged at his arm.

"Run."

"What?"

"I said run—"

A whirring drowned out the rest of his sentence. Caroline's jaw unhinged, and out spiraled a deep smoke wrapping around her face like a tornado taking form in the little shop. A new mask took place on her head of a half-skeletal face with one white eye and one missing.

Even though Bria never met him before, she knew right away who it was: the pernicious leader of the Council himself, the supposed God of Death, Ningursu.

The skull turned towards her, calm in appearance, though his one eye marked anger she had never seen in anyone else. No, not anger. Fury.

Ningursu opened his mouth. A chain woven of smoke exploded from his teeth, spiraling out of the shelves and lunging towards Brent. Bria moved faster, pushing him to the ground. And like the winds of a tornado, the chain broke open the front window of the shop.

"Brenton, the Diabolo is not gone. Come back. We'll help," Ningursu prodded, his voice overlapping Caroline's in an echo. "I feel it inside of you. It is betraying you. You are not well. Kek and their disgusting Magii have always despised Mist Keepers. Why would they help you when they would rather see the Council destroyed?"

Brent rose. The rage in his face matched Ningursu's, and Bria saw a yellow tinge flourishing in his eye. But he owned it, wearing it as a cape to propel his own confidence. "After everything that has happened, why should I trust you?"

"I only want you to succeed."

"No, you don't. You want...you want YOU to succeed. And I'm in the way of some grand idea or some shite...because I don't want to be a Mist Keeper, and I'm refusing to fucking die!"

"Why do you not want to join us, Brenton? Is it because of her?"

Bria stiffened as Ningursu stared at her. A low hum ripped through the back of her ears, pricking at her little branch. Her heart raced, fear seeping over her. *Not again. Please don't. Please, not again.*

"She's a threat, Brenton. To you. To the world. Didn't you see what she did in Newbird's Arm? Then she had the audacity to block the tunnels to prevent us from helping you. She is selfish. And you are suffering."

Brent cursed back, but to Bria, they sounded far away. The buzzing grew deafening, and the room shook. Kek had opened her back up to her magic, and now, she paid the price. She felt the minerals in potion vials, the cracks in the walls, and the trees crackling outside the shop. Everything wrapped around her. She suffocated, and she wanted to cry, to scream.

Hold back. If you give in to the pain, he controls you.

Count the lights.

The surrounding mist thickened; no, not mist, a putrid smog that might as well have blocked out the last ray of sunlight. Past it all, Bria counted the lanterns on the ceiling.

One...two...three...

Ningursu's voice echoed, repeating phrases in a foreign tongue. Did Brent hear it? Was she alone?

Four...five...six...

It was as if a Diabolo was standing right beside her.

She prayed it wasn't Brent.

Seven...eight...nine...

Finally, Ningursu's voice echoed in her ear, hissing. "Come, Briannabella. Let lose like you always wanted. It's bubbling inside of you."

Ten lanterns.

You can't control me. I know there are ten lanterns.

"I'm not a puppet!" Bria screamed and threw her arms back. A tree branch blasted through the walls, knocking down all ten lanterns while sending glass shattering and wood flying. Vines crawled through the already broken windows with roots pummeling beneath the floor. Whatever spell had captured Todd momentarily broke, and his cursing ripped through the air.

Nix howled and ran about the room in circles.

Bria fell back with the force, collecting dust in the air with the mist. She saw Brent run forward out of the corner of her eye. He pushed Caroline to the ground, sending the skeletal illusion shifting in every which direction. The pounding in Bria's head ceased, and with her confusion fleeing, the floral chaos of fauna and earth retreated.

She breathed out.

But she didn't rest for long.

Brent darted back over and helped Bria to her feet.

"Are you still you?" Bria patted Brent's cheeks. "You're still Brent?"

"For now, yeah, but we gotta go. Before Caroline gets the mask back...we gotta go."

Bria agreed.

Before the two of them stepped through the broken rubble, Todd approached them, climbing over the fallen shelves and Caroline's contorting body. He held a pistol in his hands, nostrils flaring, mouth pulled back in a sneer. "Where are you two going?"

Brent flinched. "Please. We're not...we don't mean to... we're not your enemy."

"You stole from me! Destroyed my shop! Sent my wife to the hospital! I fucking hate all you damn Magii and shite, and now...you better stay here so I can turn you into the coppers or...or...or..."

Bria wiggled her fingers. A few vines climbed off the walls, snagging Todd by his wrists and pulling him into the air. Another branch slapped the pistol to the ground. He hung in the air by his arms, kicking his feet while spewing vulgarities Bria didn't even recognize.

"I'm sorry," Bria whispered.

"You two are gonna pay for—"

With another flick of Bria's fingers, the vines covered Todd's mouth, leaving him repeating muffled phrases.

"C'mon, we gotta get out of here." Brent took her hand. In his palm still rested that green gem. This time, Bria sensed the magic loitering in the gem's heart. It pulsed through her, relaxing her nerves and pulling her away from the fear left by Ningursu's voice.

Nix raced out the door in front of them, and together, they fled from the shop and away from the impending mist.

CHAPTER TWENTY-EIGHT

TERRORIZED

B rent sprinted down an alleyway on the western end of Celosia with Bria. His head spun. The stories danced around him, filling his thoughts and clawing at his skin. Nix bounded around him in circles, mimicking his own anxiety.

"Why can't they leave you alone?" Bria panted.

"I didn't get a read on the story...Caroline, I mean... she's been kind of wrapped up in all of this. Ningursu has a grip on her..." Brent flinched. "He doesn't like Magii. But I hardly know anything about him. I mean...he wants control and all...and...shite."

"But he can't control *you*?"

"I dunno how his magic works. But if he could, he should've been able to make me obey. Like what he almost did with you…" Brent pushed back a strand of Bria's sweat-riddled hair, glancing at her little branch. It had healed since Ningursu cut it for his own advantage, but there remained a fear in the air. Brent asked, "Are you okay?"

"I'm fine."

"Bri."

Bria nodded, sadness drifting across her face. "I'm okay, really. It was frightening, but I'm okay now. Really."

"Promise?"

"Promise."

Brent looked at her hard one last time. It'd be easy to tell if she was lying, but he held himself back from reading the stories. It was easier said than done with so many spinning around the boardwalk and through the city. The mist thickened with each passing moment, blocking the late afternoon sky with thunderheads and smog.

Brent glanced at Bria. "What…what can we do? I mean, the tunnels aren't an option. If we stay here, the Council will…I mean, they'll terrorize Mert."

Bria focused for a moment. "We can't run. Not again…"

"What do you mean?"

"In Newbird's Arm...after the Diabolo...I fled. I'm wanted now, Brent, and I can't go home."

Brent stared at her. "And if we abandon Mert after the same chaos, it'll be the same story. History repeats." He sank back against the boardwalk, his heart rate rising. The mist grew thicker with every fleeting moment. "What can we do, though?"

"We should probably get to Kek and the others. They can help," Bria whispered.

Brent nodded. With every second of deeper smoke, his mind swirled. His hair stood on end; he sensed something deep in the core of the city. What was it? The Council? Something bigger?

Or just the stories spinning around him?

"Brent, you okay?" Bria asked as they climbed to their feet.

"Yeah."

"Do you need another dosage of the medication before we get moving?" Bria reached into her bag.

Brent shook his head, squeezing the green gem tight in his hand. "No. I've... I'm a'ight. I think I'm just...the adrenaline is high or something."

Really, Brent had no clue how he'd kept his head together through all of this. The stories spun in circles, leaving his stomach churning, but he kept a grip on his identity. But he didn't want Bria to worry.

My name is Brent Harley.

I am not Kip of Mert, the old merchant selling bow ties.

I am Brent Harley. The Mist Keeper.

I am here.

After a few more moments to catch their breaths, Brent followed Bria into the shadow of the trees and buildings, hiding from the clouds above, watching with Ningursu's detrimental gaze. The only place to go was the Sanitorium to seek Kek's help.

To Brent's relief, parts of the city remained untouched by the chaos on the corner of Myrtle and Celosia. Other than the storm clouds, all remained quiet.

Brent only hoped that what happened in the little shop wouldn't extend into the City Centre.

He and Bria said little as they ran. Bria wove him in and out of alleyways, avoiding the bustling walkways. While the wind bellowed, most city folk minded their own business, interested more in the wares of the shops or their day-to-day conversations.

They didn't avoid the City Centre, though. Bria tugged Brent through the merchants and crowds. Unlike in the winding streets, the wind here was stronger, catching papers and goods, sending them flying in the air. Many patrons stopped in the middle of the square with their attention fixated on an airship rising behind the City Hall. Brent slowed, catching their gazes.

The airship struggled during its ascent into the air, spinning with each gust of wind. A few times, the ship nosedived before stabilizing with a sigh of relief. Brent held his breath for a long moment, his knuckles tightening as he clenched the gem in his hand before finally, the airship passed through the clouds.

This isn't just wind.

Brent didn't have time to ponder it further as Bria tugged him towards the white beacon of the Sanitorium. Finally, they were safe!

No.

Brent's moment of excitement vanished with the next step forward. Beneath his feet, the ground shook.

"The tunnels..." Bria stiffened. "That's coming from the tunnels. I can feel it."

"What is it?"

"I don't know. They're shaking, though. And they're...following us. Come on...this way!" Bria tugged Brent around the outside of the Sanitorium towards the canal. The trees along the walkways swerved back and forth. As they reached the edge of the water, one of the tallest trees toppled over, hitting the spot where they had just stood. Uprooted, it left a gaping hole in the path.

Nix howled.

Seconds later, a thick yellow mist, wreaking of iron and sulfur, poured from it.

Brent froze.

He recognized that mist. That smell.

It haunted him for months. It remained tethered to his heart.

His soul bathed in it daily.

His knees buckled as the mist climbed higher over the city.

A new Diabolo with its monstrous smile, its elongated fingernails, and gnarled body rose from the steam. It bore a new face with a nose too large for its body, yellow eyes crossed, and no hair along its head. Laughter exited its mouth in a high-pitched moan while its stories—its nightmares—danced around it.

And the Diabolo in his head cackled along with the song.

Go back to it. It's calling to you now.

You would become the strongest of them all.

Join it.

Go.

"Fuck off!" Brent threw back his arms and stumbled backward, nearly falling backward into the canal. His green gem flew from his hand.

Bria picked it up and rushed over to him, pushing it again into his palm. "Focus."

"I'm trying."

"Harder. I won't lose you to the monster again."

Brent gritted his teeth. *Right. Focus. I know who I am.*

Yeah, you belong with the monster. Go to it.

No.

Brent trailed behind Bria as she walked towards the bridge crossing over the canal and into the black-and-white tulip-covered plains. Nix bolted ahead, stopped, turned around until they caught up, then raced ahead once again.

As they reached the edge of the plains, another tremble ripped through the ground.

More trees fell, lightning struck from the air, and yellow smog covered the tops of every building in Mert.

"There's more than one!" Brent shouted over the wind. "How's there more than one?!"

Bria yelled back, "Weren't there multiple jars?"

"Yes, but this is...why are they doing this? It can't be because of me..."

"Varden mentioned a treaty, didn't he?"

"And it's broken."

"See? This isn't just about you."

"No... it's war." Brent's stomach turned as the words exited his lips. This was all his fault. He climbed into that cellar beneath the library. He set the first Diabolo free. And he attempted to save Newbird's Arm despite not knowing a thing about the monster. Because he had to act on impulse over thought, he dragged Bria to Mert and exposed them both to Kek and the Council.

But that didn't mean the deaths that followed were on his hands; the world was always a mess.

Maybe he'd just uncovered it.

"They're going to destroy Mert. All the magic here... everyone's at risk." Bria's voice fell. "What do we do?"

"I...I dunno..."

Of course, you don't! You're a stupid freak! You know nothing!

Give yourself to the Diabolo already, boy.

It's not like you can tell a story, anyway.

"Shut it," he hissed at the voices. "I CAN tell a story!"

"What're you talking about?" Bria asked.

"Sorry...I mean...I...I could tell a story."

"Brent..."

"No, no, listen..." Brent forced himself to recall. "Back in Newbird's Arm, with Caroline, there was a day with the Diabolo. When we tried to capture it, I created a story from the mist, and it got distracted by it and all. I'm not gonna try absorbing the story again; I couldn't right now. But if I distracted it and sent it off in another direction away from Mert, it might disperse. Like...a small storm is easier to weather than...than this..."

He jumped as a thunderclap stormed through the air. Another Diabolo spiraled out of the mist, wearing a half-formed jaw upon its head.

Bria stared at him. He saw the gears turning in her head, the fear in her eyes. Her lips trembled with her next words. "I don't want to lose you again."

Brent stroked back her hair. "You won't. I'm here. I'm not going anywhere."

A beat of silence passed. Then another. And one more.

"Okay," Bria whispered. "But...you need to get to higher ground."

Brent glanced towards the city. Yellow smoke continued to pummel over the buildings. "We don't have time."

"Brent—"

"Bria—"

"Let me at least get you into the trees, please?"

"Oh, um... a'ight."

Bria took his hand, and with a tug, a branch wrapped around them from a nearby oak. It hoisted them up high into its branches, overlooking the tulips, watching over the canal, and peering into the city. The tree's limbs twisted together to form a platform.

"Be careful," Bria whispered.

"I'll be a'ight, I promise." He glanced back at Bria, then stepped forward onto the platform above the tulips. "Because... I'm gonna tell you a story."

CHAPTER TWENTY-NINE

THE STORM OF STORIES

Bria gripped the tree, listening to Nix bark from the ground and watching Brent balance at the edge of the platform overlooking the city. He straightened his back and opened his hands wide to the world. Out of his palms exploded droves of mist. It trickled like a drizzle, then with a single thunderclap, boomed like a storm. A story of a war fought out of the foliage, breaking free to decorate the landscape and paint the sky. Warriors marched across all the land and into the city. Decked in white and black, like chess pieces, they came together to spread words of love against hate. The characters shouted with the wind, and with each blade crashing, the mist twirled.

The story shifted. Behind each of the armies soared a dragon, each with a sorcerer on their back. The dragons breathed fire and smoke while the sorcerers sent magic tricks over the armies. From the black side, the sorcerer decorated the sky in fireworks in the shapes of flowers and victory. On the white, the sorcerer spread music through their fingertips, capturing the sky in a melody. They fought alongside their armies, and in their wake, they cast aside all normalcy for nothing but magic and pride.

No suffering took place, but the story created that ongoing illusion of chaos. Airships teetered in the air, some spiraling to the ground while others climbed to the sky. Were they a part of the story? Were people falling? Did the screams in the distance exist? Stories and reality became one melting pot. What did the people in the city see? What went through Brent's head? What part of the past came rising from the ashes as the stories continued, beckoning the Diabolo to follow? What was real? What was fiction?

Was this how Brent felt?

But despite the tales, the storm over Mert didn't shift, churning with prowess.

Brent continued mouthing a story, the tale growing more vivid with the passing moment. His eyes glossed over, his entire body trembled, and his knees gave out.

The story didn't yield.

But neither did the Diabolo.

Even as the minutes turned to hours.

Bria did not turn away as Brent clamored to his feet, continuing to mouth words. While the story carried on endlessly, its veracity vanished. Whales flying through the sky, warriors riding on ostriches, and ants the size of elephants joined the sorcerers. With each passing moment, reality crumbled beneath Brent's obtuse tale.

He can't keep this going forever. Bria's skin crawled as two of the ostrich warriors became embattled with the giant ants. *I have to help him.*

Brent cackled from his spot on the platform, falling back for a second before refocusing on the story in the field.

"Dammit, Brent!" Bria shouted after him, but the storm carried her voice away. The sky wreaked of the stories but also of a brewing rain, dancing with natural gusts of wind. The storm beat in her heart, rising through her like the thrill of a huntress catching her first beast.

It's a part of nature. I can help.

She ascended higher into the oak tree's canopy. From the top, rain beat from the clouds, pounding on her forehead. The wind wrapped around her hair, sending her scarf twisting behind her in the wind.

I am Rhodana. I am the Forest Queen.

I feel everything.

Yes, she sensed as the storm ripped through the world. The ground trembled beneath the prowess of the monsters, and the clouds cried in fear. The Diabolo spoke in rhythms of lightning and thunder.

Bria held her hand out to the storm. She spoke back to it.

You're just crying. Let it go. Be free. Set yourself free.

The wind picked up with her fear.

With her nervous laughter, the thunder grumbled through the sky.

She reached through the tree and into the earth below while craning her neck to the storm. While the sky wailed, the earth climbed; the tulips in the field opened wide, and the wind rocked their petals with fury. As the wind gathered the seeds, Bria ordered them to birth saplings, sending newborn trees and flowers spiraling into the stories.

Magic lived; it plodded, it showed. The ground cracked open. Roots scrambled from the earth and danced with the storm.

And while the storm moved to Bria's whim, the Diabolo turned away from the city and towards the Chessboard Plains.

Come on. Come on! A little further!

She balanced on the branches, holding her hands out as if pulling on a rope, lassoing around the storm to bring it closer. The thunder roared with her scream. Lightning bolted across the sky, dancing on the ground.

At least twelve Diabolo marched away from Mert. They howled as the storm pulled away from them, and their obscenities chanted across the landscape as they arrived in the heart of Brent's bizarre story on the plains. Rain battered, the wind swirled in circles, and more lightning struck again.

Bria's heart raced, and her head spun. She was the storm ravaging the plains; she was the lightning striking the sky, and she was the thunder unloading its anger in the air.

I am everything.

She straightened her back, unleashing the last bit of the storm. No, not just a storm, but a hurricane across the landscape. Tulips flew, branches fluttered, and stories soared.

With another crack of thunder, the lightning split open the sky. It hit the ground inches from Bria's tree, missing Nix and setting the grass ablaze.

Her nerves ran rampant. Her stomach churned. Tears dotted her cheeks.

And the sky cried with her.

Despite the rain, the Diabolo continued to move towards her.

"Brent! Send them off already!" Bria shouted over the wind.

Brent didn't reply, but she saw his eyes light up, and he mouthed a few more words. With a sudden wave of his hand, the story changed. Out of the storm rode the whales, the ostriches, and the sorcerers on the back of dragons; they ran in at least sixty different directions, away from Mert like criminals fleeing from the scene of a crime. The Chessboard armies followed.

Confusion struck the Diabolo as they followed the stories. Every which way they, turned in circles. Were they trying to decide where to go? Who to follow?

The Diabolo let out pitiful shrieks, childlike, before spiraling into the sky wrapped in the storm. With another detrimental scream of thunder, the storm parted, sending clouds in every direction across the sky, carrying an ugly tint of yellow upon their surface.

A clear sky emerged through the clouds. Tulip petals fluttered by in the breeze.

Bria sighed, letting the remaining vines and roots fall. She jumped out of the tree, landing on the last few embers of fire. They fizzled at her feet. With a single wave of her hand, the tree lowered its platform to the ground. Brent slid off it and onto the charred grass where Nix waited, her tail wagging as she bounded in his direction.

"Brent?!" Bria limped over Brent and Nix.

"Heh...ostriches..." He laughed into Nix's fur.

"Brent...are you okay? Please be okay. Please tell me you're okay."

He opened his eyes. Still silver.

Still him.

His laughter continued to rock the air. "You ever noticed how weird ostriches are? They're kinda terrifying. I mean, like...are they even birds? They just...run around with their long necks. Ostriches, Bri, ostriches!"

"Oh, thank goodness." Bria knelt beside him, her own energy fleeing like the storm overhead. Her head pounded, and her eyes hung with exhaustion, but one thing was certain: he was still Brent Harley.

And they'd won this battle.

CHAPTER THIRTY

ALOBY

Jemma thought her worries would be over once they crossed through the Newbird Mountain range into the Opal Region. Yet the voyage proved more than she expected. Every bump in the road caused nausea to climb through her stomach and into her throat. Over the course of their two days' worth of travel, she told Micca to pull over at least every other hour to gag on the side of the road.

By the second day, after spending the night in some profuse tavern on the side of the road, Jemma spent most of her waking hours dreading the next bout of nausea. Even Micca's incessant chatter did little to keep her nerves at bay. It didn't help that, frankly, Micca was a terrible driver. He wove on and off the road, buckling through the forest and swamp, then kicking up dust behind him as they crossed into the plains. He babbled on and on about his time in the Pit and remarked on old classmates, never taking a chance to let the subject develop naturally.

"Y'know," Micca continued, rambling as they turned onto a smooth paved road, "I heard something. Someone said Captain Carver and his meathead son are still alive somewhere and up in the Capitol. Mighta thought it was stupid if it came from a vag, but a guard back in Newbird said somethin' about Captain Carver's orders and all. Plus, there was a photo in the newspaper in that town yesterday. Did you see? It had Senator Cordova on there with a guard at his side. Funny fellow with a bushy mustache...but he got those creepy Captain Carver eyes. Too blurry to make out, though. Wouldn't surprise me if they survived all that madness, yeah?"

Jemma squirmed in place, focusing more on the queasiness in her stomach than what Micca said. "It is a possibility. Oh, dear—pull over!"

Micca slammed his breaks. Jemma leaned out the window, upchucking her lunch before pressing her head against the door.

"Ya a'ight?" Micca asked, a softness in his voice.

"Are we almost at Opal's Canyon? This trip has been disastrous." Opal's Canyon marked the halfway point between Ab Aeterno and Newbird's Arm. If she could make it there, then Ab Aeterno would only be a few more days of travel. She had to take each leg one bit at a time; she had to cling to what was in view.

Like the Effluvium.

And soon, the mythical tower of Ab Aeterno would be more than a figment of her imagination.

"Eh. Another day or so, probably. We're gonna have to stop for the night. I think Aloby is up ahead from the map I looked at back this morning in the tavern."

Jemma settled into the seat and closed her eyes again, trying to imagine she was sitting on her parents' porch reading scripture while her father smoked his pipe and read the paper. Her mother would return from the fields as the sun set, angered by the vagrants or bantering with a vagabond traveling through town. Life used to be so simple.

Why did Jemma put herself in this situation?

She held her eyes shut for the rest of the trip, ignoring Micca's babbling. He really wasn't that bad of a fellow; a little vulgar, sure, but not what she ever considered a vagrant.

Granted, she never considered Brent Harley as one either.

Micca slowed the truck to a halt behind a hill within a ten-minute walk away from Aloby. The town glistened in the distance like a mirage, bordering along the legendary canyon that carved the land in two.

The tension Jemma had harbored the past two days loosened as she climbed out of the truck. Her grip on her bag eased, and her shoulders relaxed. She walked a few paces away from Micca in silence, following the road along the canyon. The town in the distance didn't bustle with the exuberance of Newbird's Arm, but it was far livelier than the villages they'd encountered during the journey. Even from the distance, she saw a small tower gazing over the town with the signature gray uniforms of the guard walking along the outskirts of town.

Micca grew visibly more distraught with each step, his gaze falling towards the canyon. Jemma hadn't taken a moment to marvel at the beauty of it; glistening stones coated the walls of the canyon while shrubs grew along the sides. But as much as Jemma marveled at it, she couldn't figure out what Micca saw.

Jemma joined him at the edge of the canyon. "What is it?"

"Look."

"Yes, it is lovely—" Jemma peered down into the canyon. Her jaw dropped.

Yes, it was true; the canyon sparkled with iridescent stones that painted the walls like a rainbow. But, further down below in the canyon, hundreds of vagrants worked on the ledges. Their houses, made of clay and soil, sat perched over the edge, with old garments waving in the breeze. A few bodies hung over the edges, slipping...falling...

Into the piles of corpses at the bottom of the canyon.

"I guess the Pit's literally a pit here, eh?" Micca's jovial tone had vanished.

Jemma nodded, unsure how to respond. The canyon wreaked of demons, of the Effluvium's damned and of half-deserved death. Surely, under the Effluvium's guise, only the worst met such a cruel fate.

This canyon made Newbird's Pit seem like a paradise.

Micca stared for a few moments longer, then turned back toward town. Jemma followed. She redirected her attention to the setting sun as it cast an orange glow over the buildings, turning the walls of the clay houses from beige to gold.

Despite the putrid livelihoods existing mere steps away, the town of Aloby continued to buzz. Hums crossed their lips, rocking through the streets towards the small Temple perched in the center of town. Jemma gazed at it in awe. It wasn't as big as the one in Newbird's Arm, carrying instead the welcoming arms of the Effluvium. The Year Glass gazed above everyone, the last few days of the year trickling down the sides of the fixture.

Year Birth was days away now. Soon, everything would be reborn.

Jemma didn't realize how much she missed it. Newbird's Arm had been suffering; here in Aloby, people basked in the Effluvium's embrace.

It's so beautiful. The Effluvium will bless Newbird's Arm again someday. And I will lead it home. She kissed her fingers and raised them up towards the Year Glass.

"The fuck are you doing, Jem?" Micca prodded beside her, squinting at the Year Glass.

"Praying." She stared at Micca. "Do you not pray?"

Micca crossed his arms over his chest. "What's the Effluvium ever done for me?"

"Maybe if you prayed a bit more, you wouldn't have ended up in the Pit. Besides, you could have had it worse. You could have ended up...here...in the canyon."

Micca's face soured, and he spat, "You don't know nothing about why I was there. And don't go belittling the ones here either. You know shite!"

"You smoked and vandalized the Temple!"

"That's only half of it."

"Then pray tell, why were you in the Pit for four years, Micca?"

"Because of my pa." Whatever happy façade Micca usually wore vanished, replaced instead with the seriousness of a man locked away for years. He looked older than twenty-two, his brown eyes like mud, his lips forming a straight line on his mouth.

"Your father?" Jemma scoffed.

"You remember the vandalism and shite that I was accused of, yeah? That ain't my fault. Yeah, I smoke, and I like them good tonics and serums, but I ain't a vandal. That was my pa."

"Why would your father vandalize the Temple?"

"Cause he was having some shellshock shite!"

Jemma blinked. She heard rumors of men suffering from shellshock after the Smoke Riots over twenty years ago. Everyone knew about the Smoke Riots, the infamous altercation between the men of Knoll and the rest of Rosada. No one agreed on who won; there was no true victor. Men returned from the riots in anguish, giving into vices and abolishing virtue. Over time, most of those men vanished, either locked away in the Pits or taken by their own insanity. "If he is shell-shocked, then why wasn't he in the Pit in the first place?"

"Cause it don't work like you think it does! One day, I came home from the market, and he was kind of throwing a fit. Went on like that for weeks. Ma tried to calm him and all. I followed him one night and saw him vandalize the Temple, crying like he was back in Knoll during the Smoke Riots or something crazy like that! So, I sent him home, the Guard caught me, and end of story. I was probably gonna end up there anyway, so whatever, y'know. Ma sent Pa to an institute far away to help his head. He came back two years later while I was still in the Pit and don't remember nothing. So, if you wanna think those of us in the Pit belong there cause we're some sort of demon shite, then so be it. Just shows you ain't no better than Elder Don Van and the Carvers and shite like that."

Jemma glanced away from Micca. "I'm sorry, Micca. I didn't know."

"Yeah, well, now you do." Micca turned. "I'mma get a drink at the hostel we passed a few streets back. I'll see you later."

Jemma held up her hand to stop him, then lowered it, watching as Micca turned on his heels and trampled down the road.

A part of her always knew the vagrants didn't deserve their treatment. Well, most of them didn't. Yet, they carried that stench of addiction and slander to a point where she often looked down at them like insects beneath the tips of her feet. Her parents belittled them in conversation. The kids threw rocks at the Pit's wall, and everyone spat at those with the black stamp.

She wanted to prove, back during her betrothal, that she could change a vagrant.

Jemma never believed Brent was bad; he was just too far in his own head. Was he deserving of the Pit? Probably not. But did he welcome the Effluvium? Not quite. Now, as far as everyone was concerned, Brent Harley was dead.

It wasn't too late for Micca.

Jemma darted after him. She wouldn't lose him to his vices.

She wove between the roads queuing back to the hostel at the entrance to town. It was a small place with a worn-down sign and guards crowding the entranceway. She kept her head down as she passed them. One guard whistled at her while another beckoned for her with drunken words.

Jemma didn't make eye contact. Her heart pounded in her ears as she walked past them.

It didn't get much better inside the hostel. Other than the Guard, individuals clad in scandalous clothing passed around drinks and smokes. Micca sat in a corner talking with a red-headed man. They laughed together as Micca removed a little wind-up toy before downing a glass of whisky.

She took a seat at the far end of the counter, where she could observe Micca. As soon as she sat down, the bartender rushed over to her, a grin spreading ear-to-ear.

"What'cha pretty lass like ya doing here?" He leaned forward. His breath smelled of smoke.

"I'm here with a friend," Jemma retorted.

"Ah, yeah, *sure*. Ya want a drink or something? Ya look like ya need one."

"I'm fine. Thank you."

"Ya sure?" He tilted his head to the side, his eyes piercing Jemma.

She recoiled. "Yes. I am sure. Please leave me alone."

The bartender raised his hands and walked away, grumbling to himself as he tended to a guard on the other end of the counter.

Jemma stayed in her spot for a bit, watching Micca from the corner of her eye and sending the bartender away each time he made an advance. She wasn't afraid of these men and women, but the squalor of the tavern caused her stomach to boil. A pungent odor of sweat and liquor danced in the air, tainting the Effluvium. The patrons harmed it more than the vagrants in the Pit, dancing with their vices and tossing aside the virtues.

Micca and his red-headed friend eventually rose and vanished up a set of stairs, leaving Jemma alone in the hostel. She debated following them upstairs, waiting by their door, and cornering Micca when he emerged but decided against it.

Instead, she left the tavern, taking a seat by the rim of the canyon. She didn't see the vagrants below, eaten away by the darkness. It contrasted the sky's beauty. The stars sparkled with passion out here, far more than the smoggy atmosphere of Newbird's Arm. Unlike the greenery that wove its way through her home, the area around Aloby was brown and dead. Not even an owl hooted, nor did a cricket chirped.

Empty. Lifeless.

Mundane.

Jemma didn't have magic to bless it with life, but she had one thing: The Effluvium. Quietly, she whispered a nighttime prayer into the darkness, begging that green would one day return to the fields of Aloby.

Goodnight, old son,
Goodnight, old lass,
Sleep well, tucked in,
While the Effluvium does pass,
Into dreams
And horrors, more
It'll rock you,
Bless you,
And keep you tight.
So breathe,
Believe,

Even at night.

She bowed her head, mumbling her prayer over, setting her mind onto a peaceful blanket in her head. The Effluvium waited as it always did; she would be in its embrace soon.

"SHOVE 'EM! KICK 'EM!"

Jemma's trance broke, and she glanced down the road. At least twelve men and three women gathered in a circle by the hostel, cheering and cursing up a storm.

"Get 'em!"

"Show those damn vags what they're in for!"

"Kick 'em! KICK 'EM!"

Jemma rushed over and pushed her way through the crowd. Guards with steel-toed boots kicked two men on the ground. One was the man with stunning red hair. The other, without a doubt, was Micca.

She restrained a scream.

"You damn vags know by now...this ain't the place for your tomfoolery!" One guard kicked Micca in the stomach.

"You don't got no money! No dignity! Go back to fucking around in the Canyon!"

Jemma burst into the center of the commotion. "Stop! That's my friend! You cannot harm him!"

"Step aside, lass," a guard with a curly mustache ordered. "Don't go defending vags like this."

"I am a Sister of the Order! You cannot treat my friend like this!"

"Oh, yes? Prove it."

"I have an official Year Glass right here." She reached into her bag. "Look—" Her eyes widened. Instead of pulling out her Year Glass, she'd removed her father's pistol from her bag.

Another guard with yellow hair laughed. "Oh, yeah, that's definitely proof, m'dear. Do you even know how to use that?"

"I—"

The guard with the curly mustache grabbed Jemma's arm, pulling the pistol from her hands and throwing it to the side. His comrade lifted Micca and the red-headed man up by their hair.

"It's time for ya'll to get back to the Canyon where you belong."

"I'm not a vagrant!" Jemma shouted.

The guards ignored her, dragging her away from the tavern. One of them rummaged through her bag, pocketing the money she brought. Another tossed her Year Glass on the ground. It shattered in pieces, the silver liquid inside seeping into the ground.

Jemma's head spun. She lost track of Micca as the group grew, with at least fifteen guards joining in the commotion. The Guards passed her between themselves. They touched her, unpinned her hair, and pulled at the buttons on her dress. Each scream came with further detriment. She wanted it to be a nightmare, to end, to wake up at home. *I'm sorry, Ma! I'm sorry, Pa! I shouldn't have left! I'm sorry!*

The guards continued to toss her around like a rag doll. She begged as they teased her with threats of humiliation.

The Effluvium will protect you. It'll protect you. They are just a bunch of drunken guards.

You are safe.

To Jemma's relief, despite the Guard's threats and unwarranted touches, the Effluvium sheltered her from the vilest deeds.

It listened as Jemma screamed, and wallowed, and begged, and cried. Their touches stopped, replaced with a single nudge. The Guards threw her down the steps and into the Canyon.

Jemma hit the ground with a thud. Her head hurt, her heart rang, her body throbbed, and her lips ached. Would she ever be able to speak again? The guards' hands on her left an odd ghost of fear itching across her body.

Micca and his friend landed beside her.

"Enjoy your stay, *Sister*." The guard with a curly mustache cackled. "Maybe we'll have more fun next time we see you."

Before she moved, the Guard marched back up the stairs and slammed the gate shut.

Jemma clutched the ground, digging her nails into the dirt. *I wish I had Bria's magic. I wish I could just destroy this entire Canyon.* She shook her head. *Don't be ridiculous. That would insult the Effluvium.*

"Hey, Jem…" Micca crawled over to her.

"Go away." She snarled. "I don't want to talk to you!"

"I just wanted to thank you for, y'know, standing up for me back—"

"GO AWAY, MICCA FEIN! IF YOU JUST BEHAVED YOURSELF, NONE OF THIS WOULD HAPPEN!"

Micca stared at her. "I didn't break any rules—"

"You should've stayed in the room, not flaunt your stamp. Then we would be fine!" Jemma climbed to her feet, shaking. "You couldn't keep your head down!"

Micca rose to meet her. His nostrils flared, "I ain't gonna live my life hiding! That's a shite life if you ask me."

"I'm not saying to hide—"

"Yeah, you are. It ain't me who's the problem, Jemma; it's your fucking system."

"It's not my system!"

"*Your* Order started it!" Micca turned. "C'mon, Neddle. I ain't dealing with this shite."

The red-headed man shrugged, and with Micca at his side, they walked away into the commotion of the Canyon, leaving Jemma alone to fend for herself.

CHAPTER THIRTY-ONE

AFTER THE STORM

Daylight.

It returned on the back of birds flying in the sky. Their songs broke through the constant bellowing, leaving a peace over Mert from the highest buildings to the deepest cellar. Down beneath the earth, Todd hid with Lex and Garrett in their cellar, surrounded by nothing but frozen meats and wines. A pregnant silence sat between them, with Lex never looking in Todd's direction while Todd remained fixated on the floor, not abandoning his thoughts deep into the night. Never sleeping. Only with his thoughts.

And his regrets.

I had every right to turn them into the coppers. Todd rubbed his hands as he squinted at the dull light trickling through the cellar. How was he supposed to know that Detective Walsh was crazy? Or that the plant girl would lose control? His wrists hurt at the thought of that damn girl. After she left, the vines collapsed, sending him hurling to the ground. He hadn't checked himself for injuries, instead ushering Lex and Garrett into the cellar to avoid the sudden terror-filled storm.

Not that Lex thanked him.

I'm doing what's right for you, Lex, whether you agree with me or not.

The singing of birds signaled the end to the day of terror. He glanced once at Lex. The magic storm left her exhausted, but that medication Dr. Kafele gave her seemed to do the trick. Other than weariness captured by the bags beneath her eyes, Lex appeared unharmed.

Todd didn't wait for her to wake, though. His longing to climb out of that damp basement trumped all else, and after Lex showed no sign of stirring, he gave into the daylight's call.

Yet, despite the songbirds, the sky basked in a thick gray cloud, locking the city beneath a faux nighttime. Around him, his shop lay in shambles. Vines and roots crawled through the walls, leaving shelves strewn about and debris scattered on the floor. To Todd's surprise, the roof remained intact. Though he hated to imagine what the second floor looked like after yesterday's storm.

He walked around the back of the counter, picking at one of Garrett's scribbled drawings and turning it over in his hands. At his touch, the soaked paper hung over like a wet noodle before falling to the floor in a single heavy clump.

A moan escaped from behind the counter.

Todd snatched his tattoo gun from the counter and held it out, his neck tense as he spoke. "Who's there!?"

Another moan.

He held out the tattoo gun and walked around the counter.

Detective Walsh lay amongst the rubble, her once blonde hair turned black, face drooping like the distorted drawing in his hand. She opened one bright blue eye.

"Help," she begged, blood sputtering from her mouth.

"What are you?" Todd trembled.

"Please help me." The woman coughed up blood.

Todd backed away, his heart rising in his ears. It had to be a trick. The woman would spring up in a second, lunge at him with a skeletal face, and he'd be dead.

Would Lex even care?

Brriiinngg. Todd jumped at the sound of the bell. The dilapidated doorway opened behind him. In, with her uniform covered in dust and soot, marched Detective Locasta.

"You!" Todd jumped. He clutched the tattoo gun tighter. "Do you realize how much *bullshite* you and your partner have caused?

"Where is she?" Detective Locasta spat. "Did she run off? Is she safe?"

"Tildy..." Detective Walsh groaned.

Before Todd moved, Detective Locasta jumped over the counter and knelt beside her partner. "Oh Caroline, Caroline, Caroline. Didn't you learn lying only causes you to drown?"

Detective Walsh mumbled.

"Come, up. We should discuss what you have done." Detective Locasta helped her partner off the ground, arm around her waist. "I had hoped it wouldn't come to this."

"I had no choice," Detective Walsh replied.

"Oh, Caroline, what has become of you? Where's the girl who always fought? You were never so defeated."

Todd hopped in front of the two women, arms spread out, "Ey! You two ain't leaving here without an explanation! What the fuck happened?"

Detective Locasta shook her head. "Mr. Dray, this ain't something for you to worry about—"

"My home's destroyed!"

"You saw what happened. That's your answer."

"Yeah, but *what* happened? Why were you two so obsessed with the Story Collector—"

"The Story Collector's wanted for questioning, for disrupting the peace. Nothing more. My partner and some of her superiors escalated the case." Detective Locasta glared at Detective Walsh. "It was never supposed to get this big. So I recommend you silence your lips and forget about it!"

"But why the FUCK does Detective Walsh's face change?" Todd already anticipated the answer.

"Magic. What else?"

Todd huffed.

Detective Locasta pushed past Todd, her partner held close, voice as professional and orderly as the Guard. "I'm sorry you lost your house. File a report with the Mertoni Chamber of Treasury, and they will provide you monetary compensation. That should give you enough to get out of Mert like you want."

He didn't have time to ask how Detective Locasta knew what he wanted. The two women stepped out into the street, distorted by the fog, leaving Todd alone in his little broken shop.

"Fucking shite!" He kicked the ground as the detectives left. The gems, the ones the Story Collector returned, jumped at his anger, rolling every which way through the rubble.

Why does everything have to be magic?!

He released another stream of profanity, punching the wall once and proceeding to kick the bench. Only when the cellar door opened did he stop.

Lex stood with Garrett, her eyes bloodshot and lips quivering. The events of the previous night had left her pale and feeble, but a slight fire still glowed in her eyes. How did she still look so beautiful while so worn? Todd wished he could express his admiration, but it remained buried beneath his anger and discontent.

"Lex..." He reached out to her.

She shied away. "No."

"Lex, they destroyed our home. Magic is gonna kill you if we don't leave. You gotta understand."

"What I understand is that YOU turned over those two kids!"

"The Story Collector—"

"For the gods' sake!" Lex threw up her free hand. "If YOU didn't turn them in, then this wouldn't have happened! None of this would have happened! This is YOUR fault, Toddle!"

"How was I s'pose to know that the detective was some crazy magic demon?"

"By trusting me! You never trust me! You treat me like that girl you met back in Knoll. The one who needed your help. I'm not her anymore, Toddle! You still don't trust me after all these years!"

"You didn't know she was a demon!"

"Yes, but if you trusted me, then you wouldn't have called the coppers in the first place!"

"Lex..."

"Don't *Lex* me!"

"I'm trying to protect you!" Todd cursed.

"From what? My *disease*? Dr. Kafele said I will live for years as long as I take my medication. Magic isn't the enemy. I thought you learned that! But you're still a guard at heart, aren't you? Ten years later, you're still...filled with hatred."

Todd gawked. Perhaps she was right. Maybe he hadn't changed since leaving Knoll. Was it even possible to change now? Since he was fourteen, he'd heard it all: magic was evil, silver eyes belonged to demons, and storytelling built riots. Lex had worked with him to toss aside most of those prejudices, but he still struggled to shake a distaste for magic. And with everything that happened, how could he? Sure, sometimes it was beautiful, but after everything...would it make sense to taper it?

"Lex, everything is for you and Garrett. After we lost Preston—"

"Oh, shut it! This has nothing to do with Preston. This has to do with a selfish desire to be a hero!" Lex turned to the stairwell, her body shaking as she spoke.

"*Protect my family, avenge my son*, blah blah blah! This does nothing but PISS your family off! Consider that." She exhaled, sharp and uneven. "I am going to go to Madame Owiti's for a few days with Garrett and Preston. Don't bother coming by. You need some time to think about what you've done."

"Lex," Todd groaned.

"I said don't *Lex* me!" She started up the stairs to their abode, "I'm getting my stuff. I'll see you in a few days."

With the slam of the door, the conversation ended. It rang through the little shop and deep into Todd's soul. He had to remind himself why he made his choices. Why had he been so convinced they were right? Lex was just disoriented and hysterical. Why couldn't she see he wanted to protect her?

Todd's mind raced as he collapsed onto the stool. Fog and grime covered his window, leaving empty shadows passing in the streets. But they were merely phantoms of life from another day. No one passed by to shop. Children didn't play. Lovers didn't kiss. Empty. Dead.

Just as the lamppost outside of his shop sat dark.

CHAPTER THIRTY-TWO

A BATTLE WON, A MOMENT LOST

Ostriches.

Brent only saw ostriches.

They marched through the room, squawking and kicking up dirt with trails of mist in their way. Brent closed his eyes, trying to shake them away from him. *They're not real. Just a dream. Go away.*

Yet, they wouldn't go away. Since he woke on the stiff mattress, every time he opened his eyes, the ostriches were there. *This is what you get for telling a story, Brent.*

Stupid boy. The Diabolo in his head snarled.

Go away, dammit!

He rolled off the bed, unable to see anyone. Hear anyone. Sense anyone. He needed to escape the ostriches before they pecked open his head.

They're terrifying. They're huge. Get them away from me!

Crawling across the floor, he avoided the misty birds, closing his eyes as they neared and willing them away. But they kept getting closer...and closer. They towered over him, ready to peck him to death. He rolled onto his back and held his hands over his head.

Go away! Go away!

My name is Brent Harley.

And I'm terrified of ostriches!

Go away!

Then, pain ripped through his arm. The ostriches faded.

And he was lying in the Sanitorium, covered in sweat and shaking. After blinking away the tears, once again, he could see. Varden stood over him, needle in hand, a sly smile on his face.

"Oh, um...thanks." Brent relaxed. He was back in the Sanitorium in the small room above the hospital, wearing dirt-covered clothes and with a pounding headache. It was as if he never left.

Except Nix lay at the foot of the bed where Bria slept.

And he still knew his name.

"How'd I get here?" Brent asked, staring up at Varden.

"Your dog came and found me. You and Bria passed out in the tulips together. The two of you put on quite a show. Dr. Kafele is extremely impressed!" Varden grinned. "They'll be in shortly. The Council injured several people before you deterred the Diabolo. It has kept our hands full, that's for sure."

"Oh. I'm...sorry. I mean, I can't help but feel like I did something and—"

Varden waved his hand. "You did nothing. Ningursu was bound to go ballistic one of these days. We should have been prepared, but, alas, we fall into contentment, don't we?"

The giant continued to babble as Brent pulled himself off the floor. His head continued spinning, the shadows keeping tall necks like ostriches. *Go away.* He closed his eyes.

Varden placed a hand on Brent's shoulder. For a moment, the stories of a giant walking in the Chessboard Plains filled his head. But the medication fought it back.

"We've tripled your dosage while you recover," Varden said. "You'll be okay, but you told quite a story, didn't you?"

Brent nodded.

"Try to get some rest. I'll be back in shortly."

With that, Varden left, ducking under the doorway and into the main room. Brent settled back onto the bed. Nix scooted over, resting her boxy head on his thigh. He scratched behind her ear, glancing down at Bria. *You don't realize how powerful you are, Bria.*

She shifted. One eye fluttered open. "Brent?"

"Hey, Bri." He smiled at her.

"You're still you."

"I mean...yeah...for now." Brent pinched at his skin. "Don't think I'm anyone else. Maybe an ostrich wrangler or something, but...nah, I'm me."

She sat up and peered around the room. "How'd we get back to the Sanitorium?"

Brent recanted what Varden told him as he helped Bria climb out of bed. She wobbled on her feet before sitting back on the bed and nestling into his shoulder. Personally, Brent didn't remember much of what happened. But as she stroked his bony hand, the memories out on the tulip-covered hills returned. Bria conjured and controlled a storm while he danced with ostriches and obscure stories. Together, they forced the Diabolo away. All before Nix led Varden to them in the dark of night.

They'd won this battle.

"You were amazing." Brent pushed back Bria's hair. Her little branch sat nestled behind her ear as always, budding with a single white camellia flower.

"You were too." Bria's fingers crossed the scars on his arm. "We make a good team."

Brent smiled. For the first time in a long time, he really felt like himself. He was back with Bria, wrapped in her embrace. The Diabolo continued to knock at his head, but overall, his thoughts belonged only to him.

He knew who he was.

He knew his name.

Bria tried to rise again, this time stumbling forward a few paces before Brent caught her. He guided her back to the bed. "You need to rest."

"I'm fine."

"No, you're not. You used a lot of your magic." Brent brushed a strand of hair from her face. "Rest. We're safe."

Bria stroked his cheek. She looked like the earth, flourishing with a single camellia flower behind her ear. The way she stared at him with oak-colored eyes warmed his heart. She gave him life.

"We're safe," Brent promised again, pressing his forehead against her brow.

Bria met his eyes. Slowly, her fingers danced along his jawline, stopping just at the corner of his mouth. She poked a blemish on his chin. Brent wished he could read her mind. Emotions trickled over her face, bordering between happiness, relief, melancholy, and sadness.

"Do you think I can kiss you without you eating my face?" Bria asked, half-giggling.

Brent grinned. Instead of responding, he kissed her lightly on the lips. The Diabolo screamed obscenities in his mind.

Slice the bitch.

Go away, you...have I named you yet? I should name you if you're not going anywhere.

Kill her!

Shut up...Frankie!

The Diabolo went quiet. Brent laughed mid-kiss.

Bria pulled away. "What's so funny?"

"The Diabolo...he was...it was being a bastard. So, I...I named it Frankie, and it shut up and..." Brent fell back in a fit of laughter. "I named it Frankie! What kind of name is Frankie?"

"It's a better name than Brent!"

"Oi! My name is wonderful. It's better than your name, *Briannabella*. What a mouth full!"

"Oh, you love my name." Bria leaned in and kissed him again.

Kek waited for them in the lounge, a grin so wide, it almost sliced their face in two. "There's my powerful little couple!"

Brent glanced at Bria. She pulled her cowl up to her chin. Once again, despite being given a set of white clothes, Bria insisted on wearing the cowl and long jacket. Well, Brent recognized it as *his* jacket, but she probably got better use out of it.

"You two did amazing! Everyone in the city is talking about the Storm of Stories!" Kek placed a hand on Bria's shoulder but stopped short of Brent's arm. "I have not seen such cohesiveness between a Magii and a Mist Keeper since...well, me!"

"Since you?" Brent couldn't gather the story around Kek with a single glance. There were too many elements, thousands of years of stories spiraling in one place.

To Brent's surprise, Kek humored the answer. "I've known many Mist Keepers. You don't get to be my age without a run-in. Do you honestly think I was born into hating the Council?"

"You're talking about that war, right? The One War or whatever it's called?"

Kek nodded. "Yes. I suppose the Council voiced concerns over it when you released the Diabolo?"

Brent recalled the conversation, deep down in the heart of the Library, a week after the Diabolo escaped from its jar. Caroline mentioned it to him before then too. The Council always remained elusive, not detailing the events, leaving Brent with one key idea: a war happened, and now the Mist Keepers and Magii hated each other.

"They didn't say much," Brent muttered.

"I shall tell you. It isn't fair for you two to navigate this environment without knowing the truth. But please, first, sit down! You two must be starving!" Kek motioned to the platter of cheeses and fruit on the table.

Bria picked up two pineapple rings and held them up to her face like glasses. Brent fake gagged before grabbing an apple and taking a bite.

"How long were we out?" Bria asked.

"About fourteen hours, I would say." Kek counted on their fingers. "Yes, about that long."

"Fourteen?!" Bria rose. "Why did you let us sleep that long? We should make sure everyone is okay."

"Bri..." Brent touched her hand.

"What about Madame Owiti? Or Lex? Or...everyone? They were all out and about when this started!" Bria stared around the room. "People might have died..."

"No one has died because of the Diabolo attack, as far as we can tell," Kek replied.

Brent verified that statement's truth. There was no strong pull outside of the Sanitorium. The stories continued to pulsate outside the building, but they were soft, constant, not screaming. He whispered, "Bri, sit down, please. Relax. Everything's a'ight."

Bria sank back into the cushion beside him. Her entire body continued shaking, though.

"What? What's wrong?"

"I'm fine." She glanced down at Nix, lying on Brent's feet, and scratched behind the dog's ears.

"Bri..."

"Can we talk about it later?"

"A'ight, yeah, later." Brent frowned. He removed a piece of pineapple from the tray, sniffed it, then handed it to Bria with disgust.

For a few minutes, they ate in silence. Brent hadn't noticed his own hunger until the first taste of a bitter apple touched his tongue. As he took another bite, the door to the suite flung open. Nix woofed, and Brent's stomach flipped.

Edith entered the room like a fire, her eyes sharp and the knife in her hand sharper. It dripped with blood. Brent could hardly look at her; her face haunted the recollections of the ward. Her fingers left nefarious phantoms prodding at his skin.

But he didn't rest on his fears for long. The blood from the knife dripped on the floor, trailing behind her to a body with wild hair lying on the floor.

Brent jumped. "Malaika!"

He recognized her in an instant. Brent only met her briefly after he encountered the Diabolo in the mountain all those months ago. Malaika saved his life and patched his skin, then took him on her airship, the Mystical Cheer, back to Caroline.

What was she doing here?

"Found this reaper after her airship crashed on the plains." Edith snarled and kicked Malaika into the room.

"Fuck off!" Malaika cursed, spitting blood on the otherwise pristine floor.

"Great, we will need to clean again." Kek sighed as they approached Malaika. "You're one of Tilda's friends, yes?"

"That's what I was telling her, but she ain't wanna listen to me!" Malaika barked in Edith's direction. "We saw the outburst on my map and headed on over here, but then the storm caused us to crash! Dobroslawa and her crew are busy fixing up the ship, but I was trying to find Caroline and Brent when this fucker ambushed me!"

"Edith, let Malaika go."

Edith gaped. "But—"

"Let her go. She is not a threat to us."

"You don't know that! She could be their eyes right now!"

"I ain't Ningursu's eyes! I haven't been to the Library since I rescued Brent here!" Malaika pointed in Brent's direction. "Ningursu's got nothing on me!"

"You're just saying that!" Edith snarled.

Brent glanced over at Malaika. The mist sat calmly around her face. "She's not lying."

Edith shot a glare at him.

"C'mon," Malaika groaned, "I ain't here to pick a fight! 'Sides, Tilda's expecting me! Was communicating with her when this red-head thing came attacking."

"Edith." Kek glared again.

Grunting under her breath, Edith dropped Malaika on the ground and stormed into the other room. With her gone, the tension left Brent's shoulders, and he relaxed next to Bria again.

"Brenty, my boy!" Malaika clamored to her feet and grinned widely. "You don't look crazy like they were telling me!"

"Oh, um, I got better." Brent flushed.

The woman laughed. "I can see! That's good! So good! You look good! And you!" Malaika spun to face Bria. "Must be the Breee-uhhh he kept moaning about when I saved him that one time from the Diabolo."

Bria turned back to Brent. "So that's how you survived? You never told me!"

"We were kinda...dealing with shite." Brent flushed harder.

"So Malaika saved you?"

"Yeah, she found me on the mountain. She uses the mist to create maps."

Bria's eyes widened in wonder. It was easy for Brent to forget how little exposure Bria had to the Mist Keepers. Sure, Brent had little more experience, but he'd seen the way Caroline disguised herself face with mist, or how Aelia read medical history through it, or Malaika's ability to construct a map from it as well. The mist contained more magic than just stories.

"Why didn't you come months ago if you knew where Brent was?" Bria asked.

Malaika chuckled. "Just because I can create maps doesn't mean I know how to read them."

Kek interjected themself into the conversation. "This reunion is wonderful, but I must ask...why did Tilda want to speak with *you?*"

"Cause she's got Caroline!"

Brent stared at Malaika. "You mean Ningursu didn't take her?"

"Nah. Tilda found her in the rubble. It means we got a chance to get that damn skull out of her head!"

CHAPTER THIRTY-THREE

LIMITATIONS

Bria trailed towards the back, watching as Kek and Malaika led them out of the Sanitorium and into the streets. Brent stayed by her side with Nix at his heels, silent since they left the suite above the wards. She hugged herself and kicked the ground. Her mind raced. Sure, Mert survived this atrocity, but the scent of destruction remained. The trees along the road didn't sing. The shops lay barren and vacant but for the streetlamps flickering every few paces. Otherwise, all was dead.

"Bri..." Brent tapped her shoulder.

She jumped.

"You a'ight?" He stabilized her with his palm. Bria didn't want to bother him with her own disparities. Already Brent appeared worn down from their conversation before, his eyebrows pressed together in his usual thoughtful expression. "You told me you'd say what's bothering you or...or something."

Bria frowned. "It's...I was worried, that's all."

"Bria."

She stopped walking, turning to face Brent in the pathway. "I was...worried...that we would leave Mert in the same disarray as I left Newbird's Arm. I fled in the middle of rioting and never fessed up to my crimes or anything. And I killed Cadet Lawry!"

"After he attacked you. Who knows what he would've done!"

"But I didn't want to kill him! I should have thrown him into the trees or...or something!" Bria threw her arms back. A few seeds flew from her coat pockets and latched onto the nearby wall. "That's not all, though! I caused riots in town! The few times I snuck back, it was an utter nightmare! I could've been smarter. I didn't have to start riots or...or...when Ningursu controlled me, I—"

"Stop. Stop it!" Brent took her hands delicately and squeezed them. "That's the word right there, isn't it? Control? He controlled you; you didn't have a say in it. And if it wasn't Newbird's Arm, it would've been somewhere else. We saved our home...and we saved Mert."

Bria met Brent's gaze. He smiled.

"You're a hero, Bria, whether or not you want to admit it. You see the world's beauty even in the darkest times."

"Because when life gets a little petty...I try to replace it with something pretty," Bria whispered.

"Yeah, exactly. You taught me that."

Bria sank into Brent's arms, restraining her own tears again. *You're stronger than this. Stop falling into this self-loathing trap already.* She didn't want to remove herself from Brent's arms. There, she was safe; there, she could cry.

There, no one could control her.

"Can you two stop snogging and hurry? Tilda's waiting for us!" Malaika shouted from the end of the block. Kek stood beside her, arms crossed and smirking.

"Sorry!" Brent called back. With his arm around Bria's shoulders, the two of them rushed to the corner.

"Bout time," Malaika grumbled and waved her hand in the air. The mist spiraled before her, forming what appeared to be a bird's-eye view of the Mert. Bria gaped. The unique magic of the Mist Keepers always amazed her. While Brent performed fantastical feats, the other Mist Keepers had their own abilities. Magic always came in an array of surprises.

Malaika traced her finger over the mist and stopped above a building. "Looks like she's here. You know where this is?"

Bria peered over Malaika's shoulder. "That's Madame Owiti's place."

"Then I'll let ya'll lead the way because God knows I'll just get us lost, and we'll somehow end up in Evylain!"

With Bria at the front of the pack, they walked back towards Mert. Brent stayed beside her, not saying much, his eyes constantly tracing over the landscape as they walked. Kek stayed behind them, silent and observant. It was odd seeing Kek out of their doctor's uniform and out in broad daylight rather than in the unnatural lighting of the Sanitorium. Their dark eyes showed their age, worn with lines creasing their otherwise pointed face. Their oily curls poked out of their usually slicked-back hair. It differed from when they collected the Copper Periwinkles. There, at least, Kek seemed alive. Here, walking the streets of Mert, they were like a ghost transplanted in unfamiliar territory.

Meanwhile, Malaika trailed further back, occasionally muttering in foreign languages. Sometimes when Bria glanced back, the woman vanished, standing instead at a tree or an intersection, scratching her head while looking at the map.

"Sorry 'bout that." Malaika grinned sheepishly after the fourth time. "I get distracted by the mist and all. Gets me thrown about."

"How did you manage as a Mist Keeper if you get turned around all the time?" Kek asked.

"I wandered a lot and hoped I came across a dead person needing my help. Think that's why I get lost. I can see all the paths to the dead and all, and I try to follow 'em but never go where I'm supposed to." Malaika's face hardened. "There've been a lot of those paths lately."

"That's why I must...I hear so many stories..." Brent pinched his brow. "They're...it's noisy, and I can't...I dunno where they're coming from half the time."

"Everywhere. They're coming from everywhere. No one is releasing souls regularly anymore. They're struggling."

Bria glanced at Brent. "Didn't Caroline mention something like that?"

"It just doesn't make sense to me," Brent clenched his fists as he spoke. "Just from a story level or something! Why the shite would fate or the Effluvium or whatever put ONE person in charge of releasing the dead! That's...that's punishing people who don't deserve to be in Hell or...or anything! I just...I don't want to believe that the world is that...evil. And the stories are screaming...I hear them and—"

Bria stopped Brent as he strode forward a few paces, making him sit down against a wall and breathe. She pressed her fingers into his knuckles, begging for him to calm down, focus on himself before the stories gripped him again.

"You're okay. Breathe. You're okay."

"I am...I'm here. I'm a'ight." Brent closed his eyes and exhaled.

Malaika interjected, "He's gotta point, though. It's messed up and all. I think it's gotta do with control or something ridiculous like that."

"Ningursu always had a...perplexing way of doing things," Kek added.

Brent took another moment to exhale, then he rose to his feet, and they continued through Mert. While the buildings still stood, the few trees lining the streets had fallen. Foliage lay strewn across the ground while merchant booths sat on their sides. A few windows were shattered. Debris decorated the streets.

Bria gripped Brent's hand tight as they ventured deeper into the city. She once again had to stop every few seconds to make sure Malaika was nearby, only misplacing her once rather than the multiple times near the Sanitorium.

To Bria's surprise and utter relief, Madame Owiti's building sat untouched, like a beacon of hope amid the carnage. She led the way up to the apartment and knocked on the door once.

Madame Owiti answered the door in an instant and pulled Bria into a hug. "Oh, Rho! I was so worried! You're fine though, yes yes? Oh, you look fine! C'mere!"

Bria stiffened. "I'm alright. Really."

Madame Owiti cupped Bria's cheeks. "You are an amazing girl. You too, lad!" She grinned at Brent before continuing, "Yes yes, you two were absolutely amazing! I watched it all happen! And—oh, where are my manners?" Madame Owiti dropped Bria and turned to Kek and Malaika. "Hello there, Kek! And you must be the Malaika that Tilda has told me all about, yes, yes?"

"It is nice to see you too, Awiti," Kek bowed their head.

"Where are Tilda and Caroline?" Malaika strode past Madame Owiti and peered around the room.

"I put them in the back room. But would you like any tea or coffee? I have a kettle brew—"

"Not the time. Brent, my boy! C'mon!" Malaika grabbed Brent by his sleeve, and before he objected, she dragged him down the hall into the back room.

Madame Owiti ushered Bria and Kek into the living room. Nix bounded onto the sofa, twirled in three circles, then parked herself on the cushion.

"What brings you out of hiding, Kek, my dear?" Madame Owiti bumbled about the room as she spoke. "You rarely venture far from the City Centre."

"I would like to speak with the Mist Keeper once she is willing." Kek strolled across the room, peering at Madame Owiti's orb sitting on the shelf. They poked it once and scowled.

"That is not wise, deary dear."

"I'm not here for your opinions, Awiti. Trust me. I have years of experience."

"Sometimes, all of you immortals consider age experience. Dear, let me tell you—"

Kek glared.

"Very well." Madame Owiti popped her lips. "Well, would either of you like coffee or tea? I apologize for not cleaning up. It has been quite a day, hasn't it? Yes, yes. Tilda brought Caroline by a few hours ago and contacted Malaika and then..."

"Coffee would be wonderful, Awiti," Kek replied.

"Of course." Madame Owiti strode towards the kitchen.

Bria followed Madame Owiti. Already the old woman bustled by the stove. Before Bria had the chance to offer help, the old woman abruptly cut her off without turning.

"How have you been the past couple of days, Rho? Is your fellow doing better?"

"Oh yes, things seem better. He has his head on his shoulders," Bria said. "You know, you don't have to keep calling me Rho..."

"No, no, I think I'll keep calling you Rho. It suits you. If you don't mind, of course."

Bria didn't protest.

"Can you grab a few mugs from the cabinet, please?" Madame Owiti removed the kettle.

Bria obliged, placing them beside Madame Owiti. She offered the old woman a hand with pouring the kettle, but Madame Owiti waved her away.

"I got it, I got it. Yes, yes." She poured the first cup. "But how are *you*, Rho? Are you happy now, at least?"

Bria pondered that. "I...I don't know if happy is the word. I feel...safer, and there is some normalcy, but..."

"You've been through a lot, and even the deepest love cannot heal those wounds. It is all a part of the process, yes yes?"

"I suppose."

Madame Owiti began rummaging through her drawers for silverware. "I apologize I wasn't at the shop when you arrived yesterday. Kek took their sweet time sending additional vials over for Brent, and then a strange sensation told me to stay home. I do apologize...but I am yet to be wrong about a gut feeling."

"Oh. It's okay. Really."

"Hm." Madame Owiti grunted. "It was peculiar. I still am not sure what the snafu was, really. Kek is usually quick on their feet and on time for everything. I recommend you be wary."

"What? Why?" Bria's throat tightened.

"I think Kek sees something in you."

"Yes, I know that."

"Just be wary. Sometimes Kek can be a little selfish in their desires."

"What do you mean?"

"They train people for their benefit. But I am sure you are fine, yes yes. You understand your limits." Madame Owiti shrugged, then her demeanor changed, replaced with her usual wide grin. "Could you help me bring the tea and coffee out, dear?"

"Yes," Bria gathered the mugs and carried them out into the main room. Her mind continued racing. What Madame Owiti said bothered her; what was Kek hiding? Did Brent see the story? Or was it masked by a thousand years of commotion?

Did it really matter right now?

For now, at least, they were all safe.

APPRENTICE AND MASTER

The room sat dark, kindled by only a single lantern on the far wall. Shadows danced beneath it, cast by the woman in black herself sitting on a chair in the corner of the room. Brent stepped in slowly, afraid that any move might cause her to flinch. Old cloth tied Caroline to the chair, her eyes covered with a rag. Tilda sat on the bed across from her, legs crossed, glowering.

Malaika sliced open the silence. "She say anything?"

"Not since I sat her down." Tilda's eyes narrowed. "I've been methodical trying to get her to talk. She doesn't want to, though. It's like something is holding her back. Her aura is very...dull. Usually, it has a bright blue around it, but right now, it's just...gray."

Brent peered over at Caroline. The mist continued mingling around her, clinging to her skin and pores. "Like smoke, you mean?"

"Brenton. It is so nice to hear your putrid voice," Caroline hissed. As her chapped lips curved into a smile, stories spun around her. They danced with inconsistencies and lacked coherency, leaving Brent's head spinning. One moment, he saw Caroline standing by the water; the next, her story mingled with that of a skeletal figure dancing across an empty field. *The stories don't fully belong to her. She's not herself.*

Brent glanced at Tilda and Malaika, then with their permission, turned back to Caroline. "What happened to you?"

"You happened to me."

"What?"

"You decided to be...you. You refused to change for me. For us."

"I...what?"

"Die. You need to die." Caroline's mouth hung ajar on the last word.

"What? But...I..."

"Cursed. You're cursed. Die already."

"Caroline!" Brent stared hard at her. The stories around her head continued to spiral. "I thought you...I mean...it seemed like you...I thought you cared! You acted like it! Act like it now!"

Caroline's voice softened, her body sagging. "I *do* care, Brent. I am trying to protect you."

"Protect me? You...you sent Diabolo after me!"

"Look at my story. *I* care about you." Her voice was a mere whisper now, a sudden change in demeanor washing over her as she spoke.

Brent stared hard at Caroline. The mist whisked around her head. He saw her coming to Mert. Tilda welcomed her with open arms and a kiss, then led Caroline to the police precinct under the guise of Detective Walsh. The goal was simple: find the Story Collector and protect him.

But then something switched. A deep fog coated the story, different from the Diabolo but enough to send anyone's head spinning. Brent squinted, watching the story spin, but he struggled to make sense of it. The story flashed with Ningursu's face, echoing overlapping commands which Brent struggled to fathom. Throughout the tale, Caroline stiffened, her face hollowed, her magic tamed. She lost control of herself, dragged forward with one goal circling her mind: bring the Story Collector back to the Council...at all costs.

"You understand now?" Caroline asked.

"He controlled you," Brent whispered. "Like he did with Bria."

"I cannot confirm nor deny. He is listening. He is watching. He always is." Caroline gritted her teeth, her tone changing again. "So be fearful. You cannot hide from him, Brenton. He is you as you are him. Everywhere...watching. You should have thought about that a long time ago."

"Caroline, please fight it. You're more than just a mask!" He gripped her hands, ignoring the sudden wave of three hundred years' worth of stories traveling through her palms and into his skin. "You need to fight, Caroline. Recite your...recite your mantra. Your name. Your home. Your constant." He glanced behind him, half expecting Bria to be standing in the doorway. "Always remember what is constantly there..."

"It is a load of hogwash!" Caroline spat.

"It worked—"

"Only for you! Everyone else has to deal with Ningursu's constant nagging!"

"You mean...Aelia...Tomás—"

"Every one of them! Aelia, Tomás, Jiang, Alojzy! They are Ningursu's eyes...and they cannot shake it."

"I ain't!" Malaika interjected. "I keep away from all that shit!"

Caroline nodded. "I suppose that is for the best."

"What about Julietta?" Brent asked.

"Julietta..." Caroline's voice cracked. "No, no, of course not. She is too pure to be Ningursu's eyes. She cannot be his eyes."

Brent sucked in his lips. His old teacher shrank in on herself, her lips opening and closing like a fish, her cheeks hollow. He never imagined her as weak. She was the woman in black, the one who assaulted him in the tunnels, and the one who introduced him to this magical world of mist and fantasy. "You can fight it, Caroline. I believe in you. Just like...I mean...you believed in me."

"I am not as strong as you, Brent. I apologize. It is impossible for me to fight it. It seems I am too old to change my ways." Caroline's head fell.

Defeat cradled Brent as the desire to help Caroline remove the mask she'd created reigned. Perhaps that was the true curse brought to the Mist Keepers; death was stagnant, unable to change, stuck forever in one mindset. He could help her stand up, but she had to walk on her own.

And beside them, Malaika and Tilda stood helplessly.

"Ningursu is your Diabolo," Brent mused.

"Pardon?" Caroline's face flickered.

"He's constantly nagging you, trying to get you to behave and everything; you're struggling to fight him. He's like my Diabolo. Um...Frankie."

"Frankie?"

"That's, um, his name. He's not going anywhere, so I gave him a name." Brent rubbed the back of his neck and flushed.

It's a stupid name.

Be quiet!

Caroline smirked. "If you insist."

Brent shook his head, ignoring *Frankie's* sudden mocking. He needed to focus on Caroline. This was her turn to shine. "A few things have helped me fight...*Frankie*." Brent scowled. "Sure, I got some medication from Kek and such, which kinda cleared the fog—"

Caroline's face shriveled up for a moment in disgust. A wispy, echoing voice exited her mouth. "They gave you poison!"

"Caroline! Focus!" Brent grabbed her hands. "Focus on YOU!"

Her nails dug into his skin for a moment, then relaxed.

"Find your identity in the fog! It didn't matter if the fog cleared if I didn't have a sense of myself!" Brent released Caroline's hands. "Who are you, Caroline? You're not some pernicious woman in black. You're a klutz; you make mistakes...but you have a heart. Are you just unsure where that heart belongs?" He focused on her. "You told me once...back when I first found out about the curse...to kiss that girl and smile more. And I have been. And it's given me the ability to fight...because there's more than what the Effluvium or Ningursu says. Fight it. Because if a sap like me can fight the fucking God of Death, so can you. You can be the hero of your story."

Caroline said nothing. Brent wished he saw her eyes beneath the veil but knew for his own safety it had to stay. He wanted to comprehend what she was in her mind, understand her expressions...but how much did Ningursu see through her eyes?

"I will try, Brenton," Caroline whispered.

"The first thing you gotta stop doing is calling me Brenton. You never do that. That's Ningursu."

"Right...you go by Brent. What a terrible name for a Mist Keeper." She smiled.

Brent grinned back. "Well, this Mist Keeper chucked Ningursu's head against the ground."

"I am still flabbergasted you got away with that."

"Once you're back to normal, we chuck it to the wall together."

Caroline's smile widened. "It is nice to hear you be yourself, Brent. I hope we can reconvene as teacher and apprentice one day."

"Or if not...as friends."

Caroline nodded. It might have been the lighting, but Brent swore tears fell from behind her blindfold.

"I am so sorry I failed you those months ago."

"You didn't fail me. You...I mean...I told my *own* story, and you weren't expecting that, you know?"

"Perhaps..." Caroline bowed her head. Her lips quivered. When she spoke again, her voice held that same echo as before. "Now, let me see you, Brenton. Please."

"We cannot do that, Caroline," Tilda said. "It puts us at risk."

Caroline cackled. "Does it matter? You are already at risk, Tilda, my dear."

Tilda backed away and glanced between Brent and Malaika. Brent squinted at Caroline's story, once again murky around her head.

"The Diabolo are gone. Mert is safe. The only risk now is Ningursu," Tilda reiterated.

"That is what they want you to think."

Malaika eyed Tilda, then Brent, as she ran her fingers through the air. A new global map made of mist came to life before them. She spun it around on her fingers, fixating on different locations. "Oh crud. This isn't good."

"What is it?" Tilda asked.

"Caroline's right. We're in a crapload of trouble. There are at least seventy Diabolo loose."

"Seventy?" Brent gawked. "How? There weren't...we didn't...there weren't that many when they attacked or anything! Did I...did we...did I create them when I sent them flying off?"

"Nah, not all of 'em by the looks of it," Malaika pointed to a couple smaller blobs meandering across the Chessboard Plains across the Blood Sea. "See the small ones? Those are the ones ya'll made. Not much of a problem, if you ask me. It's these new ones. See 'em?" She then indicated a spot on the map where a large plot hovered over Rosada, Heims, and Spinzoa. "A lot of them are just kinda...waiting. But there are a few heading to Mert." Malaika paled. "Ningursu's pissed off!"

Caroline cackled again. "Of course he is angry! Brenton and Briannabella have messed up all of his plans."

"Caroline, please fight back!" Brent begged again.

But Caroline's laughter continued to shake the room.

"You've done all you can do for now, Brent," Tilda whispered. "I think it's time to leave Caroline alone for a bit."

"No! Do not leave me, *Brent*. I need you!"

Brent lowered his head, and with Malaika and Tilda at his side, he turned back to the doorway. "Keep fighting it, Caroline. I'll be back."

"Brenton!" Caroline continued to call after him as he left the room. He held his head tall. For now, all he'd provided was that vague bit of advice. How else could he help her? Stories didn't trap her. A Diabolo didn't run rampant in her head. This was more sensitive. If Brent broke the window Ningursu peered through, it would become a door.

Brent hunched his shoulders in defeat, wearing the silence like a blanket as he entered the parlor. Bria lay on the sofa in the main room. Madame Owiti sat beside her, braiding her hair, while Kek stared out the window. Tilda collapsed onto the love seat across from them while Malaika ambled into the kitchen. No one said much of anything. The truth hung in the air: Caroline suffered, and the Diabolo were loose.

Nix was the only one who reacted to his presence, bounding across the living room and jumping up, so her paws hit his stomach.

The silence remained, though. It sliced the room. Sometimes silence was all anyone needed to understand their surroundings.

Malaika joined them a few moments later, carrying out a bottle of copper liquid and a handful of glasses. She collapsed on the floor and poured herself a glass. "I think we're gonna need this."

Bronze glasses and liquid serenity. It washed away worries. It created stories. After Brent and Malaika detailed what they learned about both Caroline and the Diabolo, drinks became the staple for the day. Brent nursed a glass of rum while the others drank, laughing and dancing on the tables. Who knew what alcohol would do to *Frankie* or the stories? He didn't want to risk it. A single drink was good enough.

Bria danced with the others, Nix running between her legs. *We should be celebrating.* Brent frowned and watched Bria twirl between Kek and Madame Owiti. *Not drinking to accept our fates.*

When Bria noticed Brent, her face sparkled with happiness. She hopped to her feet, giggling slightly, and danced over to him, holding a half-filled glass of rum. "Mr. Harley! Why are you standing there being boring?"

"What? Oh. Nothing. I'm fine." Brent raised his eyebrows. "You're drunk, though."

"Listen, I've been running in circles for months. I can have a drink if I want!" She poked his chest, then pulled Brent forward in an awkward twirl. She spun him in circles, then hopped on the table where Malaika lay inebriated and planted her lips against his mouth.

"You're my boyfriend, and I like you..." Bria giggled and kissed him again. "I like you a lot."

"No more alcohol for you," Brent whispered.

"At least I can hold it better than you!" Bria prodded his chest. "You're two drinks in, and you think you're a cow!"

"I think I'm a cow even when I'm sober. *Moo!*" Brent threw his voice, laughing. Focusing on Bria and no one else, he was himself, though he still sensed the stories bounding through the room. There were thousands of years of knowledge sitting right there, but instead, they all sat there drinking and laughing like old friends.

"You're such a goof!" Bria jumped off the table, wobbling slightly.

"We should go home, a'ight?"

"Mhm..."

He led Bria to the door with Nix on their heels. They said their quick goodbyes to Malaika, Tilda, Madame Owiti, and Kek, then left the apartment.

On their way down the stairs, Bria's composure changed. With each step, her face fell, and her eyes grew hard. Outside the building, she stopped and knelt to the ground, running her fingers over the dirt on the corner of the road.

"Bri?"

"We're not safe." There was sudden soberness in her voice. "We will never be safe..."

"It'll be a'ight. We...we can fight them. We'll be a'ight."

"Will we, though?"

"Yes! C'mon, Bria, this isn't you." Brent frowned. "You're a fighter. Don't give up."

"I'm not giving up! But it's hard." She wiped her eyes with her sleeve. "The world is dying, and everything is shit! You don't feel it like I do. I know you have the stories, but you don't feel the way these trees are gasping for air or the dirt quivers from lack of nutrients. I could bring it all back to life. But that puts Mert at risk...and...and..." She traced the ground with her fingernail. "I'm so tired."

"You don't have to fight it alone. I mean...we're together, right? And we got Kek and Malaika and Tilda...and... I mean, we're here. A'ight? We're here." Brent helped her off the ground and brushed the dirt off her jacket. "We're gonna...we're gonna figure this out and make the world pretty."

"Because life is petty?"

"Yeah. That." Brent squeezed Bria's hand. Together, they walked down Myrtle towards Celosia in silence. The little shop on the corner of Myrtle and Celosia proved to be the epicenter of the destruction. The stop still stood, but the windows sat broken, the door hanging on a hinge. Inside, the shelving lay in shambles, everything scattered and frayed.

As they walked by, Lex stormed out of the doorway, holding her living son's hand. He held his arm outstretched, so his brother stayed close.

"I told you, Toddle! I'm going! You can't change my mind!" Lex shouted.

"Let's talk about this!" Todd followed her out the door.

Brent glanced at Bria, and they ducked down Celosia away from the shop before the shopkeepers noticed them. They continued to bicker, their voices ringing through the road, bouncing against the buildings.

It was weird, walking back into their apartment building. Only a day before, Brent thought he'd never return to this small studio again, but here they were, once more climbing the stairs, surrounding themselves in stories of the past few days.

Nix bounded into the room and jumped on the bed, tongue hanging out of her mouth, tail wagging.

Brent grinned. "Someone's happy to be back."

Bria smiled slightly, removed her jacket and boots, then sat on the bed. Brent joined her. They sat quietly for a few minutes with Nix between them. The stories floated about the room, calm, pulsing...always there.

"Tell me a story," Bria finally begged.

"What? I mean...I don't know...I...I—"

"Try. Please."

"A'ight, yeah, I can try," Brent mumbled. Carefully, he chose each word, waving his hand through the mist. He concocted a story about a Prudish Prince in a castle who cast away every woman he called a wife. None were as pretty as the sky, he declared, so he cast them away from the window in the tallest tower. Down, down, his wives descended, but they never hit the ground. For the moon and the sun watched the Prudish Prince, and to save his wives, turned them each into fairies before they hit the ground.

"The fairies, they did not stay around to entertain the Prudish Prince, oh no!" Brent waved his hand through the air. Mist drizzled over his fingers, continuing with the tale. The mist itself showed the fairies traveling far away from the Prudish Prince, where they met the Ugly Princes of Insects, Slugs, Snails, and Spiders. The Ugly Princes were kind, though, and over and over, the fairies found love in their arms. Together, they formed the kingdom of Fireflies, where they ruled the skies, the stars, and everything between them.

"So, what became of the Prudish Prince, you ask?" Brent twirled his fingers through the mist, showing a grumpy king sitting alone in the throne room. "Well, he grew up alone and without a kingdom to rule. They all left, hearing of treasures in the south. Towards the end of his days, he sent his last loyal knight south, expecting to receive riches in return. But the knight only returned with a jar of fireflies."

Brent glanced back at Bria. Little fairy lights dotted the room, singing songs of freedom from tyrants and hate while dancing in the mist. "So that's a...that's the story...sorry...it was bad."

"Bad?" Bria gripped his hands, "You're being *you*. That was...you told a story!"

A stupid story.

Shut it!

"Yeah, guess I did..."

"You're getting better! You've finally beaten down the Diabolo!" Bria cupped his cheeks in her hands. "You did it!"

"I told Frankie to shut up is all." Brent fidgeted.

"But you're back!"

"Yeah, I'm back. I'm...I'm me again."

For the first time in ages, Brent truly felt like himself.

CHAPTER THIRTY-FIVE

A VAGRANT SISTER

Jemma didn't believe in luck. She had faith in the Effluvium's prowess, its guiding hand, and the fortune it blessed on those who proved loyal. Yet, after a couple days passed in the Canyon, she considered herself lucky. Sure, the Guard humiliated her, but she kept her dignity, her skin remained ungarnished, and she was alive.

It could have been much worse.

The Effluvium protects those who pray. She sighed in relief, pulling herself up off the ground of her tent, surrounding herself with the serenity of the prayer.

After her arrival, a kind old woman with five missing teeth and a tendency to talk in the third person provided

Jemma with a tent and a flimsy cot. She thanked the woman with the Effluvium's grace.

Despite being in proximity, she didn't see Micca for over three nights. During the day, Jemma often sat at the foot of the tent, praying to Aloby's Temple that light would guide her to freedom.

As Jemma finished her prayer, the old woman approached, placing a plate of stale bread on the ground. "You need a good old meal. The Guards threw the food at Miss Kelly, and Miss Kelly thought you'd need to eat. Eating makes you strong and wise."

"Thank you." Jemma scowled as she broke off a chunk of bread, the crumbs falling over her skirt.

The old woman stared at her. She had these odd burgundy eyes that sent shivers through Jemma's spine. Had those eyes once been clear? Did a demon stroke them and turn them red? Yet the old woman appeared kind enough, unphased by Jemma's stares. "Miss Kelly wonders why the dear girl stays in here. The world beyond here is beautiful, yes. The Canyon stretches wide and far. If Miss Kelly's legs weren't so old, she'd go exploring. Yes indeed."

"Oh." Jemma paused, holding the bread to her lips. "I apologize for your predicament then."

"Do not apologize. Just go do a living for Miss Kelly!"

The old woman gimped from the tent, leaving Jemma alone with her piece of bread.

Miss Kelly was right; she'd spent the last couple of days hiding away in the tent, fearful of what lived in the Canyon. If she wanted to embrace the Effluvium, Jemma had to break out of this self-pity-filled shell.

Jemma gathered herself and strolled away from the campsite, holding a coarse blanket around her shoulders as a wind funneled through the stacks of adobo homes. The sunlight painted the buildings orange, and a gentle glow from Aloby left a bitter reminder that life continued above the Canyon.

Unphased.

Unlike the Pit, the Canyon ruled itself; the Guards watched from above, but the vagrants created their own rule of law. A market sat in the center of all the homes, where vagrants traded goods and services, just like Madame Gonzo's market back home. Micca had told her to look beyond the obvious, and while Jemma continued to see the vagrants in their torn clothes and tangled hair as vagrants, she also saw a society beginning to emerge from the ashes of hatred. People spoke about their day-to-day, not deterred by the stamps on their bodies, while a group gathered in the center square to pray.

They still pray! How wonderful! Jemma followed their gaze. They gazed toward the shadow of Aloby's Year

Glass on the Canyon wall. The same prayers she memorized, welcoming the Effluvium and promising a better future, crossed their lips.

Remember Effluvium is watching,
It kills the Year clean,
The evil shrivels,
The demons falter,
And you can speak, alas.
Say it loud.
Louder.
Say it now.

"I shall not be your agent, for I am the Effluvium's soul," Jemma whispered. She glanced back the Year Glass's shadow. *Year Birth will come in the next few days.* She hadn't been paying attention, even back in Newbird's Arm, locked in the day-to-day of Elder Lau Rel's new rule.

And what a year it has been. It wasn't quite the Year you wanted, was it, Brother Roy Al? She remembered his prayer, jovial in the prospects for new lovers, new families, and boundaries crossed at the start of the year.

Oh, how things changed.

She kissed her fingers and held it up to the Year Glass's shadow. They hung in the air for a second before she proceeded, strolling along through the tents beneath the adobo homes. A child ran past, playing with a newspaper like a kite, strung together and floating in the air. A couple pages caught the wind, flew into the air, and landed by Jemma's feet.

She picked it up and scanned the pages. Yes, it was nearly Year Birth. Ab Aeterno prepared for the annual festival while the Capitol issued a warning against potential riots. An advertisement for a circus sat beneath the warning, a smiling caricature of the sun welcoming all to the adventure.

Jemma flipped the page, skimming through for any mention of Newbird's Arm. Nothing popped up, though, with most articles mentioning Knoll and the Capitol instead. A brigade of airships had left Knoll recently to investigate a huge bout of magic near the Chessboard Plains. Meanwhile, Senator Cordova issued a decree to station Towers in every major city. Jemma's skin crawled reading it; would every city undergo the same cleansing and testing requirements as Newbird's Arm?

Knoll's taking over Rosada. Jemma folded up the newspaper and shook off her fears, continuing to walk along the path. The mere idea of Knoll left a shadow in her mind of the Guards; they all came from that city's heart, spurned with sexist ideals and prejudiced against those with silver eyes. What did they endure to transform them into such scoundrels? How come they left a stain wherever they appeared?

No wonder the vagrants screamed. Their shouts echoed around her, filling every path in the Canyon. Noise polluted the air, mingling with smoke and dust, hiding the true length of the Canyon. Homes and tents scattered throughout the Canyon, like its own country, formed together beneath the edge of civilization.

Truthfully, without all the squalor, the Canyon reminded Jemma of a setting in one of Brent's stories. She always pretended not to listen, but it was hard to ignore the way his eyes lit up, and his smile sparkled when he told one. When they were first betrothed, she tried to force herself to fall in love with those tales.

Yet she struggled to accept them. Stories continued to wreak of demons and taint the Effluvium.

The glistening rocks, the adobo homes, the moonlight...none of that was a story. This was the real world. Demons didn't live in a story of truths.

She followed back along the row of tents toward where she'd been staying. This would be a haven for many vagrants, but she had to get out. Surely, somewhere, she'd be able to find a way up the Canyon again, back to freedom and to Ab Aeterno.

Jemma struggled to focus on creating a plan, though. The shouts grew as she walked, replacing her focus with annoyance and disorientation.

"YEAH, WELL, YOU AIN'T GONNA GET ANOTHER GANDER AT THIS PEASHOOTER ANYWAY!"

Jemma froze. She'd recognize that voice anywhere.

Micca stood in front of his tent, adjusting his pants while cursing into the entrance. "YEAH, AND ANOTHER THING! If it ain't for you being a drunkard, we wouldn't be here. So, you better get a good ole look at my jerry one last time cause you're why I ain't a free man on my way in my fucking auto!" As he shouted, Micca unbuckled his pants.

Jemma turned away quickly, flushing.

"YEAH, WELL FUCK YOU TOO—Oh! Jemma!" Micca's tone changed. "Um, I'm decent now."

Jemma turned back to him. She continued to feel the blood build up in her face. Sure, she'd seen vagrants and others undergo Level Three of the Cleanse, the Cleanse of Humility, plenty. But she had never seen an individual holding themselves at the mast.

A heat rose inside of her. She twisted her legs and looked to the ground, hiding her shame between both of her shoulders.

Micca approached her. "Sorry, uh, Neddle and I had a disagreement. Never make a one-night fling last more than a night. It ain't good for no one."

"Yes, okay." Jemma straightened her shoulders and sucked in her lips. As hard as she tried, the image didn't leave her mind.

"I, uh. Sorry."

Jemma shook it off, reclaiming her poise and holding her shoulders high. "It is just the human anatomy. Nothing to apologize for."

"You look like a bright red tomato, though!"

"I did not expect to see you flinging your privates around!"

"Jem, if you ever get yourself a man, you'll learn we fling our goods all the time."

"If I ever do wed, I do not have the intention to find a man so perverse."

Micca chuckled.

"What? What is so funny?"

"You gotta cut loose, Jemma. Live a little."

"My heart and soul belong to the Effluvium."

"So you keep saying," Micca laughed. "Whatever, Jem. If that's what you do, you do that. Leaves more men for me. That's the way this works, doesn't it?"

Jemma sighed.

She and Micca sat down by the firepit. Jemma said nothing, instead tearing up her newspaper and throwing strips into the fire. He didn't understand her. But, she supposed, she didn't really know him. The two of them came from different worlds. He was a free soul while she devoted her heart to the Effluvium. Did they even share the same motivation anymore? Did Micca even want to leave the Canyon? Maybe he was more attached to this Neddle fellow than he claimed? Jemma didn't want to pry.

Perhaps she should have never left Newbird's Arm. All of this was crashing down around her. It seemed so easy: steal a car, leave Newbird's Arm, and drive across the country.

Or perhaps it would have been easier to garner approval from the Elders to travel to Ab Aeterno.

Or wait for Brother Roy Al to return.

"So…" Micca fiddled with his fingers. "You got an idea how to get outta here?"

"You—You want to leave?" She stared at him.

"Why the hell would I want to stay in a shanty piece of shite like this? I just spent my time trying to get outta Newbird's Pit. Ain't no way I'm gonna spend time in the Canyon!"

"Oh."

"Oh? You only can say 'oh'? What the shite is wrong with you?! No one ain't wanna be a vagrant forever!"

"But you were with Neddle—"

"Neddle's done! Y'know how many pricks like him I slept with? More than even I can remember! It's all fun, ain't nothing serious! I'm *living* my life."

"Oh. I'm sorry. I didn't think—"

"That's your problem. You have this one way of looking that you think is right! Shite!"

Jemma stared out past the fire. Tears prickled at her eyes, but she pushed them back, holding her head tall. "I know what I want. And that is what I shall focus on."

"And that's getting to Ab Aeterno?" Micca crossed his arms.

"Yes."

"Well then, if you're so focused on that, how we gonna get there?"

"I, um..." Jemma frowned.

"Fine, let me use all my brainpower to figure this bullshite out." Micca rolled his eyes. "I'll tell you how: we walk."

"Walk?"

"They can't monitor the entire canyon. We head west until we find another town or something, then get transport to Ab Aeterno from there. Gotta be a way up or something. Or, well, that is what I intend to do."

"Anything may be out there, though. There could be wild beasts! Or the guard might be monitoring it! You don't even know if there's a way out!"

"Jemma, Jemma. Ya just gotta watch where you're going, y'know? And think smart!"

"I don't know..."

"Well, do you got a better idea?"

Jemma shook her head.

"Yeah, that's what I thought. What d'ya do without me?" Micca winked. "Go get some shut-eye. I can handle it from here."

Before Jemma could stop him, Micca darted into the droves of tents, leaving her alone about the fire with just her thoughts and prayers.

CHAPTER THIRTY-SIX

LOWERING THE SAILS

The next few days dwindled in and out, uneventful and filled with soft kisses, tender smiles, and continuous cuddles. Bria's monthly bleed arrived, and while she spent those days in and out of bed with Nix snuggled against her, Brent served as her caregiver. He completed chores around the small apartment when he was home while they waited for Kek or Malaika to tell them their next move.

They discussed the possibility of leaving Mert a few times, but with the world caught up in the Diabolo's embrace, nowhere was safe. Bria decided that Mert was probably the safest for now; at least then, they had access to the Pool and Kek.

Brent agreed.

So over the next couple of days, Mert returned to normal, picking itself up after the distress and resuming life.

For a little while, Bria could at least pretend to be normal.

During the day, while Bria nursed her cramps and slept, Brent often vanished. When she first woke up to him missing, panic heightened in her chest, only to find an illegible note on the counter. After staring at it for a few minutes, she interpreted it to say Brent went to visit Caroline at Madame Owiti's apartment. Bria's nerves settled. If anyone could get Caroline back to her old self, it would be Brent. He understood better than anyone what it was like to have voices in his head.

Yet Bria's anxieties didn't rest. Day turned to night, and the lanterns outside grew dark. She counted the flickering lamps in her apartment while lying in bed. The cramps immobilized her, her heart pattering against her ribs. What if the Diabolo dragged him down again? What if Caroline attacked him? Or worse, what if Ningursu found him? Surely Madame Owiti would have told her!

She'd prepared to force herself out of bed as the moon crowned over the rooftops when Brent walked in, his hair sticking out in random directions, dirt coating his hands. He held a box of chocolate out as a peace offering.

"I'm...sorry," Brent shuffled his feet. "I...uh...the stories of the dead...they got to me and I...I mean...I went to conduct releases and lost track of time. It was...I shouldn't have, I mean. But the stories are so strong, and I...I'm sorry."

Bria threw her arms around him. "It's okay. Just...don't scare me again. I was so worried."

"I know...I'm sorry...I mean...here." He forced the box of chocolates into her hands.

They sat on the bed picking through the box. Brent spit out a cherry-filled piece, gagging, while Bria tested the different flavors. Bria didn't harbor any anger towards him. He could go out if he wanted. There was nothing stopping him.

Especially now that he continued to carry his thoughts without fear.

"If you're not going to be home by sundown, let me know. Otherwise, I'll start worrying." Bria kissed his shoulder.

Brent smiled. Into the night, they sat together while Brent practiced weaving stories. Some stories, he finished with ease, while others left him fumbling as the Diabolo criticized his every move. He was getting better, stronger even, and if he kept building, soon no one could stop him.

The next two days, Brent held his promise. He left for Madame Owiti's after Bria woke up, and returned before sundown, usually with a present. One night, he brought a box of different pizza slices. The next, he returned with a parcel of unusual seeds. Bria spent the entire night sorting through them. Flowers bloomed as she touched each one, decorating their kitchen table with fire-lilies, ghost-lilacs, and misty roses.

She wove them together into a crown to place upon Brent's head. "Where d'you find these? They don't grow around here!"

"Traded a story for them in the market." Brent grinned.

"So you told a story?"

"Yeah...I did!" His eyes brightened.

Bria pulled him close to her.

Through the evening, Brent wove more stories until they fell asleep wrapped in each other's arms.

They woke again at morning's light. Finally, the cramps subsided, and Bria climbed out of bed before Brent to take a long hot shower. The fire-lilies remained strewn across the floor, dancing with the lilacs and roses. These flowers belonged to a world of magic but not to Mert.

After she showered, Bria collected the seeds in her bag. She let the flowers dance across her fingertips and watched them jump into her pouch. They glowed like flames with the piles of lemon seeds, grass clippings, and nuts she collected.

Brent woke up, joining her by the kitchen counter. He kissed the top of her head and boiled a pot of coffee. It felt *normal*.

Almost.

Except for the injection Bria inserted into Brent's arm and the way he quivered as the liquid shot through his veins.

And there the hidden anxiety that the Diabolo or Council would return remained in Bria's stomach.

"Ugh, I hate that shite." Brent leaned against the counter and closed his eyes, waiting for the kettle to boil.

"I know. I was thinking of stopping at the Sanatorium today to see if we can adjust it. You're doing better. And..." Bria met his eyes. "We could see if there are any plans about how to deal with the Diabolo. I feel like we may have to deal with it on our own. They haven't said anything to you, right?"

"I've only seen Madame Owiti, Tilda, and Caroline...and that shopkeeper. Lex is her name, right? She's been staying with Madame Owiti."

"Lex, yes. How's she doing?"

"She's quiet, mostly. She hasn't made up with her husband..." Brent poured his cup of coffee and sniffed it.

"They're a strange couple." Bria crossed her arms, staring across the room at Brent's green gem sitting on the table.

"And we're not?"

"I mean, yes, but at least we...talk."

"Unless I go a little mad."

"Yeah, except then."

Brent wrinkled his nose as he smiled, then leaned in for a kiss.

Bria pushed him away. "Go rinse out your mouth. You smell like coffee!"

"Oi! You kissed me with pineapple breath!"

They continued laughing and bantering as Brent got dressed. Together, they headed out into the streets with Nix on their heels. Bria let the sunlight enthrall her. It was a weird, misty light, dancing between the buildings and debris. The streets didn't bustle the same way anymore, with children hiding in their homes and those passing by keeping their heads lowered. Brent flinched at random moments as they zigzagged through the streets, taking the long way towards the Sanitorium. He'd point out stories and statues, commenting that one represented Merta, the city's namesake, while another showed the founding members of Mert's first City Council. He absorbed the history like a sponge.

Rosada misses out on people like you, Brent. You might've been a scholar if they looked past your eyes.

Commotion picked up as they passed through one of the smaller plazas. A couple people in pinstriped suits bickered beneath an awning. A few women sat on the benches beside them, their large sunhats and fuzzy winter coats redolent of giant pillows.

Brent slowed, his attention drawn to a woman in a bright pink hat. Bria followed his gaze, but before she asked anything, the woman shouted in their direction.

"REGGIE!"

The woman in the bright pink hat raced over to Brent and squeezed him.

"Um..." Brent stumbled back.

"Reggie! There you are! You just vanished a month ago!" The woman gripped Brent's cheeks as she spoke. "I was so, so afraid that I lost you again!"

"I'm sorry, I don't—" Brent met Bria's eyes.

"Who are you?" Bria interjected. Brent was too flabbergasted to find the correct question.

"The better question is, who are *you?*" The woman glared. "Reggie! Did you find yourself a new woman!

You didn't even have the heart to reject me, you bastard!" She smacked Brent. "You terrible bastard!"

"Mitzi!" one individual in a pinstriped suit shouted.

"Look, Freddie! It's Reggie! He up and vanished and—"

"I told you that we found him!" The one called Freddie marched over to them. "His name ain't Reggie; it's Brent. He's got his head together finally!"

"No reason he had to up and leave us hanging! We were his family!" Mitzi banged her fist into Brent's chest. "We was your family, Reggie, and you disappeared!"

"I'm sorry...I don't...I don't remember. I really am..." Brent squirmed.

Bria stepped in front of Brent, preventing Mitzi from hitting him again. "Brent was sick for a while. He didn't mean to hurt you."

"Oh, fuck off, ya slut!" Mitzi pushed Bria to the side.

Bria landed on the ground with a thud. Freddie shouted as Mitzi lunged again at Brent, shrieking at him. As she screamed, Nix jumped forward, standing between Brent and Mitzi while snarling.

"Get outta the way, you damn dog!" Mitzi screamed.

Nix growled.

"Aw, forget it!" Mitzi spat in Brent's general direction before storming away from them.

"Sorry about that, Reg—Brent." Freddie shrugged. "Billie and I was telling her you ain't no Reggie no more, but she ain't wanna listen. Gotta hope and all, I guess."

"It's a'ight," Brent shifted. "I wish I...I mean...she obviously loved Reggie...."

"She lusted him, ain't love. Reggie didn't want nothing to do with her."

Bria watched Brent's eyes fall. Was he trying to find Reggie's story? Was that the man he channeled back in the morgue?

"You look even better, though, Brent. Glad to see ya being happy. Gonna miss ya being around, though. Was a huge help," Freddie said as they began walking away.

"Um, hey Freddie?" Brent called.

"Hm?"

"Be safe, a'ight? With all these storms and all, I mean...and...yeah. Just be safe. There's gonna be some weird shite going on."

"Yeah, there already is! Like there was that crazy storm." A smile caught Freddie's lips. "You did that, didn't ya? Knew you had all that special magic and all."

"Yeah, um, sorta, yeah." Brent reached for Bria. She took his fingers and squeezed them. "But, um, I don't think it's over."

Bria turned to Freddie. "Mert's in danger. There are people who want it destroyed."

"Rosada's desire to annex us ain't a new issue. Think they've been sending spies if you ask me." Freddie looked over his shoulder, lowering his voice. "We seen some funny-looking characters lately. Our guy in the Mertoni City Council's been busy poking and prodding, and there's this newcomer who's tryna get the Sanitorium shut down and all. Said it's inappropriate healing magic. And Billie saw this Giant the other day who got tried to take control of the police precinct...he mighta been drunk, though. I dunno. Could be nothing. I think Rosada is sending some people here to mess with us too. But me and the Stripes'll be ready. We'll fuck 'em up if we gotta."

Brent's face paled as Freddie spoke. "Do you know any of these newcomers' names?"

"Dunno about the weird giant guy, but there's a new minister in the City Council. Calls herself Victoria or Lia or something like that. It ends with an 'ia' is all I got!"

Brent nodded slowly but kept his eyes on Freddie. "Listen, be careful...a'ight? It's...I...I think something's gonna happen."

"You was always saying funny things like that." Freddie cackled. "All good, mate. You take care of yourself, and we do the same, yeah?"

"Yeah, a'ight."

Freddie nudged Brent's shoulder once before wandering off, confidence brimming on their shoulders.

But Brent did not show the same confidence. He shrank in on himself before glancing at Bria. She read him like a book. That worry and fear scoured his face like none other.

"The Council is still here," he whispered.

"That doesn't surprise me, to be honest."

"Why wouldn't they attack, though?"

"I'm not sure. But... we have to decide about what to do next."

Brent bit his lip. What did he see in the mist? Was he looking for signs?

She touched his arm. "We should keep going to the Sanitorium. We can talk to Kek then..."

"No, you do that. I'm...I should go talk to Caroline. I mean...I might be able to coerce some information out of her or something."

Bria didn't like the sound of that.

"I'll be a'ight. I promise. A'ight?"

"Okay," Bria replied.

"And if I'm not," Brent squeezed her shoulder, "you can force-feed me pineapple all you want."

Bria reached the Sanitorium, her mind racing. Nothing validated her suspicions. It was hunch: a drunken

Giant causing a fuss and a woman with a name oddly like Aelia. Sight in Mert was strong. Most people saw the Mist Keepers as if the City of Mert granted sight to its citizens. Was the Council influencing the affairs in the city? Her mind raced as she summoned a branch to lift her to the window at the top of the Sanitorium.

She tapped her fingers a few times on the windows. After a moment, a shadow rushed over and opened the murky windowpane.

Varden pulled her inside the suite. "Bria! What are you doing?"

She collapsed into the kitchen chair and shook her head. "I was coming by to talk about Brent's medication."

"Is he doing okay? What happened?"

"He's fine. More than fine. He's doing great. I was wondering if we could reduce his dosage—"

"Ah, that is a question for Kek."

"Yes, I know. But...that's not the point right now." Bria shook her head. "We overheard something is all..."

She detailed what Brent's acquaintance told them about the Giant and the Councilwoman. Varden listened intently, never interrupting, his eyes soft and kind.

He spoke only when Bria finished. "There are lots of Giants and strange people in the government. Think of the Rosadian Senate. You can't say any of those senators are right in the head."

"I know..."

"It is something to watch. I will consult with my comrades and the Pool. There is tension in the air, but a huge onslaught of magic just filled Mert. It would take the Order weeks to ready an attack on us. And the Council, well, they would have to readjust their command over the Diabolo. They're rogue players. But..." Varden scowled. "I will investigate it and speak with Kek."

"Thank you."

They sat there in silence for a moment. Maybe her anxiety got the best of her. Why should one drunken giant make her worry about the Council? Sure, Giants weren't common, but here in Mert, the unusual thrived. People lived. Stories bloomed.

"Here, we were talking about Brent before, yes? Well, if I recall, Kek was working on something for him. Hold on!" Varden jumped up and bounded from the room. He cast a tremendous shadow over the kitchen.

A giant shadow.

Bria shuddered. She had tried not to forget the Council's Giant, Jiang, and how he tossed her over the ledge into the Library. She tried to forget about her temporary imprisonment. But it was there, nagging, and now climbed back to the front of her mind.

She counted the lights in the room, then counted backward from ten. The tree branches banged on the windows, pleading for her attention.

Bria approached the window. She hadn't noticed before, but the sky bore a yellow tint, a soft mist stroking the air. And the clouds choked. They cried as if a monster sliced through them, ripping them open at their hearts.

"Okay!" Varden bounded back into the room. "Kek has finished it! They created a tablet form of Brent's injection. One of these a day, and he should have his head under control. Kek created enough to last a couple months."

Bria glanced back at Varden. She took the jar, but Varden must have seen the worry sprawled across her face.

"What is wrong, Bria?"

Bria pointed to the shadow riding above the clouds. She half expected it to be a Diabolo turning over the horizon.

What she saw was much worse.

At least twenty airships lowered out of the yellow-tinged clouds, descending on the heart of Mert.

And on their sails sat the one symbol Bria knew better than any other: the Black Stamp.

CHAPTER THIRTY-SEVEN

TODD

Airships flooded the sky over the Mertoni Chamber of Treasury. For eight hours, Todd queued with others to claim the financial relief promised by the government. He walked away with barely enough to pay rent for the month, but if he sold the shop, it'd be sufficient to get out of Mert.

Now, ships loitered in the air.

Todd paused as the airships lowered from the sky. He recognized the insignia in an instant; he wore it on his wrist, he dreamt of it daily, and he tried his hardest to push it from his mind.

What is the Order doing here? He gripped his envelop of treasury notes to his chest. His mind raced. Did the magic really attract them? Hadn't they always let Mert be?

But then again, with the announcement that Knoll fell under new leadership, there were rumors of the Order's interest in the city.

I gotta warn Lex. Todd bolted out of the city square, down Dogwood, towards Myrtle. He didn't bother stopping by the shop, continuing to count as not only one airship arrived, not two, but at least ten lowered from the clouds. Behind them, a yellow tinge of smoke followed. The Order would recognize his brand in an instant. They would rip his and Lex's freedom from them in a moment.

Madame Owiti's building glared like a fortress. Yet, his own fright over the Order's arrival, as well as the leftover terror from that storm the other day, trumped any weight that hung on his feet. Every day he tried venturing to the building only to have his own anxiety push him back. Now, it didn't matter.

He slammed his fist against Madame Owiti's door.

"Oi! Open up!"

Madame Owiti answered, her crimson eyes heavy. "Ah, Toddle. I should have known, yes yes."

"Is Lex here?" Todd panted. He didn't wait for Madame Owiti to reply, pushing straight past her and into the main room.

Lex sat on the loveseat with her legs crossed, Garrett on her knee. She didn't meet his gaze.

"Lex, we have to leave! The Order is here—"

"We saw," Lex said with no emotion.

"Good, let's go—"

"It doesn't mean I want to leave with *you*." Lex glared at him.

"Lex—"

"Why don't you go back to the Order where you belong? They're obviously here for you!" Lex spat, and with Garrett in tow, rushed into the back room.

Madame Owiti sighed. "Toddle, maybe if you were softer, she'd hear you. Stop being a prick, yes yes? Show her what scares you. No one likes a hard head."

Todd didn't how to respond, resorting to picking at his tender new tattoo on his right forearm. Over the last few days, he'd dedicated his artistic energy into creating a woven tattoo reminiscent of the monster that had torn through the city. Plumes of smoke, towering over highrises, decorated his arm. A constant reminder of the day the world went dark.

"Toddle, your mind is in the clouds." Madame Owiti turned back to him. "Why do you ignore what is so clearly in front of you? The world is much grander than it."

Todd crossed his arms. "I'm not stupid."

"Then why do you act ignorant, Toddle Dray?"

"I don't! I... it's hard, a'ight? I've seen so much and wanna protect Lex and Garrett after everything that has happened."

"But you're wrapped in your own agenda." Madame Owiti paced to the far side of the room and opened a window. "You are hiding from something, Toddle. You do not want to *see* the truth."

"What're you going on about?" Todd snarled. "If you're talking about magic, I'm sick of it! I came here to have a quiet life—"

"A quiet life? Here? In Mert? That is not possible." Madame Owiti chortled as she left the room. Todd stared after her but didn't follow, watching as she vanished into the kitchen.

He collapsed face-first onto the couch and cursed into the pillow. Great. What was he supposed to do now? He thought the Order's arrival would send Lex back to him with little fight. Things were never that simple, though, were they?

The front door swung open. Todd sprung to his feet, grabbed the book from the table, and threw it at their intruder.

In the doorway stood the Story Collector with a dog at his heels. The book hit him on the head, and he stumbled for a second before kneeling on the ground to gather the book. "Oi! Don't abuse books. What have they ever done to you?"

"What the shite are you doing here?" Todd growled.

"I...need to talk to Madame Owiti and her friend. I..." The Story Collector glanced around the room. "What're you doing here?"

"The Order's back. Wanted to get my wife."

"Yeah...I saw..." Fear struck the Story Collector's face as he replied. Todd noted the black stamp embroidered into the kid's skin. If the Order came, he would be in as much danger as Todd's family.

Todd wasn't sure if he cared.

"What d'you do to piss the Order off?" The Story Collector motioned at Todd's wrist. "You got a black stamp like me, I mean. I didn't notice it at first, but it's there...right? Sorry...I shouldn't look, but..." The kid looked away, fidgeting with the ends of his coat's sleeves.

"I disobeyed orders. That's all," Todd muttered. "You collected my story. You can see."

"I only see parts of it. The stories aren't always clear."

"Hmph."

The Story Collector grew quiet, scratching the dog's ears as he stared beyond Todd. His silver-tainted gaze made Todd uncomfortable. These eyes almost terrified Todd more than the yellow slits he had a few weeks ago.

Both saw more than Todd wanted. But at least the yellow eyes belonged to a monster. These silver eyes belonged to a man.

"Listen, I really am... I'm sorry for breaking into your shop," the Story Collector whispered. "I wasn't myself."

Todd didn't acknowledge him.

"If there's anything I could do—"

"Fuck off!" Todd snarled. "Ever since you showed up, life has been a shitshow! I came to Mert for safety, and now the fucking Order is here! Dammit! I want my family to be safe, and you fucked it all up!"

The Story Collector recoiled. "I'm sorry. It's obvious you...you care immensely for your family."

"No shite! They're all I have! I don't have nothing else! I ain't got family back in Rosada! There is no *Dray* family! That ain't existed. My name is Toddle Riley Drayton! But no one can know that, because if they found out... I'm screwed! They'd know I've got this damn black stamp, plus I'm probably on some sorta list or some shite because of everything I did! So yeah, I care about my family!" Todd paused, watching as the Story Collector's eyes traced him. "And DON'T go collecting my story now, ya hear me?"

The Story Collector's gaze fell.

Todd continued ranting. There was something about the Story Collector that made him want to keep going.

Perhaps to prove a point. Or maybe that was part of the Story Collector's power: he got people talking. "Y'know, I never had much of anything growing up or shite. So I gotta protect my family. Ma died when I was a kid and never met my Pa. So I joined the guard, y'know, got involved with rounding up those accused of magic right before the Smoke Riots.

"Lex was one of 'em even though she ain't got it. She was a pale little thing, only twelve years old when we met, so I didn't pay much attention to her or nothing. I coulda stopped all her suffering there if I told 'em she ain't magic. She's just a pathetic girl; she woulda been able to stay home. But I didn't do nothing."

"You were a kid," the Story Collector stated.

"I was sixteen or something, I dunno. I SHOULDA got right from wrong, but instead, I obeyed orders, not giving a flying two shites what happened to Lex or none of the others we took. They got thrown into one of the Towers in Knoll. And I just accepted it! They were kids!"

Todd stopped. *Like Garrett.* How had he been so heartless? Had the Guard really ripped his soul out, thrown it into the wall, and left him but a shell?

"I just went with it over the years and shite. The Guard made me a perfect shoulder, taught me to shoot, garner a whip, beat vagrants, and give orders. I lost my virginity to some harlots, treated women like pigs...cause, y'know, that's what they make you think. No one is worth it."

The Story Collector's irises flashed.

Todd continued. The words flew from his mouth one at a time. "When I was twenty-two or something, they put me on duty in the Barracks beneath the belly of the Prime Tower. That's when I think I regained humanity or some bullshite like that." Todd rose, walking across the room, trying to keep his nerves at bay. The years of trying to forget flooded over him. "I didn't realize how bad everything was or nothing until then. Thought, y'know, they interrogated these saps, threw some in the Pit, let the others go. But no, that ain't the case. The Guard kept hundreds of people, young and old, beneath the Prime Tower. My senior officers took the most impressive of the lot out of the barracks. I remember a man who could turn gold into food, a woman who seemed to teeter on invulnerability, and a child who could freeze people in their track, to name a few. I never found out what they did. It don't matter. Cause they ain't ever come back."

The Story Collector paled. He squirmed. Todd almost took pleasure in the reaction. At least some stories were even too much for the Story Collector.

Todd took his silence as permission to continue. He didn't know why he bothered, but the story was halfway through the air now. It was better than having his story unwillingly collected. "When I was down there, I saw the pale girl with white hair: Elexis...my Lex. She seemed strangely...peaceful. A pretty thing, really, and I was absolutely enchanted. All my Guard training told me she was mine for the taking...but for once, I guess my conscious spoke or something and told me to stop. So, after a week or so, during my lunch break, I sat down before her cell and offered her an apple. I'd never seen someone so enthralled with fruit, I swear.

"We talked. A lot. She was young. Smart. But kind of...aloof? She was convinced she could see things—the present, the future, the past. Each time the Guards took her away, she only came back with more wild ideas. Unphased. Unflinching. Until one day..." Todd closed his eyes. "One day, one captain called order in the Barracks. He said the Capitol was investigating mistreatment out in Knoll for logistic purposes. To adhere, they wanted to deplete the barracks, leaving behind only those who provided what they needed. They procured a list of names to take upstairs one last time. They either got shot or sent to the Pit based on the results...whatever that meant."

He glanced at the Story Collector. The kid opened his mouth to say something but stopped himself, instead stroking back his dog's ears again.

"They handed me a pistol and ordered me to wait outside. Hours passed until they led a disoriented bunch outside. To my relief, Lex was not in the group. So, I took aim...and I..." Todd felt nausea enter his throat. He tried so hard not to think about what happened.

If someone asked, he ignored them.

If someone prodded, he denied the allegations.

"You shot them," the Story Collector finished. "The story is potent. I can't... I'm sorry, but it's hard to ignore."

Todd clenched his fists and looked away. "I didn't have a choice! It was my job! I killed three of them. I killed them...shot 'em right in the head!" He shook his head. "But then I reached this child. Must've been thirteen or so. I couldn't—I couldn't do it. I objected. My captain hit me. I continued objecting...so the captain had the other cadets around us drag me away while he finished the job."

"Because you're not the monster you think you are," the Story Collector mumbled.

"Nah, I was! Don't matter if I stopped; I'm still a monster, and...I ain't ever was the same! They beat me! Broke my ribs! Bloodied my face. And branded me.

When I woke up, I was in the Pit, and Lex was nursing me back to health." He wiped his face. "She was my angel, my sweetheart. We became more than a girl in the barracks and her guard. We fell in love. It seems stupid—I was her captor. But...we didn't fall in love for a couple years at least. I fooled around with the harlots and such, y'know, like you do. But Lex always was there. And soon, we were together, trying to make a life in the Pit. I did some odd jobs to get food. She made small amounts of money telling *fortunes*. They weren't real, but over the next five years, she made enough to...to purchase *my* freedom. Because she has a heart of gold."

He choked for a second, keeping back a few tears. Why did he bother telling this stupid story?

"So, the Guard let me out. But...me being the impulsive idiot I am... as soon as they closed the gate, I kicked the Guard in the face. A riot broke out, and Lex and I snuck away onto a passing train filled with a bunch of animals and shite, with no idea where we were going. It was on the train I proposed to her, and we married once we arrived in Chelidae's Mark on the coast of Rosada. We made a home there for a few years...until the Guards found us. It was Lex's idea to book a ride on an airship to Mert. We found out while we fled that she was pregnant, made landfall before she gave birth. With the money we salvaged, I bought the store so we could set shop.

"Our sons were born a couple months later. We were delighted! But...then we found out Preston was sick and there wasn't much we could do but make him comfortable. He died just shy of his second birthday. It did a number on Lex...and me. But... we've stayed here for these last four years, but now—now—" Todd banged his knuckles against the wall, "Now she's sick, and it's a mess, and...we gotta leave again. We gotta find a place where we can be all healthy and happy and...and shite like that!"

"Have you ever stopped to consider what makes Lex happy?"

Todd paused. It wasn't the Story Collector who spoke. No. He recognized that whimsical voice, and with each pronounced syllable, his heart rang.

Lex stood in the hallway, arms crossed, somehow looking even frailer than she had moments earlier.

"Lex..." He glanced at his feet. "How much of that did you hear?"

"Enough." Lex strode past the Story Collector, stopping a few paces away from Toddle. "It is about time you opened your heart again, Toddle. You claim I'm the one affected by Preston's death, but you're the one who has shut down for years. I want you back, not a statue. You."

"I want what's best for you and Garrett. And Mert is—"

"You've expressed your thoughts on Mert. And I've chosen to ignore them. But now...the Order's back. So, you're right, finally. It's not safe." Lex shook her head. "But we're a team, Toddle! You're not the leader of this household... we're supposed to work together! We're a team!"

"I only do this 'cause I love you, Lex. I'm a prick, and I love you. Please..." He gulped down his tears. "You and Garrett are everything to me. Please come back to me."

"I know, Toddle." She smiled. It caused Todd's own emotions to bubble. "Let's ask Garrett if he's ready to see his Daddy, okay?"

Lex took Todd's arm, guiding him down the hallway. Before he left the living room, Todd turned to the Story Collector. "Thank you."

"I did nothing." The Story Collector half-smiled. "You just started talking and told a story. I didn't ask for shite."

Todd grimaced.

"Thanks, Brent. You're a sweetheart." Lex kissed the Story Collector's cheek. "You might have a future as a counselor."

Brent flushed, paying attention again to his dog instead of meeting Todd's gaze. "Gotta work out my own problems first."

Lex led Todd into the backroom, where Garrett napped on the bed. For the first time in a while, Todd didn't need to force a smile. It came naturally.

Crayons and lay scattered on the bed beside. He had an artistic knack, and Todd missed the days he spent coloring with his son. That was before the robbery, before this mess.

Todd pieced through the drawings. One scribble looked like Lex, while another looked like Brent and his dog. Most notably, though, there sat an image of the airships in the sky. The Black Stamp sat as a fixture in the image.

"We can't stay here," Lex whispered. "You're right. For Garrett, we need to leave as soon as possible."

"Yeah...guess we gotta get packing."

CHAPTER THIRTY-EIGHT

COUNSEL AND ORDER

Bria watched as the airships rose over the city. Behind them, a trail of yellow smoke filled the clouds. A buzzing rose in her ears, and dizziness washed over her, only broken by the sound of the door flying open as Tilda burst into the suite.

Bria jumped, hitting her head against one of the lower shelves.

"Varden! Do you see—Oh! Bria! Good! You're here too!" Tilda relaxed slightly. "We should have known this would happen. *I* should have known. Caroline has been going on about the impending doom of it all, like a pure drama queen, but there is a method to her madness. She kept saying how 'those consarn milksops in the west' were going to make a fool of this city, just like they made a 'fool of her apprentice.' I ignored her. I'm sorry I did! But...I didn't think the Council reacting would cause the Order to come, and now..." Tilda blinked, continuing her incessant babbling. "One of our coppers got into a drunken tirade the other day and threatened to hold a coup over the Chief! Can you imagine...a coup over our police department! When I told Caroline, not that she is being very responsive, she said that of course Jiang would. Jiang? Who's Jiang?"

Varden answered in stride. "He is one of the Mist Keepers. Malaika's master."

"Malaika never told me his name! She always called him her Old Boozer!" Tilda continued ranting. The few times Bria saw her, she kept poise and confidence, analyzing everything in her path. The façade broke. Her red eyes darted about the room. "I didn't think that some fool drunkard calling himself John was Jiang the Mist Keeper. I was trying so hard to derail this. We've been doing such a good job keeping the Council and Order out of the city. I should have worked more with Caroline...but I...consarn it, I shouldn't be rekindling an old flame!"

"Love makes us do strange things, Tilda, my dear friend," Varden reassured her. "What is done is done. But I am glad you are here now."

"Caroline was going on a tirade about her head spinning and that she was going mad or something. I came by to see if Kek had anything that might help. Are they here?" Tilda glanced around nervously.

"No, Kek is with Edith and Malaika checking on the airship's repairs. They've been working on an escape plan idea, although they have said little." Varden headed towards the kitchen's archway. "Let me check if Kek has anything for Caroline."

Varden vanished from the room again. Tilda continued pacing while Bria continued fidgeting. She hated being debilitated by her monthly bleed. Some months were better than others, but lately, her cramps left her vomiting into the loo for days. Stress, exhaustion, all of that was to blame, but it didn't keep her from feeling at fault for not helping Kek with their preparations for leaving.

Tilda glanced again towards the window, where another airship lowered itself from the sky. Most of Mert's ships left during the Diabolo storm a few days earlier. Now, the city waited defenseless. "There's no way they would have known to come now. I bet that's what Caroline meant. They're in cahoots... they've gotta be."

"The Council and the Order?"

"Yes. It would take a few weeks to ready an attack like this."

"They probably just wanted a reason to attack." Bria's voice caught on a lump in her throat.

Tilda gripped the table so hard, her knuckles paled, "The world ain't that simple."

Bria shook her head. "I...I should go find Brent."

"Where is that silly man?"

"He was going to visit Caroline..."

As Bria turned to the doorway, Varden rushed back in, nearly tripping over Bria as he carried an orb in his hands. The texture swirled in circles, showing shadows of someone looking through at them. Varden dropped it into the sink and turned on the water. A metallic steam rose from the sink, decorating the small kitchen, before settling into a calm miasma.

Bria blinked, watching as Varden's outline tapped the top of the water.

"What's going on, Varden?" Tilda pushed past Bria.

"Tom's calling me."

"Tom?" Bria asked. *He can't mean... that'd be silly.*

Varden tapped the surface of the water a few more times.

"Tom? Tom, are you there?" He called out.

A tranquil voice replied. Bria swore she recognized it.

"Vardy, mi amore, are you safe?"

It was a man's voice. Calm. Smooth. Like melted chocolate over ice cream.

"Yes," Varden replied. "What is going on? The Order just arrived here. I thought—"

"I apologize, Vardy. I did not expect Ningursu to act so soon!"

That piqued Bria's interest. She peered inside the sink.

Her heart almost collapsed.

None other than the scarred-faced Mist Keeper, Tomás, stared back at her. His face softened as he met her gaze.

"Hello, Briannabella," Tomás said. "How are you?"

"You...you tried to...you..." Her head spun, just like back in the Library. Tomás had attempted to mess with her mind, leave her in a dreamlike state after her first time entering.

Tomás read exactly what was on her mind. "I apologize for our previous encounter. Things are far more complicated than I let on."

Bria hugged herself. "You could've killed me."

"But I did not."

Varden placed a hand on Bria's shoulder. "We can trust Tomás. I have trusted him for hundreds of years...with my life. He is playing his role as a peace-keeper."

"Well, he could have come and helped with Caroline and that consarn nightmare!" Tilda interjected. "This is an utter mess."

"Hello, Tilda," Tomás responded. "You are aware I cannot act outside of Ningursu's orders."

"For sard's sake!"

"Tilda, this is a delicate situation. Tom and I have been trying to prevent this outbreak for many years. It was only inevitable that it would occur." Varden glanced into the sink. "Now, we must quell the flame."

"All we can do is attempt to delay Ningursu," Tomás added.

"Wait! Wait!" Bria held up her hands. "What exactly is going on!?! There's all of this stuff, and no one explains everything. I am sick of being in the dark!"

Tomás stared at her with his good eye. "It is long and complicated. You and Brenton are in danger, though. You all are."

"Just tell me what's going on!" Bria slammed her hand on the counter. The silver liquid reacted, sending a few peonies fluttering to the surface.

Tomás sighed. "I wish I had the answers. I know that Ningursu has been in contact with individuals who have ties with the Order. I don't know the extent of the communication, but I came across it recently after Brenton's episode with the Diabolo."

"What? Why didn't you say something? Or try to stop it?"

"That is what we've been doing with me working at the Station House," Tilda interjected. "But everything is in the air. We don't know who has what influence or who is a Mist Keeper...or any of that consarn malarkey!"

Varden added, "Ningursu has been trying to get Kek to slip for a while. The Order wants Mert to fall. Their interests aligned, so they formed some pact. Whether the Order knows they're working with a Mist Keeper is another issue entirely."

Bria clenched her fists and shook her head. "And we're pawns in their game."

"Ningursu is playing a game, yes."

"Kek too!" Bria shot back. "They're trying to...meld me into something. Sure, they keep praising my powers, but they're no better than Ningursu."

"They only want to help you and Brent," Varden promised. "They are not trying to take advantage of you."

"Then they'll let Brent and me do what we want in this battle, right?"

"They want you safe."

"What if I want to stay and fight?"

Varden said nothing.

"That's what I thought." She straightened her back as she stared up at Varden. "Whatever is going on here, Brent and I are our own players. Not anyone else's."

"Where is Brenton anyway?" Tomás interrupted, his voice bubbling beneath the pool.

"He went to visit Caroline."

Tomás cursed under his breath. "Then it's already too late..."

"What? What's already too late?" Bria clenched the edge of the sink.

"Ningursu must have his location."

"But she's blindfolded!" Tilda exclaimed.

"Does that matter?"

Bria grew silent, staring between the three others. Why did she bother arguing with them? They were so much older. But that didn't make them wiser. In fact, they seemed almost childlike.

Varden pulled on Bria's arm. "We need to get you out of here before the Council arrives. You're in danger."

"We're all in danger! I'm not more important." She shoved Varden's hand away.

"Kek wants you safe."

"I don't give a damn! Everyone's in trouble! I have to help!"

"Kek can handle the Order and Mert. You don't need to—"

"I said, I *want* to help! The Council and Order can't keep stomping on top of us! I don't want my life dictated by this!" She waved her hand in the air between Varden and Tilda.

Tilda smirked at Varden. "Always knew there was a reason I liked her."

I don't have time to warn Brent. I have to figure out how to find him and stop this from getting any worse. What can I do, though? If Ningursu grabs Brent, then...oh! Bria scrunched her face. "If Ningursu knows where Brent is...then he'll bring him back to the Library, right?"

"Most likely," Tomás said. "The Library is where he is the most powerful."

Bria stared at the sink. It was a large fixture, big enough for her to fit. She pressed her fingers over the water's surface.

"What are you planning, Bria?" Varden peered into the basin with her.

"An advantage..." She tapped the silver liquid, letting it dance over her fingers. "I could take them by surprise."

"You mean go to the Library?"

Bria nodded.

Tomás's face drew into a straight line. "It's risky."

"Trust me. Please. This will work," Bria begged. "Please."

Varden patted her shoulder again, causing her to recoil slightly. "I agree with Bria. It's worth the risk. It's unorthodox, but... that's why it might work."

"Okay. Give me a moment to get ready." Tomás shifted, and the pool grew dark.

Bria stepped back and glanced up at Varden. The Giant shrugged and turned to Tilda, remarking something under his breath that she couldn't quite make out. Bria tried to find a question to ask, avoiding the long pause of silence, but her own heart and mind flurried. Was Brent already in Ningursu's clutches? What did the Council have to do with the Order's arrival?

Before she asked anything, Tomás's image flashed again in the sink. "Okay. I am in a better location now. I didn't see any other Council members while I trekked downstairs. You're safe."

Bria pushed a chair over to the sink, checked that her bag was safely at her side with Brent's medication, then with Varden's help, she climbed inside the sink. She glanced once at Tilda and smiled.

"Good luck," Tilda mouthed.

"Same to you."

The silver liquid seeped around her, dragging her beneath the surface, first by her ankles, then her knees, and up towards her waist. It ate her like the quicksand in Brent's stories, tugging away at her skin, pulling her down, deeper...

Deeper...

Deeper...

She emerged in a deep lake, gasping for air.

And surrounded by a field of red peonies.

CHAPTER THIRTY-NINE

HOW TO DEFEAT A MONSTER

B rent stayed in the lounge, stroking Nix's head, staring at the spot where Todd had stood. The story was a lot to take in, and it relieved him that he hadn't used his magic to discover it. Each emotion that wove its way through his head locked him in tight, a wave of empathy transforming him from Brent Harley to Todd Dray.

While Brent was sympathetic towards Todd's plight, an uneasiness remained about the man's time in the guard. Could years of habits die so easily? On top of that, what was going on in Knoll? Brent tried putting together the pieces together, but it made his head hurt.

Vague memories flickered in his head of Elder Don Van, back before the Diabolo riddled his mind, preparing him for the lucrative Level Five Cleanse: The Buzzing. He saw a story of Elder Don Van working in a tower by an odd machine.

But Brent never learned what happened next. The story faded. It was probably for the best.

With Nix on his heels, Brent headed through the hallway toward the back room where they kept Caroline. Madame Owiti sat in the kitchen, staring out the window, half asleep. He didn't bother waking her. His mind trailed elsewhere. *I shouldn't have gotten distracted by the story.* But even Brent admitted he loved a good one. Todd's tale was one he would ponder for days to come.

Caroline sat, as usual, on the chair in the corner, her wrists tied together. For the past few days, it had been the same circumstance. She barely moved, her face hardly ever staying on one identity. Brent understood, too; the medication helped the stories not be so loud, but the whispers of every story remained. The dead called for him. It wouldn't stop.

"What is going on?" Caroline perked up as his footsteps clicked into the room.

"The Order has arrived in Mert."

"Oh. That's a shame."

"A shame?! You know what they did to me! You..." He gritted his teeth and winced. Phantom pains from his wounds after Level Four of the Cleanse stabbed at his side. Elder Don Van's voice climbed in his ears.

"It has never affected me. They are a bunch of mortal fools," Caroline whispered.

"Never affected—you're in Mert now! Everyone's affected here!" Brent cursed under his breath.

Caroline scowled. Her face momentarily shifted from its melting façade to that of an old man, then back to normal. "They are merely mortals."

"Sight is strong in Mert."

"Then why not leave?"

"You asked me that in Newbird's Arm. It's not that simple. We can't run forever."

"I think running is the only way I can escape him now."

"Ningursu, you mean?"

Caroline nodded. "I still hear him."

Brent sat on the ground before Caroline, taking her hands. "Repeat your mantra. Your name. Your constant."

"My name. My constant."

"What is your name?"

"Caroline Elisabeth Walsh."

"What is your age?"

"Oh, for sard's sake, Brent, I lost track."

Brent laughed.

"I must be over three-hundred-twenty!"

"Good..." Brent grinned. "Where are you from?"

"Heims Norte."

"And what is your one constant?"

Caroline's lips twisted as she tried to find the right word.

Her mouth opened to speak.

And she let out an inhuman screech.

Brent flew back into the wall. Nix howled. As Caroline continued to shriek, a profuse yellow smog twisted around her. The smog drifted about the room, out into the hallway, and towards the open window in the lounge.

In an instant, Caroline vanished.

And all fell quiet.

Brent blinked. *Ningursu.*

Todd popped out of the back room. "What the shite was that?"

"Just...um...stay here! It...stay here!" Brent jumped to his feet and bolted out of the apartment with Nix.

He stumbled down the stairwell and into the streets where the sky beat with a yellow tinge. *I have to warn Bria. Where was she going? Right! The Sanitorium!* He paused on the corner of Myrtle and Celosia. *If I head this way, then I go straight through the City Centre and...shite!*

He zigzagged through the alleys. In the back of his mind, he recalled days spent sleeping behind trash bins or running into the Pinstripes on the corners. Now, he pushed past individuals ducking for cover in the storm. If Ningursu attacked, if a Diabolo appeared, he needed to get as far as possible from these innocent bystanders.

He would not let them be victims in this game.

His heart pounded as he ran, climbing into his ears and shaking his head. Brent ignored everything, even the stories building up in the passages. The mist grew thicker. Everything pounded. The world was nothing more than clay, and Ningursu melded it around Brent.

His ears rang.

Brenton. I know you can hear me.

The voice sounded like Caroline mixed with the Diabolo.

But it belonged to Ningursu.

"Go away," Brent hissed, coming to the end of an alley a few blocks from the Sanitorium.

You and your little lady have been a thorn in my side, Brenton. I never believed two children would cause so much trouble! If you had kept your head down and listened, we would not have a war brewing on the horizon.

Brent turned. Ningursu's voice sounded like it was right there in his ear. "There doesn't need to be a war!"

If you had not released the Diabolo—

Brent laughed. "Don't pin this on me! If YOU hadn't kept those monsters...if you destroyed them like you told Kek, you wouldn't have caused this! You're...I don't know what you hate about the Magii or Kek or anything! They're just like you!"

Immortality and magic impact the balance of this earth. Your little lady should not have so much power. Kek should not be alive any longer. There is an imbalance caused by magic...and hence, the world is dying.

"Lies! You sound like the Order! I've seen the stories!"

Brenton, they have deceived you. The Diabolo has ravaged your mind, and Kek and their Magii have manipulated you.

"No. You're lying." Brent scanned the alley, half expecting Ningursu to emerge from the mist sinking out of the sky.

Come back to the Library. We'll talk.

"No."

If you come back, we may facilitate an end to this war before it begins. Come now, Brenton. Think about this. We are your family. Mist Keepers die to support the network of the dead. We are one.

Brent quivered beneath Ningursu's words. They pulled on his convictions and heartstrings. He fought them back, and his stomach leapt in circles. "I will not die."

Brenton—

"I've survived this bullshite! You want me dead! I won't die!"

You must die to become a true Mist Keeper. The longer you wait, the more others will suffer. You saw Caroline. You felt the dead screaming. Do you want it to continue?

"It's not my fault."

Do you want others to suffer? Don't make us drag you back, Brenton.

"Fuck off!" Brent threw open his arms. The mist parted at his command.

On the opposite end of the alleyway stood none other than the giant, Jiang. His long black hair floated in the breeze while a scowl hid beneath his overgrown beard. He bore a copper's uniform, a club at his side, and each of his steps rocked the air. Brent shrunk, stumbling back against the wall. Stories pulsated around the giant.

"I thought Caroline and Malaika were bad enough." Jiang stumbled forward, the dingy smell of liquor on his breath. Before Brent understood what happened, the giant lifted Brent up by his arms and held him above the ground.

Nix barked.

Brent strained against Jiang's grip, but he slipped back into a story. It wrangled his head, and for a flitting moment, he did not remember if he was Brenton Harley or Jiang of Tencauri.

He exhaled sharply, letting the mist expunge from his body.

A tale formed in the air. In a city, young Jiang prepared to marry his darling fiancée. But a week before the ceremony, an evil sorcerer with silver eyes took her. He and his wife, in a fit of fury, slaughtered Jiang's fiancée and many others in a plea to save their dying son. Jiang drank away his woes. He vowed to destroy the sorcerer and abolish magic for his fiancée and all those who died at the sorcerer's hands.

In the area around Jiang's head, Brent watched the story unfold. A battle waged with many lost and a sorcerer who set a lush green forest ablaze. The fight never stopped; there was never a winner. Jiang kept in his pursuit.

"You don't need to fight..." Brent met Jiang's glare. "Magic isn't the enemy."

"Just because you can see my story doesn't mean you understand."

"It was one bad person."

"They're all bad."

"And Ningursu's any better?"

Jiang's face contorted. "I said they're all bad."

"Then let me go."

"I can't—gah!"

A figure rushed from the end of the alleyway, barreling straight into Jiang's legs. He went flying, hitting the far wall.

Brent landed on the ground with a thud. He grunted, pushing himself off the ground, and looked to meet his savior.

Edith stood over Jiang. She pressed her hand into the wall, and a long sword emerged from the stone.

"Always wanted to slice up a reaper. Guess this one'll do just fine." She grinned in a way that made Brent's skin crawl.

"You think you can beat me?" Jiang rose. He removed an equally sharp blade from his coat.

"Oh, yes. I've got years on you."

Jiang raised his sword. Edith lunged forward.

It was an odd sight, really. Jiang was at least twice as tall as Edith, but the woman moved with the smoothness and daintiness of a ballerina. She parried each of his swings while he leaned away from her as she struck. Brent stood there in complete shock, watching the two fight.

Edith broke the trance. "Hey, Reaper! Get your ass out of here! Kek is dealing with Malaika. Don't know where anyone else is, but you better get the fuck outta here! I'm not fighting for fun!"

"Oh, um, right!" Brent darted past the commotion with Nix right beside him. At the end of the path, he turned back. "Thank you!"

"You owe me big-time, Reaper!"

The mist caught her voice and lowered on the scene.

But it didn't end the commotion.

Brent turned to face a storm waiting on the other side of the alley. The sky bled orange, pulsating with the rage of the Diabolo. He saw it now, clear as day, soaring through the clouds. Its mouth dripped with blood, leaving a crimson shadow on the sails of the airships. It appeared to look directly at him.

His head seared as he met its gaze.

Join it, his Diabolo hissed.

Shut it, Frankie! He watched as the Diabolo lowered itself from the sky. His mind raced. For a moment, his memories dragged him back to Newbird's Arm, fighting again. Falling...fading...

What was he supposed to do?

I can stop them. I can keep pushing them away...keep distracting them. But they'll keep coming back. I gotta stop it. He glanced down the road. *I need to get its attention.*

"Nix, c'mon!" Brent turned and darted down the street towards the beach. People rushed past him, looking for shelter, fighting against the bellowing winds and the oozing nightmares from the Diabolo's skin. They grappled towards him but didn't wrap around his head the same way. He'd seen so much; what more could the Diabolo do?

He skidded to a halt at the edge of the boardwalk. The Diabolo in the sky moved with him, lowering every second, so near now.

Its breath tasted like tobacco and corpses.

"Oi!" Brent shouted, waving his arms. "Down here!"

The Diabolo extended its jaw, revealing its sharp pearly teeth.

"Okay, a'ight, cool...um..." Brent glanced at Nix. "Catch me if you can!"

Brent ran again. He had no clue what he was doing. No plan. Nothing. His adrenaline pulsated through his body, his head seared, but he had to keep going.

His feet carried him along the sand, kicking against the water, as he approached the dunes. The sand blew, catching the air, spinning. It danced around him.

The Diabolo clamored down to the beach. It crawled behind him like a spider.

And screeched.

"Yeah, c'mon! Right here!" Brent backed into the dunes. He stepped in the crevasse between the twist of grass on the hills...

...and to his shock, he emerged in the Council's Tunnels beneath the earth.

He didn't have time to get his bearings. The red and yellow smoke piled in after him, filling the cavern.

Whining, Nix bolted down the tunnels away from the commotion.

"Nix!" Brent pivoted away from the Diabolo and raced down the Tunnel. Behind him, plumes of smokes continued to grow. Tendrils wrapped around him, grappling at his arms, legs, neck, and face. He pushed them back.

Give in!

Shut up, Frankie!

It will be easier.

Dammit, Frankie, go away!

He pulled away, racing straight into the junction where Nix waited for him, her misty form pulsating in and out in front of the Library door.

Brent slowed in the center of the junction. He'd spent so much time here, but now he was no more than a stranger in an unknown land, encompassed by a whirlwind of orange. He heard the Diabolo; it whispered his name, stroked his face with fallacies, and promised improbable victories.

I'm the only one who knows how to fight it. Brent faced the monster. Up close, it was less human than his own

Diabolo. Its face was not one, but twelve different countenances piled onto one body. It moved like an arachnid, crawling on multiple misshapen arms and legs.

And even worse, Brent sensed its suffering. It screamed beneath hundreds of personalities trying to dominate. No one story remained stable for long. Someone had woven them all together into a disfigured knot.

Brent reached forward. "I'm gonna help you."

The Diabolo screamed.

"I need you to stay still, a'ight? I'm gonna help."

As he inched towards the monster, it didn't recoil. Instead, it lowered its head and closed all eighteen of its eyes.

Brent placed a finger to the top of its head. He found a single thread of a story about a boy who chased a cat up a tree.

One by one, he began unwinding the stories, letting the red, orange, and yellow mist pile around him. He held onto one thought:

My name is Brent Harley. And I am here.

CHAPTER FORTY

THE BATTLE FOR THE TUNNELS

Bria rejected Tomás's assistance out of the pool, blinking away the silver liquid. She arrived in a room filled with peonies. The flowers encircled a large silver pool, knitting their way across the floor and up the walls. They pulsated, bled, and reached for her as she marched towards the exit on the far side of the room.

"Briannabella!" Tomás shouted. "Where are you going?!"

"To stop this!" Bria shouted. The peonies seethed around her.

"No one is here but me and—"

"I thought you said they had Brent!"

"They do! They know where he is, and once they have him, they'll—"

"Then I'll catch them when their guard is down."

"Briannabella, please." Tomás sighed. "I know you and I did not have a favorable first encounter. You have no reason to trust me, and I can tell you are scared and angry. But please, do not act in haste. Ningursu is powerful."

"I'm not scared of a talking skull." Bria clenched her fists. That was a lie. He haunted her every day. But she wouldn't drop her guard. Not now.

"Bria—"

"I can't stay complacent. I'm not like you or Caroline or even Kek. This needs to end." Bria marched towards the end of the room. The peonies followed her. "You can help, or you can stay here talking to Varden. But... I'm going to stop this."

She didn't wait for Tomás to reply. With a single step forward, she hurried out of the peony-filled room and into the heart of the Library.

It was just as miraculous as she remembered. Shelves reached towards the incandescent glass ceiling above while lanterns flickered and footsteps pattered. But to Bria, more than anything, she loved the way the walls pulsated. Bark and leaves composed the walls, and as she strode forward, the peonies continued to explode behind her.

She ignored the sudden nausea in her throat as she walked. As much as Bria wanted to forget, she still remembered how the walls circled around her in a maze composed by the Mist Keepers' guile. She wandered aimlessly those months ago, her head spinning, pounding with incoherent demands.

Bria shook away the fears, putting them in the back of her mind, and rushed to the doors at the front of the Library. She half expected to see Alojzy in his slick suit, with his voice like ice, emerge from the shelves. But no one did. Not even Tomás followed.

They're all cowards.

She jumped as the door to the Library shook. An inhuman scream rumbled from just beyond it.

A dog barked.

"Nix?" Bria rushed to the door and thrust it open.

Bria didn't have a chance to take in the junction's familiarity. Her attention at once fell to the red smoke dancing before her. It spun in circles around a tall, lanky figure in the center of the junction, arms outstretched, eyes shut. Nix bolted around in circles, yapping and whining.

Then the smoke dissipated, leaving a calm miasma gathering about her ankles.

There, Brent stood. He stumbled back, his body shaking.

Bria acted fast. She removed a vial and syringe from her bag. While preparing it, she rushed over to Brent, grabbed his arm, and before he protested, jammed the needle into his skin. His eyes widened, then his knees buckled, and he collapsed on the ground, hyperventilating.

"Brent?! Brent, are you okay? Please be okay. Please." Bria collapsed beside him. "Please...I can't do this again. Please..."

He glanced at her, face pale, lips quivering.

His eyes remained silver.

"Bri...hi," Brent croaked.

She threw her arms around him, holding back sobs. Nix trotted over and lay her head on Brent's leg.

"How d'you know I was gonna...I didn't even know I was gonna be here."

Bria opened her mouth to reply, then paused. Muffled voices echoed from the northwestern tunnel.

A few moments later, Jiang entered the tunnels, dragging Edith by her hair. Beside him walked a ghost with a bushy beard carrying none other than Ningursu's head. A long chain of mist poured from Ningursu's mouth, connected to Caroline's wrists as she teetered her way through the tunnels. Her bright blue eyes darted back and forth, fear marking her melted face.

Alojzy took the rear, poised and calm as ever. He noticed them first. "Look, Master Ningursu. We are blessed today."

Ningursu turned his head. His single white eye fixated on her. Bria's head rang. The world spun.

"No! Stop! Stop it!" She gripped her head, falling to her knees. "Go away...go away..."

It kept spinning. The wind bellowed again. A dog barked.

She was everywhere.

She was nowhere.

She belonged to Ningursu.

"No!"

You are nothing but a weed. Now flourish. Flourish.

She gripped the ground. Vines crawled along the walls and towards the floor.

I am not a weed! Bria lifted her head and met Ningursu's gaze. "I am not your toy."

"It appears she is stronger than we thought, hm?" Alojzy glanced at Ningursu.

"She doesn't matter to me. Bring me the boy."

No one moved. A mist-made chain exploded out of Ningursu's mouth. It wrapped around Brent's ankles and dragged him across the ground. He sputtered, pulling against it. But his strength faltered. His eyes hung with exhaustion.

"Brent!"

Jiang yanked Brent from the ground, holding him up by the collar of his shirt. Edith squirmed over his shoulder.

"Wait!" Caroline shouted. Her voice belonged to her again, her blue eyes stark and trembling. "What are you doing to him? He looks terrible!"

"Caroline, behave," Ningursu hissed.

Alojzy peered at Brent with curiosity from his position. "He might've fought a Diabolo, but his mind is sound. He won't be ready."

"Ready for what?" Caroline spun. "He is not a monster! Do not treat him like one!"

"Be quiet, Caroline!" Ningursu boomed. Another chain made of mist sent Caroline flying into the wall. His ghost-aid flinched.

Bria shrunk. But no one watched her. No one cared.

She was in control.

These were her tunnels.

Bria gripped the ground. The vines pulsated through the tunnels, bolstering with excitement. *I am not a weed. I am a forest.*

She kicked her foot against the nearby wall. The vines burst out from all angles, grabbing each of the Council members and throwing them in every which direction. Jiang dropped Brent and Edith, and they both hit the ground.

Bria raced over and helped Brent up, glanced at Edith's unconscious body, and then turned. She didn't have time for first aid. Now was her chance. Instead, she rose to confront the Council of Mist Keepers.

"We're not done yet," Bria shouted.

"Stand aside!" Jiang rose, his voice booming. "You're nothing!"

"If I'm nothing, I wouldn't be able to do this!" She jumped in the air. A few stones fell, blocking the pathway to the west.

As a third rock tumbled, though, the surrounding walls shook and twist outside of her control. For a moment, everything spun, and when everything stopped, the junction was but a single room, with no doors, no exits.

"You're trapped," Alojzy stated from his spot by the wall.

Ningursu motioned for his ghost lackey to approach Bria. She'd never seen the skull up close and in person. The little skin that remained on his face had rotted; his empty white eye was as soulless as the skull half of his face. "Little girl, I would hate to mess with your head again. Leave. This is beyond you. You are trapped."

Bria glanced at the spots where the tunnels had vanished. In their place stood walls, traced over by vines and roots from the ceiling. They squirmed and inched towards her. She smirked. "Everyone keeps saying this is beyond me. But trapped? I'm not trapped."

She launched her hand off to the side, and her tunnels called back. Her vines attacked. They latched onto the array of Mist Keepers, stringing them up by their feet. Ningursu's lackey tripped. The ancient head fell and rolled across the floor. It wouldn't last long, though. She sensed Ningursu's powers crawling over her, trying to get her to cede.

The charade wouldn't last, though. The Mist Keepers had only one true weakness.

The mist.

"Brent!" She darted back over to him.

He held his head, pale as ever, looking as if he might vomit.

"Are you there?" she pleaded.

"Yeah..."

"I need a story...now!" She hated that she needed to demand something from him now, but it was the only plan she had concocted.

"What...what?"

"I'm so sorry. But it's the only thing I can think of...please! Just any story!"

"Right...yeah..." His fingers shaking, he held out his hand.

The mist reborn, the story fledged, an army of men and women in furs from the north, fighting, screaming. At the same moment, the vines she used to hold back the Council broke. The story was powerful, but not enough. Confusion was but a mild inconvenience, and as the mist thickened, Bria still saw the Council reaching towards them. She called her vines closer, and just as they wrapped around her fingers, they tackled the mist. They transformed into an army of plants and vines, capable of scarring and tearing skin away. They marched with vigor, and the Council dispersed about the junction. Jiang used his blade to ward off a few of them, but with every slice, each of the vines Bria sent out became stronger.

Nix darted among the stories, and as it faded, Bria kept her head above it all, grabbing Brent's wrist and tugging him into the center of the junction. He panted but stayed standing, relying on the same adrenaline Bria felt coursing through her body as she stared down at the Council. Caroline had fallen to the side near Ningursu. Alojzy's focus had yet to unhinge. The tunnels continued to spin. Jiang inched forward on the defensive, his eyes on fire. She'd lost track of Edith and

Ningursu's lackey in the fray, though, dust mingling with the mist, blinding...

Darkening...

Sinking...

They all waited for Bria's next move.

The last of the story dissipated, leaving Bria alone with her vines and roots. From the center of the junction, she saw all the tunnels hiding behind the illusioned walls. As Alojzy took a step forward, the ground beneath her shook, but by her own step, the entire junction roared back. It shook as the man reached out towards her, and with a single whip of vines, he fell back onto the ground.

"Bria! Watch out!" Brent yelled more alert than she'd imagined.

Jiang came barreling towards her with his blade outstretched. She leapt away from him, the vines grabbing him by his feet and turning him upside down. At another skip of her feet, the tunnels trembled again, dirt and rocks scrambling from overhead. The tunnels opened along the wall.

She paused, holding her hand out and grinning. "Don't mess with me or *my* tunnels!"

A single snap of her finger and roots climbed out from all ends, gripping each Mist Keeper by their feet. One vine lassoed onto Ningursu's head, tossing it down a tunnel to the west. The rest of the Mist Keepers tried to scramble, but Bria was faster, ordering her vines to take them away.

The roots above loosened. A landslide brought rubble and debris into the tunnels, locking the junction in silence.

She kept her energy alive, pulling Brent by the arm into the open Library. Nix raced in after them.

Once inside, she told the bark from the walls to cover over the doorknobs, locking it tight.

All was finally quiet.

And with the last beat of the nerve-riddled drum, she collapsed.

CHAPTER FORTY-ONE

OPAL'S CANYON

The trek through the canyon took far longer than Jemma had hoped it would. Micca babbled relentlessly, hopping over rocks, juggling the conversation with one hand and his navigation with another. He had a knack for direction and survival, and throughout the week, bargained with travelers to receive food, goods, and other necessities. It might not have taken as long if Jemma's feet didn't start blistering on the third day. In the middle of the voyage, they made a pit stop in a small vagrant-ridden village to get a healing cream for her skin.

At first, uncertainty lathered their voyage. They had no money, no belongings, just the skin on their back. But Micca bartered with his skills, trading his ability as a mechanic for other goods. Jemma had never felt so useless. Prayers didn't equate to money. No one cared about a Sister of the Order in a lawless land.

Much to Jemma's amazement, they saw no wild beasts or animals in the Canyon – human or otherwise. For the most part, this crack in the earth bore no life.

Even the shrubs struggled to breathe.

No wonder the Guards do not watch us. Most could not survive such a trek, Jemma realized as they walked.

After a couple days into their journey, Year Birth blessed the skies with hail. They ducked between caverns, and when they stopped, Jemma sat and prayed. Micca continued pacing, muttering to himself, uncaring about the world reborn.

By the time nighttime fell, Jemma sat alone by the fire, staring at the stars and counting the clouds mingling in the sky. Occasionally, they pulsed with the essence of the Effluvium, glowing yellow, to white, to orange. Micca ventured off to a group of trucks overlooking the edge of the canyon, leaving Jemma to her prayers.

Her journey would be over soon. They were so close to the city of Opal's Canyon, and then it wouldn't be long until she arrived in Aeterno. Whenever she closed her eyes, she almost visualized Ab Aeterno waiting for her. Stories told how its tower glowed on the landscape, pulsing with red and silver gems. Its Year Glass cast a painted glass shadow over the sea. It was so near now.

The next day, with the hail subsiding, they continued along the endless stone path. They spent their days arguing about the direction, weather, Effluvium, and the well-to-do of vagrants until civilization finally emerged on the horizon. Opal's Canyon, the pinnacle city of the southern edge of Rosada, waited for them like a beacon. White buildings, glimmering with opulent stones, climbed towards the sky.

A caravan of foreign trucks waited for them above the canyon. One foreigner, with a thick Heims accent, guarded the entrance to the hoist ascending the canyon. Despite the foreigner's gruff exterior, Micca managed to strike up a bargain with them. He agreed to fix one of their truck when they arrived in the city in exchange for passage up the lift.

At the top of the canyon, the Caravan's Leader, a stick-like man with a braided beard, welcomed Jemma and Micca onto the back of his wobbling trucks towards Opal's Canyon.

Jemma prayed as she huddled with the other passengers, begging that her stomach stay in one place. But, without a doubt, as soon as the truck skidded to a halt on the outskirts of the city, Jemma clamored off the back of the truck and vomited on the ground.

"I am not riding in any more of these vehicles!" she sputtered and wiped her mouth.

Micca laughed. "Woulda thought you'd be used to trucks by now."

"Never." Jemma wiped her mouth with the kerchief. "Forget that, though. What do we do now? You are the one with all the ideas, it seems! Now that we've arrived in Opal's Canyon, how do we get to Ab Aeterno? We cannot walk!"

"Relax, relax." Micca shook back his hair, still chuckling. Why did he always laugh? "I've gotta hold my end of the bargain here and fix up their truck. Why don't ya go into the city, find a train schedule or some shite like that, a'ight? If that ain't gonna work, I can always finagle my way into getting one of these trucks."

"No more stealing!"

"I ain't gonna steal!"

"It sounded like it!"

"I ain't!"

"We'll take a train or hitch a ride."

"I know! Stop being so strung up or whatever." Micca turned as he spoke. "Go get a train schedule and maybe, I dunno, relax or something too. It'll be good for you to do something like that."

Jemma straightened her back. "Fine. I'll make myself useful."

"I didn't say—"

"You implied it." Jemma left Micca and headed down into the city.

The canyon cut the city in half with a long bridge arching over it. It wasn't just cutting it in the literal sense but also in the figurative sense. On the southern side of the canyon rested the shacks and slums, overseeing the Canyon's vagrants. A single tower fixated itself at the end of the bridge, peering over everything, a mere beacon inside their one green oasis that gave the city its water. This tower was far older than the ones that came to Newbird's Arm. Gears churned and puffed with steam as she walked over the bridge. The Guard in its watchtower eyed her, but she kept going, ignoring their repugnant stares.

Just beyond it sat the train station, lined with rows of tracks. A brightly colored train occupied the tracks. An odd-looking bunch in leotards and glittery suits unloaded tents and carried them out to the empty field just past the train station.

Jemma stopped at the board on the outside of the station and grabbed a schedule. Flyers hung on the bulletin board: an advertisement for Santiago's Cirque Sunrise, a call for new recruits, and a worn-down wanted ad for Rhodana, the Forest Queen. Jemma stared for a moment at the blurry picture of Bria Smidt on the page.

Shadows covered the girl's face, hiding her in newsprint ink. She could walk straight into the city, and no one would know.

Jemma wondered if, soon, wanted flyers with her own face would cover these walls.

After pocketing the schedule, she turned towards the city. Her heart fluttered at the sight. There Opal's Canyon's Temple stood among the iridescent buildings, glistening with the same colorful array of the stone below its watch. The Effluvium danced around it, with dust gathering in the air. Jemma's feet carried her straight to its doors, her attention only on the Year Glass above the pews.

As Jemma stepped through the door, the windows shimmered, and the marble pillars dripped in the stain-glassed grasp of the sun.

Brothers and Sisters of the Order waltzed past, unphased by Jemma's presence. In pedestrian clothes, she looked like any other patron praying in the pews.

"My dear." One Brother approached her. "Welcome to the Temple of Opal's Canyon. Can I help you?"

"Oh, hello. I'm..." Jemma paused. "My name is um, Annabella...I just got here from Grover's Marsh. I am just passing through to admire your glorious Temple. You know, ours is so small and pitiful."

Jemma hated bashing another Temple, especially one she only ever heard about in rumors. She almost hated it as much as lying. But she couldn't tell them her actual name, not when she and Micca had fled Newbird's Arm like fugitives.

The brother smiled. "Please make yourself at home and stay as long as you wish."

"I worry my visit will be short, but thank you, Brother."

He bowed, then continued along the pews, greeting the patrons in their prayer. Jemma loitered in the rear of the Temple, marveling at the stained-glass windows and the tapestries on the wall. Yet, what drew her attention the most, even more than the Year Glass, were the odd mirrors that hung on the northern wall behind the podium. She circled through the pews and over to them, bowing again to the Brothers and Sisters she passed before reaching the far wall.

Her reflection awaited her distorted in the mirror. It was almost liquid in movement, causing her reflected orange hair to weave through the image. Her face floated between normal and perturbed.

Jemma reached her fingers to the mirror. When her fingers slipped over the surface, it bubbled like liquid. It shifted at her touch, spiraling. For a moment, her reflection vanished. In its place, haunting the mirror like a ghost, appeared a set of dark eyes. They stared at her for a moment, blinked, then reopened as a pair of blue eyes.

They blinked once more and disappeared.

Jemma stared, half expecting someone to step out from behind the mirror, claim it as a trick. But part of her believed, just slightly, that magic was afoot.

Magic! Of all things! In the heart of the Order! It was preposterous.

But what else explained it?

You're tired, Jemma. It has been a few days.

She sat upon a bench and bowed her head. The evening prayer came as the sun fell behind the canyon with a gentle haiku preached through the Temple.

Here, in the shadow
Of the mist's loving embrace,
We learn of true sleep.

"For I am the Effluvium's Soul," Jemma recited.

She will come to all,
Her arms outstretched in adore
To rock, rock, sleep now.

"For I am the Effluvium's Soul."

Come to bed now, dear,
She'll be here in the red morn,
Do not fret, you know

"For I am the Effluvium's Soul!"

The lyrics drifted into a soft hum, and each patron bowed their head in unison. Jemma brought her lips to her Year Glass. All the peace in Opal's Canyon, it was all she wanted to bring back to Newbird's Arm. Brother Roy Al would help bring this; he had to have seen this all in Ab Aeterno. Surely, surely, he would know how to bring this prosperity back home.

As the prayer dwindled, Jemma glanced back at the mirrored wall one last time. The images didn't shift again. Only reflections stared back at her, mimicking the activity in the pews. She bowed to her own reflection, then paraded out of the Temple and back into the streets.

The sky turned an odd shade of yellow as she left. *It must be the dust,* she thought, bowing her head. Though the wind left an odd taste in her mouth, reminiscent of sleeping too long or eating garlic. She winced and continued back towards the caravan. Assuming Micca had finished his work, they could find a place to stay for the night, then reconvene in the morning.

Jemma yearned for a proper bed too.

Micca waited for her, covered in oil, his hair slicked back into a ponytail. He smiled at her, showing his misshapen teeth. "Ay, Jem! You find anything worth sharing?"

She paused, then remembered the schedule in her pocket and removed it carefully. "This was all I found. I went to the Temple instead."

Micca grunted and took the flyer. He skimmed over it, and his smile spread across his face, widening ear-to-ear. Jemma didn't know what had excited him. She hadn't even looked at the schedule, to be honest. The Temple drew her to it instead, as always.

"A'ight! This is perfect! A'ight!" He laughed.

"What? What is it?"

"Ya didn't read this shite?"

"No. I did not."

Micca rolled his eyes. "Well, whatever, I think I got an idea of what we can do, a'ight?"

"Oh...okay..." Jemma blinked, taken aback by Micca's exuberance.

"This here schedule, it says that only one train is leaving tomorrow towards the west, yeah? It's heading to Laysan's Beach, which ain't that far from Ab Aeterno if my map is right. We can hop on it tomorrow."

"Oh, wonderful! But..." Jemma frowned, "How will we get tickets? We haven't any money."

Micca chuckled again, that overly exuberant, heartfelt laugh that often left Jemma uneasy. "Tickets? Oh, Jem, this train ain't got tickets."

"Pardon?"

"It's a circus train! They don't go taking passengers. We're gonna have to hop on tomorrow before they load up the show, a'ight?"

"That's freeloading!" Jemma argued. *I am so sick of these illegal activities!*

"I'd think you'd be up for it by now. You've already broken a bunch of rules." Micca winked and pocketed the flyer. "I'm gonna head to a tavern to get a drink."

"Please, don't get in trouble."

"I ain't gonna get in trouble! I'm gonna go to the crummy one on this side of town. No Guards give a damn about nothing there."

Jemma raised her hand to object, but Micca had already turned down one of the narrow roads, leaving her alone. As usual

Except for the watchful eyes of the Effluvium.

CHAPTER FORTY-TWO

THE GHOST IN THE LIBRARY

Where am I? It took Brent a few moments to get his bearings. He lay on a stiff bed in a bright room, his body aching, head pounding, light stabbing into his retinas.

He blinked a couple times, then rolled onto his side. Everything remained foggy, but except for the dull beating in his head, he was all there.

After a couple minutes, his vision stabilized. Once it did, the room came into view. He recognized this room, though it took a few stories to get it right. *I'm in the Library's infirmary. Right. I remember now.*

Brent grunted as he sat up from the bed. The door to the hallway remained open, and on the other cot, Bria slept with Nix at her feet. She looked tiny, covered in dirt and sweat. He called out to her, but she didn't stir.

After the Battle of the Tunnels, Bria passed out at his feet. He got her up the stairs and into the infirmary. His head spun in circles as he carried her, his mantra pounding in his ears, but he retained a sense of identity before sleep cradled him into the night.

Brent crawled out of bed. Other than his joints creaking as he walked, he didn't have any injuries. His head seared with yellow as the Diabolo tried to pry at his thoughts, but a hint of tranquility continued its reign. The medication worked. His head belonged to him and him alone.

Although, it took much longer to cross the room than he would have liked.

"Bria?" He stroked back her matted hair.

She stirred slightly but didn't wake.

Her story danced on his fingertips. He avoided intercepting her story in most cases, but this one remained prominent on her skin. For a moment, he absorbed parts of the tale, complementing them with the fuzzy recollections he had of the Battle in the Junction, then pushed the rest away. Those deeper terrors belonged to Bria, not him.

Brent sighed. Paleness encapsulated Bria's face. She looked unbelievably frail beneath her layers of wilting fauna armor. "What'd you do to yourself? You can't keep this up forever."

She still did not wake.

Brent leaned forward and kissed her forehead. "Listen, I'm gonna go find us some clean clothes and...um...food and such. You're gonna be starving when you wake up. Just...stay asleep. I'll be right back, I promise." He glanced at Nix. "Stay with Bria, a'ight?"

The dog didn't even bother lifting her head.

"Lazy." Brent scratched behind Nix's ears, then slowly left the infirmary. He stopped in the doorway, watching Bria for one last moment, then turned into the hallway.

The Library itself looked exactly as Brent remembered it. He paused, leaning over the railing. A barricade of chairs, vines, roots, and shelves lived against the entranceway. They were safe. No one chasing them, no one in their heads.

We're alone. Brent grinned. He was king of the castle, wandering along the droves of books and dancing on the glass walkways, mingling with hundreds of years of stories.

He dragged his fingers along the walkway, trying to pick up the stories hidden amongst the ancient wood. It was too much, though; moments of arguing, of Mist

Keeper's walking, and of ghosts meandering bombarded him at once, and he pulled back, reciting his mantra and stabilizing himself in the present.

Brent found a washroom and cleaned himself. He looked just as bad as Bria with dirt smudged across his face, dark pits beneath his eyes, and his curls mangled in all directions. After tugging at a few of them, he stepped into the shower, humming an off-key tune while washing and brushing away the grime.

It was only after he stepped out that he realized there were no towels in the room, and his old clothes had seen better days.

Shite.

He bolted out of the bathroom, stark naked, and into the neighboring room. To his relief, he found a silk nightshirt in one drawer. It was far too tight for him, but it did enough to cover him.

Even though the Library was empty, Brent didn't want to risk the possibility that *someone* might be watching.

Let em look, one of his voices cackled. *It ain't that bad.*

Brent grimaced.

It's true.

Brent pushed the voices to the back of his mind and peaked out of the spare room again. All remained quiet. He followed along the walkway, checking rooms for a potential closet or anything he could use for real clothes. When his search failed, surrendering his mind to his growling stomach, he gave up and headed downstairs towards the galley.

He gathered a few loaves of bread, fruit, cheese, and a jug of water then returned to his room. While he saw no one, when he returned, he found a fresh set of clothes at the foot of his bed and a simple dress on the table for Bria.

Relieved that Bria wouldn't see him in the hideous gown, he changed into the trousers and tunic, then downed a glass of water and ate some fruit.

Once his stomach finally stopped gurgling, he lay down beside Bria. When would this all stop? He wanted to give her everything: a small cabin in the woods with no stories just so they could make their own. A place where she could dance and smile untethered by the harsh realities. It was as they were if caught in a vicious cycle, locking them into every unlucky situation. Perhaps it was his curse. It still crawled on his skin, crawling like spiders, constantly trying to kill him or make him go insane.

They might not break it, but at least he could outlive it. Perhaps.

Brent scratched Nix's head, his mind drifting over an array of thoughts about elephants, long-term memory, and old methods of war. The dog snored and stretched, kicking Bria's stomach.

"Dammit, Brent," she mumbled.

"It wasn't me. Blame the dog."

Bria opened her eyes and smiled at him. "Oh. Hi."

"Hey." He smiled back.

"Are you...are you okay?

"Mmm." Brent poked her nose. "Just spent the last hour lying here, pondering how elephants function."

"Goof." She smiled and closed her eyes again. As her eyes shut, a tear trickled down her cheek.

"Bri?"

"It's nothing." She wiped her eyes and rolled over.

"Talk to me."

She shook her head.

"Bria."

She didn't budge.

He redirected his energy. "Eat. A'ight? You need food."

"Okay..." She tried sitting up, only to collapse back into the bed. "Fuck!"

"Bri?"

"I can't...I..." She burst into tears, rolling onto her side and hugging herself. Every inch of her body trembled. Nix inched up to her face and licked her chin.

"Bri. Please talk to me. I can't help if you don't tell me what's wrong," Brent begged.

She sniffled.

"Here, let's get you some food." This time, Brent helped her sit up, placing a few pillows behind her to elevate her back. He brought a plate over to her, and one piece at a time, she ate. The tears didn't stop.

"We're a'ight. We're safe. A'ight?"

"It's just been... it's been so much. I'm so tired." Bria dragged her fingers over his arm, stopping where the 'reaper' scar cut into his body. "And I was worried about you."

"I'm fine, Bria. Really. I mean, I beat that damn Diabolo." Brent looked away, ignoring the distant stories playing in his head.

"Are you sure?"

"Yes, I'm sure."

Bria sniffled, gripping Brent's shirt as she held back another round of sobs. "I keep worrying I'll lose you. The Diabolo could have sent you back six months. After everything...I thought...I was so scared."

"But I'm here."

"You're here," she recited.

Brent smiled. "I think people should avoid trying to hurt me. They should fear you. You'll do anything to protect those you care about."

Bria snorted. "Not anything."

"You just fought the God of Death."

"I don't believe in a god."

"Still fought a crazy ancient head and won."

Bria shrugged. "I guess so."

Brent stroked back her hair again, focusing solely on her face. She grounded him in the present, keeping his attention from dwindling into the past, both his and others. When he stroked the side of her cheek, she leaned into the touch. She was always gentle, kind, but like the way the wind can transform from a gentle breeze to a shrieking storm, Bria could topple the world.

A knock on the door brought Brent back to reality. Nix barked.

"Who is that?" Bria gulped. "I thought we were alone..."

"Who's there?" Brent called.

No response.

"Um... I'll take a peek..." Brent rose while Bria grabbed a handful of grapes from the plate by the bed. Nix growled by Brent's feet as he cracked open the door. Everything told him it was a bad idea. But would a foe be so courteous?

A literal ghost stood in the doorway.

Brent blinked a few times. He recognized this ghost.

"You! I've met you!"

Before them stood Ningursu's ghostly companion. Usually, he moved about as a mere shadow of mist, carrying the God of Death's head about the Library. But this time, his features took shape, a man with dark hair and a thick beard, tired gray eyes gazing at Brent with equal attribution.

Brent also recognized him from the streets in Mert, stopping him from throwing the door shut in the ghost's face.

"Shite! Um...hi." Brent stepped back. "You...I saw... You're...you were in Mert! But... you're also...if you're Ningursu's...I should've...shite! Is Ningursu here? Did they get in? What...when did they get back?"

The ghost waved his arms as a sign of disagreement.

Brent breathed out in relief. "Oh, okay. Good. Um. Good."

"Who is it?" Bria asked. She held herself against the wall, knees shaking as she watched the ghost.

"Uh, it's Ningursu's ghost...but... Ningursu's not here. I...um..." Brent glanced at the ghost. "What are you doing here?"

The ghost pursed his lips, then signed with his hands and said, "I have things to tell both of you."

Bria stumbled forward, her bushel of grapes in hand, "What is he saying?"

Brent rushed over to Bria's side and helped her stand. "He wants to talk to us."

"About what?"

"It is important for you to understand the truth," the ghost remarked.

Brent was even more confused. "About?"

"Meet me by the pool once you are ready. There is much to discuss."

"Pool?"

The ghost vanished into the Library's mist, leaving a trail of stories in his wake.

"What was that about?" Bria gripped Brent's arm.

"He wants to tell us something...but I dunno what..." Brent frowned. "You can stay here if it makes you more comfortable—"

"No, I'm coming with you."

Brent helped Bria to the lavatory, finding a towel for her before she moved into the shower. Her steps were careful, light, and uneven. After hearing her fall in the bathroom, he helped her sit down in the tub, letting the water fill up while brushing back her hair and promising it was okay. He'd never witnessed her so distraught and uneasy as she sat there, letting the dirt and leaves fall from her skin while her little branch retreated behind her ear.

"I used too much of my magic in the tunnels," she said as Brent helped her out of the tub and handed her a towel.

"We'll walk slowly, a'ight? Just take it easy."

After she got dressed, they headed into the Library. Brent paused, marveling at the shelves. Peaceful, empty, the Library was a natural wonder, composed of trees and pages galore. But beside him, Bria grew stiff. Tension coated her skin. She didn't let her emotions breathe.

"Bri?" He touched her shoulder.

"I'm okay."

"Do you want to talk about what happened here?" He'd seen the stories of her time imprisoned in the Library, but that didn't matter.

"No. Not really. Not now, at least."

"A'ight."

They continued away from the door. Nix followed them, a trot in her step as she bounded at the various spider webs and insects in the mist.

Climbing down the steps proved too tenuous for Bria, and Brent carried her on his back down each step. At the bottom, the story of Ningursu's ghost greeted him. Brent followed him, weaving through the towers of books to the far back of the Library. Hints of the earth with the stench of a swamp and bark coexisted with the books. Bria perked up as they surrounded themselves in the walled bark of cypress trees, mangroves, and mosses. Doors hid, their brass knobs rusting away, wood rotting by the tepid humidity in the air.

"I always felt so much here..." Bria gawked, walking again while holding onto Brent's arm. "It's more than a tree... it's an entire ecosystem."

Brent squeezed her hand in reassurance, his attention set on the story as it led him to a door in the far back. He might never have noticed it, blending seamlessly with the walls.

A field of red flowers waited for them beyond the door, dazzling all the way toward the thick wall on the other end of the room. As Bria stepped forward, the peonies danced about her feet, parting to reveal a silver pool in the center of the room. From it poured the scent of lemon cakes and dust after a rainstorm.

Bria fell to her knees, trembling and hugging herself, gazing into the pool.

"Bri!" Brent raced to her side.

"This is the pool I came through before when I was trying to find you. I didn't have time to look at it, though. I was...distracted." She smiled slightly at him. "But...I didn't notice at the time how...strong this pool is."

"Are you saying it's the original pool or something?"

"I don't know, but... it's old. These peonies are ancient. Their song is so much softer."

Brent helped her up again as he peered about the room. There were few stories save for the occasional shadow of Mist Keepers visiting the pool, collecting its liquid. The further he looked, the deeper the stories struggled to form. Was that Kek standing by the pool? Or Tomás talking into it? Was that Bria climbing out of the liquid or someone else?

Eventually, his attention situated to the far end of the pool, where Ningursu's ghost lackey stood. He waved his hand. "I am glad you could join me."

Brent approached, keeping his head high. For both him and Bria, he had to be the strong one today. "What's this about? Who are you?"

The ghost looked sadly into the pool, then replied, "It is time for someone to learn the truth."

"About what?"

"My name is Nedo. I was one of the first ghosts released under Ningursu's reign. I've been by his side for thousands of years...as I'm bound by blood to him." He stared at Brent, not blinking. "For I am his brother."

Brent gawked. It was as if a pin dropped in a silent room.

"What's wrong?" Bria asked.

"Nedo is Ningursu's... he's Ningursu's brother." Brent kept his voice low as if Ningursu himself listened.

"His brother?"

"I have many things to tell you," Nedo said.

Brent turned back to the ghost. "About what?"

"Ningursu...Kek...everything..."

"What about them?"

"I think it will be for the best if we do it this way." Nedo held out his hand, offering his stories.

Brent stared at it. How much would it risk his sanity? Thousands of years of tales and memories existed in that one handshake. Would he be able to climb back out?

But there was so much he needed to uncover.

"Brent. Be careful," Bria whispered.

"I will."

After staring at it for a few moments longer, Brent accepted Nedo's hand. Goosebumps decorated his skin, and the mist thickened around him.

The peonies vanished, and he stood in a fog-covered desert long ago.

CHAPTER FORTY-THREE

A POOL OF PEONY

Mist cloaked Brent, wrapping him in a story from long-long ago. He watched two men draped in tattered clothes, their olive skin sparkling with sand and sweat, enter the scene. The shorter man of the two shouted, raved, ranted before drawing a blade and slaughtering the other without a second thought.

The dead man lay there, the moons turned, and his body disintegrated to dust. Eventually, his killer came back, and despite the man's dark hair and gray eyes, Brent recognized Ningursu's determined stare. He released the soul from the sand, and there stood Nedo, face to face with his killer once again.

Time changed. Years turned. A monsoon flooded the desert, and mist followed, riding the winds of Ningursu's wrath.

He walked alone.

Over time, others joined Ningursu, but before they became one with the mist, they vanished. No apprenticeships. No Mist Keepers. Just Ningursu, the sole God of Death, wandering alone across the world to complete his duty.

Things changed.

Time changed.

And suddenly, Brent stood in a bustling city. A young woman ran past him. She wore a beige dress, her long black hair falling to her shoulders. Red eyes scored her face, and as she ran, she ran into Nedo.

She saw him vivid as day and reached for his face.

They talked. Nedo had a voice.

Her name was Merta.

As they spoke, their friendship bustled. Merta and Nedo spent every waking hour together. They talked, they laughed, and they became good friends.

But Merta's life was not glamorous. Every day, she worked in the fields, talking with Nedo, never telling others of her talent to view the dead. She was a lonely young woman, a sad young woman, but in Nedo, she found comfort and solace.

One night, Nedo sat beside Merta when his brother arrived in a wave of mist. Merta quivered at Ningursu's presence, her sight wide and all-encompassing.

Ningursu disregarded Merta.

"Nedo, my brother, why do you spend such time with this girl?" His voice still boomed, shrewd but somehow soft.

"She sees me," Nedo spoke.

"Does she now?"

"As she sees you."

The girl flushed.

"A dead man with a girl of life is no way to be," Ningursu spat.

Perplexed as ever, Nedo inquired, "Why are you here, brother? You were never one for small talk unless there is something you thus desire."

"Ah, my brother, yes, so you know." Ningursu sat by the fire, a long black cloak falling to his feet. "I have grown interested in the Royal Heir, Kek. They are a talented alchemist, and I believe they are trying to tamper with the balance between Life and Death."

"Then kill them. That is what you do."

Ningursu's eyes narrowed. "You hold a grudge after all these years, brother?"

"You executed me for no other reason than I inherited the more fertile plot of land."

"Times were different."

"And I have changed."

Despite their differences, the two brothers agreed, and the next morning Merta delivered Ningursu's message to the Royal Heir.

The Royal Heir welcomed Merta to their home, watching as the young woman fidgeted beneath their stare. They said nothing, listening as Merta informed them that the God of Death was watching.

"I understand," Kek stated.

"Why does Death care about you, your highness?" Merta inquired.

"Come." Kek then led Merta into their back room, where their silver pool waited in a basin. Kek poked at it once, and the image changed to show a mist-covered field of peonies.

"There is a thick mist around us. It calls to me, but I cannot see beyond it. By what you told me, you can, yes?"

Merta nodded.

"Even the Pool cannot help me, but you can."

"What is the Pool?"

"Everything." Kek stared at her. "I made it out of earth's heart, magic's embrace, and the mist's skin. Together, beneath the fingers of the alchemist, it lets me see fragments of the world. But not the truth. Not like you. Will you help me?"

"I do not know how."

"I do." Kek removed a small blade from their satchel. "A drop of blood is all I need."

"And what do I receive in return?" Merta asked, holding her ground.

"Anything you desire."

"I want peace."

"Then you shall have it."

Merta made a small incision in her finger. Kek held her hand over the liquid, and three drops of blood fell into the pool. The liquid shimmered.

"Beautiful." Kek smiled, then brought a ladle to the elixir and drank.

At last, Kek saw Ningursu. Merta left the two alone, Nedo still at her side.

Kek spent their days with Ningursu. When seen together, they walked along with pride. Equals. Similar. Kek took the role of Death's partner to heart, and as they assumed the throne above their kingdom, their reign strengthened.

Merta did not visit Kek again, enjoying the peace and prosperity gathered by their reign. No plague. No untimely deaths. Merta was free to live in the city where Nedo stayed by her side.

Yet, as the years passed, Merta continued to age. Kek did not, looking as pristine as the day Merta met them. No wrinkles, no gray hairs; young.

One day, many years later, Kek demanded that Merta join them in the palace.

"The pool is losing its luster. What you gave has faded." Kek meandered about it in the heart of the castle. Nedo watched from the side, his head bowed, fortunate that Kek did not notice him that day. "You can help me, Merta."

"With what?" Merta, now elderly, narrowed her eyes.

Kek tilted their head. "You gave it the knowledge of a seer many years ago. The last bit of magic that gave me sight. It was more than that, though, for with that sight, I took away Ningursu's cloak of invisibility and granted myself immortality. But it is fading. I feel my bones ache. You can join me, dear Merta."

"I do not want immortality. I plan to die and join my love forever, united in the mist."

"As a decrepit old woman?"

"Yes." Merta turned.

"Shame."

Kek pushed Merta backward, and she hit her head against the edge of the basin. Her body hit the basin. The woman gasped as she floundered into the water, the silver liquid encapsulating her, drowning her in blood.

When the bubbling stopped, her body floated to the surface.

Dead.

Nedo shrieked.

Ningursu emerged and stared at Merta's body, ignoring his brother's pleas as he walked away with Kek at his side.

"Brother! Help her pass through to the afterlife! Please!"

Ningursu turned to him with a smirk. "No one should be permitted to see the world of the dead. It was for the best."

"You have an individual of life beside you!" Nedo shouted.

"A god who can make liquid shine and escape thine eye," Ningursu stated. "Life itself, yes?"

"Brother!"

Ningursu shouted, "I cannot. She belongs in Hell. We must not tempt fate."

"You must try!"

"Goodbye, Nedo."

"Brother!"

The tale faded.

Time continued.

With Merta gone, Kek added one name to their collection; they became Tehuti Kek.

And with Merta gone, new individuals with red eyes emerged from the mist, and Kek kept these new seers in their purview.

The naïve seers worked together with Kek to find other Magii with a powerful inclination of magic. Kek raised these Magii and groomed them into the realm of gods. Meanwhile, the red-eyed seers died in droves, sacrificed for the Pools. Nedo tried to help each one, to help them survive, but it proved fruitless.

Kek ordered their slaughter, keeping blood off their hands in most counts.

Most.

Ningursu never released their souls.

None.

A thousand years passed.

Two thousand.

Maybe more.

Eventually, after a countless number of new Mist Keepers failed by unknown means, another Mist Keeper permanently joined Ningursu's ranks: Aelia of Merton. To complete her training, Ningursu sent her to Kek, where they trained her in the art of alchemy.

Nedo watched from the shadows, as he did for centuries. But Aelia's success caught his attention, and he dared to speak with his brother again. "Alas, you decided to keep one?"

"She is different," Ningursu said without looking at him.

"How?"

Ningursu smiled to himself. "You wouldn't understand, brother."

"I've been by your side through all of this. Try me."

Ningursu's eyes flickered, and he paced ahead. "She doesn't threaten me."

"Elaborate."

"Her magic within the mist is limited compared to the other Mist Keepers." Ningursu stared out into the mist.

Nedo waited for more.

"The other ones I dared train, they connected with every aspect of the mist – the dead, the history, the way it functions, and more. They were strong, stronger than me, and I could not let them interfere with my reign. But Aelia, well, her magic focuses on mist, medicine, and alchemy of all things. How does that threaten me?"

"It doesn't," Nedo replied.

"Precisely."

"So you are responsible for the failure of the others?"

"All I did was refuse to help them. Their failure was not my fault."

"But—"

"It is how it must be for my power to remain." Ningursu's face darkened. "Especially now that Kek's numbers have grown."

"Kek is your equal."

"Kek is an abomination!"

Nedo stared in shock. "They are like you."

"They are not a Mist Keeper. They have taken Life and Death and trumped it, walking on that ever so fine line of immortality. Every day, they find more seers to slaughter to perfect their immortality formula. With each seer, they find more Magii to add to their immortal ranks. It is a disgrace on the sanctity of Death. It is an insult to being a Mist Keeper!"

Nedo approached his brother, anger brimming in his core. "You helped Kek obtain this...now you want them gone? You killed Merta for this!"

"Because I didn't understand the threat Kek posed."

"To whom? The world...or to you?"

Ningursu turned away from Nedo, his voice flat as he spoke, "It doesn't matter. I believe Aelia will put Kek in their place. I know it."

Before Nedo dared to ask another question, Ningursu vanished into the mist.

As Ningursu expected, Aelia's alchemy and mist talents created a rift between Kek and Ningursu. Kek watched in horror as Aelia dove deeper into the potions, using the mist to brew nightmares and monsters. The creatures emerged from the Pools with a vendetta, a promise to keep the world in balance and strike fear into the hearts of Magii and Seers.

Kek did the only thing they could: they continued to grow their immortal Magii in numbers, preparing defenses against Ningursu's army of mist-made nightmares.

The gap between Ningursu and Kek grew wider. After thousands of years of friendship, their differences had grown insurmountable. Ningursu grew more and more bitter, determined to find a way to abolish the Magii and keep the world in his balance...without Kek ever knowing what he intended.

This continued under Kek's nose for another thousand years. But the two would continue to come together through the magical pools across the world in the cordial fashion of lovers and kings.

Nedo never dared combat Ningursu or Kek, at least not to their faces. Instead, he made it his goal to warn Magii of Ningursu's ploy, communicating through seers to those who lacked sight of the dead.

Most of the time, it was for naught.

Ningursu hunted the Magii in a cloak of mist, with Aelia continuing to create monsters and expand the Pools. All while Kek searched for seers to bleed, strengthening the ever-expanding pool of immortality.

The winds changed by a cruel shift of fate.

The story took them to a land filled with white tulips where a giant had collapsed on the ground.

His name, as Brent knew, was Varden.

Nedo had been watching him, intrigued by the man's red eyes, but despite his sight, Varden never quite explored his abilities.

It was there in the field, Varden collapsed, only to be awoken by an army led by a woman with dull red hair.

Edith. Brent's throat tightening as she smiled.

For a moment, the surrounding story changed, and they were back in the infirmary. She was standing over him, a bloody scalpel in her hand. Brent gasped, fighting back the memory. She held him against the ground. She carved him.

Brent sent the story back to Nedo's tale, though, where Varden and Edith stood amongst the tulips.

Edith created a sword from the minerals in the ground and threatened the giant, demanding that he guide her to treasures beyond her wildest imagination. Varden used his sight to take Edith to a pool in the middle of the field. Edith bathed in the water, drank it, then, reminiscent of Kek's own virtues, sliced Varden's stomach open as she retreated to her army.

Varden withered. Nedo arrived at his side, but in a fit of uncertainty, Nedo did the one thing he could think of: he cupped his hands and poured the liquid into Varden's mouth.

Varden awoke much later, the first known seer not slaughtered by Kek's desires or Ningursu's ambitions. He not only survived the attack, though; he drank from Kek's Pool of Immortality...like all the other Magii in Kek's army.

When Ningursu found out, his anger ripped through the entire world. Kek's army had grown too large, too horrendous; no one should stand taller than the God of Death. By now, he had obtained a third Mist Keeper for his Council that did not threaten him after countless more 'failures': Tomás, who used his magic to read and manipulate minds through the mist.

A war ensued, filled with blood and toil. Nedo kept to the shadows, as he often did, but it did not last. Aelia's monsters, dubbed the 'Diabolo' as they carried Hell and Demons on their back, wreaked havoc, following Ningursu wherever he went. Aelia acted as his loyal soldier, constructing more Diabolo and finding new ways to poison the Magii.

Yet Tomás followed reluctantly as the war raged on, his own morals causing each choice to weigh heavily on his soul. Too much needless death, too much sacrifice; he wanted it all to end.

Brent wanted it to end too.

One day, as Ningursu marched Aelia, Tomás, and the Diabolo through the droves of white tulips, Edith attacked with her army. The battle ensued, and before Tomás could run, Edith snagged him in the fury and sliced his face in two.

Ningursu, Aelia, and the monsters fled.

Yet Varden served as Tomás's savior, nursing the young Mist Keeper back to health.

They hid, and the war continued. Kek claimed the rest of their names over the years, abandoning their previous identity to become Tehuti Tarek Thelma Kamilah Kafele Kek. They fought with vigor, with determination to lead the Mist Keepers to squander—for Death had no place amongst the gods, they said.

Both the dead and living cowered in fear, the war transcending both realms. Many learned the truth. The world was at risk of dying for good.

With fear mounting too high, worries spinning, a rebellion formed at the edge of a pool by a field of peonies. Varden and Tomás led the pack, and after much debate, Nedo joined too.

They stood for one reason: to end the war.

And it did, after many years, in a spin of mist and confusion that a story did not dare explain.

In the white tulip field, now tainted with streams of black, Kek beheaded Ningursu as the living and the dead surrounded them. Ningursu survived, leaving the two leaders in a bitter stalemate, for no one could kill the God of Death.

Tomás and Varden led the negotiations. They signed a treaty with the following terms: Ningursu would destroy the

Diabolo, no more Seers would die to further the potential of the pool, the sight would die out, and the Magii would continue to live. The Council would remain a shadow to humanity, refusing to touch the world of the living. The Palaver of Immortal Magii would protect their own without altering the affairs of the general populace.

Ningursu's final demand was a servant, someone who betrayed him but whom he could trust. At first, it almost seemed like Ningursu intended to select Tomás, but then when Ningursu noticed Nedo standing there, he chose his brother instead.

There was no compromise.

But it was worth it to end a war.

Wasn't it?

And just like that, the war ended, as they always do.

Nedo lived a half-life by Ningursu's side.

He pleaded for death. A true death.

A real death.

He wanted to be part of the earth again.

Not a ghost. Not an entity.

But a tree, flourishing in the forest.

"Please kill me."

The story lashed out around Brent, returning him to the field of peonies. His hand remained locked in Nedo's grip.

Brent sensed the pain, the sadness, and the fear all in one blow. It yearned to disappear. The man had lost repeatedly and now only existed as a mere a puppet to his brother's hand.

Brent yearned to help.

He had to help.

He reached for the story, tugged on it, pulled it close. It belonged to him now. He knew it all.

Then someone screamed.

Brent jumped. The story faded. His senses returned. His thoughts were once again his own.

Nedo's fingers weighed heavy in his hand.

"Brent! What's happening?!" Bria's voice penetrated the fog.

He yanked his hands back. Before him, a faded phantom stood, flickering in and out of the mist.

A moment later, it reformed into Nedo's shape, eyes filled with melancholy and sadness.

Each of Brent's fingers shook, and his knees gave out as he knelt to the floor.

Gasping.

Shuddering

What happened? It was like when I destroy the Diabolo.

Bria stared at him, tears in her eyes, answering his own question aloud. "You...almost...killed him."

"No...no...I...I don't know what happened...I...I was showing his story and then...and then..." Brent brought his head to his knees.

"You...you...you are a...I..."

"Bria—"

"I need to be alone." Bria fled from the room before he could stop her.

Brent shuddered, unable to bring himself to follow her. He struggled to piece together what happened. One minute, the story dominated, and the next, it was like when he was with the Diabolo, pulling it apart one piece at a time.

He stared at his hands. "I didn't mean to..."

Nedo placed a hand on his shoulder. "It is not your fault. You were just doing as I asked."

CHAPTER FORTY-FOUR

KING AND QUEEN

Bria fled from the room, shaking. Her mind raced. Had Brent almost killed Nedo? It was an odd thing to think, but she had witnessed it happen. Nedo's body faded at the end of the story, and Brent's eyes rolled back as he clenched the ghost's hands. Was he tugging at the ghost's story, like he did with the Diabolo? Did he know what was happening?

If he could slip that easily, who was to say the Diabolo wouldn't come back?

Bria collapsed behind a bookshelf, holding her knees against her chest, listening as her heartbeat climbed into her ears. *He didn't know what he was doing. Brent wouldn't ever do something like that. He didn't know. Breathe. Breathe.* She exhaled once and counted the candles on the chandelier on the ceiling. Her fingers trembled. It had never really occurred to her what Brent *could* do if he put his mind to it. He was, after all, a Mist Keeper.

Dead or alive.

Bria shivered. It wasn't just Brent that scared her. Everything Nedo had shown them, the amount of weight it carried, left her head spinning.

She pressed her head against the shelf, pulling out a book and dusting it with her hands. She didn't understand the title, and the pages stuck together as she flipped through them. A few pictures of pirates filled the pages. *Breathe. It's okay. What did I just learn?*

Her mind kept racing. *Ningursu is thousands of years old...I knew that. But I didn't know he had countless apprentices that he...forced into failure. Did they have powers like Brent?*

And what about Kek? They've killed countless Seers to further their own ambitions. Can I trust them?

Or will the war between them and Ningursu trump all else?

She shook her head. The questions were relentless, and she couldn't focus on the answers.

If this is how I feel...what does Brent feel like? Didn't Nedo reveal that Ningursu prevented apprentices with a deep connection to the mist?

Wasn't that similar to the connections Brent had with the stories?

Footsteps approached, tugging Bria out of her thoughts. She wiped away her tears and put the book back.

"Brent?" She called out.

No response.

"I'm not angry with you…I was scared…" Bria sniffled. "I'm sorry…"

Footsteps continued around the bend. Light. Even. Almost musical.

They belonged to a beautiful woman, whimsical in her movements, long blonde hair falling to the small of her back. She smiled at Bria with an innocence belonging to a child.

"Oh, hello." Bria sat up slightly, reaching into her dress pocket for a seed.

"Petunia, I am so glad you are awake. You were quite the damsel lying on the floor the other day." Her voice carried the same tune as her steps. Kind. Trusting.

"Petunia?"

"Yes, that is you, dear. Do you not remember? I'm sure you had a big fall."

"No, my name is Bria."

"Oh, silly Petunia, always concocting lies."

"I…" Bria blinked. She wasn't sure how to handle this peculiar woman.

"Julietta!" someone else shouted between the bookshelves.

"I am over yonder!" the whimsical woman sang.

Heavier footsteps followed, and this time, Tomás emerged from the shelving. His face brightened upon seeing Bria. "Oh, wonderful! You are up and about."

Bria tensed.

"I found Petunia sitting here looking distraught," Julietta said with a grin.

Tomás patted Julietta's shoulder, continuing to talk with Bria. "I am glad you have had time to become acquainted with Julietta."

Bria nodded. "Are you both Mist Keepers?"

"Yes." There was an odd twinge of sadness in Tomás's voice as he spoke.

Julietta interjected, turning her attention back to Bria. "Why are you so sad, Petunia? All is lovely today in the Library, as it is every day. Every day is a gift, and we should treasure it."

"Oh, um..." Bria bowed her head. "We met Nedo."

"Oh, I love Nedo! He's a sweet man, isn't he?"

"Julietta!" Tomás stopped her. "Weren't you going to find yourself some new pigments? You have that beautiful painting you're working on, and I would hate for you to forget about it."

"Oh, yes. I need to finish the crimson sea before it dries. I wonder if I can find the right tone of red in the galley..." Julietta continued mumbling as she walked off.

Once she vanished, Tomás turned back to Bria and sat down facing her, cross-legged. "So...you met Nedo?"

"Yes." Bria glanced towards the room with the peonies.

"What did he tell you?"

"About...him and Ningursu, Kek...and you and Varden. Just...everything that led to the war a long time ago."

Tomás nodded.

"Why didn't you tell us?" *Why didn't Varden tell me?*

"It is a touchy subject. It is not something we go spread rumors about. Otherwise, Ningursu would go on another harangue." Tomás stared past Bria towards the wall. "I've stayed on his good side over the years. He might have easily eradicated me. But it was crucial for the treaty to succeed that I stay intact. Now, it doesn't matter, though." Tomás ran his fingers over the spines of the books. "Varden and I tried our best to keep the world at peace. We sacrificed our own relationship for it. But it was never peaceful. Just...strenuous. Ningursu and Kek have been playing their pieces right, navigating around the stalemate. Neither of them expected you or

Brent to come along. But it was inevitable an outsider would disrupt things."

"It can't be our fault, though." She was sick of blaming herself. A war didn't start because one domino fell; it started because the other dominoes were already loose.

"No, it is not," Tomás spoke with firmness in his voice. "I am regretful that I might have made you feel that way, especially back during the Storm of Nightmares all those moons ago. I should have fought back, but Ningursu has quite a claim over the Mist Keepers, as you encountered with Caroline."

"Is Brent at risk of being controlled like that?"

"No. Brent's a rogue player."

"Ningursu can control me, though." Bria reached up to touch her little branch. It still stung when she recalled the way her mind spun.

"Thank Jiang for that. He might not have magic, but he loves to experiment." Tomás's face grew stern. "I don't know what he did, though I do believe it has to do with your magic. I cannot say otherwise, though. I am sorry. Aelia might be able to help, but unfortunately, Ningursu has her wrapped tight around his metaphorical finger."

"Because Ningursu enjoys being in control."

"Yes."

"Is that why he has the pool here?"

Tomás said nothing. Bria's face grew numb, taking that answer to mean yes. What control did the pools give to Ningursu? Was it a mere plight against Kek? Something more?

She wondered what Brent would say. He probably perceived more in the story than she did. And while already the tale had settled in the back of her mind, Bria was sure it continued to assault Brent's mind, deepening with each moment, revealing more secrets.

Bria glanced back over her shoulder. "I should go find Brent..."

Tomás patted Bria's hand. "Once all is well, I'll come by. Take care of yourself, Bria. And if you need to talk, I am here."

After Tomás left her, Bria wandered back toward the pool of peonies. The room, but for a gentle mist drifting through the flowers, was empty. She wondered what stories loitered among the flowers, but all she heard were the songs they sang against the gentle stirring of water. Yet, as she brushed her hands over the petals, the flowers only stirred slightly, leaving her with aches in her wrists and joints. Her heart palpitated, and a knot formed in her stomach.

It's too much right now.

Bria left the pool and continued her search for Brent. Yet, with the endless sea of books, she had no clue how to find him. Brief memories skidded back of Alojzy, confusing her with bookshelves moving and the ceiling twisting. But, even with everything still, the Library remained as much of an enigma.

She kept counting the lights to make sure she didn't get lost in its mysterious embrace.

Until she heard a dog bark.

"Nix?"

Another bark.

Bria followed the sound upstairs. Nix waited outside the infirmary door, continuing her woofing tirade. There, Brent sat on a bed, rummaging through Bria's bag.

She knocked on the doorway to get his attention. "Brent?"

He looked up, pale with bloodshot eyes. "Mer..Merta?"

"Try again." Bria approached him.

"I...Merta?"

"Backtrack. What is your name?"

"Ned...no...it's um...I mean, it's..." He closed his eyes tight and muttered a few times. "Brent."

"And who am I?"

Nix approached Brent, placing her head on his leg as he blinked a couple more times. "Bria..." His face scrunched up as if he would cry, "I'm... I'm so sorry. I didn't mean to...I mean...I don't want to kill anyone."

"I'm not mad at you. It was a lot in one go, that's all." Bria sat next to him.

He refocused his attention into the bag, "I...the... where's the stuff? The liquid serum stuff... it's... there's so much...I need it to...I mean... it's pulling at me and, and, and—"

Bria took the bag from him, opening the front pocket where she hid the needles. Instead of taking out a needle, she removed the jar of pills Varden gave her. "We should only use the elixir for emergencies. Varden gave these to me. He said they're not as strong, but this supply should last a while."

She placed a tablet in Brent's hand. He stared at the silver coated oval, ran it through his fingers, then popped it in his mouth.

He scowled, and his shoulders relaxed.

Bria touched his arm, "Better?"

"Yeah." Brent didn't look at her. "It was just...there was a lot, and I...I don't know what...I mean...I keep replaying the story. It was so much, and I...I keep seeing new things. Ningursu was...he is...terrible. So fucking terrible and...shite. He went through hundreds of apprentices, Bria. Like me, and I...I...I dunno what he's trying to do. And Kek and Mert and Nedo...and Tomás and Varden. I can't... it's all... it's all so...I—"

"Yes. I saw." Bria stopped him from scratching at his wrist. Brent saw more; she hadn't seen the hundreds of apprentices or the beating of the story on Brent's skin. It spared her that outcome.

Brent stared ahead at the wall. "He's so tired."

"Nedo?"

"Yes. He wants to... he's begging to fade away. It's been a long few thousand years, and I...I mean, he...imagine being enslaved for that long?"

Bria watched Brent's expressions change every few words. There he was again, compassionate and caring as always, trying to put an explanation on hatred. Brent Harley: always empathetic, always the kind soul who wanted the world to flourish. He always put others forward first, and now, presented with an impossible task, he struggled.

"It's heartbreaking," Bria whispered.

Brent closed his eyes. "It was weird. Nedo...his stories were so close...and he was trying to give them to me and...it was...I mean...it was like the Diabolo all over again. I didn't mean to scare you. I mean...I didn't wanna kill him or anything."

"You pulled back."

"Barely!" Brent retorted. "I could have killed him!"

"But you didn't." Bria placed a hand on his chest. "You knew what you were doing."

"Did I?"

"Yes," Bria whispered. "And even if you didn't...if you did it out of pure terror, that doesn't make you a monster. I mean, I—I killed." She gulped, finally mustering the courage to say the words aloud. "I killed Cadet Lawry out of fear. One ill-placed death doesn't mean you're a bad person."

Brent dropped his head. "But...what if he wants to die? Is it wrong of me to deny him that?"

"I think that's for you to decide, Brent. You are a Mist Keeper."

"And if I decide to help?"

"I'll know you had weighed the options extensively. You might be impulsive about a lot of things, but the fate of others has never been one of them."

Bria lay with Brent on the narrow cot for hours with Nix at their feet. They rehashed the events of the day until Brent's nerves dulled and Bria could think clearly. Tomás dropped food off for them once, asking if they needed anything. It was an awkward visit, like an uncle who hadn't seen his niece and nephew in a long time.

As they lay beside each other, Bria continued to ponder Nedo's story. Something had stuck with her out of everything else: Ningursu killed countless apprentices to keep his throne above the Dead. There was no mention of curses.

Only eradication.

Only murder.

"Brent?" She nudged him.

"Hm?"

"I noticed something...in the story."

He glanced at her.

"This might sound dumb, but...in Nedo's story, he showed us that Ningursu killed or eradicated apprentices that had a deep connection to the mist, right?"

"Uh huh."

"So, doesn't that mean...he killed them? Not a curse?"

"I don't think that means anything." Brent's face hardened. "The curse is that somehow, each Mist Keeper will die before joining the Council. It's inevitable. That's what Caroline and the rest of them said, at least."

"But what if there isn't a curse? What if it has always been that Ningursu decides if you live or die? Or at least the circumstances of that death."

"That doesn't explain the current Council members, though. They all *died*. The odds are against me, I mean."

"But what if it's a lie?"

Brent didn't reply.

Bria leaned over to get a good look at him. Defeat settled into his eyes as if some bloodthirsty creature dove deep into his skin, sucking life from his heart. She placed her hand to his cheek, "You've survived for over a year now. You carry the Diabolo in your heart, and still...you are Brent Harley. And if there is a curse, though I don't think there is, you know what I say?"

"They're meant to be broken?"

"Exactly."

Brent grimaced, saying nothing else.

Silence once again strode into the room. Despite the physical exhaustion seeping over her body, Bria still did not sleep. She kept focusing on the cuts on Brent's skin, tracing the reaper scar and listening to him mumble obscure stories to himself. Sometimes he would stop talking and just breathe as if holding back tears. She wouldn't press him to speak his mind on any of their recent discoveries.

It was his choice to speak.

After lying there for hours without sleep, they abandoned their space on the bed and ventured off into the Library. Bria felt somewhat stronger as she climbed out of bed, but Brent still offered her a hand.

Nix opened one eye as they left, blinked, and closed it again.

"Lazy dog." Bria giggled as she followed Brent from the room.

He smiled. That half-cracked, kind smile that still caused Bria's heart to putter. And as they left the infirmary, he paused at the edge of the balcony, looking down into the sea of books. Bria followed his gaze, then stumbled backward. For a moment, a sensation of falling wrapped around her, rocking her body and throwing her into a spinning fit of nausea.

Brent touched her back. The spinning stopped. Only the expanse of books below remained.

"A'ight?" He glanced at her.

She blinked and tallied the two lanterns hanging on the wall. "Yeah."

"Really?"

The knot formed again in her throat, and she pointed to the opposite end of the second-floor walkway. "Jiang threw me from that balcony."

Brent grew quiet.

Bria sensed the worry. "This is the first time it made me feel like that. The Library is like a city...so not all of it brings me back to when they kept me here. When I was here, I only saw a fragment of it all, and it was so confusing. I don't remember most of it. It's a fog."

"You sure? We can leave," Brent asked.

"Yes. This Library is like paradise for you. We can stay a bit longer, especially as long as the barricade stands." She eyed the layers of bark and vines over the entrance. Some had wilted, but mostly, their blockade remained. They would be safe for another day or so unless Bria used her energy again to reinforce it.

Brent followed her gaze. "Especially now that the Council is gone. We're like the king and queen of the castle. We get to decide what we do and when, you know?"

"Well, *your royal highness*, what do you want to do?"

Brent grinned once again, so his eyes lit up and led Bria through the second floor. He pointed at different fixtures of art on the wall, marveling at the endless bookshelves and incandescent glass walkways. For a bit, without the terrorizing gaze of the Council, the weight of the Diabolo, or Kek's nagging, Bria and Brent were nothing but young lovers. They danced between the steps and laughed. Together, they were equal rulers of the castle. No one could stop them.

They checked different rooms, passing through an odd laboratory with dripping serums and bubbling potions, a training facility with an array of weapons, and another with hundreds of blank books. Brent stopped at times, taking in the stories, commenting as he always did, before returning to himself.

This was their adventure.

At the top of the stairwell, Brent slowed as they approached two ominous-looking doors. Carvings decorated the wood telling multiple tales of warriors, of forests, of castles, and of monsters. Even without Brent's magic, the stories pulsated from carvings.

"Ningursu's office," Brent stated. "I've been in here once...when I released the Diabolo."

"What's it like?" Bria asked.

"I don't really remember. I was panicking."

"What's stopping us from going in now?"

Brent eyed the door up and down, then placed his hand on the doorknob. It twisted open unceremoniously, welcoming the touch of a Mist Keeper.

The room waited for them, dark and musky. Even as Brent lit the lantern on the far wall, the darkness remained, living beside the soft glow. Scrolls, books, and papers lay strewn about the office on the desk, the couch, and disheveled on the shelves in unintelligible handwriting. Brent scanned a few of them but didn't say a word. A world map sat behind the desk with illegible markings on its surface while most of the furniture in the room sat covered in dust.

A head really didn't have much need for a couch or table.

Brent walked in ahead of Bria, staring not at any one thing. What stories captured him now? Sometimes, Bria wondered what occupied his mind; how much did he really see? Was it possible to hide a secret from him?

Eventually, Brent's attention settled on Ningursu's desk. This time, Bria didn't need his magic to understand. Clear as day, sitting on the desk, was a single basin filled with that odd silver liquid.

Why does a god-like entity need the pool? The question still hung in the air.

Brent partially answered the question, his eyes resting on a hidden story. "Ningursu uses this a lot. He talks to someone..."

"Who?"

Brent brought his fingers to the liquid and tapped it once. The liquid swirled.

An image appeared in the basin. She and Brent leaned forward to get a better view. The image showed a marble-coated room. Shadows moved among it, with a distant hum echoing in the air, chanting hymns of distant familiarity. A figure knelt at the bottom of the image. Their head hung in prayer.

"We're in one of the Order's temples, I think...inside some sort of container...or window or something..." Brent muttered.

Yes, that makes sense. Bria touched the edge of the image. It kept twisting, spinning about the room, only to relax when a door opened on the far side of the wall.

A voice boomed from the doorway, "It is time to give up, Brother."

Bria's stomach dropped. *It can't be...*

The other figure, too fuzzy for Bria to make out, raised its head from the prayer, "I serve only the Effluvium, not you, Elder."

"I am no longer an Elder."

"You always shall be to me."

"Very well." The figure in the doorway entered the window's light, revealing their face.

Bria covered her mouth.

She recognized the newcomer all too well. Those two blue eyes had symbolically watched above Newbird's Arm her entire life. She thought when the Diabolo destroyed the Temple that she would never see that face again.

She was wrong.

"There is no compromise. Our reign has only begun," The newcomer circled the vessel that held the pool.

As he passed by, the image grew dark.

Bria gawked at Brent, his face pale, his bottom lip quivering.

At the same moment, they both said his name. A name they hated. A name they feared. A name they had tried to forget.

"That was Elder Don Van."

CHAPTER FORTY-FIVE

CIRQUE SUNRISE

Micca dragged Jemma to the circus that morning. She objected on all counts. Scum berating the Effluvium filled the circus. She much rather wanted to go to the Temple for morning prayer. If her back hadn't hurt so much from the straw mat on the floor of the truck, she would have jumped up at the first crack of dawn.

Before she even brushed her hair, Micca took her by the arm and dragged her out of the back of the truck. "C'mon Jem! We gotta go check out this circus! It's s'posed to be amazing!"

"They practice magic freely! That is a complete violation!" Jemma strained against Micca's arm.

"Yeah, but they ain't got in trouble yet!" He continued tugging her along and lowered his voice. "Listen here, a'ight Jem? If we go to the circus, we'll see when those carnies are all done and can kinda hide among them as they pack up the train, y'know? C'mon, use your noggin." He poked her forehead a couple times.

Jemma groaned.

Micca continued rambling as they crossed the train tracks and passed under the sign for *Santiago's Cirque Sunrise*. Jemma didn't pay attention to what he said, putting up her guard as they passed the droves of carnies dancing in the path. One tiny little woman lifted a truck with a single hand while another big fellow with a curly mustache painted the air with sparks of color.

It was more like a showcase than a carnival. Residents of Opal's Canyon went between each miniature stage, pointing at the slights of hands and parlor tricks. None of these magical acts matched Bria's charade back in Newbird's Arm. In fact, they might have just been an illusion.

Jemma would have thought so, at least, if it weren't for the odd yellow aura resting in the sky. It collected dust, masking the Effluvium and dulling the colors of the city. It reminded her of the monstrous entity that wrapped Brent in its arms that day.

Her stomach twirled, choking down nausea as she sat down on a bench near the train station. Micca continued bouncing between the unique acts, unphased by the yellow tinge in the sky. *It's probably a dust storm. But...*Her mind rested on Brent for a moment. Part of her wondered if he was okay; she believed he was still alive. Maybe he and Bria had run off somewhere to live a life away from the Order.

They probably vanquished the Effluvium from their lives. Don't feel sympathetic. Jemma stared at the ground. *You did everything in your power. If Brent Harley handed himself over to the demons, that isn't your fault.*

She picked at a newspaper beside the bench, flipping through the pages, trying to ignore the commotion of the circus. Most of the articles spoke of the well-to-do in the Opal's Canyon region. Jemma skimmed over it, uninspired by the discussion of the weather or the local farmer's market. Even the section on the new Temple being built in the small western town of Zery left her empty. None of it mattered, really.

Especially compared to the titular world event echoing across the next page.

The Province Rosada has taken Mert

After evidence of an unprecedented magic outbreak in the Independent City of Mert rattled the eastern region of the continent, the Senate of Rosada voted to annex the city. This is the largest political move since the Smoke Riots. The notion, voted in favor by a vote of 8-to-7 with Senator Cordova leading the affirmative side, was enacted on Year Birth.

Approximately half of Knoll's Guard, coupled with allies from Kainan, left to seize the city and dispose of the City Council. There was little resistance from the city, still recovering from the fall out of the magic outburst.

Until a proper election can take place, the City of Mert will fall under the control of Knoll's Gully, led by Senator Cordova.

Jemma gaped at the page for a moment. She'd heard only snippets about Mert, but she'd knew it was a haven for magic. Even men like Brother Roy Al seemed wary of such powerful spots. Inevitably, a fallout would happen one day, right? Look what happened in Newbird's Arm after Bria's spectacle! Magic left those with nothing powerless. How could they piece together the ashes when they had no way to identify the pieces?

For once, Jemma agreed with the powers out in Knoll. Perhaps the City of Mert would flourish again, someday, under a firmer hand.

Besides, what good had magic done for anyone recently?

She started folding up the paper as she glanced back at the carnival. Everyone looked happy while basking in the magic. But eventually, the demons would come, as they always did.

If magic was so good, why did so many people suffer?

Why was the Effluvium yellow?

Why did people needlessly die?

But it was easy to forget with children smiling and Micca's foolish grin emerging from the crowd. He picked at a sticky, pink, floss-like food and held out a piece to Jemma. "Try it! They call it cotton candy!"

Jemma took a piece and tasted it. The sweetness dissolved on her tongue. Despite her own displeasure with the circumstance, she couldn't help but smile. It whisked her back to childhood when her mother made caramels while Jemma sat at the table playing with her dollies and Miss Porridge.

Things were simpler back then.

Micca, as usual, intercepted her thoughts. "I overheard 'em say they're gonna start loading up and all. We can sneak up there and hop onto the back of the train or something before they get moving. No ones gonna notice us in the commotion."

Objecting would be pointless. Why not just ask to board the train, hitch a ride? Micca had to make this difficult.

But if one thing was certain, it was that once Micca Fein decided something, there was no changing it. He was as stubborn as a mule.

With the carnival winding down, Micca took advantage and led Jemma up onto the platform, sneaking in and out of pillars, avoiding the gaze of the guard. Steam masked the engine on the far tracks, mingling with the yellow clouds in the sky.

She and Micca reached the end of the boxcars, then once the close was clear, they lunged onto the train's caboose. Micca latched onto it first, grabbing Jemma's arm as she jumped behind him, nearly falling onto the tracks. They landed against the car's wall with a thud. Despite their anxious breathing, Micca guffawed, much to Jemma's displeasure, before prying open the door and letting her inside the boxcar.

Jemma collapsed against the wall, heaving. The train hadn't even been moving, but adrenaline pumped through her veins. Did anyone see them? Would they go unnoticed the entire trek to Laysan's Beach? Her mind sped.

Micca convened beside her. They said nothing until after the train's whistle blew.

"Something smells like poo." Micca finally scowled.

"Ew! Micca!"

"No—like animal poo. Take a whiff."

"I don't want to—"

"Sniff the air, Jemma!"

Jemma took a whiff and almost vomited. "What d'you do?!"

"I said it ain't me! It's definitely an animal!"

Jemma squinted into the darkness of the boxcar. Her own fears prevented her from inspecting her surroundings, but now that her pulse rested, she saw clearly. Straw covered the ground, boxes stacked high and blocking the light from the single lantern hanging in the car. It stank, but as far as Jemma noticed, no one else was in the car with them.

"I think it's coming from over there." Micca pointed before rising from his spot and meandering toward a crate in the far corner of the room. A white tarp-covered something. "Aw shite, it smells like shite!"

"Micca, just leave it!" Jemma called.

"I wanna see what's in' ere, though!"

"Micca Fein! It's none of our business!"

"But—"

Jemma rushed over to him, stumbling as the train chugged along the rails. She tugged his hand away from the tarp. "Leave it alone!"

The tarp fell with his hand, though. A cage waited behind it.

Jemma gasped.

A reptilian creature lay curled in the cage. When the tarp fell, one silver eye opened to stare at them. Mist seethed from its pores. It might have been a beast in one of Brent's stories about a monstrous creature with wings. She thought they were only stories, but no...it was here, right in front of her, basking in the Effluvium's prowess.

Jemma blinked. "What? What is it?"

"Holy fucking shite!" Micca jumped in the air. "It's a dragon! They didn't have it out in the carnival before!"

"A dragon? But those are...those aren't real..." She shook her head. The *One Scripture* mentioned not a word about dragons, and anything passed between storytellers, historians, and vagrants was mere hearsay. *I must be dreaming!*

Micca chuckled and pressed his fingers to the bars. "Ain't ya heard of Graycott? They're across the Eastern Sea, a far way from Rosada and Mert. They've got big ole dragons there. Supposedly in other places, there're miniature dragons too or something. Jem, ya gotta be open-minded." He poked the dragon's paw. It hissed. "Ha! See! All real! Damn! This is mad! This is...wow! A real dragon! Ain't too big or nothing...might be able to carry a few people...but still a dragon! Wow! This is amazing!"

Jemma gawked at the creature. An odd beauty encompassed it, almost producing fragments of the

Effluvium from its skin. She didn't trust its silver eyes, though; if silver eyes attracted demons in humans, who knew what they did with wild beasts!

Micca poked at the dragon's face again. This time the beast roared, shaking the entire boxcar with its ferocity. Jemma yelped, jumping back into the piles of hay and holding her year glass to her chest.

It's a monster! Make it go away! Please make it go away, dear Effluvium; take it back to where it belongs.

Micca clamored back, hitting his head against a crate. A few boxes tumbled over, breaking on impact and sending droves of bottles and vegetables across the boxcar's floor. After a few moments passed, the gangway connection door slid open. A man decked out in yellow walked in, his top hat like a sun on top of his head. When his dark eyes fell on Micca and Jemma, a smile slithered across his face, two golden teeth stuck in the front of his mouth.

"Well, lookie here!" he crowed. "Looks like we got some riders in our trolly! Ya'll come take a gander! We got new meat!"

Jemma sat awkwardly on a crate next to Micca, watching the man in the yellow suit parade about the small room, arms thrown in the air as he fumed. A few members of his crew sat opposite them, watching as the discernible leader continued haranguing in a foreign language. Jemma eyed them. She recognized most of them from the carnival hours earlier. As she expected for a circus train, they were an odd bunch. The mustachioed fellow with bulging muscles that reminded her of a gorilla and the woman with puffy pink hair lounged by the wall. A few others poked their head through the door, trying to get a glimpse of the newcomers on their train.

The yellow-suited man slammed his hands down on the table and stared over at Jemma and Micca. The table trembled, already on unsteady legs from the puttering of the train on the tracks. He was a tiny fellow but with a presence as large as the big man with the curly mustache.

The man dressed in yellow sat across from them. "So what d'ya two think you're doing sneaking around in my train?"

Micca went to open his mouth, but Jemma interrupted him. "We're sorry. We just wanted to hitch a ride."

"You were bothering Zephyr."

"Zephyr?"

"My dragon."

"Oh," Jemma said.

"She was sleeping, and you disturbed her. How's she supposed to perform when we get to Laysan's Beach in the morn? She's gonna be crabby."

"Oh dang!" Micca blurted out. "That's so damn cool! I never thought—"

"Shush!" The man in the yellow suit waved his hand.

Micca fell quiet as if a spell washed over him, and he could no longer open his mouth. He pulled at his lips, and when they didn't open, he flailed his arms about in frustration.

"I'll give you your voice back soon. I have a few more questions for the lass."

Micca pouted. Jemma stared at him. *So it is real magic.*

"Give me one good reason I shouldn't turn you into the Guard the moment we arrive in Laysan's Beach."

Jemma straightened her back. "Because I'm a Sister of the Order."

"Bull!" He snarled. "Ya don't look like one or nothing."

"It has been a long journey."

"I call bull!" The man shook his head. "But even if ya are, ya don't seem all that important. Otherwise, you ain't be sneaking onto trains."

Jemma eyed down the yellow-suited man. She feigned confidence. Soon, she'd be close to Ab Aeterno, and there, she would have jurisdiction. This man couldn't control her. She was a Sister of the Order. There was no reason to be afraid.

"Yes, but isn't the guard more likely to believe *me*, a Sister of the Order, than the petulant ringmaster of an *illegal* magic circus? I understand you like passing off your feats as tricks and spectacles. But I think with what you just did to my friend, you have proven that you do, in fact, break the law. Or am I mistaken?"

"I have connections that keep me safe."

"Mine are stronger," Jemma lied. He didn't know the truth, though.

The yellow-suited man turned pale.

"That is what I thought. So why don't you let my friend have his voice again, yes?"

The man snapped his fingers, and Micca released a deep belch that rumbled the train car. The mustached fellow sitting against the wall chuckled.

"Timmy! Shush!" the yellow-suited man spat before returning to Jemma. "What do you want then?"

"Safe passage. That's all. I am trying to get to Ab Aeterno, and this is my best option." Jemma kept her confidence in tow.

"And what about your boyfriend?"

"Boyfriend? Pah! She's not my type." Micca guffawed. He winked in the direction of Timmy.

Jemma swore she saw them flush.

"I see. So you're not together." The yellow-suit man leaned forward, his nose inches from Micca's face. "What threat do you have for us then, pal?"

"I ain't got a threat!" Micca's composition changed at once, glowering at the man. "I like you a lot. Always thought myself sort of a clown if you know what I'm saying."

There was that dazzle in his eye again.

"We ain't a free ride, kid."

"But I can fix shite up!" Micca offered. "I done fixed trucks and shite all along the way here. You can ask Jem! I know what I'm doing! See!" He removed a little wind-up toy from his pocket.

"That won't make us a dime!"

"Sir!" Timmy, who had an eerily soft voice in contrast to his large physique, spoke. "It'll help us cut overhead costs if we got a handyman. We won't need to hire someone at Laysan's Beach if he can fix up the pipes!"

"Keep it in your pants, Timmy!"

"Salazar!" The woman with pink hair stepped up, placing a hand on the man's arm. "Timothée has a point. If this kid is as handy as he says he is, then we won't have to pay that asshole in Laysan again. Saves us money. More than pays for him and the girl's ride on this train. They'll be gone soon."

The yellow-suited man huffed, glaring still at Micca and Jemma. "Fine."

Jemma exhaled sharply.

Grumbling, the man bowed with the grace of a performer, leaving behind his angry persona and replacing it with the façade of a ringmaster. His frown became a smile, his eyes brightened. It was a change as quick and easy as blinking. "Well, welcome aboard the transport for Santiago's Sunrise Cirque. I am the ringmaster, owner, and controller of voices, Mr. Salazar Santiago. You can just call me...Master Santiago." He leaned forward, his eyes narrow now, the entertainer gone again. "And that's the only jovialness you'll receive from me. Just stay out of my way, and we won't have a problem, alright?"

"Yes, sir," Jemma whispered.

"Good. I don't like you lot, so the sooner you're outta here, the better." He turned to leave. "Lolli! Come!"

The woman with puffy pink hair skipped after him. The door slammed shut behind them.

"Well, that was something, ain't it?" Timothée twirled his mustache around his finger and smiled again at Micca.

"It worked out, though," Jemma stated.

"Ay."

"Sure did." Micca grinned.

"I'm Timothée, by the way. Not Timmy. Timothée."
He held out a hand.

Jemma curtsied. "Sister Jey Ma of the Order."

"And I'm Micca!"

"Do you want me to show you the…pipes…that are giving us the problem?" Timothée asked, speaking slowly as he continued staring at Micca.

"Absolutely." Micca smirked at Jemma. "You'll be a'ight for a bit, yeah?"

"I will be fine." Part of her had hoped Micca would stay by her side, but he had his own interests. No point in being jealous.

"A'ight, thanks, Jem! You're amazing!"

Jemma didn't bother objecting. Micca was out the door with Timothée in a heartbeat.

Something told her they were doing more than just checking the pipes.

CHAPTER FORTY-SIX

ONLY ONE FLIGHT

Smoke encapsulated the City of Mert. The sky blazed. Sirens and gunshots pounded in the distance. Magii ran through the streets in fear and fury. The guards tainted Mert with a detrimental taste, wreaking of death and hatred. A smog settled.

The night the airships arrived sliced the tension in Todd's heart. He kept Lex and Garrett close all night, even allowing Madame Owiti to sleep in their room, listening as magic screamed and the sirens blared. They had to leave. It wasn't even a question anymore.

He had no time to spare. As soon as the commotion settled, Todd bolted from Madame Owiti's home and made plans to sell the shop. With the Order taking hold of the City Council, it wouldn't be long before they started knocking on doors. He wouldn't let that happened.

Within a day, Todd booked a flight out of Mert to Evylain on an airship. He sold most of their products to other shopkeepers at a steep discount. Two individuals in pinstriped suits offered to buy up the shop. While Todd didn't want to think what illegal goods they might front behind the counter once he left, he didn't care. The sum was enough to secure passage out of the city for his family and pick up at least a year's worth of Lex's medication from the Sanitorium.

Now, the shop looked large and empty with silence etched on the wall like drawings. Todd exhaled as he walked along the back of the counter. He pulled the last of Garrett's drawings off the counter and folded them into his pocket. The images had improved over the years, migrating from basic scribbles to resembling stick figures and animals. A few more years of practice and his talent would surpass even Todd's mediocre artist ability.

Tap. Tap. Tap.

"Toddle! Open up!"

Madame Owiti tapped again on the front door.

Todd yanked the door open and glared at the old woman. She carried a bag on her side, her long hair woven back into over thirty different braids.

"What do you want?

"I'm coming with you, of course!" She patted Todd's cheek and walked inside the shop.

"Wha—what? No! I didn't—I'm leaving with my family!"

Lex emerged from the back room, Garrett on her hip. "I invited her."

"Lex!"

"She's helped us the entire time we've been here; it is only right! Besides, Garr-Bear loves her!"

Garrett waved at Madame Owiti and laughed.

"We don't have the money to pay for her flight," Todd grumbled.

Madame Owiti laughed. "I have already secured my ticket."

Todd cursed under his breath.

"Lex dear, may I use your lavatory, yes?"

"Of course!" Lex opened the curtain.

Once the old woman ventured into the back room, Todd exploded. "Why didn't you tell me you invited her?!"

"She's family!"

"Bullshite!"

"Toddle, she's like a mother to me! I wasn't going to leave her behind!"

"But—"

"She's coming!" Lex held her ground.

Todd decided not to argue and refocused on packing the last few keepsakes in the shop. Lex waltzed about the room, once again as gorgeous as a moonbeam. Todd knew how close she was to Madame Owiti. He wouldn't deny her that friendship, but he intended to make this a fresh start.

No more Mert.

No more magic.

Once Madame Owiti returned, Todd did his last sweep of the shop. All their belongings fit into three bags, and he hoisted them each over his shoulder. It was weird looking back at the little shop. This had been home. As ridiculous as Mert had been, for years, they were happy here.

A bunch of dreadful men took this away from them.

Lex paused in the entranceway as they left, staring at their empty little shop. "I will miss it here. I thought we'd found a home."

"We'll find a new home in Evylain. We're together. That's all that matters." Todd took her hand. He stared down the rows one last time, twisted the dial on the gas lantern, then turned into the road. Someday, they'd find solace. Just not today.

They huddled together as they hurried through the streets, heads down, staying out of the lantern light. He didn't enjoy wandering around Mert like this. At night, usually, the streets bustled. Now the men of Knoll occupied every corner, and those who dared to brave the streets kept their heads lowered. No magic. Nothing. It was as if Rosada reared its ugly hands around the nation of Mert and shook it, leaving but a skeleton. Within days, they'd taken Mert's livelihood; with the collapse of the City Council, the snatching of Magii, and the positioning of Senator Cordova as interim leader, who was to say what would happen next? With a mere order, Mert might soon burn to the ground.

Todd wouldn't risk it. Not for his family.

To his dismay, a queue formed from the City Centre towards the airships. Guards marched around the perimeter of the field, shouting and cursing. It was business-as-usual; they would check papers, then let the passengers aboard the airships. Simple.

It didn't stop nerves from decorating the air. Children cried, women paced in lace, and Todd gripped Lex's hand tight. One wrong move might end their freedom. One right move might bring them to victory. Todd kept reminding himself that they weren't looking for him; no one knew he had ventured here. This had nothing to do with him.

But why did it feel like they were staring right at him?

Todd shook his head and peered ahead. Families huddled together, most never bothering to look the Guards in the eye, keeping their heads down as they weaved together through the plaza. Guards pointed in different directions, shouting at the top of their lungs.

He clutched Lex's arm tighter as they took another step forward. Lex grew clammy beneath his arm, and she hopped from one foot to the other as they waited in place. Garrett had fallen asleep with his head on Lex's shoulder, a crayon in one hand, arm hanging over her back. Todd wanted to take them both and run. He'd steal an airship and fly into the sky, away from this mess.

Or become a dragon.

Once, when he was a young boy, he dreamed of turning into a dragon. That was all he remembered. Perhaps he'd live that dream now. If he focused hard enough, maybe he would turn into a dragon, and they could escape.

But that was a dream.

He wasn't a dragon.

He wasn't magic.

He was at the will of the Order now.

The guard at the front of the line came into view as they rounded the bend. He stood where women and men split, his beady eyes like daggers, "Oi thar! Yeh gotcha papers?"

Todd and Madame Owiti removed their documents and showed them to the guard.

The guard looked over the papers, "A'ight, ya three can go. Not her, though." He pointed at Lex. "What's wrong with her?"

Lex shifted, rubbing her paperwhite hands together.

"Nothing's wrong with her," Todd answered. "She's fine."

The guard sniffed Lex. "She sick?"

Todd shoved the guard. "Fuck off!"

The guard shoved him back. "Ain't no diseased fucker allowed passage."

"I paid for her passage!" Todd tightened his fists.

Lex touched his arm and said, "Toddle... it's fine. Just take Garrett and go."

"Lex!"

"I'll be fine. We still have rent on the shop for a few more weeks."

"I ain't leaving you here!"

"I'll be okay," she reiterated as she placed Garrett in Madame Owiti's arms.

"No, I'm not leaving you here. I'm not—FUCK IT!" He twisted and punched the Guard in the jaw.

"Fucking shite!" The man stumbled back.

Lex screamed, "Toddle! You'll get in trouble!"

"You're not a second-class citizen, so I don't give a damn. C'mon!" Todd grabbed Lex's wrist and pulled her into the airship's cargo bay, slamming the door behind him after Madame Owiti climbed inside with Garrett. To his relief, the door locked from inside the cargo hold.

A few families gathered among the cargo, staring at Todd in awe. He pushed away their stares. By now, he had grown accustomed to ignoring others. Their thoughts were no secret, though: *What is this asshole doing?*

He collapsed amongst the cargo freight, refusing to let go of Lex's hand as they hid behind a pile of boxes. He didn't care. It didn't matter. They were on the ship.

Solace had no place here. Eventually, the Guards would open the door.

Wouldn't it?

The Guards bickered outside the door. He didn't make out what they said, their voices bouncing off the hull like bog horns. Curses flung, slanders were drawn, then silence settled. Todd held his breath, waiting for the door to reopen.

Instead, the banging stopped, and all that remained was the creaking of pipes. It would surprise Todd if the airship even managed to fly.

Silence remained. No one spoke.

Could anyone speak?

Fear acted as a genuine agent in the cargo hold. It strangled them, giving a voice to the rickety pipes and churning gears.

And with fear came shock. So, by a sudden jolt, the engine roared to life. The steam whistled, and with a singular lurch, the airship shivered and rose.

"They're not looking for us?" Lex asked.

"Guess not..." Todd rose, walking over to the porthole. Mert shrank beneath them, with plumes of smoke and darkness wrapping around the city. It looked strange from the air. The last time they had seen the city like this was on their arrival. Then, colors captured the city, and a sensation of hope rose from the rooftops.

Now, looking down at it, dread worked its way into Todd's core. The spires on the top of City Hall burned, all the colors in the street replaced with a drab gray of nighttime smoke, and the stars painted blacks.

"Why did they let us go?" Lex whispered, joining Todd and placing a hand on his back.

"I dunno."

"Because, this isn't a ship to Evylain anymore," Madame Owiti interjected.

"What? What do you mean?" Todd snapped.

"I heard them, yes yes. All ships are heading to Rosada before their primary destination. They're gonna go and find you, Toddle, yes yes."

"That doesn't make any sense. Evylain isn't near Rosada."

"The Order doesn't have to make sense. Sure, they'll probably go and set this up in Mert soon, but for now, they don't want magic or dissonance to escape. So off we go to the belly of the beast!"

"Shite!" Todd sank against the wall. How did he mess this up too? Why couldn't he do anything right?

How could he ever look Lex in the eyes again after this?

.

CHAPTER FORTY-SEVEN

THE CRYPTS

Brent lay in bed beside Bria, unable to sleep as the night dragged forward. Or maybe it was daytime? It was hard to tell while in the Library. All he knew was he wanted to lie on the bed with Bria until all fatigue vanished. Someday, they'd be able to sleep without worry.

They barely spoke since they left Ningursu's office earlier, both trembling and walking in a haze. In the infirmary, they pushed the thin cots together, holding onto each other as if the world would crumble around them. If either had the energy, they would have found an empty bedroom and hid away in there.

To Brent's relief, Bria eventually fell asleep with her head against his chest. Sleep avoided him as he continued to ponder what he had learned, though. Ningursu was talking to the Order.

How have I been so blind? He'd held onto this unfounded belief that the Council understood him, that he would rise to become a great Mist Keeper and be something more than a vagrant from Newbird's Arm. But hadn't it always been clear?

The Council hated magic. The Order hated magic.

And he was an outlier pestering both groups.

Perhaps they were unrelated, but the signs remained. It was as if the entire world tried to beat Brent down, test how much he could take before he collapsed; the curse was relentless at that. Sure, he survived a Diabolo, certain death, and terror on multiple occasions. But the Mist Keeper's curse continued to ride on his back, play with his hair, and coo in his ears.

Unless, as Bria insinuated, the curse never existed. What if it had been a ploy Ningursu used for control over the Mist Keepers?

No. That doesn't make sense. Caroline told me that Mist Keepers obtain their powers with the promise to die. Wouldn't Ningursu just let their powers fade? Brent's mouth grew dry, and he brought a glass of water to his lips. *Of course, he wouldn't. Because maybe they don't fade...and that was another lie. Shite.* As his frustration mounted, he dropped it on the floor with a clatter. Nix looked up from her spot on the foot of the bed, groaned, then fell back to sleep.

Bria stirred. "Brent?"

"Go back to sleep."

Bria didn't, sitting up beside him and stroking his cheeks. "Talk to me."

"I... it's...I..." Brent hid his face in his hands. "I give up. I dunno what to believe in anymore. This... they're working with the people who've chastised me since birth!"

Bria's face grew hard. Brent tried to get a read on her, but she held her opinions steady.

As she did with her voice. "Tomás said you were a rogue player. I don't know what that means."

"It just means I've fucked up a ton and—"

"No. Not like that." Bria shook her head. "You need to talk to him about it. It might help us figure out what to do next."

Brent stared hard at her. Did she trust Tomás? He still wasn't sure how he felt about any of the Mist Keepers at this point. The only one who seemed trustworthy was Julietta.

"Do you trust him?" Brent asked. He witnessed the story of her emerging from the Pool with Tomás's help, the peonies chasing after her, but was there an ulterior motive? Is that why Tomás had avoided him?

Stories always told the truth.

"I think we can. Varden trusts him. Nedo does too, by the looks of it."

"Yeah, guess so." Brent agreed and climbed out of the cot. Bria trailed behind him. Her energy had returned, and she walked without help after recovering from the battle, but she didn't have that same confident stride. As she walked, she dragged her fingers over the railings, watching the bark climb around her fingers. She swore she was fine, but Brent didn't quite believe her. Her story of being tossed over the edge, of being dragged through the Library, and of being sent into a frenzied maze haunted the facility.

Bria held herself high, though, as she always did.

They found Tomás sitting by a fire on the first floor, parsing through a book, legs crossed in the chair. He glanced up as they approached.

"Brenton! Briannabella! Hello!" He put the book down and bowed. "I thought you two would sleep the day away."

Brent glanced at Bria, and she nodded once. His mind raced with questions.

"I am sure you have questions," Tomás interjected. Perhaps he'd already read Brent's thoughts.

"I do." Brent scowled, picking the words with care. "Last night...we saw Elder Don Van in the pool. The one who...he sanctioned my cleansing and..." Brent flinched. For a moment, he was back in the Temple. Lashes bombarded his body. Ice coated his skin. He drowned in history.

Bria's fingers on his wrist brought him back to the present.

"He...he was the one who cleansed...I mean...he ruined my life."

Tomás closed his good eye. "Ah."

"So...I guess...the question is...is Ningursu talking with the Order? Are they...are they in cahoots or something?"

"I apologize, Brenton. I do not know the full extent of this relationship with the Order, as I mentioned to Bria a few days ago."

Brent raised his eyebrows at Bria.

She fidgeted. "Honestly, I forgot. There was so much going on. I didn't think it had anything to do with Elder Don Van."

"Oh... a'ight."

Tomás reopened his eye and focused on them. "I can tell you this. Ningursu desires control. He has been known to reach out to powerful leaders throughout the world, manipulate their beliefs and understandings, and play power moves and chess. He uses the pool to communicate."

"Why not go in person?" Brent asked.

"Because he's a head," Bria responded.

Tomás leaned into his chair. "Yes, it is hard to travel as a head, so he chooses a way to speak instead. The pools are everywhere throughout the world, so he has eyes watching. Always seeing. Always able to control. Just like with Caroline. He thrives on control and respect."

Brent exchanged a glance with Bria, then asked, "And that's why I am a...rogue player? Because he can't control me?"

"Yes. He can't control either of you, and that's why he is scared."

"He has controlled me, though," Bria stated.

"He took something from you to solidify his control. Yet, you've always broken his grasp."

Bria scowled.

Brent fumbled over his words as he asked, "But why does that terrify him? I mean...I understand, Bria. She's this amazing Magii who is powerful and—"

Bria nudged him.

He flushed and picked at his wrist. "Right. But... I'm a Mist Keeper. What makes me so different?"

"Because your magic manifested before he intervened. He wants to stop you before you come into your true self like he did with all the others."

"The...others?" Brent asked. *Didn't Ningursu destroy the others?*

Tomás climbed out of the chair. "It might be best if I show you."

After exchanging a confused glance, Brent and Bria followed Tomás through the Library. Bria walked slower than usual, her fingers tight around Brent's sleeve as they perused the shelves. Stories continued meandering, wallowing between the shelves, telling tales of Mist Keepers reading, of ghosts cleaning, of magic constructing, and of Bria running.

Only their breaths spoke as they walked. All remained quiet. Even as they passed Julietta in the back of the Library, enamored with a few paintings on the wall, no one said a word. She smiled at them, then continued on her way, vanishing back into the shelves.

Like a ghost.

Tomás led them to the darkest corner of the Library, where a thick iron fence masked a set of dark, rickety stairs between the bookshelves. A rusting lock sat on the bars. Vines hung from the wall, tight around each bar, while mist flourished from beneath the gate itself.

When the doors opened, the darkness that peered back stared like demonic eyes, glimmering slightly in the torchlight. Bria whimpered beside him.

"Briannabella, you spent a few harrowing days down there. Are you sure you want to come with us?" Tomás asked.

"Yes, I'm fine." Bria straightened herself, but her fingers remained tight on Brent's sleeve.

"Bria..."

"Really! I'm fine. I want to be by your side going down there..."

"I'm not going to slip if that's what you're thinking."

"Brent."

"A'ight. Fine." He didn't pester her anymore and nodded to Tomás.

Tomás took a torch from the wall as they entered the darkness. Their footsteps echoed.

Followed by moans pouring over darkness, like sobs of the most decrepit vagrants.

Shadows moved. Fog snored.

Tomás stayed quiet, letting Brent take it all in and letting the stories soar.

Brent struggled to push away the stories with each step. Even when he didn't see them, their shadows remained, occasionally flickering into the candlelight and dancing against the steel bars: individuals dragged down, by Ningursu, by Aelia, and by Jiang. Never by Alojzy, but he often came and looked. The individuals seethed and roared from the cages.

But they also whispered and cried like children.

Brent squeezed his eyes shut as they passed an empty cage. Bria's story, of her lying on the ground and sobbing, haunted him. He didn't want to look.

He didn't need to look.

They passed each cell. Skeletal individuals occupied each one with haunting silver, yellow, and white eyes. Some mumbled incomprehensible stories while others raved about the endless collection of souls in his head. Brent's throat tightened at each step. *They sound like me. Who are they? What are they?*

Who am I?

What am I?

Where do I belong?

Most of the time, the monsters spoke in garbled tongues. Stories pulsated off their bodies, of learning to release souls and collecting stories. But their minds wavered, their bodies fell, and screeching in pain, the Council led them into the crypts.

Help us.

   Help us.

      Help us.

Bria tugged at his arm. "Are you okay? You're pale."

"Yeah... I'm fine... I'm...shite!" He gripped his knees, gagged a few times, then pressed his hand against the wall.

Help us.

Help us.

Help us.

"Help me," Brent gasped.

Bria caught his arm, then turned to Tomás, "Who are these people? What's going on?"

Brent barely heard Tomás speak. "They're the remnants of Mist Keepers who Ningursu failed to control. He left them to rot in their uncontrolled powers."

"They're not human," Brent choked.

"Not anymore."

Brent stared at one of the monsters in the cage. Its silver eyes gawked at him as if reading him like a book. Its stories reached for him. He could hardly breathe.

"Brent? Do you want to leave?" Bria whispered.

"Yeah...please..."

"I understand. It is a lot to take in," Tomás replied. He continued to stare at the cage, his expression emotionless. "Go rest. Both of you."

"Thank you." Bria helped Brent from the crypts. He winced at every cell, holding his head in his hands and shaking. Each time he tried to tell Bria, his mouth ran dry. He would stop to bang his fist into the wall, then slid down and hugged his knees.

It must have taken twice as long to exit the crypts as when they entered. Bria guided him over to the nearby couch, where Nix joined them. The dog nuzzled her head into Brent's lap, and he brought his nose against her fur, inhaling and exhaling until the spinning headache disappeared.

Bria lowered herself into the chair across from them. Only then did Brent notice Bria's own discomfort; her eyes were wide and tearful. He might have seen it, but she lived in those crypts for days.

His stomach churned again. "I'm sorry...I mean...that was hard for you, and I was being shitty and... I'm sorry."

She wiped her face. "No. It looked like something smacked you in the face. What happened?"

"I saw you—"

"There was something else. You were responding to a story."

Brent stared at his trembling fingers. "I dunno. But it...I mean, in the stories...it felt like...I mean...shite!"

"Take your time."

Inhaling, Brent found his next words. "That could be me in there. One wrong move and...I could end up just like those Mist Keepers." He stared hard at Bria. "They're just like me."

CHAPTER FORTY-EIGHT

AB AETERNO

Jemma pulled her red hair up into a symmetrical bun on the top of her head as she stared at herself in the mirror. One girl on the train gave her a blue dress. It was nowhere near as beautiful as the gown she had packed for the voyage, but it was far better than the rags she wore climbing aboard the train. All-in-all, other than Mr. Santiago and Lolli, the others on the train welcomed their presence, offering them meals and company to help the day-long journey move just a tad faster.

She loved her small, windowless sleeping cabin. Jemma hadn't realized how much she missed the luxury of privacy and a warm bed. It gave her a chance to toss away her worries and refocus on the goal: Ab Aeterno was less than a couple hours away.

Ab Aeterno had always served as that mythical place far away with its tower watching over the western seashore. There were no photographs, but the artwork Jemma had seen painted a picture of a glistening marble tower with a Year Glass hanging high above the town. Rumors said gemstones, silver, gold, and treasures galore highlighted the tower, and in it, Brothers and Sisters learned the true peace of the Effluvium.

Jemma brought her fingers to her lips and held them toward the doorway. Soon, she and Brother Roy Al would reunite. They'd bring peace back to Newbird's Arm. Elder Lau Rel would leave the town, and the Guard would follow; they would be the new talk of the town.

An authentic hero always returned.

Jemma gathered herself as the train slowed. She paced the windowless cabin, trying to picture Ab Aeterno in the distance. Would she see the tower from Laysan's Beach? This was the moment she'd waited for since she was a young girl. Her heart raced with giddiness as she bounced between each foot with excitement.

When the train screeched to a halt, Jemma ran to the door. Micca came out of one of the other rooms in the car with Timothée right behind him.

He joined her by the exit. "You look excited. Don't think I've seen you like this ever. Guess you have a bit of a personality, huh?"

Jemma glared.

Micca responded with a melancholy grin.

The door opened. They exited out to a platform overlooking a courtyard of autos. The sea glistened just over the grassy dunes, matching the morning fog of yellow and gray with awkward waves. The carnies began unloading the train, moving like a well-organized machine to prepare for the next show.

Jemma glanced at Micca, her smile wide, exuberance bubbling in her chest. "I've wanted to come here since I was a little girl. Finally, I'm here! And I hope you'll understand when you see it—"

Micca interrupted, "Jem. I'm not going to Ab Aeterno."

Jemma stared at him. "But...you traveled all the way here."

"I left Newbird's Arm. The destination ain't what got me to come with you. I coulda gone anywhere, but I'm a good person and helped ya. This is where my journey ends, though."

Jemma blinked. Despite Micca's despicable nature, abhorrent attitude, and relentless crude mouth, she'd grown accustomed to him traveling beside her. In the back of her mind, she pictured Micca walking into Ab Aeterno with her and marveling, with his stupid smile, at its grandeur.

"But...where will you go?" Jemma whispered.

"I think I'm gonna stay with Mr. Santiago and the lot. They liked what I did with the pipes and all last night and want me to stay on. Gives me a warm meal and some shelter. A vagrant ain't able to ask for much else, y'know?"

"But you won't be able to go home. You'll be alone."

"You abandoned your home on a wild goose chase to find Brother Roy Al," Micca responded point-blank. "What will you do if you don't find what you're looking for, Jemma?"

"Brother Roy Al will guide me."

"That ain't the question."

Jemma straightened her posture. "I'm a Sister of the Order. I'll go where I am needed. If I am not needed here, I'll find another Temple to serve. Or I'll return to Newbird's Arm. But I am sure Brother Roy Al will be happy to see me."

Micca scowled.

"Come with me, Micca, please."

"I ain't a part of that life." Micca kicked his foot against the platform. "Just, Jem...if you change your mind or anything, Mr. Santiago said we'll be here in

Laysan for at least a bit to get supplies before we head north and all. You can always come back."

"I don't think that will be necessary. Thank you, though." Jemma didn't mean to sound bitter, but her voice cut the air, and by the time she started the sentence, she had committed.

"It might be, though!"

"It won't be!"

"You don't know that!"

"Sister Jey Ma!" Timothée spoke at last. "I think it is best you look behind you."

"What? Why?"

Timothée took her by the shoulders and turned her in a half-circle.

Jemma gasped.

Plumes of smoke rose in the distance, past the roofs of Laysan and upon the mountains climbing over the landscape. Jemma's heart fell as she watched them gather. A shadow of a tower sat deep beneath them. Waiting. Watching.

Burning.

"Ab Aeterno..." The words hung from her mouth.

Timothée bowed his head. "I'm sorry, Sister. We saw the smoke as we approached. Didn't know how to tell you."

Jemma didn't hear the rest, rushing off the train platform and toward a car parked by the tracks.

"Jem!" Micca raced after her. "What're you doing?!"

She ignored him, finding a car with an open door. Without the slightest idea of what to do, she started fidgeting with the wheel and panel, hoping something would start.

Anything.

Micca grabbed her arm. "Jemma! Stop!"

"I need to get there! I need to—"

"And do what, exactly?"

"I don't know! But I need to get to it before it burns!"

"Y'know, most people run away from a fire!"

"Please!"

Timothée joined them, shaking his head. "No need to steal a car. We got one in the caboose. Was gonna head to Aeterno Village to pick up some goods and such. Might as well head there now."

Jemma stared at Timothée. Unable to speak, she nodded.

"Alright. Give me five minutes, and we'll be on the road."

While the ride to Ab Aeterno took only thirty minutes, Jemma swore a lifetime passed between climbing into the car and their arrival in Aeterno Village.

Timothée and Micca bantered, already interacting like an old married couple. If fear hadn't encapsulated every one of Jemma's thoughts, she would have found it amusing. But now? No. She had to reach Ab Aeterno before it burned.

If she didn't, would this be for naught?

Timothée parked the car at the edge of the village. Despite the flaming exterior of the tower, the village appeared unscathed. Villagers pointed to the scene on the hill in the distance, huddling together in groups and shouting while the guard filled the streets in droves.

This is more guards than necessary for a small village.

Jemma recognized the insignia on their arms, the determination in their eyes. *Of course, the men of Knoll would be here,* Jemma realized. But they obeyed and loved the Order...they couldn't be responsible for the destruction of the sacred tower.

Right?

"Shite, I ain't able to get out here," Micca grunted, rubbing his arm.

"Stay low. I'll be back." Timothée unhitched his seatbelt. "Sister, you might want to stay—"

Jemma didn't let him finish his sentence. Before Timothée could even open the door, she bounded out of the car. For a moment, nausea from the trip washed over her, but she shooed it away, pushing through the crowds towards the tower.

Timothée and Micca shouted after her, but soon, just like the tower in the smoke, their voices vanished.

Jemma had never run so fast in her life. She kicked off her shoes, ignoring the way dirt caught the edges of her skirt, and her hair fell from its perfectly perched bun. Each step brought another pounding ache to her chest. She would get to Ab Aeterno. She would save it.

Foolish, perhaps, but it was the only thing keeping her going.

It took about five minutes to reach the hill beneath where the tower burned. The flames continued to plume, puff, and whip against her face.

A group of Brothers and Sisters gathered at the top of the hill. Jemma slowed to join, wheezing and puffing to catch her breath. Their numbers were few, certainly not all of those who occupied the tower, and they gazed at the fire in both awe and fear. Brother Roy Al was not among them.

Jemma's throat tightened, and she followed their gaze to the Tower. The fire ate away at the wooden externalities while the marble tower itself, with the towering ruby and silver Year Glass, remained intact. If it weren't for the flames, it might have been a glorious moment; the gems on the tower's exterior basked in the orange while the marble reflected the sun's glow through the clouds. For a moment, Jemma absorbed it; Ab Aeterno was just as she imagined it, watching over all else, standing so tall that it stroked the Effluvium's arms in the sky.

But now, it burned beneath a crackling blaze.

"What happened?" Jemma asked one of the younger Sisters.

The Sister didn't look from the tower. "We are unsure. The Senator came to visit with some of his guards. Then a fire started, and we all fled. We pray the Effluvium will bring us rain soon."

"I wouldn't be surprised if a Magii started it," a young brother added. "Brother Roy Al was trying to reform a few of them down in the Pit. Perhaps one was a little crazed and set the fixture ablaze when the Senator came here."

Jemma stared hard at the Sister, praying that they would do something. But they both had to be younger than she was, filled with even more fear. They hadn't seen what Jemma endured in Newbird's Arm.

"We must stop the fire!" Jemma cried.

"We already called the guard. They're bringing the Fire Company," the young brother said.

"But this will all be burned by then! And the other Brothers and Sisters—"

"The Effluvium will protect them."

"As it protects us all," another added.

"From fires and smoke it does fight."

"And we will keep our heads held high."

"To the Effluvium."

"For we are its soul."

Jemma stared at her peers, astonished by their nonchalant attitude. Ab Aeterno was on fire! How could they just let it burn?

People would die.

Brother Roy Al!

She pushed past the Brothers and Sisters and sprinted straight towards the entrance. They screamed after her, but their pleas did not stop her from pushing open the charred doors and rushing inside the Temple.

Smoke filled the pews. It masked the beauty Jemma had imagined, a dark soot coating the stained-glass windows while the charcoal smoke spiraled up with the stairwell that wrapped around the tower. At the very top hung the Year Glass, looking down at the scene below, its silver interior twisting and churning. A shadow stood on the catwalk, gazing with the same intensity as the glass.

Jemma stepped forward and nearly tripped but not because of the smoke.

A thick substance coated her foot.

Red.

Blood.

She covered her mouth to restrain a scream.

Blood dripped throughout the room. Bodies lay strewn in the pews.

Not just any bodies.

They belonged to Brothers and Sisters, those who believed in the Effluvium and its words. But the Effluvium did not protect them. Instead, it let them wither here, dosed in blood, their Year Glasses broken around their necks.

She strode through the rows, choking down each scream and sob. *This isn't because of the fire.* As Jemma examined each body, she noticed the wounds in their heads, their unwavering gazes, and the blood.

So much blood.

And there, among the benches, her worst fear bubbled into actuality.

There, amid the slaughter, lay Brother Roy Al. His glasses sat cracked on his face, his eyes open, a gunshot wound bleeding from the top of his head. He gripped his year glass with both his hands, his mouth parted as if in the middle of a prayer.

Jemma cried, "No!"

It was like everything crashed down at once. She fell to her knees, spreading her arms over Brother Roy Al's body, begging for it to be a joke or a nightmare. He did not stir.

He must wake! She couldn't have traveled here just for him to be dead! *No! No! No!*

She sobbed loud and ugly, clenching Brother Roy Al's robes and letting the tears hit his skin. What in the Effluvium's name had done this? And why? Over twenty Brothers and Sisters lay dead in Tower's pews. Why? *Why? Why!?!*

Her tears took her away from the present. She thought of her time sitting with Brother Roy Al, listening to him spread the kind word of the Effluvium. Had that left a bitter taste in someone's mouth? Or was he just an unnecessary casualty?

She couldn't wrap her head around the reason any of this would occur. It made little sense.

The Effluvium protects.

"Halt! Who goes there!?!"

Jemma heard no one approach, but now their voice rang through the pews.

"Stand up! Now!"

One step at a time, she rose from Brother Roy Al's corpse and turned to the guard standing at the end of the aisle.

The guard's voice cracked. "Jem—Jemma?"

She glanced in his direction. "Christof…"

Cadet Christof Carver stared at her, lowering his gun slightly. A deep cut dug into the left side of his face, his lips slightly crooked while his blond hair stuck out from beneath his cap. She hadn't seen him since that fateful day in Newbird's Arm. Some people thought he died, but others, like Brother Roy Al, vehemently believed that he and his father had survived the events.

And here he was now, still a guard.

Still upholding a distorted belief.

"Are you going to shoot me, Christof? Just like you did to your uncle?" Jemma sniffed.

"To my uncle..." His glare caught Brother Roy Al. "Shite..."

"What? You didn't know?"

"No, I..." Christof shook his head, then repositioned his pistol. "What're ya doing here, Jem?!"

"I could ask you the same thing."

"You need...you need to leave!"

Jemma shook her head.

"Don't make me drag ya outta here."

She stood her ground.

Christof cursed as he rushed over to Jemma and dragged her out of the tower by her wrist. But she didn't scream. She didn't protest. Instead, Jemma closed her eyes, accepting whatever fate handed to her.

For Newbird's Arm and for the Effluvium.

CHAPTER FORTY-NINE

FOUR LANTERNS

The airship hit the ground with a thump. Todd jolted awake, his head hanging to his chest, while Lex slept with her head on his lap. Garrett had fallen asleep in his mother's arms, tearful and crying as they rose into the clouds. After Todd's own ears stopped popping, he removed one of his son's drawing pads from the bag with his crayons and lay them out on the ground before him. That seemed enough to preoccupy Garrett, and soon, they all drifted to sleep. Only Madame Owiti remained awake and alert, scanning the room with her lips pursed, unusually quiet.

The other families in the loading bay huddled in bunches. No one looked at each other, everyone whispering as the gears and pipes bustled. Todd's stomach rumbled with the noise. In all their planning, he hadn't thought to pack much food. The flight to Evylain would have only taken a half-day. Rosada took longer.

Madame Owiti thought ahead and provided snacks for Lex and Garrett. She offered some to Todd earlier, but he declined; his wife and son needed them more.

"So, you've figured a way out of this situation yet, Toddle?" Madame Owiti raised her eyebrows. Her maroon eyes examined him as if looking into his soul.

Todd frowned. "Only thing I thought of is I'll go out there and create a diversion. They might shoot me or some bullshite like that, but at least you, Lex, and Garrett can get away."

"Is that wise?"

"You got any bright ideas?"

Madame Owiti sucked in her lips.

"Didn't think so. This is the best bet I've got to getting Lex and Garret outta here in one piece. If it means I get dead, I get dead."

The airship thudded again, this time waking Lex and Garrett beside him.

Todd stroked the top of Lex's hand. "Hey, love. We've landed."

"Oh." She rubbed her eyes and kissed the top of Garrett's head.

"Lex, dear," Madame Owiti said as she rummaged through her bag, "you should take one of your pills—"

"I need to conserve them. I'm fine."

Todd frowned at Lex. Now wasn't the time to argue with her. He had no clue what would await them when the cargo doors opened. Would guards be waiting to escort them? Would they shoot them on sight? If this was the end, Todd didn't want his last words to be an argument with the love of his life.

"I really do feel fine." Lex stared back at Todd. "Really."

"A'ight. I'll trust you."

She smiled but not a real one. It told a story instead, hinting at her sadness, at her worry, and at her fear. It surged through her eyes, her lips, and down to her posture.

Yet before Todd had the chance to quell her, another thud rocked the cargo hold. The doors opened moments later.

He braced himself for an onslaught of guards, of gunfire, and for death. If he believed in the power of the Effluvium, he might have prayed. Todd instead grappled for those he knew and believed in: he reached for Lex, for Garrett, and even for Madame Owiti. Damn, he even reached for Preston.

Wherever he may be.

To his surprise, no guards came through the cargo hold door. All was quiet but the whirring engines of nearby airships.

The other families rose from their spots and filed out, unphased by the developments. Todd glanced at Madame Owiti. She shrugged in response.

"Something is off. Stand your guard," he muttered to Lex.

Todd waited until the remaining families left, then gathered his bags in one hand and Lex's fingers in the other and led his family out of the cargo hold into the unloading bay. At first glance, it looked like all other warehouses, filled with boxes and supplies. Todd's attention drifted away from the boxes towards the guard standing a few paces away. He motioned to the families as they approached.

"Women and children on the right, men on the left!" the guard chanted.

An older gentleman, who'd been on the same air carrier as Todd, glared at the guard, poking him in the chest. "Now what in tarnation is going on here, young man? This ain't what I done did when I was last here!"

"Get to the left, sir, or I will find you in contempt!" the guard barked.

"No, I want me some answers, and I—"

Whack.

Faster than Todd could blink, the guard hit the old man with a club. He fell to the ground, and two more guards came over to drag the man away.

Todd turned back to Lex, keeping his lips sewed tight. Neither Lex nor Madame Owiti gaped. They'd all seen this.

It still never failed to leave his body aching with fear.

They took another step forward, watching another family split up by the guards. Everyone kept demanding answers with few responses: "get to the left," "it's standard procedure," "you'll be with your family soon," and the most jarring, "it's only questioning."

Only questioning? Todd scoffed at the remark.

No. This was more.

With one family ahead, Todd turned to Lex. "Listen. If they recognize your name, if they ask about me, say you don't know. Lie your ass off, a'ight? Say I kidnapped you, raped you...I don't care! All that matters is you and Garrett get the hell outta here, a'ight?"

"Toddle..." Lex placed a hand on his cheek.

"Promise me you'll lie."

"And get you in trouble?"

"Lex—"

"Next!" The guard called and motioned for them to split with Todd heading to the left while Madame Owiti and Lex with Garrett heading to the right. He followed the women with his gaze, praying it would be a short time until they'd see each other again.

In the name of the Effluvium or whatever almighty power watched over him, he would return to Lex.

As they disappeared behind the crates, Madame Owiti mouthed to him a couple words. "I'll take care of Lex. Don't worry."

"Oi! Stop loitering around! Get moving!" The guard prodded him with the end of the club.

Todd grunted and took a step forward. Each step weighed heavier, the boxes towering over him like a city. He shrank alone beneath the eyes of the Order. It reminded him of when he was a kid, stepping onto the old worn-out train car to join the Guard. He was nothing then.

He was nothing now.

The line of at least fifty men from various airships wove through the boxes. People yelled, shouted, and threw their arms back. Guards stopped altercations. It was like a prison yard, the Pit, or a dark alleyway in the middle of the city. Todd kept his head down, holding his bag tight, and with each step, he hoped that all would be well when he reached the counter at the end of the line.

A tall guard with a narrow face and a curled mustache manned the desk. He bore the captain's insignia on his uniform with his name inscribed beneath it: Carver.

"Papers, please," the captain said, not looking up from his own notes.

Todd kept his hands steady, passing the papers to the guard.

The man took the papers, then poured the pitcher on his desk into the thin dish beside him. An odd silver liquid, reminiscent of Madame Owiti's orb, filled the bottom of the plate. "Index finger out."

Todd didn't quite understand, but he obeyed.

The captain pricked his finger with a small needle and dribbled the blood in the liquid. It intermingled with the liquid, a slight twinge of red highlighting its surface.

"Hmph." The captain turned to the papers. "Very well, you are free to go, Mr. Dray—" The captain trailed off, staring intently at Todd. His beady eyes narrowed. "Your name is Mr. Toddle Dray?"

"That's what the papers say, don't they?"

"Don't be coy. Is your name Toddle Dray?"

Todd glowered. "Yes, that's my name."

"Very well." The captain rose. He was taller than Todd, not by much but enough, so Todd had to strain his neck to meet his gaze.

Todd, of course, knew what the captain's words would be next.

"Toddle Dray, you are under arrest."

"Yeah," Todd said as he raised his hands. "I figured that would be the case."

The captain left him alone in a solitary holding cell. Todd occupied himself by pacing, punching, and cursing. He could only hope Lex and Garrett were safe.

They were all that mattered.

Outside, the door in the hall opened. Footsteps followed. The door to his holding cell slid open.

The captain from the loading bay entered the room and lit three lanterns on the wall.

"Up," the captain said, monotone.

Todd rose, blinking a few times as his eyes adjusted.

The captain sat on the bench across from Todd. "How many lanterns are there?"

"Wha—what?" Todd processed the question.

"How many lanterns are there?"

"Um...three."

"What if I said there were four?"

"I'm... I'm sorry? Four?" Todd looked at the lanterns again and counted to himself twice. "No, there's definitely three."

"Hmph." The captain removed a notepad from his front pocket and flipped through it. For a few long pauses, he read through his notes, his nose nearly touching the page, before returning to Todd with that same concrete stare. "Mr. Toddle Dray...or should I say Drayton?"

Todd blinked. "How did you—"

"Not very creative, are you? It would have been safer to go with a last name like Smith or Wood." The captain flipped through his notes. "After you assaulted that guard in Mert, we sent a telegraph to Knoll for your files. Quite a record you have here, hm?"

"I don't want to talk about my *record*." Todd snarled.

"You were a good boy for a long time before you disobeyed orders, assaulted a guard, and escaped the Pit. What a shame. By now, you would be a senior lieutenant or even a captain! Where did we go wrong with you?" The captain put his notebook away and looked straight at Todd. "How many lanterns are behind me, Mr. Drayton?"

"I see three!"

"I'm telling you, there are four."

Todd threw his hands in the air. "Maybe your fucking big ass head is blocking the fourth one! I only see three!"

Whack.

Captain Carver reacted with the dexterity of a cat. He hit Todd, sharp and hard enough that Todd fell to the ground.

"Are you done?" the captain snarled.

Todd grunted.

"I cannot hear you!"

"Ay!"

"Good." The captain sat back down and stared at Todd. "It's quite a shame what happened with you, Mr. Drayton. You still have the Guard's influence deep inside of you."

"Can't get rid of something that fu—that influenced me for ten years of my life." Todd rubbed his head.

"It makes me wonder what you noticed while in the City of Mert. You ran a shop there, yes? In fact, the Yellow Demon emerged from your shop, correct? We have witnesses who believe so." The captain raised his eyebrows. "And aren't you friends with Madame Awiti Owiti, the Seer? Has she not been influencing your wife and child?"

"My wife..." Todd tensed. "Where are they? What did you do with them?"

"They are safe. No harm will come to them if you cooperate."

"What do you want from me?"

The captain smirked. "I want your unrelenting cooperation. I would hate to send you through re-education so we can learn a bit about your time in that asinine city. It's such a grueling process. Why go through it when all I want is the truth?"

Todd stared hard at Captain Carver. The man didn't blink. "If I cooperate, do you guarantee their safety?"

"I guarantee we will take care of them." The captain turned away from Todd. "So, tell me, Mr. Drayton, how many lanterns are there?"

Todd gazed at the lanterns on the wall. Everything he'd ever done was to protect his family. It was never for him or anyone else.

Always Lex.

Always Garrett.

Always Preston.

Todd closed his eyes, his voice a mere whisper when he answered, "There are four."

CHAPTER FIFTY

WHERE MONSTERS ARE BORN

B rent wandered through the next day in a haze. He tried to stay upbeat, but at night, the night-mares haunted him, lurching him awake. He often wandered down to the crypt's entrance and stared at the gates. What made him so much different that he survived while the others wilted away in prison? Why did he get to survive? How long would he be able to by-pass Ningursu's gaze? He kept pondering it with every passing moment but found no answers.

Bria joined him most nights, keeping him in place while her attention drifted to the barricade blocking the Library's entrance. She'd done well to keep it standing, but the vines began pulling back, and the bark withered. Soon, the barricade would collapse. With every sleep, Brent knew the Council would not let it stay much longer.

Their time in the Library was coming to an end.

Bria leaned into him one morning while Nix slept by his feet, following his gaze to the gate. "We need to stop Ningursu."

"I know." Brent scowled.

Bria stared, her attention turned back to the room with the pool on the other side of the Library. "What if we destroy the Pools?"

"What? Kek would hate that."

"To Hell with Kek! This has to do with Ningursu! If we get rid of his ability to see, his reign ends." Bria rose.

"Do we know what that will do, though? Destroying them, I mean? Aren't they kind of...part of the world now?"

"We don't have to destroy all of them, just the important ones. Like the ones in the Library or the one that we saw near Elder Don Van. It'd be impossible to destroy them all."

"Yeah...but...we dunno how to destroy them...or find them...or..." Brent hesitated. "But Malaika might be able to help! If we find her, she could make a map and—"

"And I can destroy them!" Bria exclaimed. "They're made of the earth. I feel it...and if I can feel it...I can destroy it."

"Are you sure?"

"If I focus, I think I can do it. I just have to have the intention to destroy them. It might take time to figure out, but we have time while we search for them! It's just part of the next adventure."

"You're... you're a genius! It's a crazy idea, and usually, I come up with those, but this time... you're a genius!" Brent laughed.

They embraced and kissed hard. The sudden taste of victory brushed over Brent's mouth; there was hope. It was distant, almost unreal and impossible, but there.

As much as Brent wanted to keep kissing Bria for hours, they both pulled back, removing themselves from the spot near the crypt to discuss their next steps. They meandered through shelves with Nix rushing ahead of them, forming a comprehensive plan as they bantered back and forth. It came down to one simple idea: they would leave in the next couple days via the pool in the Library. That would be the best way to start because inevitably, they would end up somewhere with a Pool. Bria detailed how she almost destroyed Madame Owiti's orb. If it hadn't been on accident, and she had instead embraced her magic in that moment, she might have destroyed it completely.

The plan wasn't foolproof. In fact, it wasn't even a plan, just an idea. But it was something, and that was what they needed.

"What do we do about the...Mist Keepers...in the crypt, though?" Brent asked as they strode into the galley. Julietta stood at the counter and smiled in their direction as she collected an odd array of fruits and dyes before vanishing again in a plume of mist.

"What are your ideas?" Bria asked as she retreated into the pantry to search for seeds to add to her collection as she did each evening.

Brent sat at the table, pondering, "I want to help them...but I don't think I'm strong enough yet. I mean, I can try to help them find their stories or free them or something, but..." He stared at his hands. "They're not as straightforward as the Diabolo. The Diabolo is just... it's madness and evil. But...the...the ones down there are people and...I can't do it yet."

Bria sat down across from him with a pile of seeds. She took his hand. "It will take time. I understand you don't want to leave them struggling, but you can't do it all."

"Neither can you."

"I can try." Bria kissed him again.

There were these moments when they kissed that transported Brent back to their early romance, when they hid in the Senator's Garden, giggling. He stayed with those memories even after Bria pulled away, returning to her pile of seeds and examining each one with excitement. One at a time, he helped Bria organize them, pretending they were two farmers like in one of the stories he'd collected, preparing for the upcoming harvest. As he told the tale, Bria laughed, watching as the farmer and his wife appeared beside them at the table.

It was something normal, at least.

For the rest of the day, they continued like this, making plans to leave, collecting seeds, playing with Nix, and telling stories. The day passed as if nothing bad would happen. Things were okay. They even went to bed at a reasonable hour, where Brent told a story until the candles waned. Yet while Bria fell asleep, Brent did not welcome sleep's blessing. He tossed and turned before giving up and climbing out of bed. He kissed Bria's forehead. She stirred once, rolled over, and pulled the blankets around her like a cocoon.

Nix was up and by his side, though, galloping at his heels as he once again returned to the metal gates of the crypts. He only paused once, glancing at the Library's entrance. The lattice of vines hung, wilted and frayed, but the door remained shut.

It's fine, Brent told himself. Even with the vines shriveling, the bark created a shield over the doorway. No, their barricade stood. For now.

Upon reaching the crypt, he paused and gripped the gate, tracing the leaf-like patterns along metal bars before moving his fingers above the handle. The stories beckoned him.

This time, he didn't stop himself.

He took each step slower this time, leaving the gate open a crack in case Bria came searching for him. With each step forward, he immersed himself in the stories. Of Ningursu, Aelia, Jiang, and Alojzy visiting the crypts; of skeletal individuals dragged to and from their cells; of screaming and tears; of Bria begging; of everything.

By each of the cells, he paused. Flashes of Bria's confinement washed over him, but he shook it off, trying to avoid infringing on her privacy. But it was there: her crying and sobbing as she navigated the maze-like crypts, only made more confusing by an architectural mist.

Yet, as he swerved deeper into the crypt, the eyes of the prisoners haunted him even more than Bria's tale. They sent him back to moments in the Sanitorium, locked away in the hallway with the flickering lights, with screams, with pain, and with Edith. But their stories also brought him into a void of the unknown. The prisoners screamed and wailed, shouting and withering at his steps. None of the doors had locks on them; in fact, most didn't even have doors.

Most of the prisoners hid in the mist and shadows. They didn't flinch as he walked by, talking to themselves. A few displayed misshaped, malnourished stories. Others told tales of Brent as he walked by: *Here he goes walking. Walking. Walking. Dog at heels. Waves. Stutters. Tremors. Walking.*

A woman with a skeletal exterior and sickly yellow eyes watched him from her cell. Brent slowed his pace and touched her hand as she reached out. Stories flew through him of a young girl training alongside Tomás. She was brave, kind, and empathetic...but then the stories came, and she locked herself in a chamber, begging them to stop until she pulled out all of her hair. The stories told her to stop eating. The nightmares told her to stop sleeping.

When she died, Hell kept its fury; she did not escape until Tomás offered her the key.

She was but a skeleton of her former self when she emerged. Tomás tried to help her see, to hear, to breathe, but she wanted to lie on the floor and crumple like paper.

Brent saw violence; he saw peril. Someone offered the girl an odd brew from delicate hands. Her mind vanished, replaced by the evil discourse of the worst individuals to walk the planet.

Screaming.

Shrieking.

Shouting.

"Shite!" Brent released the woman's hand and stared at her. The Diabolo in the back of his mind momentarily invaded his thoughts. *Choke the woman. Kill her. Then kill your lass, too. Blood...dripping...feel it...blood...* "Stop it, Frankie!" He gritted his teeth and reached for Nix. The dog licked his hand. "My name is Brent...and I am not a monster!"

The skeletal woman in the cage tilted her head to one side.

"I know, I know!" Brent's lip quivered as he spoke. "It hurts...the stories...they don't stop. I can't imagine what you're seeing...or what you've been through. Your story is so jumbled..." He sniffed. "I wish I could help."

"You strong stay you. Strong must be, stay." The woman receded to the back of the cage like the others.

Brent hugged Nix, breathing in the dog's fur. *It's okay, it's okay. You're still here.*

The urge to go back rocked his stomach, but he kept on pushing with Nix on his heels. Darkness thickened.

Black like a crow. No stars. No nothing. Just endless oblivion with each step.

He held up the torch and peered further down the path. The crypt forked off into two smaller paths, one with empty cells and few stories to guard the way and another with a basin at the far end.

Brent paced towards the basin, past the few occupied cells where more skeletal-like individuals cried, and a few ghosts moaned. The basin stunk, not like the usual crisp air of the pool above but more like rotten milk and sewage.

When he peered into the liquid, a murky yellow coagulated on top. His finger burned when he poked it, and rather than the comfort he often found in the peonies, it left him distraught.

Like when the Diabolo first screamed into his face.

A knot formed in his throat, and he gagged. The nightmares of those in the crypts pulsated through the pool, feeding off the terrors and screams. Like a Diabolo.

Someone touched him on the shoulder.

"Shite!" Brent spun around. "Julietta? What're you doing here?"

"You looked scared, Quincy. I thought I'd make you a pie." She held out a half-baked pastry in her bare, blister and paint-covered hands.

Brent stared at her. Her empty gaze sent a sadness through his chest. "Julietta. You need to go back upstairs."

"What is this place, Quincy? It is dark. You shouldn't be here."

"You're right." Brent placed a hand on Julietta's shoulder. "Let's go back upstairs."

Julietta stared hard at Brent, then towards the basin. Her nostrils flared. "Oh, Quincy! That is vile! Perhaps we should clean it before it gets out of hand, yes?"

"No, it's okay, Julietta!" Brent grabbed her wrist. Nix barked.

"Now, now Quincy, it's rude to leave a mess." She pulled away from Brent, stronger than he thought she'd be, and moved towards the bowl. Her fingers skimmed the top of the liquid.

"Julietta! Please!" Brent croaked.

Let her do it. Let her go.

She deserves it.

"No!" Brent pushed past his own nightmares and once again took Julietta's hand.

She didn't turn this time, raising her hand out of the liquid and up to her face. The yellow liquid dripped over the tips of her fingers and down her hand to mingle beneath her scabs and blisters. Julietta cocked her head to the side as if watching it, not budging as the liquid continued down her wrist.

"Julietta?"

No answer.

"Julietta! Answer me!"

The woman hit the ground with a thud. Brent rushed to her side, turning her body up from the ground. As she breathed in rapid gasps, foam gathered at her mouth. The liquid finally stopped traveling up her skin, evaporating like steam in the air, leaving behind a gray tint on her skin.

"No...no...come on! Wake up!" He gripped her shoulders. "Julietta! Answer me!"

She coughed. Blood pooled from the corners of her mouth.

Then, with a single blink, her eyes opened.

They were not green anymore.

Instead, they glowed yellow.

Brent released her. "No..."

Julietta simpered insidiously.

Shite. It was like looking in a mirror. *Is this what Bria saw?*

When Julietta finally spoke, her voice arrived in a series of rapid whispers, warped into a bundle of a thousand voices. "Forgotten. I'm forgotten."

"No... you're not forgotten. You...we...I...I tried to stop you! What happened? No...please come back...please!"

Julietta's lip curled. "We received a blank slate. Now, she shall reign."

"Julietta...please... you're stronger than this. Fight!"

"Julietta was a shell. She's whole now."

"No... she's not... she's—"

Julietta lunged at him, her nails scratching his face. Brent stumbled up and back, hitting the wall with his back. Nix barked.

"Nix!" Brent shouted back. "Go get help! Bria! Or Tomás! Or someone! Get help, a'ight!?!"

Nix tilted her head.

"Go!" Brent shouted, dodging another one of Julietta's pursuits.

The dog woofed once, then bolted out of the crypts. Brent hoped it wasn't out of fear.

Julietta's mouth extended into a wide, perverse smile as she approached him again. He wiped his forehead, blood trickling down the side of his face from the cut on his cheek.

She cackled. "Poor baby boy. Needs to get his dog to help. Shame."

Brent didn't take her bait. Instead, he stepped along the wall, reaching into his surroundings.

He might not have been able to fight, but there was one thing he could do.

The surrounding stories, from all the nightmares and prisoners, took root at the forefront of his mind. He did the only thing he knew to block Julietta from her pursuit.

He told their stories.

CHAPTER FIFTY-ONE

INVASIVE

Bria woke up with a jolt to Nix licking the bottom of her feet. "Ew! Nix! Stop!"

Nix whined.

She rubbed her eyes. Once again, she was alone.

While Bria had gotten used to Brent's late-night escapades, this time, it felt different.

The dog whined again.

"What is it? What's wrong, Nix?" She turned on the one lantern and squinted. The dog had already started to the door. "Okay, okay, wait!" She pulled on her jacket and shoes, pausing to snatch her bag and place a handful of seeds in her pockets.

Nix ran across the second-story corridor. Bria chased after the dog. The silence in the Library made her queasy as if expecting a monster to strike. *Why didn't you wake me, Brent?*

She followed Nix to the stairwell. As she began her descent, she almost walked straight through Nedo as he meandered up the stairs, his eyes vacant.

"Nedo! I'm so sorry!" Bria held up her hands.

A gentle smile crossed Nedo's lips.

"Have you seen Brent?"

Nedo motioned behind her. She spun, her momentary relief turning to a deeper dread. Up on the third floor, visible from where she stood, the door to Ningursu's office sat cracked open.

She turned back to Nedo. "Is he in there?"

Nedo shook his head.

"Then—"

Nedo held up his hand, pointed at Bria with one hand, and jabbed the other towards the door.

"I—"

He then pointed at himself and shot his other finger downstairs.

"You'll find him? Promise?"

Nedo nodded.

Bria fidgeted with her bag, removing her cowl and a small sack of seeds. She stared at the stitching on the cowl, running her fingers over the wool. Her mind battled over whether to listen to Nedo, but the barricade stood, so was it Ningursu up in the office? Or something else?

She trusted Nedo, though. She'd seen his story, and it flooded her veins. After a moment of hesitation, Bria handed the satchel to Nedo. "He might need this."

After taking the bag, Nedo motioned again for Bria to go up the stairs. She stared hard at him one last time, then turned, while Nix followed on Nedo's heels.

Bria's anxiety ran rampant as she took each step up to Ningursu's glowing office. Her heart pattered. She counted the number of lanterns hanging from the ceiling as she walked up the stairs. *Eighteen. There are eighteen lanterns on the ceiling here. We're safe. Remember. We're safe. There's nothing to worry about. It could be Tomás. Or Julietta. Or nothing!*

Her mind kept going. Perhaps Tomás had betrayed them! Maybe there was another entrance!

She got in using the pool, didn't she?

She sucked in her breath at the door. Her ears buzzed in anticipation, sending sparks of nerves down her spine and itching along her fingertips. With an inhale, she pushed open the door.

None other than Kek themself sat on the edge of the desk, picking at their nails. Yusef stood on a chair beside them, gazing into the basin without flinching. Two candles illuminated the desk.

And with a slam, the door closed behind her. A blade pressed into her shoulder, followed by that immoral voice. "I wouldn't move if I were you."

Bria tensed and reached into her pocket for the seeds, letting them dance around her fingertips.

Kek looked up from their nails. "Now, now Edith. We do not want to harm Briannabella."

"She's got plants on her." Edith hissed and poked Bria's back. A few seeds toppled from her pockets.

"Bria is a rational person. She won't attack. Lower your blade."

Edith snarled but obliged, releasing Bria from her hold. The fear remained in Bria's stomach, but her tension loosened. She rubbed her shoulder before approaching Kek. She ran through each question in her head before settling at last on, "How did you get in? We have a barricade. I didn't realize you had access to the tunnels."

"We do not," Kek stated. "*You* let us in."

"What?"

Yusef perked up from behind the basin. "I saw you by the Pool with Nedo. It's a window, after all. You have the same magic as me, so the connection was much more prominent, and we were able to latch onto it."

"I—"

"Thank you, Bria!" Kek grinned as they spoke. "You have given me access to where I've been trying to get for years. And what luck! You've even knocked the Council out of here! You are something fantastic."

"I'm not here to be your weapon or spy." Bria stared hard at Kek, recounting the warning Madame Owiti passed to her. *Be wary. They train people for their benefit.*

"I never said you were."

"Then why train me?"

Kek scowled. "Because I see your potential. Yusef has too. We all have."

"Just like with Merta and all the others you slaughtered?"

"Ah. So you've met Nedo?" Kek raised their eyebrows. "You should not trust everyone you—"

"No! Don't give me that!" Bria spoke over Kek this time. "Brent showed the story to me! Stories don't lie! What happened in the past happened and cannot change."

Edith cackled. "What if Brent manipulated the story to show you what he wanted?"

"He didn't," Bria replied, confident in her answer.

"But—"

"Edith! Silence!" Kek glared before returning to Bria. "I have changed, Bria. That was thousands of years ago when I slaughtered Merta. And yes, I will admit that all those deaths were not sacrifices, they were slaughters. I was wrapped in my head. But people change. I changed. I learned. And I have many, many regrets. Merta was my friend. She gave me this life. So did the others."

Kek turned their attention to the ceiling. "After the One War, I reflected. I ordered the slaughter of many. I started what the world became today; magic has faltered, Ningursu is all-powerful, and people have grown fearful. I dedicated myself to the preservation of magic. So, I founded a safe haven and named it the City of Mert after her...because anyone with magic should be safe." Kek blinked, pushing back what looked like tears. "I made mistakes. But I learned. My job now is to protect Magii, Seers, and anyone under threat by ridiculous men like Ningursu! Whatever you might believe, I am not here to use you, Bria. I only want the best for your magic. If you were to walk away, I would not stop you."

Bria watched Kek. There was a genuine sincerity in Kek's voice, in how their eyes glistened, and in the slack in their stance. But Madame Owiti's warning, Nedo's story, and the events from the past couple months weighed heavily over Bria.

"I'm not sure if I can trust you," Bria admitted.

"Because you're smart. You question things. That is a necessity," Yusef chimed in, poking again at the basin.

He turned to Kek. "I've contacted the others. They're ready."

Kek waved their hand. "Good. Tell Varden to keep ground in Mert. We need eyes there. And tell Tilda to keep a watch on Malaika. She's no use to us if she runs off." Before Bria could inquire about Malaika or the rest, Kek turned back to her. "I would not expect you to trust me. Yusef is right; you are smart and guarded. It is why you are here now instead of lying dead in the tunnels. But, if you claim stories are true, could Brent confirm the veracity of my statements?"

"Depends. Where is he?" Bria glared.

"Pardon?"

"What did you do with him? Nix woke me up whining! Nedo went to go find him so I could talk to you. So, what did you do to him?" Bria reached into her small pouch. The pumpkin seeds grew along the tips of her fingers. She wanted answers!

"That is unrelated to my presence."

"Bullshit!"

"Bria—"

"Excuse me, Tehuti," Yusef interjected himself again, "the others are preparing for arrival. They should be here soon."

"Who?" Bria demanded.

"The other immortals, of course." Kek walked over and placed a hand on Bria's shoulder. "We're claiming the Library as our own."

Bria opened her mouth, then shook her head. She wouldn't be a part of this war any longer. "I am going to find Brent, and we're going to leave. If you meant what you said, then you will let me."

"As you wish."

Bria left the room without another word. Part of her expected Kek to send Edith after her, but no one followed. Bria paced forward a few steps, and once sure no one followed her, she sprinted down the stairwell for Brent. She hoped Nedo was already sitting with him at the bottom of the stairs, but upon reaching the first floor, there was no change.

She called out again for Brent and Nix, but no one answered.

Only her voice echoed back.

As her voice bounded, the surrounding Library hummed.

It captured her voice and used it as its own.

The hair on the back of her neck rose. Had the walls suddenly gotten closer? Or were the bookshelves closing around her? No, it had to be nerves, right? Or the rest of Kek's Palaver had arrived. That had to be it. *The Council isn't here!*

Bria glanced at the Library's doors. They remained standing, branches and vines wrapped around them. But had the door shrunk? Didn't it used to reach the ceiling? Why was it only the size of the shelving now?

"Oh no..." She stepped back. *Alojzy. The Council. They're here. They must have learned about Kek! Shit!*

How? Bria didn't dwell on it. Ningursu had eyes everywhere.

She called out Brent's name again. This time, her voice hung in the air.

Suffocating.

Twisting.

Vanishing.

From above, she heard shouting, footsteps, and thuds.

From below, the world quivered.

From the walls, she sensed the doorway quivering.

Her barricade fell. Vines slithered to the ground while the roots were dismantled.

Bang.

Bang.

Bang.

Bria rushed away from the crypts towards the barricade, throwing her hands up to send her vines and roots back. With each command, her breaths strained, her tears fell, her mouth numbed. This couldn't last for long;

her body couldn't handle the fight. It was running on reserves. What if she collapsed again? Would she even wake?

"Stay!" she shouted.

But her voice got caught in her throat. The vines retreated. The roots crumbled.

"Come on!"

Nothing. She was talking to the wind.

And like the wind, the air grew stale.

Empty.

Then exploded.

As the doors flew open, a tornado of mist garnished the Library, throwing Bria back into the shelving. Books scattered.

Once the mist cleared, the Council stood in the entrance. Aelia held Ningursu, front and center, while Jiang stood behind her. Caroline waited a few paces back. Alojzy did not join them, nowhere to be seen.

Bria locked her eyes onto Ningursu. What looked like a smile wove across his mouth.

"No... no....please don't," Bria begged.

Her entire body seized. The world tightened around her as the pounding drums rumbled in her head. She couldn't fight it like she had in Mert. Once again, it was like she was back in Newbird's Arm, completely and utterly locked in Ningursu's grasp. She couldn't move. She couldn't see. Only madness.

Vines...

Forests...

Beating...

Beating...

Her tears swelled in her eyes as she fought the voice. The pumpkin seeds left her pouch in a dance, finding homes on the wall. Mingling with roots, frolicking in newly born storms, the Library caved around her.

Please go away, please go away... She exhaled. A thunderstorm nestled on the distant ceiling of the Library. Thunder boomed with her tears.

"I'm not your puppet!" She screamed and held her head. "Go away!"

Lightning erupted from the sky. Rain fell in a thick sheet. They might as well have been outdoors, stuck in the mountains, rather than inside a library.

Perhaps they were.

Another bolt hit the ground, setting books aflame. She saw no one in the storm save for Ningursu. Was he locked in her mind now? Had she already died and gone to Hell? The lightning continued to explode, hitting the ground beside her, combing the floor below, and sending frizz through her body.

Let go... let go...

She couldn't. It was as if someone turned her powers into overdrive.

Vines.

Roots.

Water.

Wind.

Thunder.

And lightning.

One pounding after the other. The electricity, the vibrations, the pouring rain; it all hit her at once.

Each one brought her withering beneath its force.

Was that Nix barking in the distance? Or Brent calling her name?

It had to be rain.

Or were they her tears?

CHAPTER FIFTY-TWO

SENATOR CORDOVA

Jemma waited in a locked prayer crevasse beneath the tower of Ab Aeterno, praying and fasting as she had been for the past couple days. She cleansed herself of worry, of fear, and focused only on the Effluvium's loving embrace. If she kept her head high, then the Effluvium would bless her with a second chance. Deep in her heart, Jemma knew she did nothing wrong. The Tower of Ab Aeterno burned. She chose to save it.

Or at least try.

Her mind kept floating back to Brother Roy Al. His bloodied body stained her thoughts, his mouth ajar, his eyes lifeless. What did he do to deserve such a fate?

It had to be a mistake. He just got caught up in the fray.

She'd concocted a myth in her head that a vagrant had caused the ruckus. The guard was only there to dull the flames. That had to be it, right?

But she'd seen what had happened in Newbird's Arm. Ab Aeterno was no different.

Jemma resorted to praying. She begged the Effluvium to come save her, to guide her to the answers, and show her captors she'd done no wrong. With each prayer, she reflected upon the days that passed, the days to come, and what she would say to her captors. The Effluvium would guide with open arms. It always did.

Meals marked the passage of time. Not that she ate. She fasted and waited.

When the door finally opened, she figured only two days had passed based on her hunger. It was almost a relief when Cadet Christof Carver entered the crevasse.

He threw a loaf of bread at her. "Eat, and then come with me."

"If I refuse?"

"You'll come with me, anyway. Ya might as well have a full stomach. Stupid to not be eating."

"I was cleansing."

"Yeah? Well, you was fasting too long." Christof crossed his arms. "Eat. The senator won't wait long."

Jemma picked at a few pieces of bread. At first, it hurt to eat, but soon she devoured the loaf whole. She then gathered herself off the ground and strode from the room behind Christof.

The cadet led her up the winding stairwell, out of the cleansing crevasses where they'd kept her and into the heart of the tower.

To Jemma's surprise, the tower looked as pristine as ever, as if devastation had not touched it those couple days earlier. Char marks garnished the floors while workers unhinged the wooden fixtures outside the windows, but inside, the pews bore no mark of fire and blood. Ab Aeterno stood tall.

At least the Effluvium answered one of her prayers.

The staircase wrapped around the tower, the stone steps stable against the wall, up toward the Year Glass that hung in the atrium. It was more obvious from above how the fire had primarily attacked the wooden structures beneath the physical tower. The rest stood tall, steady, and together.

"Christof?" Jemma asked.

"What?" he spat.

"How did you survive?"

"Survive what?"

"The Storm of Nightmares."

Christof glared at her. "Don't be stupid. I survived how everyone else did! I took cover from that bastard's onslaught."

"But afterward...you avoided arrest and—"

"It's easy to get out of the town, Jemma. You should know that better than anyone."

Jemma blinked. Did he know that she and Micca stole a car? Was her face plastered all over Rosada like a common criminal, like Bria? What about Micca? Was he safe?

It was the first time since coming to Ab Aeterno that she'd thought of Micca. Did they capture him? Was he being tortured? Why hadn't she thought of him during her days of prayer?

She shook the thought away.

Christof continued marching her up the stairs, past the droves of prayer crevasses and toward the catwalk that circled the tremendous Year Glass at the top of the tower. A door sat on the northernmost side against the Year Glass's wall.

Christof knocked on the door once. "Sir! I have her."

"Bring her in." The voice that responded cut the air like a paper cut: soft, slithering, but pained.

Christof opened the door. Wonder replaced all of Jemma's fear. The door led inside the Year Glass itself. While the silver liquid trickled down the dual-paned sides, there was a vacant center in the middle of it all. A mere room surrounded by glass. The windows towered above, and a small stairwell led to a platform peering out over the village below the Tower.

The figure on the platform turned.

Jemma gasped. "Elder Don Van!"

"That's Senator Cordova now, Sister Jey Ma." He turned to Christof with his blue eyes sharp enough to cut stone. "You can leave, Cadet. Please inform Elder An Drew we are ready to depart."

"Ay." Christof saluted, then left.

The Elder-turned-Senator smiled at Jemma. It still bore no trust, no genuine kindness. He motioned to a chair. A tea kettle and a few lemon cakes sat steaming in the center of the table. "Sister, please sit. You must be worn from your cleanse."

Jemma sat down, staring at the meal.

Senator Cordova shrugged and served himself. "I am so happy we found you, Sister. After reports traveled that a vagrant kidnapped you, we thought you disappeared for good."

Jemma retorted, "Micca didn't—"

He stopped her. "Because if you *were* working with the vagrant, we would have to strip you of your Sisterhood and send you to the Pit. You are too pure to commit such treason against the Effluvium, yes?"

Jemma closed her mouth.

"Eat," Senator Cordova insisted.

They ate in silence. An occasional bump below or a shout broke it, but other than that, all that remained was the wistful drizzling of the Year Glass. Jemma's mind wandered; each word she said next would decide her fate. She had to choose wisely.

As Jemma finished her lemon cake, she finally spoke. "Did you catch him? The vagrant?"

"It is not worth the efforts of my men. We came here for a reason."

"To kill all those Brothers and Sisters?"

"I am unsure what you are implying, Sister. Those Brothers and Sisters died in an unfortunate fire caused by a pyromancer."

"There was blood."

Senator Cordova continued, unphased by Jemma's remark. "A terrible, terrible fire. It is a shame, but the Effluvium protects those who believe in it. Perhaps those Brothers and Sisters had a distorted view of what the Effluvium offered. Perhaps they did not anticipate the dangers some pose to its existence."

"You mean they were kind?" Jemma snapped. *Like Brother Roy Al.*

"Kind? No. Blind." Senator Cordova walked to the Year Glass's window and looked out. "You saw what occurred in Newbird's Arm, and I am sure you learned the news of what happened in the City of Mert. Each time they open themselves to magic, to stories, and to vagrancy...they are attacked. You build a wall up to stop a predator. The moment you cut a hole in it to let in the prey, the predators follow. They always follow."

"But—"

The senator continued over her. "And it doesn't matter if one person makes the window or thousands do. Once it is there, the cracks show. Lucky for us, the Effluvium speaks. The Effluvium tells us what needs to be fixed. You wish to *hear* the Effluvium, right, Sister? That is why you abandoned your betrothal to that grifter. You want to listen to the Effluvium's song, experience the way it crumbles at the touch of sinners, and taste the fresh air it blesses upon us. Isn't that right, Sister?"

"Yes," Jemma squeaked.

"Pardon?"

"Yes, I want to be one with the Effluvium! But I always thought...I was always told that the Effluvium thrives on kindness. *Killing* isn't a kindness!"

"It is a kindness to humanity. Come." Senator Cordova beckoned her to the window. The village below glowed under the midday sun, with life bustling in the streets as yellow seeped across the buildings. But the world went on despite the terror from a few days earlier.

The senator led Jemma around to the other side of the Year Glass.

Jemma gasped.

The ocean sprawled out before her. As the sun shone through the Year Glass, it caught the edges of the sea-mist in a silver coat, glimmering like a medallion on the surface of the water.

"It's the Effluvium..."

"Part of it, yes."

"It's beautiful."

"You should see it at sunrise and sunset. The colors are phenomenal." The senator placed a hand on Jemma's shoulder. "It is bound to be like this everywhere. But when the Effluvium is tainted, we are blind."

"And you intend to help the world see again?" Jemma glanced at him, unconvinced.

"I wish to rid the world of what taints it."

"You mean magic?"

"Demons, sinners, and liars which include many Magii." Senator Cordova pressed his fingers to the glass. "There are many out there, Sister. We will have much to learn. Much to do. And it starts with moving the Tower."

"Moving the Tower?"

The senator smiled and guided Jemma to the middle of the room, where the glass walkway overlooked the pews beneath them. Guards and workers hurried about, carrying tools and dripping in sludge.

"We've unhinged the Tower from its wooden externalities. I have had my engineers reinstate the old gears installed on the tower during the Smoke Riots. We are bringing Ab Aeterno back to Knoll."

Jemma blinked. "Back to Knoll?"

"The Order built this Tower in Knoll many years ago. Before I was born, even. After the Smoke Riots, when the original tower of Aeterno burned down, we moved this beautiful fixture here. No one knew otherwise but the people of Aeterno." The senator walked over to the Year Glass and stroked its walls. "But Knoll is where it belongs. Knoll is where it will thrive again."

"Why are you telling me all of this?" Jemma looked up and met the senator's gaze.

"Because, Sister Jey Ma, there is a fire within you. You have always held your head high, always done what was right in the eyes of the Effluvium, even if it was not what you wanted. You made it all the way here against the odds. A woman abducted by a vagrant and then traveling alone across the province? That is almost unheard of! But here you are. And I want to feed your flame. So, come with me to Knoll. I will show you every single crevasse of the Effluvium. I will lead you to greatness."

Jemma stared at the senator. She couldn't decipher his stern stare. Was he lying? What did he really want from her?

What could she learn from him?

"And if I refuse?" she asked.

"You are free to leave, but where shall you go? Back to Newbird's Arm, a mere junior Sister beneath Elder Lau Rel? Or will you continue to wander across the province? There is not much for you, is there, Sister? You are here now, in Ab Aeterno; this is where many Brothers and Sisters dream of ending up! So come and join me. You shall behold the Effluvium in full." Senator Cordova offered her a hand.

Jemma sucked in her breath. He was right. Where else would she go? If she went home, her parents would kick her from the home. Sister Lau Rel had no interest in teaching her. Sure, she could return to the circus with Micca, but for what? To be some broad riding on a train?

She'd ventured to Ab Aeterno to find peace. Perhaps this was the way the Effluvium wanted her to find it.

Jemma took Senator Cordova's hand. "Okay. I'll stay."

The senator grinned.

They sat back down at the table. Jemma returned to her lemon cake and tea, gazing out the window towards the village. A knot formed in her throat, and her eyes stung, but this was the right thing to do. For the greater good, she would travel with the senator until she discovered how to save the Effluvium.

I'm sorry I didn't have time to say goodbye, Micca. And thank you for everything. Thank you so much. Jemma placed another piece of cake in her mouth.

The tower lurched. A creaking noise ricocheted up the building, shaking the walls and the table. And without anymore but that single lunge, the Tower rose from its foundation and started its journey north, away from the calmness of the sea.

CHAPTER FIFTY-THREE

A BLANK SLATE

S creams.
    Fainting.
        Spinning.
Darkness.
    He couldn't see.
        He couldn't breathe.
Only yellow.
    And white.
        And black.
His feet moved. But where?
Among stories, among mist, forever.
Where would he go?
Was that blood?
He hit a wall. Voices followed. They were coming...

Coming for him...

Coming...

To kill.

Each story shot through him. The monster in his head fed on them.

Wandering...

Wandering...

Through an endless reservoir of tulips, he walked.

Then came storms.

Confusion.

Goodbye, mind.

Goodbye.

He couldn't escape.

He wouldn't escape.

All his work for naught. Would he disappear again?

What was his name?

What was his—

A bright light shocked him. A sharp pain screamed through his arm.

He fell to the ground and withered.

My name is...

My name is...

My name is Brent Harley.

He blinked. The world came back into focus. All the stories he'd pulled from the crypts continued frolicking about and left as a gentle hum in the mist, hiding him from the figure lurking in the shadows. The Diabolo in the back of his mind continued to wither and scream, begging to go back into the stories.

But once again, Brent was in control.

How?

He blinked again. Nix sat at his fingertips, licking his hand, but that was not what brought him back. A needle stuck out of his arm.

Oh. Slowly, he removed the needle from his skin and held it. A shadow stood beside him.

"Nedo," Brent croaked.

"Are you well?" Nedo asked.

"Yeah, I'm here. I'm a'ight." He blinked. "Where's Bria?"

Nedo helped Brent off the ground. "She had other business to attend to. Let's get you out of here."

"What about Julietta?" Brent still sensed the woman moving beneath the wall's shadow. The stories were enough to distract her, but for how long? They grew fainter the more he reclaimed his mind. The horrors were but a distant nightmare.

Vanishing...

Vanishing...

Vanishing...

"We cannot do anything for her. It is too late."

Brent shook his head. A migraine inched through his head, the stories attempting to draw him back.

Nedo handed him Bria's satchel. Brent fidgeted with the buttons for a moment before removing his bottle of silver-coated pills. He downed one, shaking off the migraine, before throwing the bag over his shoulder and glancing back at Nedo. "There has to be something we can do for Julietta."

"There is not. She has been turned—"

"So was I! I came back!"

"Most are not like you, Brent."

"Bullshite."

Nedo cocked his head to the side.

"I'm sick of this bullshite that...that I'm...that I'm more special than the others. Bullshite! I see their stories!" Brent motioned to the prison cells. "They went through the same as me. I just...I had a circumstance that let me thrive. If I hadn't met Kek...or didn't have... didn't have someone like Bria to help...or any of that, I...shite! I'm not fucking special! I got lucky!"

Nedo bowed his head and played with his fingers. Brent took it as a moment of understanding and pondering.

"I need to help her. This is my fault."

"I understand," Nedo finally remarked. There was a sadness in his eyes. Brent recognized the look: one of hopelessness, of loss, and of uncertainty. How much had Nedo given when the world didn't give anything back?

"I'm gonna help her." Brent turned back to the mist. A distorted shadow moved amongst the smoke and fire-light.

One step at a time, he walked forward, gripping the bag over his shoulder, bracing for Julietta's potential attack. He had to save her. If he gave up, he was no better than the rest of them.

He took another step.

The figure was clearer now beneath the light.

No. Two figures.

"Tomás?" He squinted. "Caroline?!"

The two Mist Keepers joined him in the dim light.

Tomás spoke first. "Brent! What's going on? Why is the crypt op—ah, hello, Nedo!" He beamed as the ghost joined their side.

Brent gawked. "I—"

"What is going on, Brent?" Caroline asked, blunt and to the point, sounding more like herself than she had in weeks. Her eyes glistened, free of the ghastly mask Ningursu had placed over them, operating on her own accord at last.

"I... I'm sorry...Julietta...she..."

Caroline's face grew hollow. "What happened? Where is she?"

"She followed me and...and..." He shook his head. "I'm sorry."

"Where is she?!" Caroline grabbed Brent and shook his shoulders.

Brent flinched at her touch. For a moment, he absorbed her story with doors bursting open and the Library caught in a storm. His chest tightened. "What's happening up there?"

"Never mind that! What is happening here?!" Caroline spat into his face.

Tomás interjected, "Brent. Tell us where Julietta is, please."

Brent gave up, his body crumpling, the tears breaking from the corners of his eyes. "I'm so sorry. She followed me and I...she...I..."

"Speak up, you consarn stuttering milksop!" Caroline gripped his shirt.

"Please, she's gone... she's gone..."

As if on cue, something rattled a nearby steel cage. A figure strode towards them with calmness in her stride, broken only by her slamming a hand against the cells. The creatures, no, the people in the cages wreathed and withered. Behind her flowed a trail of yellow hair. Her jaw hung ajar, face sneering.

"Julietta!" Caroline released Brent before bolting to her friend.

Julietta snarled and lunged, knocking Caroline back and throwing her against the wall. It was as if in mere minutes, Julietta had transformed beyond a vessel and into the Diabolo itself. Her smile held no semblance of humanity, her head hanging lopsided to the left, eyes bright but lifeless.

"You abandoned me, Caroline," she spoke. The voice no longer resembled Julietta in the slightest. It came in three whispers at once like a snake hissing and a monster gloating.

"Julietta..." Caroline gawked.

Tomás joined her side, staring with the same bewilderment.

"You didn't stay beside me as I withered. You let me wither...wither away. Gone...gone..."

The story traveled with her voice. For a moment, Brent saw two women together as they kissed and danced. The curtain fell, and one left the other alone in the field. The one remaining in the field stared mindlessly until her story became nothing but watercolors on canvas.

Julietta chuckled, breaking Brent from his trance. "I'm better now. So much better..."

"No! Stop it!" Caroline spun around to face Brent. Tears stained her face. It was something he'd never seen before on his old teacher, but there she was...crying. "Fix her! You escaped the monster! Fix her!"

"I dunno if I—"

"Fix her!" Caroline shrieked. "Stop being a useless kid for once in your damn life and fix her!"

Julietta cackled, then lunged at them again. The strength of the Diabolo flourished within her, and while she usually looked so fragile, this time she towered above them. Brent felt like a child beneath her, and she made the crypts look like a playpen.

With another swipe, Caroline hit the wall again, and Brent stumbled back. Nedo caught him, keeping him up with a gentle hand on the back. Enough so Brent sensed the sadness in his story but not enough to make the mistake of eradicating the poor old soul.

"Julietta..." Caroline crawled forward.

Julietta ignored Caroline and refocused on Brent. She swung at him, her nails slicing at his skin. Brent rolled over, catching Julietta's heels with his own clumsy feet and sending her to the floor. As Julietta screamed, Nedo joined the fray, grabbing her arms, and with a swift nod of his head, he motioned to Brent.

Brent's eyes met Nedo's. They stared at each other, long and hard.

"I'm not sure if I can..." Brent glanced at his hands.

"You wanted to try."

Brent understood. *It's the only way.*

He gently brought his fingers to Julietta's palm and whispered, focusing only on her. "Let me tell you a story."

Julietta's body cringed at his touch.

The mist spun around him, detailing stories of a monster brewing with the screams of honest people. The monster churned and roared until, at last, with its fingers outstretched, it grabbed a host and gnawed into her head. Its voice cooed, whispering sweet sounds of truths and consequences.

The story spiraled deeper. It was everything.

But it was also nothing.

He searched for remnants of Julietta in the story. She was nowhere. Only the monsters.

Only screams.

Only sorrow.

There was nothing to grab. No story, just an identity stolen by a monster.

Lost.

Confused.

Interwoven.

There was no separation between Julietta and the Diabolo.

They were one.

Just like him and the Diabolo in his head.

You're useless.

Shut up, Frankie! Brent sneered. He had to help Julietta climb out of her mind. No matter how deep the Diabolo pushed her, there had to be a way out.

His head seared again. Nix whined. Caroline shouted. Julietta screeched.

There must be a way... He tugged at the strap to the satchel. *The elixir!*

He fumbled to remove one of the last two needles from the bag, uncapped it, and pressed it into Julietta's arm.

She screeched and slashed at his face. Yet, the elixir acted fast. As it moved through her body, she visibly squirmed. Her face contorted, eyes wide, lips quivering.

She gave out a pained gasp, and Julietta's body clunked to the ground.

Brent backed up, wiping the blood from his cheek. His fingers trembled, his heartbeat making a new home in his throat. He begged that Julietta would pop up, her usual cheery self, and call him the wrong name with a big old smile. That's all he wanted.

But she lay there on the ground, eyes open wide, like a blank slate. She did not speak. She did not smile.

She did not move.

"Jules?" Caroline crawled over to Julietta. "Come on. Wake up! Julietta!"

"I'm sorry..." Brent clenched his hands together and brought them to his lips. "I'm so, so sorry."

"What...what did you do?"

"I tried..."

"WHAT DID YOU DO?" Caroline barked.

"Her stories are interwoven with the Diabolo. I tried...I really tried...but I wasn't able to free them..." He looked away. "I gave her the meds I've been on, but...I dunno what they did. They kind of...they tranquilized her."

"THEN WHERE IS SHE?!?"

"I dunno, I—"

"You have her stories! You could have helped her!" Caroline held Julietta to her chest. "Where is she?!"

"I don't know!"

"FOR SARDS SAKE, BRENT! STOP BEING USE-LESS!"

"There's nothing else I can do...except..." Brent removed the green gem he carried from his pocket. He ran it over his fingers, then offered it to Caroline, "This helped me. It might help her."

Caroline snatched the gem and threw it against the wall.

"Caroline..."

"USELESS TWAT!" She roared.

Tomás intervened. "Caroline! Please take a deep breath. We shall find her, but you need to focus—"

Caroline cut Tomás off, snarling at Brent. "You took her story stories! Give it back!"

"I didn't take her story! Please believe me, Caroline!"

"Hogwash!" Caroline's anger rose. With each shout, her illusion of poise vanished, once again revealing her soggy, worn face from a death filled with water.

A distant rumble of thunder shook the crypts. Brent jumped. He turned to Nedo, and with a mere motion, a more pressing manner replaced his worry over Julietta.

"Bria..."

The ghost nodded.

Brent rose, his knees trembling, and slowly turned from the Mist Keepers.

"Brent! Where are you going?!" Caroline screamed.

"I need to... there's...up there... Bria!"

Caroline leapt to her feet as if about to attack.

Tomás snatched her wrist, glaring. "Caroline, stop. Breathe."

"Julietta is gone!"

"I do not believe she is."

Brent glanced back at her. "I'm sorry. Really, I am. I promise I'll get her back."

"LIAR!"

"I'm sorry." Brent darted from the crypts with Nix and Nedo into the fray he could hear in the Library without looking back.

PLAGUE

The rain from the storm that powered over Bria tasted like sweat and tears. While the Library's maze encompassed her, she sensed the individuals moving in its embrace. The walls threatened to cave in on them. One wrong move and the Library would collapse. She had to keep it standing, despite how much the shelves rocked. If it fell, everyone would die...

Or whatever happened to injured immortals, ghosts, and Mist Keepers.

"Please stop," Bria begged. Her voice cracked with the lightning, illuminating the fog in her head. "No more..."

She didn't hear the response.

Then it cleared like water receding on the shore.

The Library transformed into a swamp. Books sank in the muddy, bark-covered ground. The shelves stood as rotting trees. Moss grew on the walls, the rain drizzling. The sky still occasionally boomed. Wind gusts turned to tornadoes, bringing the pages into the fray.

No matter how hard she tried to stop it, the Library refused to obey. It was fighting her every move.

Somewhere, she was sure Alojzy had reclaimed control.

With Ningursu's mist in her head, the storm wasn't ever going to stop. How long would he keep command over her? Would he forever leave an imprint in her head?

Bria could hardly hoist herself from the ground. Her vision spun as she searched through the storm for something to ground herself.

She locked eyes on Brent emerging from the chaos Nedo at his side. Pale. Alert. Present.

And scared. Frightened. Petrified.

Something happened. I don't know what...but he did something.

His mouth hung open, then he glanced in Bria's direction. Did he see her?

She didn't know. Her gazed slipped. It was too foggy. Too destroyed. Too much of a mess.

The world burned. If the Library was its heart, then this was a heart attack.

Burning. Beating.

Screaming.

And I'm the plague. I'm causing the palpitations. I'm the clot. And I can't stop.

She tried to rise, but her knees gave out, and she rolled over on her back. Voices, commotion, a dog barked...

"Nix," she mumbled. As she tried to lift her head, Ningursu closed his eyes, refocusing his powers and mind. It was enough to shake free of his control, and with the chains unlocked, Bria fell back. Free at last from the spinning, the screeching, the terror...but not free from her powers.

Her fear kept the storm brewing, her nerves kept the roots and vines growing, and her sobs rumbled the ground.

She still felt every piece of the Library in the palms of her hands. Ningursu had handed her a key to it, even if it were by accident. She could feel it breathe; she could feel it move. Life permeated through the world of the dead. One did not exist without the other.

The Library, after all, was no more than a tree.

Ningursu may rule it. Alojzy may control it.

But I can destroy it with a flick of my wrist. It belongs to me.

In a way, the Library belonged to her. One incorrect movement, and it would fall.

"Bria!"

She shook her head, unable to see whoever said her name.

"Bri! C'mon, you're a'ight...look at me... you're a'ight," Brent shouted over the storm.

"I can't stop," she sobbed.

"Yes, you can," Brent spoke gently, his kind fingers on her cheeks, wiping away each tear. It only made her cry more. Everything hurt.

Breathing.

Thinking.

Existing

Bolts of lightning shot around them again. Thunder boomed like footsteps approaching. Someone screamed in the distance; was it her? Her lips weighed heavily, but her mouth was closed.

"Bria..."

"I can't." She sobbed as another crack of thunder rumbled through the Library. "You need to go... I'm going to hurt you. Please!"

"Bria, look at me." This time the voice didn't belong to Brent.

She refused.

Someone grabbed her by the shoulders and pulled her up from the ground. "Look at me!"

After a few more objections, Bria opened her eyes. Kek held her up, staring down at her with hard coal eyes. The torrential rain masked the shelving and scene behind them.

"What did you tell me before, Bria?" Kek asked over the storm.

"I...I..." She wracked her brain, but then another jolt of lightning sent her into a fit of tears.

"You said you didn't want to be a weapon!" Kek continued shouting. "So, stop being a weapon! You can stop! Focus!"

"Ningursu—"

"Ningursu jumpstarted your magic and fueled your fire, but you are in control! Focus! Search for something to focus your energy on,"

"You can do it, Bri," Brent said from beside her.

Bria reached for his hand and squeezed it. *Focus.* She glanced at Kek, then towards where Nedo stood, drifting like a cloud in a storm. Even farther, the Library breathed past the storm, and the heartbeats of a thousand peonies throbbed beneath the quenching tears of the sky.

She heard them crying, drowning, and whimpering. The entire Library sank.

And with it would go thousands of years of history.

Her head buzzed, her throat tightened, but Bria centered her energy on the peonies. She wanted them to grow, to sing, to flourish. They deserved to live. The storm needed to end; the flowers would bloom, and there would be a rainbow to cast the end of the terror.

She hummed to herself the song she lived, the song she begged would change the course of this battle.

Rhodana...
The forest queen...
She loves to laugh,
She hates to scream,
She promised the world a reverie
Rhodana.

She saw the sky,
She saw the earth,
And the way it died.
But with a step,
With some pride.
She stopped the plague,
And more than tried.
Rhodana.

Bria blinked a few times. The rain dwindled to a gentle trickle, soaking the carpet and wood like an artificial swamp. Bookcases dripped with water as the ceiling let out its last sob. Red peonies climbed up the walls and towards the ceiling, filling the core of the Library like blood.

Finally, Bria saw again.

One chandelier glimmered above them. The rest remained dark.

"Good girl," Kek whispered and released Bria.

She stumbled back and fell into Brent's arms. He gripped her tight. "I got you. I got you. It's... it's a'ight."

Bria met his gaze. His curls lay damp and matted against his forehead, nearly covering his eyes.

With the storm relieved, Bria finally breathed. Nix barked in delight, shaking off the water and stinking of wet dog as she frolicked away into the shelves. All was right again.

Until Bria's gaze landed on Nedo still standing beside them. His eyes trailed behind Brent. Bria followed his stare, where true destruction reigned. Magii and Mist Keepers fought. Jiang and Edith stood locked in an intense battle of weaponry and guile. Edith dodged each of Jiang's swift movements, weaving between the bookcases, cackling at the top of her lungs. Aelia had disappeared with other Magii filling the main entranceway and shouting.

But farther from the commotion in the path leading to the crypt, Bria's gaze stopped. Caroline sat on her knees, holding Julietta to her chest and sobbing. Beside her, Tomás knelt beside them, placing his hand on Julietta's head, before glancing in Brent's direction sadly.

Bria glanced at Brent. "Brent? What happened?"

He shook his head, so his curls covered his eyes again.

"Brent?"

Kek interjected, "Now is not the time to ruminate. We still have the matter of Ningursu. Nedo, where is your broth—"

"Oh, fuck off!" Brent shot Kek a glare. "I don't have time to deal with a talking skull right now! We're...Bri and I...we should leave. I mean...right?" He glanced at Bria for her opinion.

She half nodded. Exhaustion made its way through her body. Perhaps she'd fall asleep, then wake up huddled on a bed in a quiet abode, away from this nightmare. Safe.

"Very well. I will not stop you." Kek turned. "Good luck, though. I mean it. You two are a force to be reckoned with." Kek walked away. Nedo remained by Brent and Bria's side, staring after Kek with his lips drawn into a line on his face.

Bria exchanged a glanced with Brent and nodded again. Kek might have been telling the truth after all: they wanted the best for them, not to turn them into weapons.

Because we are not weapons. We'll never be weapons.

"Let's get outta here, a'ight?" Brent stroked Bria's hair back.

"Where?"

"We'll figure it out."

"Okay." Bria didn't let go of him.

With care, Brent climbed to his feet, glanced over his shoulder, and shouted, "NIX! COME!"

A few moments later, the dog bounded out of the shelves, her tail wagging in exhilaration.

She carried none other than Ningursu's head in her mouth.

CHAPTER FIFTY-FIVE

DOG TOY

L et go of me, you confounded mangy mutt!"
Ningursu bellowed.

Brent held back a laugh. What a sight! In all
the commotion, in all the tears, Nix must have found
Ningursu's head lying on the ground and delivered it to
him like a mere trophy. Ningursu shouted for the dog to
let him go before producing a slur of curse words that
Brent didn't recognize.

"Nix! Put it down! Leave it!" Brent shouted at the
dog.

The dog cocked her head to the side.

"Come on, Nix. Put it down!"

Nix, in a moment of playful excitement, bounded
away from them and back into the shelving. Ningursu

cursed out again, and with the last curse word, a mist-made chain exploded from his mouth and latched onto Nedo, dragging the ghost along with them.

"Shite! Nix!" The dog had already disappeared into the shelves, leaving a trail of subtle mist in her wake. "How the fuck can a dog take down Ningursu while the rest of us can't?"

"Maybe she caught Ningursu off guard?" Bria asked as she joined Brent's side, her legs trembling with each step. "Or his magic only works on humans or something?"

"Could explain it. We gotta find him, though."

"On it."

A few vines moved beneath Bria's feet. To Brent's surprise, she didn't look fragile. She looked...powerful. Tired, yes, but whatever Ningursu had done to jumpstart her powers had worked; she was a queen.

"I'm feeling...where Nix has touched the vines. Maybe you can use the stories to make sure?" Bria stared at him, her fingers shaking as the plants continued to weave through the shelves.

Brent nodded and let his hand slice through the mist. Stories congregated before them, showing Nedo dragged across the ground and Nix bolting through the aisles.

At first, Bria jogged beside Brent as they hurried after the dog, but she eventually stopped, leaning against the bookcase, huffing.

"Bri? You a'ight?"

"No...I feel like I'm going to collapse."

"It's a'ight. I got the story. C'mon!" He hoisted her onto his back and hurried through the remaining shelves. The stories remained like fog on a summer morn, guiding them back through the peonies and into the room with the silver pool.

At the edge of the lake sat Nix, gnawing at Ningursu's head.

"LET GO OF ME!" Ningursu shrieked again.

Nix spit Ningursu's head out, rolled over once, then jumped after it like a ball. As Ningursu's head tossed and turned, the chain hanging from his mouth broke, sending Nedo flying onto the ground.

Ningursu tried to use the chain to stop the dog, but Nix moved with such random agility and playfulness, it proved fruitless.

"Nix!" Brent called after the dog.

This time, Nix looked up. Upon seeing Brent and Bria, she lobbed Ningursu's head into the air and pranced over, tail wagging back and forth.

"Good girl." Brent patted Nix's head. He lifted Bria off his back, and she embraced Nix around the neck.

Leaning into the dog's fur, she looked at peace amongst the peonies. Red flowers bloomed around her, still in tune with her movements, still enamored with the Forest Queen.

Brent glanced back across the lake. Nedo had gathered himself from the ground and strode towards Ningursu's head, lying face down in the dirt. He picked up the head and stared at it before holding it over the edge of the pool.

Ningursu almost appeared to smile, his one white eye transfixed on his brother. A new crack cut into his hollow eye. "Ah, Nedo! Finally!"

Nedo blinked, gripping Ningursu's head tighter, his finger slipping in the empty black socket.

"Brother, what are you doing? Let us go."

No response.

Brent watched, transfixed on what occurred. Beside him, Bria took his hand. Neither of them said a word.

Ningursu continued, "If this is about having more freedom to exist, then we can talk."

Nedo opened his mouth. The words that came out were shrill, out of practice, but firm. "I see for the first time in a thousand years."

"Brother—"

"You controlled me."

"It was part of the treaty."

"You broke it."

"Nedo—"

"No! I speak now!" Nedo's eyes narrowed. "I've not spoken for years! Let me speak!"

He raised Ningursu's head higher.

"You use me because I took a different side!" Nedo snarled. "You harm; you kill. And you took everything!" The ghost teared up. "I want to be gone. I want to be with Merta. I loved her...you took her."

"You still hold a grudge over that?" Ningursu cackled. "That was a millennium ago! It is about time you forget."

"Forget? I'm not forgetting! I've always been here, remembering. With you. I've always been!" His fingers trembled. "I know all you do if not more. Because me? I have a soul."

"Nedo..."

"No! No more Nedo!" Nedo shook the head. "Goodbye, brother."

Brent's paralysis broke. "Wait! Nedo! What're you—"

He was too late.

With a splash, Ningursu's head vanished beneath the surface of the pool.

Brent gawked as he skidded towards the edge of the water. Everything happened so fast. He half expected Ningursu's head bob up to the top of the water.

But the silver surface remained claim.

"Nedo...What did you...what did you do?"

Nedo lowered his head, silent once more.

"You...this...you can't...I mean..." Brent blinked. "The Council... they'll..."

Brent didn't understand his own feelings. Fear? Sadness? Relief? He glanced back at Bria as she watched with her mouth ajar.

Nedo tapped Brent's shoulder and held out his hand. It wasn't a mere movement. This time, it was a wordless question. Brent knew what Nedo wanted. But could he do it now with Bria watching?

Could he do it after everything that happened today?

"No... I'm not...I can't..." Brent shook his head. "Please don't ask me to do that."

Nedo's eyes did not leave him. "Please."

"Brent..." Bria joined him, placing a hand against his back. Nix followed along, tethered by a rope made of vines. "What are you thinking?"

He stared hard at Bria. "I can't...I mean...he wants it. He yearns for it. But...I..."

"What do you think is right?"

Brent stared back at the ghost. He looked pitiful now, that determination and anger removed from his body, leaving a skeleton standing on two wobbly feet. In the mist over his skin, Brent saw the story of a man on his last leg, trapped in circling stories of slavery and dismay.

And of a broken heart.

Brent's own heart sank. He glanced once at Bria, and with her nod of approval, he accepted what he had to do.

"A'ight," Brent opened his palms. Nedo placed his hands into them and closed his eyes.

The story of Nedo's life washed over him:

Two young boys played in the fields. The bigger one with dark eyes enjoyed pushing around his brother, leaving his brother weak. Nedo thus abandoned the games of play, dedicating time to his studies. He learned, he grew, while his brother continued his jovial activities.

By the time they both grew stubble on their chins, Nedo had the knowledge of a scholar, but his brother wanted easy riches and glamor. At the turn of harvest, they went their separate ways.

Years turned.

Nedo inherited a fertile plot of land.

His brother's land sat vacant.

Nedo raised a family.

His brother returned empty-handed.

Nedo kept riches.

His brother had nothing.

And by the time they both grew full beards, their plots of land highlighted their differences. Nedo's grew and bolstered. His brother's land remained dormant and empty.

Each day, bitterness grew. He and his brother fought and argued and bickered.

One day, his brother returned from a day in the fields with a crazed look in his eye. Mist exhaled from his lips.

"You are the reason for my failures, Brother."

"What do you mean, Brother?" Nedo asked. "I stayed here while you saw the world. You chose your life."

"Because no one wanted me to stay."

"That is a lie."

"The truth is in the mist!"

"What do you mean, Brother?"

And with a swift raise of his sword, brother slaughtered brother in the field.

To rot.

To wither.

To disappear.

Only years later did Nedo return under his own brother's guise.

Where he stayed...

Where he thrived...

Where he loved...

Where he slaved...

And where he once again died...

Brent exhaled. Like with the Diabolo, the mist gathered around him. Nedo's eyes met Brent's gaze, and a calm smile formed on his lips.

"Thank you," Nedo whispered.

With a gust of wind and a puff of smoke, he disappeared into the atmosphere. Nedo's stories latched onto the center of Brent's chest, a constant reminder to remember, to recall, to learn.

And then he disappeared.

"WHAT ARE YOU DOING!?!"

Brent blinked a few times to reconnect with his surroundings. Kek stood in the entrance to the pool, gawking. Their mouth hung open, their eyes wide, their face pale.

Bria came to Brent's defense. "Nedo asked Brent! He wanted to—"

"You murdered him!"

"He asked!" Brent yelled back. "He dropped Ningursu's head in the pool then ASKED! I only did it because...because...he suffered so much...and...and... I'm sorry."

Kek relaxed suddenly, a sly smile etched on their lips. "He dropped Ningursu's head in the Pool?"

"Yeah..."

"Did it resurface?"

Brent glanced at the pool. The water remained peaceful. "No."

"So... he's gone?" Kek's lips parted wider. "Ningursu, that bastard, is gone!?!"

"I...I mean...I don't..." Brent stared at the pool. "He's not here, yeah."

"Oh, thank the gods! Ha!" Kek jumped in the air, then danced around the pool, clapping their hands together and laughing. Brent's stomach sank watching them. It was an odd moment, a weird victory lap over something so anticlimactic; Ningursu had fallen into a pool, but to what avail?

Finally, Kek stopped by the entrance again. "The Library is mine for the taking! I won! I won! Ningursu is gone!"

Before Brent could protest, Kek pranced from the room, shouting for Edith, Yusef, and the other Magii to join them. Yet, Brent could not celebrate. In his heart, in his soul, hollowness rested. Julietta's mind was stone, the Library was in shambles, and Nedo was dead.

Bria's gaze held the same grief. "The war's not over, whatever Kek might think. Ningursu is still out there..."

"Yeah..." Brent looked at her and then at the pool. The secrets hidden in its shadows were endless. Where would it take him?

Even Nedo's story gave him no answer.

"The Council won't give up. They'll search for Ningursu," Brent said.

"And then we saw Elder Don Van..."

"And the Diabolo are still out there..."

"We're not safe here."

"Then I think it's time to leave." Brent had yet to take his attention off the pool. These miraculous pools of peony held so many secrets: life and death, past and future, and the world and the grave. Everything hid beneath that lifeblood, beating softly as the world continued spinning. It held the secrets to magic and to fortune. Now, it held the one way out of this madness.

"You mean..." Bria trailed off.

Brent turned back to her. "We jump."

"We don't know where it goes, though."

"Does it matter? We'll be together. We're alive. And shite! Whatever damn curses or demons are coming our way, I think we can handle. I mean, we've lasted this long, right?"

"What if we end up where Ningursu is?" Bria asked.

Brent's gaze traced the room. "Then I think we have an advantage. He'll be alone. We're together."

"Together," Bria repeated. "We'll fight together."

"You ready then?"

"It's our best option."

They gathered at the perimeter of the Pool with Nix tethered at their heels. While they had no clue where their journey would lead them, it didn't matter.

None of it mattered.

For now, they were safe.

"I'll see you in a minute," Brent whispered.

She replied with a smile, "And not a moment longer."

Together, arms locked, they took one last look at the silver pool.

Then they jumped.

AUTHOR'S NOTE

Thank you so much for taking the time to read *A Pool of Peony*.

If you enjoyed this book, I would appreciate it if you could:

Review this book. Reviews are a great help to an author. If you enjoyed this book, please consider leaving a review on Amazon or Goodreads.

Tell Others. When you share this book with others on social media, you're allowing others to discover this story. Word-of-mouth is one of the best sources of marketing for an author.

Connect with me. If you want to find out about my upcoming releases, stop by my website at www.esbarrison-author.com or connect with me on social media.

Thank you!

E.S. Barrison

Acknowledgments

To all the following, my thanks, for your support, friendship, and kindness throughout this process:

First to Dee, for being there to bounce ideas off of when I was in a bind, as well as providing both alpha and beta feedback.

To all my beta readers, thank you for your insights to make this book shine.

To my parents, for putting up with my antics and supporting this crazy project.

To Moira, my cover artist, for being so flexible and understanding when it came to all the revisions needed on the cover.

To Charlie, my editor, for helping me create a fantastic final product with polished worldbuilding.

To Matthew, for actually reading my writing and listening to me go off on tangents on a daily basis.

And finally, to my readers, I can't wait to share the next book in the series with you.

Without all of your support, this story would not have been possible.

ABOUT THE AUTHOR

E.S. Barrison has been writing and creating stories for as long as she can remember. After graduating from the University of Florida, she has spent the past few years wrangling her experiences to compose unique worlds with diverse characters. Currently, E.S. lives in Orlando, Florida with her family.

Also by E.S. Barrison

The Life & Death Cycle
The Mist Keeper's Apprentice (Book 1)

Fairy Tale Retellings
Tuppence